THE BOYS
FROM BILOXI

ALSO BY JOHN GRISHAM

A Time to Kill
The Firm
The Pelican Brief
The Client
The Chamber
The Rainmaker
The Runaway Jury
The Partner
The Street Lawyer
The Testament
The Brethren
A Painted House
Skipping Christmas
The Summons
The King of Torts
Bleachers
The Last Juror
The Broker
The Innocent Man
Playing for Pizza
The Appeal
The Associate
Ford County
The Confession
The Litigators
Calico Joe
The Racketeer
Sycamore Row
Gray Mountain
Rogue Lawyer
The Whistler
Camino Island
The Rooster Bar
The Reckoning
The Guardians

Camino Winds
A Time for Mercy
Sooley
The Judge's List
Sparring Partners

The Theodore Boone Books
Theodore Boone: Kid Lawyer
Theodore Boone: The Abduction
Theodore Boone: The Accused
Theodore Boone: The Activist
Theodore Boone: The Fugitive
Theodore Boone: The Scandal
Theodore Boone: The Accomplice

JOHN
GRISHAM

———•———

THE BOYS
FROM BILOXI

DOUBLEDAY
New York

Book design by Maria Carella
Jacket design by Michael J. Windsor
Jacket photographs: (people) © Massimo Volonte / Millennium Images, U.K.;
(seascape) © Carmen K. Sisson / Cloudybright / Alamy; (grass) © A-Digit /
DigitalVision Vectors / Getty; (clouds) © Nguyen Trong Bao Toan /
Moment / Getty Images

Library of Congress Control Number 2022942560
ISBN: 978-0-385-54892-2 (hardcover)
ISBN: 978-0-385-54893-9 (ebook)

MANUFACTURED IN THE UNITED STATES OF AMERICA
1st Printing

LSCH

THE BOYS
FROM BILOXI

PART ONE

———•———

THE BOYS

CHAPTER 1

A hundred years ago, Biloxi was a bustling resort and fishing community on the Gulf Coast. Some of its 12,000 people worked in shipbuilding, some in the hotels and restaurants, but for the majority their livelihoods came from the ocean and its bountiful supply of seafood. The workers were immigrants from Eastern Europe, most from Croatia where their ancestors had fished for centuries in the Adriatic Sea. The men worked the schooners and trawlers harvesting seafood in the Gulf while the women and children shucked oysters and packed shrimp for ten cents an hour. There were forty canneries side by side in an area known as the Back Bay. In 1925, Biloxi shipped twenty million tons of seafood to the rest of the country. Demand was so great, and the supply so plentiful, that by then the city could boast of being the "Seafood Capital of the World."

The immigrants lived in either barracks or shotgun houses on Point Cadet, a peninsula on the eastern edge of Biloxi, around the corner from the beaches of the Gulf. Their parents and grandparents were Poles, Hungarians, Czechs, as well as Croatians, and they had been quick to assimilate into the ways of their new country. The children learned English, taught it to their parents, and rarely spoke the mother tongues at home. Most of their surnames had been unpronounceable to customs officials and had been modified and Americanized at the Port of New Orleans and Ellis Island. In Biloxi cemeteries, there were tombstones with names like Jurkovich, Horvat, Conovich, Kasich, Rodak, Babbich, and Peranich. They were scattered about and mixed with those of Smith, Brown,

O'Keefe, Mattina, and Bellande. The immigrants were naturally clannish and self-protective, but by the second generation they were intermarrying with the early French families and all manner of Anglos.

Prohibition was still the law, and throughout the Deep South most Baptists and Methodists righteously pursued the dry life. Along the Coast, though, those of European descent and Catholic persuasion took a dimmer view of abstinence. In fact, Biloxi was never dry, regardless of the Eighteenth Amendment. When Prohibition swept the country in 1920 Biloxi hardly noticed. Its bars, dives, honky-tonks, neighborhood pubs, and upscale clubs not only remained open but thrived. Speakeasies were not necessary because booze was so prevalent and no one, especially the police, cared. Biloxi became a popular destination for parched Southerners. Add the allure of the beaches, delicious seafood, a temperate climate, and nice hotels, and tourism flourished. A hundred years ago the Gulf Coast became known as "the poor man's Riviera."

As always, unchecked vice proved contagious. Gambling joined drinking as the more popular illegal activities. Makeshift casinos sprang up in bars and clubs. Poker, blackjack, and dice games were in plain view and could be found everywhere. In the lobbies of the fashionable hotels there were rows of slot machines operating in blatant disregard for the law.

Brothels had been around forever but kept undercover. Not so in Biloxi. They were plentiful and serviced not only their faithful johns but police and politicians as well. Many were in the same buildings as bars and gambling tables so that a young man looking for pleasure need only one stop.

Though not flaunted as widely as sex and booze, drugs like marijuana and heroin were easy to find, especially in the music halls and lounges.

Journalists often found it difficult to believe that such illegal activity was so openly accepted in a state so religiously conservative. They wrote articles about the wild and freewheeling ways in

Biloxi, but nothing changed. No one with authority seemed to care. The prevailing mood was simply: "That's just the Biloxi." Crusading politicians railed against the crime and preachers thundered from the pulpits, but there was never a serious effort to "clean up the Coast."

The biggest obstacle facing any attempts at reform was the longtime corruption of the police and elected officials. The cops and deputies worked for meager salaries and were more than willing to take the cash and look the other way. The local politicians were easily bought off and prospered nicely. Everyone was making money, everyone was having fun, why ruin a good thing? No one forced the drinkers and gamblers to venture into Biloxi. If they didn't like the vice there, they could stay home or go to New Orleans. But if they chose to spend their money in Biloxi, they knew they would not be bothered by the police.

Criminal activity got a major boost in 1941 when the military built a large training base on land that was once the Biloxi Country Club. It was named Keesler Army Airfield, after a World War I hero from Mississippi, and the name soon became synonymous with bad behavior from tens of thousands of soldiers getting ready for war. The number of bars, casinos, brothels, and striptease joints increased dramatically. As did crime. The police were flooded with complaints from soldiers: rigged slots, floating roulette, cheating dealers, spiked drinks, and sticky-fingered prostitutes. Since the owners were making money they complained little, but there were plenty of fights, assaults on their girls, and broken windows and whiskey bottles. As always, the police protected the ones who paid them, and the jailhouse doors revolved with GIs. Over half a million of them passed through Keesler on their way to Europe and the Pacific, and later Korea and Vietnam.

Biloxi vice was so profitable that it naturally attracted the usual assortment of characters from the underworld: career criminals, outlaws, bootleggers, smugglers, rumrunners, con men, hit men, pimps, leg-breakers, and a more ambitious class of crime lords.

In the late 1950s, a branch of a loose-knit gang of violent thugs nicknamed the Dixie Mafia settled in Biloxi with plans to establish their turf and take over a share of the vice. Before the Dixie Mafia, there had always been jealousy among the club owners, but they were making money and life was good. There was a killing every now and then and the usual intimidation, but no serious efforts by one group to take over.

Other than ambition and violence, the Dixie Mafia had little in common with the real Cosa Nostra. It was not a family, thus there was little loyalty. Its members—and the FBI was never certain who was a member, who was not, and how many claimed to be—were a loose assortment of bad boys and misfits who preferred crime over honest work. There was no established organization or hierarchy. No don at the top and leg-breakers at the bottom, with mid-level thugs in between. With time, one club owner managed to consolidate his holdings and assume more influence. He became "the Boss."

What the Dixie Mafia had was a propensity for violence that often stunned the FBI. Through its history, as it evolved and made its way south to the Coast, it left behind an astonishing number of dead bodies, and virtually none of the murders were ever solved. It operated with only one rule, one hard-and-fast, cast-in-stone blood oath: "Thou shalt not snitch to the cops." Those who did were either found in ditches or not found at all. Certain shrimp boats were rumored to unload weighted corpses twenty miles from shore, into the deep, warm waters of the Mississippi Sound.

In spite of its reputation for lawlessness, crime in Biloxi was kept under control by the owners and watched closely by the police. With time, the vice became roughly concentrated into one principal section of town, a one-mile stretch of Highway 90, along the beach. "The Strip" was lined with casinos, bars, and brothels, and was easily ignored by the law-abiding citizens. Life away from it was normal and safe. If one wanted trouble, it was easy to find. Otherwise, it was easy to avoid. Biloxi prospered because of seafood, shipbuilding, tourism, construction, and a formidable work ethic fueled by immigrants and their dreams of a better life. The city built schools, hospitals, churches, highways, bridges, seawalls, parks, recreational facilities, and anything else it needed to improve the lives of its people.

CHAPTER 2

The rivalry began as a friendship between two boys with much in common. Both were third-generation grandsons of Croatian immigrants, and both were born and raised on "the Point," as Point Cadet was known. Their families lived two streets apart. Their parents and grandparents knew each other well. They went to the same Catholic church, the same schools, played in the same streets, sandlots, and beaches, and fished with their fathers in the Gulf on lazy weekends. They were born one month apart in 1948, both sons of young war veterans who married their sweethearts and started families.

The Old World games of their ancestors were of little significance in Biloxi. The sandlots and youth fields were meant for baseball and nothing else. Like all the boys on the Point, they began throwing and hitting not long after they could walk, and they proudly put on their first uniforms when they were eight years old. By the age of ten, they were being noticed and talked about.

Keith Rudy, the older by twenty-eight days, was a left-handed pitcher who threw hard but wild, and frightened batters with his lack of control. He also hit from the left side, and when he wasn't on the mound he was anywhere his coaches wanted him; the outfield, second or third base. Because there were no catcher's mitts for lefties, he taught himself to catch, field, and throw with his right hand.

Hugh Malco was a right-handed pitcher who threw even harder and with more accuracy. From forty-five feet away he was terrifying to face, and most ten-year-old batters preferred to hide in the dugout. A coach convinced him to swing from the left side with the usual rationale that most pitchers at that age were right-handed. Babe Ruth hit leftie, as did Lou Gehrig and Stan Musial. Mickey, of course, could swat 'em from both sides, but he was a Yankee. Hugh listened because he was easy to coach and wanted to win.

Baseball was their world, and the warm weather on the Coast allowed them to play almost year-round. Little League teams were drafted in late February and began games in the middle of March; two games a week for at least twelve weeks. When the regular season ended, with the city championship, the serious baseball began with all-star play. Biloxi dominated the state playoffs and was expected to advance to the regional tournament. No team had yet to make it to Williamsport for the big show, but optimism ran high every year.

The church was important, at least to their parents and grandparents, but for the boys the real institution was Cardinal baseball. There were no professional big-league teams in the Deep South. Station KMOX out of St. Louis broadcast every game, with Harry Caray and Jack Buck, and the boys knew the Cardinal players, their positions, stats, hometowns, and their strengths and weaknesses. They listened to every game, cut out every box score from the *Gulf Coast Register,* then spent hours on the sandlots replaying each inning. Every spare penny was saved to purchase baseball cards, and the trading was serious business. Topps was the preferred brand, primarily because the bubblegum lasted longer.

When summer arrived and school was out, the streets of the Point were filled with kids playing corkball, kickball, Wiffle ball, and a dozen other variations of the game. The older boys commandeered the sandlots and Little League fields where they chose teams and played for hours. On the big days, they went home and cleaned up, ate something, rested their worn arms and legs, put on their uniforms, and hustled back to the fields for real games that drew large crowds of family and friends. In the late afternoons and early evenings under the lights, the boys played hard and bantered back and forth across the diamond. They enjoyed the cheers from the fans and chided each other without mercy. An error brought an avalanche of catcalls. A home run silenced the opposing bench. A hard thrower on the mound cast a pall over any opponent. A bad call by an umpire was off-limits, at least to the players, but the fans knew no restraints. And everywhere, in the stands, the parking lots, even the dugouts, transistor radios rattled on with the play-by-play broadcast from KMOX, and everyone knew the Cardinal score.

When they were twelve, Keith and Hugh had magical seasons. Keith played for a team sponsored by DeJean Packing. Hugh played for one sponsored by Shorty's Shell. They dominated the season and each team lost only once, to the other, by one run. With the flip of a coin, the DeJean Packing advanced to the city championship where they slaughtered a team from West Biloxi. Keith pitched all six innings, gave up two hits, walked four, and hit two home runs. He and Hugh were unanimous picks for the Biloxi All-Stars, and for the first time they were official teammates, though they had played together in countless sandlot games.

With Hugh firing from the right side and Keith terrifying batters from the left, Biloxi was the solid favorite to win another state championship. After a week of practice, their coaches loaded the team into three pickup trucks for the twenty-minute drive west along Highway 90 to the state tournament in Gulfport. Hundreds of fans followed in a rowdy caravan.

The tournament was dominated by teams from the southern part of the state: Biloxi, Gulfport, Pascagoula, Pass Christian and Hattiesburg. In the first game against Vicksburg, Keith threw a one-hitter and Hugh hit a grand slam. In the second game, Hugh threw a one-hitter and Keith returned the favor with two home runs. In five games, Biloxi scored thirty-six runs, gave up only four, and walked away with the state title. The town celebrated and sent the boys off to Pensacola with a party. Competition at the next level was a different matter because the Florida teams were waiting.

Nothing thrilled the boys more than a road trip, with motels and swimming pools and meals in restaurants. Hugh and Keith roomed together and were the undisputed leaders of the team, having been named co-captains by their coaches. They were inseparable, on the field and off, and all activities revolved around them. On the field, they were fierce competitors and cheerleaders, always encouraging the others to play smart, listen to the coaches, shake off errors, and study the game. Off the field, they held team meetings, led the pranks, approved nicknames, decided which movies to watch, which restaurants to go to, and propped up teammates who sat on the bench.

In the first game, Hugh gave up four hits and Biloxi beat a team from Mobile, the Alabama state champs. In the second, Keith was wilder than ever and walked eight before being pulled in the fourth inning; Biloxi lost to a team from Jacksonville by three runs. Two days later, a team from Tampa scored four runs off Hugh in the bottom of the sixth inning and walked away with the win.

The season was over. The dreams of playing in the Little League World Series in Williamsport were once again crushed by the State of Florida. The team retreated to the motel to lick its wounds, but before long the boys were splashing in the pool and trying to get the attention of some older girls in bikinis.

Their parents watched from under poolside umbrellas and enjoyed cocktails. A long season was finally over and they were eager to get home and finish the summer without the hassle of daily baseball. Almost all of the parents were there, along with other relatives and a few die-hard fans from Biloxi. Some were close friends, others only friendly acquaintances. Most were from the Point and knew each other well, and among that group there were cracks in solidarity.

Hugh's parents, Lance and Carmen Malco, were feeling a bit shunned, and for good reason.

CHAPTER 3

When Hugh's grandfather got off the boat in New Orleans in 1912 he was sixteen years old and spoke almost no English. He could pronounce "Biloxi" and that was all the customs official needed. The boats were filled with Eastern Europeans, many with relatives along the Mississippi coast, and customs was eager to move those folks along and send them somewhere else. Biloxi was a favorite destination.

The kid's name, back in Croatia, was Oron Malokovic, another mouthful. Some customs officials were patient and worked tediously to record the correct names. Others were hurried, impatient, or indifferent, or maybe they felt as though they were doing the immigrant a favor by renaming him or her with something that might adapt easier in the new country. In all fairness, some of the names from "over there" were difficult for English speakers to pronounce. New Orleans and the Gulf Coast had a rich history dominated by French and Spanish, and by the 1800s those languages had melted easily into the English. But the consonant-laden Slavic tongues were another matter.

At any rate, Oron became Aaron Malco, an identity he reluctantly embraced because he had no choice. Armed with new paperwork, he hustled up to Biloxi where a relative arranged a room in a barracks and a job shucking oysters in an "oyster house." Like his countrymen, he eked out a living, worked as many long, hard hours as possible, and saved a few bucks. After two years, he found a better job building schooners in a shipyard on Biloxi's Back Bay. The work paid more but was physically demanding. Now fully grown, Aaron stood over six feet tall, was thick through the shoulders, and manhandled massive timbers that usually required two or three other men. He endeared himself to his bosses and was given his own crew, along with a pay raise. At the age of nineteen, he was earning fifty cents an hour, a top wage, and worked as many hours as the company offered him.

When Aaron was twenty, he married Lida Simonovich, a seventeen-year-old Croatian girl who had been fortunate enough to be born in the U.S. Her mother had given birth two months after she and her father arrived on the boat from Europe. Lida worked in a cannery and in her spare time helped her mother, a seamstress. The young couple moved into a rented shotgun house on the Point where they were surrounded by family and friends, all from the old country.

Their dreams were dashed eight months after their wedding when Aaron fell from a scaffold. A broken arm and leg would heal, but the crushed vertebrae in his lower back rendered him a near cripple. For months he convalesced at home and slowly regained his ability to walk. Out of work, the couple survived with the endless support of their family and neighbors. Meals were abundant, rent was paid, and the parish priest, Father Herbert, stopped by every day for prayers, both in English and Croatian. With the aid of a cane, one that he would never be able to fully abandon, in spite of his heroic efforts, Aaron began the difficult task of looking for work.

A distant cousin owned one of three corner grocery stores on the Point. He took pity on Aaron and offered him a job sweeping floors, stocking goods, and eventually operating the cash register. Before long, Aaron ran the place and business improved. He knew all the customers, and their children and grandparents, and would do anything to help a person in need. He upgraded the inventory, discontinued items that rarely sold, and expanded the store. Even when it was closed, he would fetch items for customers and deliver them to their homes on an old delivery bike. With Aaron in charge, his boss decided to open a dry-goods store two blocks over.

Aaron saw an opportunity with another expansion. He convinced his boss to rent the building next door and establish a bar. It was 1920, the country was in the grips of Prohibition and the Catholic immigrants in Biloxi were thirstier than ever. Aaron cut a deal with a local bootlegger and stocked his bar with an impressive variety of beers, even some from Europe, and a dozen brands of popular Irish whiskeys.

He opened the grocery store each morning at sunrise and offered strong coffee and Croatian pastries to the fishermen and cannery workers. Late each night, Lida baked a tray of krostules, oil-fried cakes sprinkled with powdered sugar, and they became immensely popular with the early crowd. Through the mornings, Aaron hustled about on his cane, working the counter, cutting meats, stocking shelves, sweeping floors, and tending to the needs of his customers. Late in the afternoons, he opened the bar and welcomed his regulars. When he wasn't serving drinks he scurried back to the store, which he closed after the last customer, usually around seven. From then on he was behind the bar pouring drinks, bantering with friends, telling jokes, and spreading gossip. He usually closed around eleven, when the last shift of cannery workers finally called it a night.

In 1922, Lida and Aaron welcomed their first child and blessed him with the proper American name of Lance. A daughter and another son soon followed. Their shotgun house was crowded, and Aaron convinced his boss to rent him an unfinished space upstairs over the bar and grocery store. The family moved in while a crew of carpenters erected walls and built a kitchen. Aaron's sixteen-hour days became even longer. Lida quit her job to raise the family and also to work in the grocery.

In 1925, his boss died suddenly of a heart attack. Aaron disliked his widow and saw no future under her thumb. He convinced her to sell him the bar and grocery store, and for $1,000 cash and a promissory note, he became the owner. The note was paid off in two years, and Aaron opened another bar on the west side of the Point. With two popular bars and a busy grocery store, the Malcos became more prosperous than most of the immigrant families, though they did nothing to show it. They worked harder than ever, saved their money, stayed in the same upstairs apartment, and went about their ways as thrifty and frugal immigrants. They were quick to help others and Aaron often made small loans to friends when the banks said no. They were generous with the church and never missed Sunday Mass.

Their children worked in the store as soon as they were old enough. At the age of seven, Lance was a fixture on the Point, riding his bike with a basket filled with groceries for home deliveries. At ten, he was sliding cold bottles of beer across the bar and keeping tabs on the customers.

Early in his business career, Aaron witnessed the darker side of gambling and wanted no part of it. Illegality aside, he chose not to allow card and dice games in a back room. The temptation was always there, and some of his customers complained, but he held firm. Father Herbert approved.

The Great Depression slowed the seafood industry, but Biloxi weathered it better than the rest of the country. Shrimp and oysters were still plentiful and folks had to eat. Tourism took a blow, but the canneries stayed in business, though at a slower pace. On the Point, workers were squeezed out of jobs and fell behind on their rents. Aaron quietly assumed the mortgages on dozens of shotgun houses and became a landlord. He took IOUs for past-due rent and usually forgot about them. No one living in a Malco home was ever evicted.

When Lance graduated from Biloxi High, he toyed with the idea of going off to college. Aaron was not keen on the idea because his son was needed in the family business. Lance took a few classes at a nearby junior college, and, not surprisingly, showed an aptitude for business and finance. His teachers encouraged him to pursue studies at the state teachers college up the road in Hattiesburg, and though he harbored the dream, he was afraid to mention it to his father.

War intervened and Lance forgot about further studies. The day after Pearl Harbor, he joined the Marines and left home for the first time. He shipped out with First Infantry Division and saw heavy action in North Africa. In 1944, he landed with the first wave at Anzio when the Allies invaded Italy. Because he could speak Croatian, he and a hundred others were sent to Eastern Europe where the Germans were on the run. Early in 1945, he set foot in the old country, the birthplace of his father and grandfathers, and he wrote Aaron a long letter describing the war-torn land. He ended with: *Thanks, Father, for having the courage to leave home and seek a better life in America.* Aaron wept when he read it, then he shared it with his friends and Lida's family.

As the Allies chased the Germans westward, Lance saw action in Hungary and Poland. Two days after the liberation of Auschwitz, he and his platoon walked the dirt roads of the concentration camp and watched in stunned disbelief as hundreds of emaciated corpses were buried in mass graves. Three months after the Germans surrendered, Lance returned to Biloxi, with no injuries but with memories so horrible he vowed to forget them.

In 1947, he married Carmen Coscia, an Italian girl he had known in high school. As a wedding gift, Aaron gave them a house on the Point, in a new section with nicer homes being built for veterans. Lance naturally assumed his role in Aaron's businesses and put the war behind him. But he was restless and bored with the grocery store and the bars. He was ambitious and wanted to make some real money in gambling. Aaron was still firmly opposed to it and they had disagreements.

Thirteen months after their wedding, Carmen gave birth to Hugh and the family was ecstatic with the beginning of a new generation. Babies were springing up all around the Point, and Father Herbert was kept busy with a flood of christenings. Young families grew and the older folks celebrated. Life on the Point had never been better.

Biloxi was booming again and the seafood business was more vibrant than ever. Luxury hotels were built on the beaches as tourism rebounded. The army decided to keep Keesler as a training base, thus ensuring a constant supply of young soldiers looking for a good time. More bars, casinos, and brothels opened, and the Strip became even busier. As was the established custom, the police and politicians took the cash and looked the other way. When the art deco Broadwater Beach Hotel opened, its lobby was filled with rows of brand-new slot machines bought from a broker in Las Vegas, and still quite illegal.

As a father, Lance tempered his ambitions to plunge deeper into vice. Plus, Aaron was still firmly in control and serious about his reputation. The family business changed dramatically in 1950 when he died suddenly of pneumonia at the age of fifty-four. He left no last will and testament; thus, his assets were split in four equal shares among Lida and the three children. Lida was distraught and fell into a long bout of debilitating depression. Lance and his two siblings fought over the family properties and a serious rift ensued. They squabbled for years, much to their mother's dismay. As her health slipped away, Lance, her firstborn and always her favorite, convinced her to sign a will that left him in control of the assets. This was kept quiet until after her death. When his sister and brother read it they threatened to sue, but Lance settled the dispute by offering each the sum of $5,000 in cash. His brother took the money and left the Coast. His sister married a doctor and moved to New Orleans.

In spite of the family drama, and the accepted belief that Lance had managed to outmaneuver his siblings, he and Carmen continued to be well regarded on the Point. They lived modestly, though they could afford otherwise, and they were active and generous. They were the biggest contributors to St. Michael's Church and its outreach programs, and they never failed to lend a hand to the less fortunate. He was even admired by some as the smarter Malco who was willing to hustle to make a buck.

Away from the Point, though, Lance was yielding to his ambitions. As a silent partner, he bought a nightclub and turned half of it into a casino. The other half was a bar with watered-down, overpriced drinks the GIs were more than happy to pay for, especially when served by cute waitresses in revealing outfits. The upstairs rooms were rented by the half hour. Business was so good that Lance and his partner opened another club, larger and nicer. They called it Red Velvet, and erected a gaudy neon sign, the brightest on Highway 90. The Strip was born.

Carmen retired from the store and became a full-time mother. Lance worked long days and nights and was often absent, but Carmen kept the home together and doted on her three children. She disapproved of her husband's ventures into the darker world, but they seldom discussed his clubs. The money was good and they had more than most on the Point. Complaining would have no effect. Lance was old-school, his father was from the old country; the man ruled the house with an iron fist and the woman raised the kids. Carmen accepted her role with a quiet steadiness.

Perhaps their happiest moments were at the baseball parks. Young Hugh became a dominant player as an eight-year-old and improved each year. During the annual draft, every coach wanted him as the top pick. When he was ten, he was chosen for the twelve-year-old league, a rarity. His only equal was his friend Keith Rudy.

CHAPTER 4

The Rudy clan had been on the Point almost as long as the Malcos. Somewhere amidst the paperwork in the New Orleans
Customs House, *Rudic* became *Rudy,* not a common American
name but more digestible than anything from Croatia.

Keith's father, Jesse Rudy, was born in 1924, and like all the
other kids, grew up around the canneries and shrimp boats. The
day after his eighteenth birthday, he joined the navy and was sent
to fight in the Pacific. Hundreds of boys from the Point were at
war and the tight community offered countless prayers. Daily Mass
was packed. Letters from the troops were read aloud to friends and
discussed by their fathers over beers, and their mothers at knitting
clubs. In November of 1943, the war came home when the Bono-
vich family got the knock on the door. Harry, a marine, had been
killed at Guadalcanal, the first death for the Point, and only the
fourth from Harrison County. The neighbors grieved and helped
in a hundred ways, as the dark cloud of war hung even heavier.
Two months later the second boy was killed.

Jesse served on a destroyer with the Pacific Fleet. He was
wounded in October 1944, during the Battle of Leyte Gulf, when
his ship took a direct hit from a kamikaze dive bomber. He was
pulled from the sea with severe burns over both legs. Two months
later he arrived at the naval hospital in San Francisco where he was
treated by good doctors and no shortage of pretty, young nurses.

A romance blossomed, and when he was discharged in the
spring of 1945, he returned to the Coast with two fragile legs, a
duffel with all of his assets, and a nineteen-year-old bride. Agnes

was a farm girl from Kansas who followed Jesse back home with great anxiety. She had never been to the Deep South and harbored all the usual stereotypes: shoeless sharecroppers, toothless hillbillies, Jim Crow cruelties, and so on, but she was madly in love with Jesse. They rented a house on the Point and went to work. Agnes was hired as a nurse at Keesler as Jesse hustled from one dead-end job to another. His physical limitations prevented him from even part-time work on a shrimp boat, much to his relief.

To her surprise, Agnes quickly embraced life on the Coast. She loved the tightness of the immigrant communities and was welcomed without reservation or bias. Her Anglo-Protestant background was brushed aside. After eighty years in the country, intermarrying amongst the ethnic groups was common and accepted. Agnes enjoyed the dances and parties, an occasional drink, and the large family gatherings. Life in rural Kansas had been much quieter, and drier.

In 1946, Congress provided funding for the GI Bill and thousands of young veterans could suddenly afford higher education. Jesse enrolled at a junior college and took every history course offered. His dream was to teach American history to high school students. His unspoken dream was to become a learned professor and lecture at a university.

Starting a family was not in the plans, but postwar America was proving to be a fertile land. Keith was born in April of 1948 at Keesler, where the veterans and their families received free medical services.

Twenty-eight days later, Hugh Malco was born on the same wing. Their families knew each other from the immigrant cliques on the Point, and their fathers were friendly, though not close.

Five months after Keith arrived, Jesse and Agnes surprised his family with the news that they were going away to study. Or, at least Jesse would study. The nearest four-year school was the state teachers college seventy-five miles north in Hattiesburg. They would be gone for a couple of years and then return. His would be the first college degree in the Rudic/Rudy family, and his parents were rightfully proud. He and Agnes packed their belongings, along with Keith, into their 1938 Mercury and headed north on Highway 49. They rented a tiny student apartment on campus, and within two days Agnes had a job as a nurse with a group of doctors. They juggled her work schedule with his classes and managed to avoid paying babysitters for little Keith. Jesse took as many classes as possible and breezed through his studies.

In two years he was finished and they contemplated staying on and pursuing a master's. However, the fertility issue was back. When Agnes realized she was pregnant with number two, they decided college was over and Jesse needed to start a career. They returned home and rented a house on the Point. When there were no openings in the history department at Biloxi High, Jesse scrambled to find a job teaching civics to ninth-graders in Gulfport. His first salary was $2,700 a year. Agnes went back to Keesler as a nurse but struggled with a difficult pregnancy and had to take leave.

Beverly was born in 1950. Jesse and Agnes agreed that two children were enough for a while and they became serious about family planning. He finally landed a job teaching history at Gulfport High and received a slight raise. Agnes worked part-time and, like most young postwar couples, they barely stayed above water and dreamed of better things. Despite their cautionary efforts, things somehow went awry and Agnes got pregnant for the third time. Laura arrived only fourteen months after Beverly, and overnight the house became far too small. But Jesse's parents were only four doors down, and there were aunts and uncles practically across the street. When Agnes needed help or even an occasional break, she needed only to give a yell and someone was on the way. The mothers and grandmothers on the block took great pride in raising each other's children.

A favorite topic, whispered between Jesse and Agnes in one of their rare quiet moments, was the notion of moving away from the Point. While the support was crucial and they appreciated it, they also found it suffocating at times. Everyone knew their business. There was little privacy. If they skipped Sunday Mass for any reason, they could expect a regular parade of family and friends stopping by Sunday afternoon to see who was sick. If one of the kids had a fever, it became a life-and-death matter along the street. Privacy was one issue. Space was an even larger one. The house was cramped and would only become more so as their children grew. But any upgrade would be a challenge. With three small children underfoot, Agnes was unable to work, which was a blow because, when full-time, she earned more than Jesse. His salary was not yet $3,000 a year, and pay raises for schoolteachers were never a priority.

And so they dreamed. And, as difficult as it was, they tried to abstain from sexual relations as much as possible. A fourth child was out of the question.

He arrived anyway. On May 14, 1953, Timothy came home to a house full of well-wishers, most of whom were in quiet agreement that four was enough. The neighbors were tired of balloons and cake.

———•———

During his brief interlude as a college boy, albeit a married one, Jesse made only one significant friend. Felix Perry was also a history major who abruptly changed course after graduation and decided to become a lawyer. As an excellent student, he had no difficulty getting into law school at Ole Miss, and finished in three years at the top of his class. He landed a job with a nice firm in Jackson and was drawing an enviable salary.

He called ahead and said he was coming to Biloxi on business and how about dinner? With four kids under the age of five, Jesse could not even consider a night out, but Agnes insisted. "Just don't come home drunk," she said with a laugh.

"And when was the last time that happened?"

"Never. Get out of here."

Single, away from home, and with cash in his pocket, Felix was looking for fun. They enjoyed gumbo, raw oysters, and grilled snapper at Mary Mahoney's, with a bottle of French wine. Felix made it clear that the night was on him, said he'd bill it to a client. Jesse had never felt so indulged. But as the dinner progressed, Jesse became irritated with his old friend's self-importance. Felix was earning good money, wearing impressive suits, driving a 1952 Ford, and his career was arching upward with no end in sight. He would be a partner in seven years, maybe eight, and that was like hitting the jackpot.

"Have you ever thought about the law?" he asked. "I mean, you can't teach school forever, right?"

Dead right, but Jesse wasn't ready to admit it. "I've thought about a lot of things lately," he said. "But I love what I do."

"That's important, Jesse. Good for you, but I don't know how they survive financially in this state. The pay is peanuts. Still the lowest in the nation, right?"

Indeed it was, but such an observation coming from Felix was unnecessary.

They spent half of dinner talking about associates and partners, lawsuits and trials, and for Jesse the conversation cut two ways. First, it was mildly irritating to be reminded that teaching school would always be a financial strain, especially for a male breadwinner with four kids at home. Second, the more they talked the more intrigued Jesse became with the idea of becoming a lawyer. Given that he was already thirty years old, it seemed an impossible challenge, but perhaps he was ready for one.

Felix paid the bill and they set off to find "trouble," in his words. He was from a small, dry county (all eighty-two counties were still dry in 1954) and had only heard the legend of Biloxi vice. He wanted to drink, roll some dice, see some skin, and maybe rent a girl.

Like every kid from Biloxi, Jesse had grown up in a culture

and a town where some of the men enjoyed bad things—gambling, prostitutes, strippers, whiskey—all illegal but accepted nonetheless. As a young teenager, he had sneaked cigarettes in the pool halls and beers from certain bars, but once the novelty wore off he forgot about such prohibited activities. Every family had a story of a young man with gambling debts or a drinking problem, and every mother lectured her sons on the dangers lurking just across town. The night before Jesse left for boot camp and the war, he and some friends hit the bars hard and spent their last dollars on hired girls. Over breakfast the next morning, his mother said nothing about his late night. He was not the only soldier to say his farewells with a hangover. When he came home three years later, he brought a wife and his brief stint as a hell-raiser was over. Occasionally, once a month at most, he met some friends for a quick beer after work. His favorite bar was Malco's Grocery, and he often saw Lance there mixing drinks.

He wasn't sure what kind of "trouble" Felix was thinking of, but the safest place to lose cash was Jerry's Truck Stop, a fixture on Highway 90, the main drag along the Coast. In years past, Jerry had actually sold diesel fuel and serviced rigs passing through. Then he added a bar behind his café and offered the cheapest drinks on the Coast. Truckers were delighted and spread the word throughout the region that you could have ice-cold beer with your eggs and sausage. Jerry expanded his bar and was counting his money until the sheriff informed him that drinking and driving were not compatible. There were some wrecks caused by intoxicated truckers; folks were dead. Jerry had a choice—diesel fuel or booze. He chose the latter, took out his pumps, converted his shop into a casino, and began servicing soldiers instead of long-haulers. The "Truck Stop" became the most famous lounge in Biloxi.

Felix paid the one-dollar cover charge and they went inside to the long, shiny bar. He was immediately slack-jawed at the sight of two lovely dancers shimmying around a pole with moves he'd never seen. The club was loud, dark, and smoky, with colored lights sweeping the dance floor. They found a spot at the bar and were immediately accosted by two young ladies in heavy makeup, low-cut blouses, and short skirts.

"How about a drink, boys?" the first one asked as she squeezed between them and pressed boobs into Felix's chest. The other one came on to Jesse, who knew the game.

"Sure," Felix said, eager to spend some money. "What'll it be?"

Jesse glanced at one of four bartenders who was ready to mix their drinks. Within seconds, two tall greenish cocktails arrived for the girls and two bourbons for the boys.

The friendly bartender eagerly agreed and said loudly, "Remember, every fourth drink is free."

"Wow!" Felix practically yelled. So, to make the economics work, a fella would need at least eight drinks to call it a good night.

The green drinks were nothing but sugar water and each included a colorful plastic swizzle stick with a cherry on top. In due course, the girls would collect the swizzle sticks and hide them in a pocket. When the night was over and they settled up, they would be paid fifty cents per stick, nothing per hour. The more drinks they solicited, the more money they made. The locals knew the game and from somewhere the term "B-drinking" had evolved. The tourists and servicemen did not, and they kept ordering.

The girls were pretty and the younger the better. Because the money was good, and the opportunities for women in small towns were scarce, they headed to the Coast and a faster life. The stories were legion of farm girls who worked the clubs hard for a few years, saved their money, and returned home where no one knew what they'd been up to. They married their old boyfriends from high school and raised kids.

Felix was with Debbie, a real veteran who could spot a mark, though it didn't take much in the way of intuition. Felix said to Jesse, "We're gonna dance. Watch our drinks."

They disappeared into the mob. Sherry Ann moved closer to Jesse, who smiled and said, "Look, I'm not in the game. I'm happily married with four kids at home. Sorry."

She sighed, smiled, understood, and said, "Thanks for the drink." Within seconds she was working the other end of the bar. After a few minutes of bump-and-grind, Felix and Debbie breezed by and grabbed their drinks. He whispered, loudly, "Say, we're going upstairs. Give me thirty minutes, okay?"

"Sure."

Suddenly lonely at the bar and wishing to avoid another pickup attempt, Jesse went to the casino and walked through it. He had heard rumors about the Truck Stop's growing popularity, but he was startled at the number of tables. Slot machines lined the walls. Roulette and craps tables were on one side, poker and blackjack on the other. Dozens of gamblers, almost all men and many in uniform, were gambling as they smoked, drank, and yelled. Cocktail waitresses scurried about, trying to keep up with demand. And it was only a Tuesday night.

Jesse knew to avoid roulette and craps because the games were rigged. It was well known that the only consistently honest game in town was blackjack. He found an empty stool at a crowded 25-cent table and pulled out two dollars, his limit. An hour later he was up $2.50 and Felix was nowhere in sight.

At eleven, he called his brother and harangued him for a ride home.

———•———

The following year, 1955, Jesse enrolled in night classes at the Loyola Law School in New Orleans. Since the dinner with Felix, he had become infatuated with the idea of becoming a lawyer, and talked, at least to Agnes, of little else. She finally grew weary of the same conversations and set aside her reluctance. With four small children a nursing job, even part-time, was out of the question, but she would support him and together they could make it work. Both despised the idea of debt, but when his father offered a $2,000 loan, they had no choice but to take it.

On Tuesdays, after class, Jesse hurried to New Orleans, a two-hour drive, and usually arrived about fifteen minutes late for the 6:00 P.M. class. The professors understood their students and the demands on their time as full-time employees elsewhere. They were in law school, at night, going about their studies the hard way, and most rules were flexible. Over four hours, covering two courses, Jesse took copious notes, engaged in discussions, and, when possible, read upcoming materials. He absorbed the law and was thrilled by its challenges. Late in the night, as the second course came to a close, he was often the only student still wide awake and eager to engage with the professor. At 9:50 sharp, he hustled from the classroom and to his car for the drive home. At midnight, Agnes was always waiting with a warmed-over dinner and questions about his classes.

He seldom slept more than five hours a night and woke before dawn to prepare his own history lectures, or to grade papers.

On Thursday nights, he was off again to Loyola for two more classes. He never missed one, nor did he miss a day of work or Mass or a family dinner. As his children grew, he always had time to play in the backyard or take them to the beach. Agnes often found him at midnight on the sofa, dead from exhaustion, with a thick case-book opened and resting on his chest. When he survived the first year with stellar grades, they opened a bottle of cheap champagne late one night and celebrated. Then they passed out. One benefit of the fatigue was the lack of energy for sex. Four kids were enough.

As his studies progressed, and as it became more apparent to his family and friends that he was not chasing a crazy dream, a degree of pride crept into his world. He would be the first lawyer from the Point, the first of all those children and grandchildren of immigrants who had worked and sacrificed in the new country. There were rumors that he would leave and rumors that he would stay.

Would he go to work in a nice firm in Biloxi, or would he open his own shop on the Point and help his people? Was it true he wanted to work for a big firm in New Orleans?

The curious, though, kept their questions to themselves. Jesse never heard the rumblings. He was too busy to worry about the neighbors. He had no plans to leave the Coast and tried to meet every lawyer in town. He hung around the courtrooms and became friendly with the judges and their court reporters.

After four years of slogging through night school and losing countless hours of sleep, Jesse Rudy graduated from Loyola with honors, passed the Mississippi bar exam, and took an associate's position with a three-man firm on Howard Avenue in downtown Biloxi. His starting salary was on the same level with that of a high school history teacher, but there was the allure of the bonus. At the end of each year, the firm tallied up its income and rewarded each lawyer with a bonus based on hours worked and new business generated. Lean and hungry, Jesse immediately began his career by clocking in each morning at 5:00.

While the law degree at first meant little in the way of real money, it meant something more to the mortgage banker. He knew the law firm well and thought highly of its partners. He approved Jesse's application for a loan, and the family moved into a three-bedroom home in the western part of Biloxi.

As the first local lawyer of Croatian descent, Jesse was immediately flooded with the everyday legal problems of his people. He couldn't say no, and so he spent hours preparing inexpensive wills, deeds, and simple contracts. He was never bored by this, and he welcomed his clients into his handsome office as if they were millionaires. Jesse Rudy's success became the source of many proud stories on the Point.

For his first big case, a partner asked him to research several issues involved in a business deal that had gone sour. The owner of the Truck Stop had verbally agreed to sell his business to a syndicate fronted by a local operator named Snead. There was also a written contract for the land, and another contract for a lease or two. The parties had been negotiating for a year, without the benefit of legal counsel, and, not surprisingly, there was confusion and tension. Everyone was angry and ready to sue. The owner of the Truck Stop had even been threatened with a good beating.

The owners of the syndicate preferred to hide behind Snead and remain anonymous, but as the layers were peeled away, it became known, at least among the lawyers, that the principal investor was none other than Lance Malco.

CHAPTER 5

The price war began in a brothel. A small-time gangster named Cleveland bought an old club on the Strip called Foxy's. He tacked on a cheap wing for gambling and a slightly nicer one for his whores. While there was no set price for half an hour of pleasure with a girl, the generally accepted rate, and one tacitly agreed upon by the owners, was twenty dollars. At Foxy's the rate was cut in half and the news spread like wildfire through Keesler. And since the soldiers were thirsty before and after, the price of a cheap draft beer was also discounted. The place was slammed and there was not enough parking.

To survive, some of the other low-end clubs cut their rates too. Then the owners began poaching girls. The economics of Biloxi vice, always a fragile equilibrium, were upended. In an attempt to restore order, some tough guys stopped by Foxy's late one night, slapped around a bartender, beat up two bouncers, and passed along the warning that selling sex and booze for less than the "standard rate" was unacceptable. The beatings proved contagious and a wave of violence swept through the Strip. An ambush behind one joint led to retaliation at another. The owners complained to the police, who listened but were not too worried. There had yet to be a killing and, well, boys will be boys. What's the real danger in a few fights? Let the crooks take care of their own markets.

In the midst of the turmoil, which raged on for over a year, a star rookie entered the picture. His name was Nevin Noll, a twenty-year-old recruit who'd joined the air force to escape trouble back home in eastern Kentucky. He came from a colorful family of moonshiners and outlaws and had been raised to hold a dim view of the law. Not a single male relative had tried honest work in decades. Young Nevin, though, dreamed of leaving and pursuing a more glorious life as a famous gangster. He left sooner than expected and in a hurry.

In his wake were at least two pregnant girls, with angry fathers, and an assault warrant that stemmed from a vicious beating he'd given an off-duty deputy. Fighting was second nature; he'd rather throw punches than drink cold beer. He stood six feet two inches, was thick through the chest and as strong as an ox, and his fists were freakishly quick and efficient. In six weeks of basic training at Keesler, he had already broken two jaws, knocked out numerous teeth, and put one boy in the hospital with a concussion.

One more fight, and Nevin would be dishonorably discharged.

It happened soon enough. He was shooting craps at Red Velvet with a couple of buddies on a Saturday night when an argument erupted over a set of suspicious dice. An angry gambler called them "loaded dice," and reached for his chips. The stickman was quicker. A side dealer shoved the gambler, who had been drinking, and who, evidently, did not take shoving well. Nevin had just rolled the dice, lost, and was also suspicious of the table. Because so many customers were soldiers and prone to drink, Red Velvet had plenty of bouncers, and they were always watching the boys in uniform. Nothing excited Nevin more than flying fists, and he jumped into the middle of the argument. When a dealer pushed him back, he shot a left hook to the man's chin and knocked him out cold. Two guards were on Nevin in an instant and both got their noses flattened before they could throw a punch. Bodies were flying in all directions and he wanted more. His two pals from the base backed away and watched with admiration. They had seen it all before. Fully grown men, regardless of their size, were nothing but punching bags when they got too close to Mr. Noll.

The dealer with the stick leapt across the table and took a wild swing. It hit Nevin across the shoulder but did no damage. He hit the guy four times in the face, each blow drawing blood.

All gambling stopped as a crowd gathered around the craps table. Nevin stood in the middle of the pile of beaten and bloodied men, looked around, wild-eyed, and kept saying, "Come on, come on. Who's next?" No one moved in his direction.

It ended without further bloodshed when two bouncers with shotguns appeared. Nevin smiled and raised his hands. He won the fight but lost the battle. Once he was handcuffed, the guards kicked his legs out from under him and dragged him away. Just another night in jail.

Early Sunday morning, Lance Malco and his chief of security rounded up the two dealers and two security guards, none of whom were in any mood to talk, and replayed the fight. The side dealer's jaw was horribly swollen. The stickman's face was a mess of cuts—one in each eyebrow, one on the bridge of his nose, plus a busted lower lip. Each security guard held an ice pack to his nose and tried to see through blurred and puffy eyes.

"What a fine team," Lance said with derision. "One man did all this damage?"

He made each one describe what happened. All four reluctantly marveled at the speed with which they got nailed.

"Guy must be a boxer or something," one of the guards said.

"Sumbitch can punch, I'll tell you that," said the other.

"You don't have to tell me," Lance said with a laugh. "I can see it in your face."

He didn't fire them. Instead he went to court and watched Nevin Noll appear before the judge and plead not guilty to four counts of assault. His court-appointed lawyer explained to the court that his client had, only the day before, been discharged from Keesler and was headed back to Kentucky. That should be punishment enough, shouldn't it?

Noll was released on a cheap bond and ordered to return in

two days. Lance cornered Nevin's lawyer and asked if he could have a word with his client, said he might be willing to drop the charges if they could strike a deal. Lance had a nose for talent, be it slick card dealers, pretty young girls, or violent men. He recruited the best and paid them well.

For Nevin Noll, it was a miracle. He could forget the military, forget going home to Kentucky, and instead get a real job doing what he dreamed of—working for a crime boss, handling security, hanging out in bars and brothels, and occasionally cracking a skull or two. In an instant, Nevin Noll became the most loyal employee Lance Malco would ever hire.

The Boss, as he was known by then, demoted the security guards with broken noses and put them in a truck fetching liquor off a boat. Noll was moved into the office upstairs, a "corporate suite," at Red Velvet, and began learning the business.

Cleveland, the owner of Foxy's, had withstood numerous threats and was still selling sex on the cheap. Something had to be done and Lance saw the opportunity to show real leadership. He and his boys devised a simple plan of attack, one that would elevate Nevin Noll to new heights, or get him killed.

At five o'clock one Friday afternoon in early March 1961, the Boss received word from a lookout that Cleveland had just parked his new Cadillac in its usual place behind Foxy's. Ten minutes later, Nevin Noll entered, went to the bar, and ordered a drink. The lounge was practically empty, but a band was setting up in a corner and preparations were underway for another busy night. Security was light but that would change in an hour or so.

Noll asked the bartender if Mr. Cleveland was in, said he wanted a word with him.

The bartender frowned, kept drying a beer mug, and said, "Not sure. Who wants to know?"

"Well, I do. Mr. Malco sent me over. You know Mr. Lance Malco, right?"

"Never heard of him."

"Of course not. I wouldn't expect you to know much at all." Noll was off the stool and headed to the end of the bar.

"Hey asshole!" the bartender said. "Where do you think you're going?"

"Going to see Mr. Cleveland. I know where he's hiding back there."

The bartender was not a small man and he'd broken up his share of fights. "Wait a minute, buddy," he said, and he grabbed Noll's left arm, a mistake. With his right, Noll spun and landed a crunching blow to the bartender's left jaw, dropping him like a brick and into oblivion. A thug in a black cowboy hat materialized from the shadows and charged at Noll, who snatched an empty beer mug off the bar and bounced it off his ear. With both on the floor, Noll looked around. Two men at a table gawked at him in disbelief. The band members froze in place and were not sure what to do, if anything. Noll nodded to them, then disappeared through swinging doors. The hallway was dark, the kitchen was further ahead. A former bartender had told Malco that Cleveland's office was behind a blue door at the end of the narrow hallway. Noll kicked it in and announced his arrival with "Hello Cleveland, got a minute?"

A thick boy in a coat and tie was bolting from a chair. He never made it, as Noll pummeled him with three quick punches to his face. He fell to the floor, groaning. Cleveland was behind his desk and had been on the phone, which he was now holding in midair. For a second or two he was too surprised to react. He dropped the phone and reached down to open a drawer, but he was too late. Noll lunged across the desk, slapped him hard in the face, and knocked him out of his chair. The objective was to beat soundly but not to kill. The Boss wanted Cleveland alive, at least for now. Using nothing but his fists, Noll broke both jawbones, split lips, knocked out teeth, closed eyes, lacerated cheeks and forehead, and separated the nasal bone from the cranial cavity. When the thick boy made more sounds, Noll took a heavy ashtray and drove it into the back of his skull.

A small side door opened and a platinum blonde of about thirty appeared and, seeing the carnage, almost screamed. She covered her mouth with both hands and looked in horror at Noll. He quickly removed a revolver from a rear pocket and nodded to a chair. "Sit down and shut up!" he growled. She backed into the chair, still unable to utter a sound. From a front pocket, Noll pulled out an eight-inch tube, a silencer, and screwed it over the revolver's barrel. He fired one shot into the ceiling and the woman shrieked. He fired another shot into the wall three feet above her head and said, "Listen to me, dammit!"

She was too horrified to react. He fired another shot into the wall, the same muted thud.

He stood above her, pointed the pistol, and said, "Tell Cleveland he's got seven days to shut this place down. Got it?"

She managed to nod. *Yes.*

"I'll be back in seven days. If he's here, he really gets hurt." He unscrewed the silencer, tossed it into her lap as a souvenir, and stuck the revolver under his belt. He walked out of the office, ducked into the kitchen, and left through a rear door.

———•———

The price war was over.

Cleveland spent three weeks in a hospital, with lots of tubes and a ventilator. His brain swelled from time to time and his doctors induced one coma after another. Fearing another visit from Noll, his girlfriend, the platinum blonde, closed Foxy's to await orders from Cleveland. When he was finally released from the hospital, he couldn't walk and was rolled out in a wheelchair. Though brain-damaged, he had enough sense to realize his ambitious venture onto the Strip had come to an end.

Because Nevin Noll was new to the scene, no one recognized him and an identification was not possible. However, his one-man assault on Foxy's became an instant legend, and left no doubt that Lance Malco was indeed the Boss.

A bank foreclosed on Foxy's and plywood was nailed over its doors and windows. It remained boarded up for six months, then was sold to a corporation out of New Orleans, one controlled by Lance Malco.

With four clubs now under his thumb, Lance Malco controlled the largest share of vice along the Coast. The cash poured in and he shared it with his gang and the politicians who mattered. He believed in spending money to meet the demands of his customers, and he offered the best booze, girls, and gambling east of the Mississippi.

Competition was a constant problem. Success bred imitation, and there was an endless line of operators angling for a foothold. Some he managed to close down by leaning on the sheriff. Others were more resilient and fought back. There was always the threat of violence, and often the threats materialized.

The Malco family moved away from the Point and into a fine new home north of Biloxi. They lived with gates and guards, and the Boss seldom went anywhere without Nevin Noll by his side.

CHAPTER 6

Hugh Malco's once promising athletic career came to an abrupt halt one hot day in August. As a sophomore at Biloxi High, he and a bunch of other fifteen-year-olds were suffering through preseason two-a-day practices and dreaming of making the varsity. Things were not going well. There were at least one hundred players on the field, most of them older, bigger, and faster. The Biloxi Indians competed in the Big Eight, the state's elite conference, and talent was never a problem. The team was stacked with seniors, many of whom would play in college. Sophomores rarely made the varsity and were usually relegated to the JV.

Long gone were the glory days of Little League baseball, when Hugh and Keith Rudy dominated every game. Some all-stars at that age continued to grow and develop, others were left behind. Some athletes peaked at twelve or thirteen. The luckier ones kept maturing and got better. Hugh wasn't growing as fast as the others, and his speed, or lack thereof, was a known liability.

On that day he twisted a knee and limped into the shade. A trainer put ice on it and informed the coach, who had little time to worry about a lowly sophomore. Hugh saw a doctor the next day and the diagnosis was strained ligaments. No football for at least a month. He hung around practice for a few days on crutches but soon tired of watching his pals sweat in the heat and dirt. The more he watched, the more he realized that he really didn't love football.

Baseball was his game, though he feared it too was slipping away. The summer season had not gone well. The right arm that had so terrified batters from forty-five feet was not nearly as intimidating from sixty feet. He had struggled on the mound and at the plate and failed to make the all-star team. Keith was now four inches taller and even faster around the bases. Hugh was proud of his pal for making all-stars, but he was also sick with envy. Their friendship grew even more complicated when Keith made the cut in August and became the varsity's third-string quarterback, one of only five sophomores on the roster. In a football-crazed town, his status was elevated and he gravitated to a different crowd. The students admired him. The cheerleaders and pep squad girls deemed him even cuter.

With his afternoons free, Hugh loafed for a few weeks until his father cracked the whip. Lance had never been idle and couldn't tolerate the notion of lazy kids. There were plenty of odd jobs around his clubs and properties and he put his oldest son on the payroll. Cash, of course. Lance controlled more hard cash than anyone in the state and was generous with it. He gave Hugh a used pickup truck and made him an errand boy. He hauled nothing illegal, mainly food and supplies for the restaurants and building materials for construction projects.

Carmen loathed the idea of her son hanging around the clubs and mixing with the shady crowd, but Hugh liked the work and the money. She complained to Lance and he promised to keep an eye on the kid and avoid trouble.

The underworld, though, proved irresistible to a curious teenager, especially the owner's son, and before long Hugh met Nevin Noll at a pool table in the rear of the Truck Stop. Nevin gave him a pack of cigarettes, then a cold beer, and they quickly became friends. He taught him how to shoot pool, play poker and blackjack, and the basics of betting on horses and football games. Before long, Hugh was booking games for his friends at school. While Keith slogged through daily practices on the field and sat the bench on Friday nights, Hugh was making money handicapping college and pro football games. Lance knew the dangers the kid faced, but he was too busy to care. He was building an empire, one that

Hugh would likely inherit one day. Sooner or later, his son would be exposed to all manner of criminal activity. Nevin told the boss that he was watching his son and there was nothing to worry about. Lance doubted this but went about his business, hoping for the best.

Hugh's life changed dramatically when he saw Cindy Murdock, a perky little blonde with comely brown eyes and a gorgeous figure. She bounced through Red Velvet one afternoon when he was unloading crates of soft drinks, and said hello in passing. Hugh was smitten and asked a bartender who she was. Just another girl who claimed to be eighteen, same as the rest, though no one ever checked.

Hugh mentioned her to Nevin, who immediately saw some harmless trouble and found it too good to leave alone. He arranged a tryst, and Hugh, at the age of fifteen, entered a new world. He was immediately consumed with Miss Murdock and thought of nothing else. While his classmates told dirty jokes, swapped girlie magazines, and fantasized, Hugh was enjoying the real thing at every opportunity. She was more than willing and thought it hilarious that she had Mr. Malco's son on a leash. Nevin became worried that the little romance would be talked about by other employees and found the lovebirds a safer place in one of the cheap motels owned by the company.

Lance was impressed by his son's deepening interest in the business, while at the same time Carmen noticed an ominous change in behavior. She found his cigarettes, confronted him, and was told not to worry because all the kids were smoking. It was even permitted at school, with a note from home. She smelled beer on his breath and he laughed it off. Hell, she drank, Lance drank, everybody they knew enjoyed alcohol. He didn't have a problem, so relax. He was skipping school and Sunday Mass and running with a rougher crowd. Lance, when he was home, ignored her concerns and said the kid was just being a teenager. His new direction in life, and his father's indifference, added another strain to a marriage that was slowly unraveling.

Cindy lived in a cheap apartment with four other working girls. Because their nights were long, they often slept until noon. At least once a week, Hugh skipped classes and woke them up with cheeseburgers and sodas. He became one of the gang and enjoyed listening to their bitching sessions. They were often hassled by the bartenders, bouncers, and security guards. They told hilarious stories of old men who couldn't perform and drunks with strange requests. Hanging out with a bunch of hookers, Hugh learned more about the business than the gangsters who ran it.

He arrived at the apartment late one morning and found everyone still asleep. As he unpacked their lunch, he noticed Cindy's purse on the kitchen counter. He tipped it over and some things fell out. One was her driver's license. Real name of Barbara Brown, age sixteen, from a nowhere town in Arkansas.

Every girl was presumed to be younger than she claimed. The eighteen-year threshold was the going rule, but no one cared. Prostitution was illegal anyway, so it didn't really matter. Half the cops in town were customers.

Her age bothered him for a day or two, but not for long. He was only fifteen. Everything was consensual, and they were certainly compatible. With time, though, as he became more attached to her, he began to resent the thoughts of his girl sleeping with any man with the cash. For several reasons, primarily his age, he was not welcome in the clubs at night, and he had never seen her hustle the soldiers in her skimpy costumes. When he learned that she had started stripping and lap dancing, he asked her to stop. When she refused, they had a good fight, during which she reminded him that the other guys were paying cash for the companionship he was getting for free.

Nevin warned him that Lance was asking questions about his relationship with the girl. Someone inside a club had snitched. Hugh told her they needed to cool things, and he tried to stay away. He went a week without seeing her but thought of nothing else. She welcomed him back with open arms.

She failed to show for a rendezvous one afternoon, and Hugh burned up the streets trying to find her. After dark, he checked her apartment and was shocked at what he found. Her left eye was bruised and swollen. Her lower lip had a small cut. Through tears, she described how she had been slapped around the night before by her last customer, a regular who had become increasingly physical. Given her appearance, she would miss work for several days, and she, as always, needed the money.

It was serious in more ways than the obvious. A teenage girl had been beaten by a brute who was at least forty years old. Criminal charges were in order, though Hugh knew the police would not be called. If she chose to tell her supervisor, the matter would be dealt with "in-house." Lance protected his girls and paid them well, and he relied on a steady stream of them from places unknown. If word got out that they weren't safe in his clubs, his business would suffer.

Cindy had left in a hurry the night before and had not told the manager. She was afraid of squealing on anyone; she was afraid of everything at the moment, and needed a friend. Hugh sat with her for hours and kept ice on her wounds.

He found Nevin Noll the following day and told him what happened. Nevin said he would handle the situation. He checked with the club's manager and learned the identity of the customer. Three days later, with Cindy back at work and hiding the damage under even more makeup, Nevin asked Hugh to take a ride with him.

"Where to?" he asked, though it didn't matter. He admired Noll and wanted to get even closer. In many ways he thought of him as a big brother, one who'd been around the block a few times.

"We're going over to Pascagoula to look at new Chryslers," Noll said with a smile.

"You buying one?"

"Nope. I think our boy sells cars over there. Let's drop by and have a word."

"This sounds like fun."

"You just stay in the car, okay? I'll do the talking."

Half an hour later, they parked near a row of beautiful new Chrysler sedans. Nevin got out, walked over to one, looked it over, and was studying the sticker in the window when a salesman approached with a big hello and a toothy smile. He stretched out a hand as if they were old friends, but Nevin ignored it. "Looking for Roger Brewer."

"That's me. What can I do for you?"

"You were at Red Velvet Monday night."

Brewer lost his smile and glanced over his shoulder. He shrugged, gave a smart-ass "So what?"

"Spent some time with one of our girls, Cindy."

"What is this?"

"Maybe I want to buy a car."

"Who the hell are you?"

"She weighs a hundred and ten pounds and you slapped her around."

"So?" Brewer had the appearance of a man who'd slapped around others and was not shy about violence. He squared up to Nevin and showed him a sneer.

Nevin took a step closer, within striking distance, and said, "She's a kid. Why don't you slap people your own size?"

"Like you?"

"That's a good place to start."

Brewer had a second thought and said, "Get outta here."

Hugh inched even lower in the front seat, but didn't miss anything. His window was down and he was close enough to hear the conversation.

"Don't come back, okay?" Nevin said. "It's off-limits for you."

"Go to hell. I'll do what I want."

The first punch was so quick Hugh almost missed it. A short right cross landed square on Brewer's jaw, snapping back his head and buckling his knees. He fell onto the front of a new sedan, caught himself, and threw a wild roundhouse right hook that

Nevin easily ducked. His next shot was a hard right to Brewer's gut that made him squeal. A left-right-left combo ripped his eyebrows and lacerated his lips. A hard right hook knocked him onto the hood of the sedan. Nevin yanked his feet and pulled him off the hood, crashing the back of his head on the bumper as he went down. On the asphalt, Nevin kicked him square in the nose and appeared ready to beat him to death.

"Hey!" someone yelled and Hugh saw two men running toward them.

Nevin ignored them and kicked Brewer again in the face. When the first man was close enough, Nevin whirled with a left hook and dropped him cold. The second one stopped, froze, and had a quick afterthought. "Who are you?"

As if it mattered. Nevin grabbed him by the knot of his necktie and rammed his head into the left front hubcap of the sedan. With all three on the ground, Nevin returned to Brewer and kicked him twice in the groin, the second blow crunching his testicles and making him grunt like a dying animal.

Nevin jumped in the car and calmly drove away as if nothing had happened. As they left the lot, Hugh glanced back. All three were still down, though the second rescuer was on all fours and trying to collect himself.

Minutes passed before they spoke. Finally, Nevin said, "You want some ice cream?"

"Uh, sure."

"There's a Tastee-Freez just up the road here," Nevin said nonchalantly, as if nothing had happened. "Best banana shakes on the Coast."

"Okay." Hugh was still in disbelief but had some questions. "Those guys back there, will they call the police?"

Nevin laughed at such foolishness. "No. They're not stupid. If they call the police, then I'll call Brewer's wife. The laws of the jungle, son."

"You're not worried about them?"

"Why? What's to worry about?"

"Well, that first guy, Brewer, he might be hurt."

"I hope so. That's the point, young Hugh. You hurt 'em but you don't kill 'em. He just got a message he'll never forget, and he won't be slapping around our girls anymore."

Hugh just shook his head. "That was pretty amazing. You took down three of them in no time flat."

"Well, son, let's just say that I've had some experience."

"So, you do this all the time?"

"No, not all the time. Most of our customers know the rules. Occasionally, we'll get an ass like Brewer back there and have to run him off. More often, though, it's some flyboys who get drunk and start fighting."

Nevin turned in to the Tastee-Freez and parked at the drive-in. He ordered two large banana shakes and turned on the radio to WVMI Biloxi, which happened to be Hugh's favorite too.

"You ever boxed?" Nevin asked.

Hugh shook his head.

"I used my fists a lot when I was a kid. Had to. One of my uncles boxed in the army, before he got kicked out, and he taught me the basics. And we didn't always use gloves. When I was sixteen I knocked him out. He said I had the quickest hands he'd ever seen. He encouraged me to join the army or air force, primarily to get the hell out of the mountains, but also to box on organized teams."

Nevin lit a cigarette and glanced at his watch. Hugh looked at his hands and fingers and saw no signs of the beating.

Hugh asked, "Did you box at Keesler?"

"Some, yeah, but it was more fun fighting the Yankees who were always putting us down. I stayed in trouble and they finally kicked me out. Plus, I hated wearing a uniform."

A cute girl on skates rolled to their car and delivered the milkshakes. When they were back on Highway 90 and headed for Biloxi, Nevin felt the need to offer more worldly advice to his young protégé. After a long pull on his straw he said, "This girl you're seeing, Cindy. Don't get too attached, okay? I know, I know, right now you're all aglow with puppy love, but she's nothing but trouble."

"You fixed me up."

"Sure I did, but you've had your fun, so move on. As you'll learn, there are plenty of women out there."

Hugh worked his straw and absorbed this unsolicited advice.

Nevin said, "She'll be gone before you know it. They come and go. She's too pretty to hang around. She'll go back home and marry some old boy from church."

"She's only sixteen."

"How do you know?"

"I just know."

"I'm not surprised. They all lie."

Hugh grew quiet as he considered life without Cindy Murdock. Nevin had said plenty and decided it was time to shut up. He was only twenty-three years old and, though he'd seen a lot, he had never fallen hard for a woman.

A siren startled both of them. Hugh turned around and saw a deputy in a blue-and-white patrol car. "Shit!" Nevin said as he pulled onto the shoulder of the busy highway. Then he looked at Hugh with a smile and said, "I'll take care of this."

Nevin got out and met the deputy between the cars. Luckily he was from Harrison County. They had crossed from Jackson County less than a mile back.

Harrison County was the domain of Sheriff Albert "Fats" Bowman, rumored to be the highest-paid public official in the state, with precious little of his income ever hitting the books.

The deputy began as a hard-ass. "Your license, please."

Nevin handed it over and tried not to be cocky. He knew what was about to happen. The deputy did not.

He said, "Gotta call outta Pascagoula, said a guy driving a car just like this one needed to answer some questions. Something about an assault at the Chrysler place."

"So, what's your question?"

"You been to the Chrysler place in Pascagoula?"

"Just left. Had to see a man named Roger Brewer. He's probably at the hospital right now, getting sewed up. Brewer was at Red Velvet Monday night and slapped around one of our girls. He won't do it again."

The deputy handed back the driver's license and glanced around, not quite sure what to do next. "So, I take it you work at Red Velvet."

"I do. Lance Malco is my boss. He sent me to see Brewer. Everything's fine on our end."

"Okay. I guess we got no problem with that. I'll radio Pascagoula and tell 'em we ain't see nothin' over here."

"That'll work. May I ask your name? Mr. Malco will want to know."

"Sure. Wiley Garrison."

"Thank you, Deputy Garrison. If you need a drink sometime, let me know."

"Don't drink."

"Thanks just the same."

CHAPTER 7

Baricev's was a well-known seafood restaurant on the Biloxi beach, near downtown. It was a popular place, with too few tables for the demand that was fueled by locals who favored it and tourists who'd heard of its reputation. Reservations were frowned upon because record-keeping was not a priority, so there was usually a long wait at the front door. Some locals, though, got their preferred tables with no waiting whatsoever.

Sheriff Albert "Fats" Bowman was a regular and insisted on the same corner table. He ate there at least once a week, with the check always grabbed by a nightclub owner or hotel operator. He loved the crab claws and stuffed flounder and often stayed for hours.

He never dined in his official uniform, but chose a nice, loose, rumpled suit for these occasions. He didn't want folks to stare, though everyone knew Fats. Not everyone admired him because of his well-earned reputation for corruption, but he was an old-school politician who shook every hand and kissed every baby. It paid off with landslide reelections.

Fats and Rudd Kilgore, his chief deputy and chauffeur, arrived early and sipped on whiskey sours as they waited for Mr. Malco. He arrived promptly at eight and had with him his number two—a lieutenant known only as Tip. As usual, Nevin Noll was the driver and would wait with the car. Though Lance trusted him implicitly, he was still too young to take part in business meetings.

The four shook hands, exchanged greetings like old friends, and settled around the table. More drinks were ordered as they dug in for a long dinner.

Lance had arranged the meeting for a reason. Some of the dinners were nothing but a nice way to say thanks to a corrupt sheriff who took their payoffs and stayed out of their business. Occasionally, though, there was a matter of concern. A large platter of raw oysters landed in the center of the table and they began eating.

Bowman needed to get a trifling issue out of the way. He asked, "Ever hear of a boy named Winslow? Goes by Butch."

Lance looked at Tip, who instinctively shook his head. In response to any direct question, especially one from a cop, Tip always began with a curt "No."

Lance added, "Don't think so. Who is he?"

"Figured. They found him in a ditch last weekend beside Nelly Road, half a mile off Highway 49. He was alive, but barely. Beat to hell and back. Still in the hospital. Last known place of employment was over at the Yacht Club. We checked around, got the word that Butch was dealing blackjack and had sticky fingers. Somebody said he once dealt for you guys at the Truck Stop."

Tip smiled and said, "Yeah, now I remember. We caught him stealing and ran him off. 'Bout a year ago."

"No follow-up?"

"It wasn't us, Sheriff," Tip said.

"Didn't think so. Look, you boys know I don't get involved in disciplinary matters, unless there's a dead body. Somebody came within an inch of killing this boy."

"What's your point, Sheriff?" Lance asked.

"I don't need one."

"Got it."

Tip ordered two pitchers of beer and they worked on the oysters. When it was time to get down to business, Bowman asked, "So what's on your mind?"

Lance leaned in a bit lower and said, "Well, it's no surprise, but this place is getting crowded. Too crowded. And now we're getting word that a new gang is taking a look."

Bowman said, "You're doing okay, Lance. You got your clubs

and joints, more than anybody else. We figure you're running at least a third of the business on the Coast." He lobbed this across the table as if he were speculating as to the numbers. Fats kept his own meticulous records. When he said something like "we figure," the message was that he knew precisely the share of vice Malco was controlling.

"Maybe so, but the challenge is keeping it. I'm sure you've heard of the State Line Mob."

"Heard of them, but I haven't seen them."

"Well, they're here. We caught a rumor about a month ago that they're moving in. Seems as though things are getting too hot up on the border and they're heading south. Biloxi seems attractive, given the business-friendly environment."

The sheriff waved over the waitress and ordered gumbo, crab claws, and stuffed flounder. When she left, he said, "A nasty bunch, by reputation."

"Yes, by reputation. We got a guy who worked up there and knows 'em well. They ran him off for some reason, said he was lucky to get away."

"They got a joint?"

"Rumor is they're trying to buy O'Malley's."

Bowman frowned and looked hard at Kilgore. They didn't like the news, primarily because they had not been contacted by the new guys in town. The rules of engagement were simple: To operate any illegal establishment in Harrison County, approval had to be obtained from Fats Bowman. Dues were required, and he then spread the money around to the police and politicians. Fats wasn't bothered by competition. More clubs and beer joints meant more money for him. The gangs could fight among themselves as long as his bottom line was protected.

He said, "You're pretty good at protecting your turf, Lance. You've done a nice job of consolidating. What am I supposed to do?"

Lance laughed and said, "Oh, I don't know, Sheriff. Run 'em off?"

Fats laughed too and lit a cigarette. He blew a cloud of smoke and put it on the ashtray. "That's your game, Lance. I don't regulate the commerce. I just make sure you boys stay in business."

"And we appreciate it, Sheriff, don't get me wrong. But staying in business is my goal too. Right now things have never been better, for me and for you, and I'd like to keep it that way. Everybody's playing by the rules, nobody's getting too greedy, at least for the moment. But if we allow this gang to move in, there's gonna be trouble."

"Be careful, Lance. If somebody gets killed, then there's the payback. Tit for tat and so it goes. Nothing fires up the do-gooders around here like a gang war. You want your business on the front page?"

"No, and I think this is the perfect moment for you to prevent a war. Put the clamps on these new guys and get rid of them. If they buy O'Malley's, then close it down. They won't shoot at you, Sheriff. They're not that crazy."

The gumbo arrived in large bowls and the oyster shells were removed. Tip refilled the four beer mugs and the men enjoyed their food. After a few bites, Bowman said, "Let's wait and give it some time. I'll have a chat with O'Malley, see what he'll tell me."

Lance grunted, smiled, and said, "Nothing, same as always."

———•———

O'Malley's Pub was in an old warehouse one block off the Strip. Two weeks after the meeting at Baricev's, Deputy Kilgore stopped by one afternoon and went inside. The bar was dark and quiet, too early for happy hour. Two bikers were shooting pool in the rear and one regular was holding down the far end of the bar.

"What'll it be?" the bartender asked with a smile.

"Looking for Chick O'Malley."

The smile vanished. "This is a bar. You want something to drink?"

"I told you what I want." Kilgore was wearing a coat and tie. From a pocket he pulled out a badge and waved it in front of the bartender, who took a long look.

"Chick's not here anymore. Sold out."

"You don't say? Who's the new owner?"

"She's not in."

"I didn't ask if she was in. I asked who is the new owner."

"Name's Ginger."

"I arrest women with only one name."

"Ginger Redfield."

"Now we're making progress. Get on the phone and tell her I'm waiting."

The bartender looked at his wristwatch and said, "She should be here any minute. Can I get you something to drink?"

"Black coffee. Fresh."

"Coming right up."

Kilgore sat at the bar and stared at the bottles below the mirror. The coffee wasn't fresh but he drank it anyway. Evidently Ginger used the rear door because no one else came through the front. Fifteen minutes later, the bartender reappeared and said, "Ginger will see you now."

Kilgore knew where the office was because he had been there several times to collect dues. He followed the bartender into the back and up a flight of narrow stairs that opened to a long, dark hallway with a row of small doors to the left. Prostitution was not a focus at O'Malley's. Chick had made his money on booze and poker, but almost every joint had a few rooms upstairs just in case. The walls smelled of fresh paint and the shag carpet was new.

A woman's touch. At the end of the hall, Ginger opened the door to her office as they approached and nodded for Kilgore to enter. The bartender disappeared. She was a heavyset woman of about fifty, with a dress that was too tight and cut too low in front. Her breasts were pushed up close to her chin and looked somewhat uncomfortable, though Kilgore tried not to notice. Her hair was dyed black and matched her thick mascara. She shook hands like a man and was all smiles. "Nice to meet you. Ginger Redfield." Her voice was low, raspy, as if ravaged by nicotine.

"A pleasure. Rudd Kilgore."

"I was wondering when you guys would stop by."

"Here I am. Mind if I ask when you took over?"

"Couple of weeks ago."

"You from around here?"

"Here and there."

Kilgore smiled, almost let it pass, but said, "Answers like that only lead to trouble, Miss Redfield."

"Call me Ginger. I'm from Mobile originally, spent the last few years up on the state line."

"Call me Kilgore. Chief Deputy, Harrison County Sheriff's Department."

———•———

Within twenty-four hours, Fats and Kilgore would learn that Ginger Redfield and her husband had operated a lounge on the Tennessee–Mississippi state line and had a long history of criminal activity. Her husband was serving a ten-year sentence in Tennessee for the second-degree murder of a bootlegger. Her older son was serving time in Florida on federal gun charges. Not to be outdone, her younger son was suspected in two murders but was currently in hiding. He was rumored to be a contract killer.

This background was provided by the sheriff of Alcorn County, Mississippi, a twenty-year veteran who knew the family well. According to his rather windy narrative, Ginger and her crew had been at war with other club owners along the state line. "Sumbitches always shootin' at each other" was how the sheriff described it. "Wish they were better shots. Don't need 'em around here."

Anyway, someone raised a white flag, a truce was agreed upon, and things settled down until Ginger's husband killed a bootlegger in a fight over a truckload of liquor. She sold out, disappeared, and for the past year had not been seen in those parts.

The sheriff signed off with "Glad she's all yours, buddy. Woman's nothin' but trouble."

"Where's Chick?" Kilgore asked.

Ginger smiled, and it was a fetching little grin that softened her hard face considerably. Twenty years and thirty pounds ago she was probably a real looker, but a life in lounges added plenty of wrinkles and hardened her features. She lit a filterless cigarette and Kilgore lit a menthol.

"I don't know," she said. "He didn't say and I didn't ask. Got the impression he was leaving town."

"That so? Did you assume this joint's liabilities?"

"That's prying a bit, don't you think?"

"Call it what you want. Chick was behind on his dues."

"His dues?"

"Look, Ginger, I'm not stupid enough to believe that Chick sold you this place without covering the basics. And the most basic is that the door stays open as long as the business license is current."

She smiled again, took a long drag, and said, "He may have said something about a license. I take it you can't get one from the chamber of commerce."

"Ha ha. We control them and they cost a thousand dollars a month. Chick was two months behind. You want to stay open, you need to get current."

"That's pretty steep, Kilgore. A hefty price for protection."

"We don't deal with protection and we don't get involved in street battles or turf wars. Your license simply allows you to stay in business and behave yourself, more or less."

"Behave? Everything we sell is illegal."

"And you'll sell a lot of it if you keep your prices in line, protect your girls, and keep the fighting and cheating to a minimum. That's what we call good behavior."

She shrugged and seemed to agree. "Okay, so we owe two grand, right?"

"Three. Two past and one current. All cash. I'll send a guy named Gabe around this time tomorrow. You'll recognize him because he has only one arm."

"A one-armed bandit."

"Ha ha. Speaking of slots, that's where the money is, in case you're doing any long-range planning."

"Already got 'em ordered. No limit on the number?"

"We don't have limits. How you run this place is strictly up to you. Just behave, Ginger." Kilgore stubbed out his Salem in an ashtray on her desk and turned for the door. He stopped, gave her a smile, and said, "Look, just to give you a little welcome. Your reputation precedes you and may get an icy reception from some of the other licensees."

"Trouble already?"

"Possibly. Some of the boys know about the State Line Mob and are a bit worried."

She laughed and said, "Oh that. Well, tell 'em to relax. We come in peace."

"They don't understand that concept. They don't like competition, especially from other organizations."

"We're hardly an organization, Mr. Kilgore. That mob is far from here."

"Be careful." He opened the door and left.

CHAPTER 8

After three years of hustling as the law firm's only associate, Jesse Rudy was ready for a change of scenery. The two older gentlemen who hired him after he passed the bar exam had practiced law at a leisurely pace for two decades and were content to shuffle paper and handle matters that did not require contested litigation. Jesse, though, enjoyed the excitement and challenge of the courtroom and saw his future there. He was almost forty years old, had four kids to support, and knew that drafting wills and deeds would not provide the income he needed. He and Agnes decided to take the plunge, get a loan from a bank, and open their own shop. She worked part-time as a secretary when she wasn't juggling her duties as a mother. Jesse put in even longer hours and used his contacts from the Point to find better cases. He volunteered to represent indigent defendants and honed his skills in the courtroom. Most lawyers in Biloxi, as in most small towns, preferred the stability of a quiet office practice. Jesse was more ambitious and saw money in jury verdicts.

But his new office on Howard Avenue remained open to all, and he turned away no one in need of a lawyer. He was soon busier than ever and enjoyed keeping the fees for himself. As a sole practitioner, he was not expected to share his income with anyone but Agnes. She kept the books and was better at culling the riffraff than her husband.

Early one morning Jesse was alone in his office. The bell on the front door rattled and he couldn't ignore it. No appointments were scheduled at that hour, so the disturbance meant another drop-in.

He walked to the front and said hello to Guy and Millie Moseley from Lima, Ohio. Mid-fifties, nicely dressed, late-model Buick parked at the curb. He showed them to the conference room and fetched three cups of coffee.

They began by apologizing for barging in but something terrible had happened and they were broke and far from home. They were near the end of a two-week trip to Tampa and back, had been headed to New Orleans for a night on the town when tragedy struck the day before.

It was obvious they were not injured. Their nice car parked at the curb seemed undamaged. As a busy lawyer hustling the streets of Biloxi, he immediately suspected trouble from the shadier side of town.

Guy began the narrative and Millie wiped her red and swollen eyes with a tissue. He kept glancing at her as if desperate for approval, and absolutely none was forthcoming. It was obvious he had screwed up, he was the villain, she had tried to talk him out of whatever nonsense he'd fallen into, and so it was up to him to confess and seek absolution.

After five minutes, Jesse knew exactly what had happened.

The first clue was the location. The Blue Spot Diner on Highway 90, with a view of the beach. It was an old greasy spoon that advertised homemade biscuits and cheap steaks. A few years back a hustler named Shine Tanner bought the place, kept the café as it was, and added a room in the back where he put on Bingo & Beer nights that drew crowds. He also had card games and a few slots but no girls for rent. He preferred to prey on an older crowd and keep the soldiers and college boys away.

Guy was saying, "And so we had a nice breakfast, late in the morning, the place was empty." That was the second clue. Shine liked to swindle out-of-towners when the traffic was light.

"And the bill came to two dollars. I was getting ready to pay when the waitress, her name was Lonnie, asked if we liked to play games of chance. We weren't sure, so she said, 'Look, everybody plays games around here. It's all harmless fun. Here's a deck of cards. I pick one. You pick one. If your card is higher, then breakfast is free. A simple game or double or nothing.' "

Millie managed to say, "She had a deck of cards in her pocket. I'm sure they were marked."

Guy smiled at his wife, who did not return one of her own. Guy said, "So she shuffled, I mean this gal could really shuffle, and after three rounds I was up four dollars. Then eight. Then I lost, back down to zero. Back up to eight. Another customer came in and she took his order. I couldn't leave because she owed me eight bucks."

"I wanted to leave," Millie said.

Guy ignored her and became fixated on his coffee cup. When he continued his voice was lower. "This guy shows up, I think he owned the place, real friendly type, asked if we wanted to see his casino."

Jesse asked, "Short, bald, not a hair anywhere, really brown and tanned?"

"That's him. You know the guy?"

"He's the owner."

The next clue. Shine Tanner arrived on the scene to lay the trap.

"She paid us the eight dollars and we followed him through a door to the casino stuck to the side of the diner. It was dark and empty. He said the casino was closed, didn't open until six o'clock, but he had a new game he wanted to show us."

"Bolita?" Jesse asked.

"Yeah, you been there?"

"No, but I've heard about the Bolita table. It's also called Razzle."

"That's what he said. There was this green, felt-like table, like a big checkerboard, with squares numbered one through fifty. He said the game was all about dice and arithmetic and easy to win. He asked if I wanted to put down a few bucks and he'd sort of walk me through the game. Lonnie popped in and asked me if I wanted a drink. The owner said the bar was closed and they went back and forth, making a big deal over whether they could offer me a drink. I didn't want one, but after all that chatter I felt obliged to ask for a beer."

Millie shook her head and stared at a wall.

"So, he rattled eight dice and rolled out the 'bones,' as he called them, then scooped them up almost as fast. Said it totaled thirty-eight. He put down two of my dollars on number thirty-eight. If the next roll was higher, I'd win. If it was lower, I'd lose, but there were other rules he threw in as the game progressed. He said the only way to lose was to stop playing before I won ten games. I'm not sure I ever understood all of the rules."

"You did not," Millie added helpfully.

"Lonnie brought me a beer."

"It was only ten thirty," Millie interjected again.

"Yes, dear, it was only ten thirty, and I should've stopped. We've had this conversation, more than once. I should've walked out and gotten in the car, saved our money. Now, feel better?"

"No."

Jesse had heard enough. These stories were common along the Coast—upper-middle-class tourists in nice cars with out-of-state tags getting whipsawed and duped by card sharks and table cheats. He raised both hands and said, "Look folks, let's get to the point. How much money did you leave behind at the Blue Spot?"

Millie couldn't wait to blurt, "Six hundred dollars, everything we had. We can't afford to buy gas to get home. How could you be so stupid?"

Poor Guy caved another inch or two at this latest onslaught. It was obvious that he'd heard much worse in the preceding hours.

"Can't we do something?" Millie pleaded to Jesse. "He was nothing but a slick con man who tricked us and stole our money. There must be a law on the books of this backward state."

"I'm afraid not, ma'am. All gambling is illegal in Mississippi, but I'm ashamed to say it's ignored here on the Coast."

"We just went in for breakfast."

"I know. This happens all the time."

They clammed up as Millie cried some more and Guy stared at the floor as if searching for a hole to climb in. Jesse glanced at his watch. He'd wasted almost twenty minutes with these poor folks.

"Tell him the rest," she snapped at her husband.

"What?"

"You know, this morning."

"Oh, that. Well, we can't afford to go on to New Orleans, so we got a cheap room down the road. First thing this morning we went back to the diner because I didn't sleep a wink last night and I wanted to give that man a piece of my mind and get my money back. But when we pulled up we could see two cops inside having breakfast. I walked in and glared at Lonnie. She gave me a real smart-ass look and asked, 'What do you want?'

"I said, 'I want my money.'

"She said, 'You ain't starting no trouble. I'll ask you to leave.'

"'I want my money.'

"Before I knew it, the cops were coming at me. They shoved me a little, told me to hit the road and never come back."

Millie had been quiet long enough. She said to Jesse, "He almost got arrested, on top of everything else. Wouldn't that just be great? Tough Guy Moseley in the drunk tank with a bunch of winos."

Jesse raised his hands again and said, "Okay, folks. I'm real sorry about what happened, but there's nothing I can do."

"You can't sue him?" Guy demanded.

"No, there's no legal cause of action."

"What about stealing?" she asked. "It was a con game, just waiting for another sucker to come along. Boy did they hook one."

"Knock it off," Guy growled at his wife. "You saw those cops. Hell, they're probably on the take too."

Jesse suppressed a grin and thought: *You're finally right about something.*

She mumbled, "He even took our traveler's checks."

"Please be quiet," Guy said.

But she ignored him and said, "He got in deeper and deeper. I kept saying, 'Let's get outta here.' But, no, Mr. High Roller here wouldn't quit. The crook would let him win every now and then, just enough to keep him hooked. I got mad and went to the car and waited and waited and I knew damn well he'd lose everything. He finally came out, ready to cry, looked like he'd seen a ghost, lucky to still have his shirt on."

"Please, Millie."

Jesse really wanted them out of his office before a catfight started. For a second he thought about recommending a good divorce lawyer, but they needed to get home for that. He looked at his watch and calmly said, "I have to be in court at nine, so we have to say goodbye."

Now Guy appeared ready to cry. He wiped his face and said with a dry voice, "Can you loan us fifty dollars to get back to Ohio?"

"I'm sorry, but it's unethical for a lawyer to loan money to a client."

"We'll pay it back, I swear," Millie said. "As soon as we get home."

Jesse stood and tried to be polite. "I'm sorry, folks."

They left without saying thanks. He could hear them sniping at the curb when they got to their Buick and could only imagine how much worse the situation would become as they begged their way north.

He poured another cup of coffee and returned to the conference room where he sat with a view of the street. He was sympathetic to a point, but a good dose of caution would have saved them the time, money, and trouble. Many folks came to the Coast looking for trouble and knowing damned well where to find it. Others, like the Moseleys, drifted through and accidentally bumped into the world of vice. They were innocent lambs in the hands of wolves and they didn't stand a chance. There were plenty of Shine Tanners making money by their wits instead of honest work.

Corruption never stays in a box. It spreads because greedy men see easy money and there is an endless demand for gratification and the promise of a quick buck. Jesse didn't resent the clubs and bars and the illicit trade they provided to willing customers. Nor did he resent men like Lance Malco and Shine Tanner and their ilk who profited from the vice. What Jesse loathed was the bribery of those entrusted to uphold the law. The corruption was enriching men like Fats Bowman and other elected officials. Most of the police and politicians had dirty hands. The treacherous part was not knowing who to trust.

The current district attorney, also elected, was a decent man who'd never shown an interest in tackling organized crime. In all fairness, if the police didn't investigate and go after the criminals, there were no cases for the DA to prosecute. This frustrated the reformers—the honest officials, preachers, law-abiding citizens—who wanted to "clean up the Coast."

A month earlier, Jesse met with a retired circuit court judge and a minister. It was a quiet meeting over breakfast in a café with no slot machines in sight. The two men claimed to represent a loose-knit group of civic-minded people who were concerned about the ever-growing criminal enterprises. There were rumors that drugs, especially marijuana, were being smuggled in and were readily available in certain nightclubs. The old-fashioned sins had been around for decades, and though still illegal, they had become accepted in certain circles. But drugs presented a more ominous threat and had to be stopped. The future of the children was now on the line.

The men were frustrated by the politicians. Fats Bowman was deeply entrenched, ran a well-organized machine, and was virtually untouchable. He had proven that he could buy any election. But the DA was another matter. He represented the State, was considered the people's lawyer, and thus was charged with the duty of fighting crime. They had met with the DA and voiced their concerns, but again he showed little interest.

They floated the bold idea that Jesse Rudy would make an excellent district attorney. He was a well-known product of Biloxi and had a following on the Point, one of the largest precincts in the three-county district. His reputation was stellar. He was considered above reproach. But would he have the courage to fight the mob?

Jesse was flattered by the idea and honored by the trust. It was early in 1963, an election year in which every office from governor to county coroner would be on the ballot. As usual, the DA's race was uncontested, for the moment. Fats Bowman was expected to get another four years without serious opposition. Nothing would change unless a new DA took office with an entirely different agenda.

Jesse promised to consider the race but had serious reservations. He was trying to establish a practice, one that needed him hard at work every day. He had no money for a campaign. He had never for a moment thought of himself as a politician and wasn't sure it was in his blood. The biggest drawback would be the promise that he would go after the criminals. He had known Lance Malco his entire life, and though they were still polite to each other when the situation called for it, they were living and working in different worlds. It was almost impossible to imagine threatening his empire.

Jesse had no interest in jeopardizing the safety of his family. His son Keith and Hugh Malco were still friends, though not nearly as close as they had been as twelve-year-old all-stars. Among the boys, it was well known that Hugh was showing signs of following in his father's footsteps. He was hanging around the clubs, smoking and drinking, and boasting of knowing the girls. Hugh had given up team sports and called himself a boxer.

But once planted, the idea would not go away. After some hesitation, Jesse had finally mentioned it to Agnes. The reception was lukewarm.

CHAPTER 9

After four club fights in Buster's Gym, Hugh had one win, one loss, and two draws. The fact that he had survived without getting knocked out emboldened him to take the next step. Buster, his coach, wasn't so sure, but seldom said no when a new fighter was eager to get in the ring. The Golden Gloves tournament was in late February in the gymnasium of St. Michael's Catholic Church, and Buster, the undisputed ruler of amateur boxing along the Coast, controlled the card. He tried to protect his novices and make sure they would survive, at least through the first round.

Hugh's first lesson was not in a gym. Nevin Noll found two pairs of sixteen-ounce gloves, and they squared off behind Red Velvet one afternoon for a friendly lesson. Just the basics: stance, position of hands, head back, foot movements. Hugh was terrified because he had seen Nevin in real action and knew how quick his fists were, but he accepted the reality that a few bloody noses were part of the training. No blood was drawn in the first few lessons as Nevin patiently taught Hugh to keep his hands up. He also warned the kid to lay off the cigarettes and beer while in training.

During Hugh's first workout at Buster's, the old coach liked what he saw. Though his feet were a bit slow, the kid was an athlete who was willing to work. Hugh sparred with some experienced boxers and finally took a hard one on the nose, but it only made him more determined. He would never contend for an Olympic medal, but he was a natural fighter who relished contact and wasn't afraid to get hit. Before long, he was in the gym almost every afternoon. He enjoyed juggling his part-time job, trysts with

Miss Cindy, and an hour or two at Buster's. Schoolwork became even less of a priority.

Lance liked the idea that his son was learning to box. Every kid needed the discipline and he was never much of a football player anyway. Carmen was horrified and vowed to avoid all fights.

After a lousy football season sitting on the bench, Keith was suffering through an even worse winter as a second-string forward on the JV basketball team. Playing time was scarce, but at least he was sweating every afternoon. Like most of his friends, he viewed basketball as a means to stay in shape between football and baseball seasons. They became intrigued by Hugh's sudden interest in boxing and were delighted to learn that their buddy would actually get in the ring at the annual Golden Gloves tournament. Hugh did not broadcast the news. While he was itching for his first real fight, he also worried about the possibility of getting knocked out cold in front of his friends.

The tournament drew a large crowd every year, and when the *Gulf Coast Register* ran a story that featured two of the local favorites, it also listed the first-round bouts. In the 145-pound welterweight division, Hugh Malco would fight Jimmy Patterson in the opening card's tenth bout. As always, Keith read the sports page over breakfast, and when he saw Hugh's name, he was proud of his friend and decided to take action. At school, he organized a cheering squad and Hugh became the man of the hour, receiving far more attention than he wanted. The knot in his stomach grew tighter and he had little interest in lunch. By mid-afternoon, he was having second thoughts, which he shared with Nevin Noll.

"It's only natural," Nevin said, trying to reassure him. "I vomited twice before my first fight."

"Gee, that makes me feel better."

"The butterflies will vanish the first time you get hit."

"What if it's a knockout punch?"

"Hit him first. You'll be fine, Hugh. Just pace yourself. It's only three rounds but it'll seem like an hour."

Hugh lit a cigarette and Nevin said, "I thought I told you to quit smoking."

"It's my nerves."

The tournament began on a Tuesday afternoon, with the finals set for Saturday night. The first bouts were novices in the lighter divisions and were uneventful. Most of the boys seemed reluctant to mix it up. By seven o'clock, the gymnasium was packed and the crowd was ready for some action. A thick layer of cigar and cigarette smoke hung not far above the ring. Vendors sold hot dogs and popcorn, and in one corner a bar offered cold beer.

Alcohol was still illegal everywhere in the state, but it was, after all, Biloxi.

Keith and his gang of rowdies arrived and waited excitedly for the big match. When Hugh stepped into the ring, his pals cheered wildly, making a nerve-racking experience even worse. The PA announcer introduced the fighters and the crowd roared for Hugh Malco, the obvious favorite. His opponent, Jimmy Patterson, was a skinny kid from Gulfport with only a few fans.

Just before the bell, Hugh glanced down at the front row and smiled at his father, who was sitting next to Nevin Noll. His mother was at home, in prayer. There were no women in the crowd. Buster rubbed Vaseline on his cheeks and forehead and said, for the umpteenth time, "Go slow. Pace yourself. You'll get him in the third round."

Buster knew exactly what would happen. Both novices would dance for the first minute, then one would land a punch that would start an old-fashioned street fight. It took at least five fights before the kids learned to pace themselves.

Keith, the cheerleader, stood and started a chant: "Let's go Hugh! Let's go Hugh!"

Hugh jumped to his feet, pounded his gloves together, and flashed a big, confident smile at his friends. The bell rang, the fight was on. They met in the center of the ring and bobbed a few times, sizing each other up. Jimmy Patterson was three inches taller, with longer arms, and danced away from Hugh, keeping his distance. The long arms became a problem as he popped Hugh with some harmless left jabs. Nevin was right. Getting hit settled his nerves. Hugh kept his hands high and backed Patterson into a corner where they flailed away at each other while doing little damage. The flurry excited the crowd. The chants of "Let's go Hugh!" drowned out all other noise. Patterson spun away and danced to the center where Hugh stalked him. Halfway through the first round, Hugh was surprised at how hard he was breathing. *Damned cigarettes. Pace, pace, pace.* Patterson found his rhythm and peppered him with left jabs. He was scoring points but doing little damage. Hugh was crouching and leaning in, and from the corner Buster kept yelling, "Head up! Head up!"

Lance found it impossible to sit idly by and watch his kid in the ring. He kept yelling, "Hit him, Hugh! Hit him, Hugh!" Nevin Noll was also on the edge of his seat and yelling.

Hugh heard nothing but his own breathing. He pinned Patterson in a corner but he covered up and got away. The first round seemed to last for an hour and when the bell finally rang Hugh walked to his corner and flashed another smile at Keith and the boys. Buster sat him down as a second poured water in his mouth. Buster said, "Look, when he throws that left jab he drops his right hand, okay? Fake a right hook, then throw a left one. Got it?"

Hugh nodded but found it hard to concentrate on anything. His heart was pounding, his blood was rushing. He had survived the first round with no damage at all, and as the crowd chanted he realized how much he was enjoying the fight. All he needed now was to kick Patterson's ass.

Patterson had other plans. He opened the second round with the same dancing and punching from long range and Hugh couldn't pin him on the ropes. He missed badly with a couple of wild rights and Patterson countered with more jabs to the nose. Halfway through, Hugh got frustrated, ducked low and tried to charge. Patterson hit him with a hard right that stunned him and buckled his knees. He didn't go down, but the referee stepped in and gave him a standing eight count. By the end of it his eyes were clear and he was fired up. By allowing Patterson to bomb away, he was losing the fight. He had to get inside and land some body blows. Buster kept yelling, "Head up! Head up!" But the problem was Patterson's long arms. Hugh practically tackled him and they grappled on the ropes until the ref broke it up. Patterson took a step back and threw a wild left that missed. Just like Buster said, he dropped his right hand, and Hugh spun a left hook that had no chance until Patterson stepped into it. The hook smashed into his right jaw, popped his head back against the ropes, and Hugh was quick enough to land a hard right as Patterson was falling. He fell in a corner, and would be there for some time.

It was the first knockout of the evening and the crowd went wild. Hugh wasn't sure what to do—he'd never scored a knockout—and had to be pushed by the ref to a neutral corner. As he began counting it was obvious that Patterson wasn't getting up anytime soon. Keith and his friends were screaming and Hugh flashed another smile as he bobbed on his toes. He was almost as stunned as Patterson. Minutes passed and Patterson finally sat up, took some water, shook his head, and got to his feet. His coach walked him around the ring a few times as he came to his senses. At the appropriate time, Hugh stepped over and said, "Good fight." Jimmy smiled but it was obvious he wanted out of the ring.

When the referee raised Hugh's hand and the announcer declared him a winner by knockout, the crowd roared its approval. Hugh basked in the glory and smiled at his father and Nevin, and also at the crowd from school. Oddly, he thought of Cindy and wished she was there for his greatest moment. But no, she was back at Red Velvet hustling soldiers. Nevin was right. It was time to stop seeing her.

Wednesday was a regular school day. The knockout artist arrived a few minutes earlier than usual. His name was in the morning's paper and he was anticipating a pleasant day being admired by his peers. Word spread quickly and different versions of his dramatic victory were making the rounds. Keith, always with plenty to say, announced the knockout in homeroom and invited everyone to the second round of fights Thursday night. Their new hero would fight a guy named Fuzz Foster, who, according to the paper, was undefeated after eight bouts.

The paper said no such thing. Keith was exaggerating and trying his best to whip up enthusiasm for the fight. With a nod from the teacher, Keith went on to say that, after watching at least a dozen fights the night before, he was now of the opinion that their new hero, the knockout artist, was in bad need of a catchy boxing nickname. "Hugh" just wasn't sufficient. Therefore, it was incumbent upon them, as his biggest fans, to find one. All manner arose from the floor. Hack, Duck, the Assassin, Bazooka, Scarface, Bruno, Rocky, Sandman, Babyface, Razor, Lazer, Machine Gun Malco. As things were getting out of hand, the teacher listed a dozen of the better ones on the chalkboard and called for a vote, but the bell rang and nothing was accomplished. Hugh trudged off to first period with no change of identity, no colorful nickname that might intimidate opponents or make him famous.

He completed his classes that Wednesday without skipping a one, and left after the final bell to see Cindy. She was not at her apartment, and one of her roommates finally admitted that she had left town. "She quit, Hugh."

"What do you mean she quit?"

"Gave it up. Gone home. I think her brother found her and made her leave."

Hugh was stunned and said, "But I need to talk to her."

"Let it go, Hugh. She ain't coming back here."

He left and went searching for Nevin Noll. He was not at the

Truck Stop, Red Velvet, Foxy's, or any of his usual hangouts. A bartender whispered, "I think they're having some trouble with O'Malley's. Nevin might be there but you'd better stay away. Things are heating up."

Hugh took his advice and drove away from the Strip, alone in his little truck, where no one could hear him mumbling to himself about losing the girl. They'd been together for over five months and she'd taught him things he'd never dreamed of, and, as much as he despised what she did for a living, he'd found a way to forgive her and carry on. She couldn't just disappear without saying goodbye.

He drove to Buster's and went through the motions of a light workout, but only because Buster expected him to. He poked around to see if anyone had seen Fuzz Foster in the ring, but came away with no scouting report. His mind was on his girl, not boxing. He knew Nevin was at Red Velvet, on duty, every night at 5:00 when happy hour started and the cover charge went into effect. He found him at the bar drinking a soda and having a cigarette with one of the waitresses.

Nevin frowned when he saw him and said, "You looking for another fight?"

"No, just need to talk."

"Well, not here. You're still too young, Sugar Ray."

"Let's go outside."

Behind the club, both lit cigarettes. "What happened to Cindy?" Hugh asked.

Nevin shook his head as he blew a cloud. "I've been telling you to forget about her."

"I know, but please, what happened?"

"Yesterday, we got a call from some cops over in Arkansas. Somebody tracked her and knew she was working here. As you know, she's only sixteen. We didn't admit that and told the police the girl had an ID that said she's eighteen. You know the drill. So, this morning two cops from Arkansas showed up with her brother. We had no choice but to cooperate, and now she's back home where she belongs. Forget her, Hugh. She's just another hooker. There'll be plenty more where she came from."

"I know."

"You need to be thinking about the fight tomorrow night. They only get tougher."

"I'll be ready."

"Then toss away that cigarette."

———— • ————

At first glance, it wasn't clear where the nickname "Fuzz" originated. No bushy head of hair, certainly no whiskers to speak of. He was only sixteen, and had casually mentioned to one of the Biloxi boxers that he had won five of his six fights. No one had yet asked about the nickname, not that it mattered at all. What mattered was his stocky frame and oversized biceps. Impressive for a teenager. If Jimmy Patterson had been as skinny as a rail, Fuzz Foster was as thick as a fireplug. Nor did Fuzz have any patience with dancing and jabbing. What Fuzz wanted was a first-round knockout, preferably in the first thirty seconds, and he almost got it.

At the bell, while Hugh was still smiling at his friends from school, Fuzz shot across the ring like an angry bull and began unloading roundhouse rights and lefts that could've wounded a heavyweight if they had landed anywhere near Hugh's head. Mercifully, none did, and, startled, he covered up and tried to stay away from the ropes. His survival instincts kicked in immediately and he ducked and dodged the onslaught as best he could. Fuzz was a madman, slinging leather from all directions while hissing and grunting like a wounded animal. Buster shouted, "Cover up, cover up. He's crazy!"

Hugh, along with every other person in the building, knew that

Fuzz was unloading everything and wouldn't last for three rounds. The question was whether Hugh could survive the onslaught. Regardless, the crowd loved the unbridled action and was roaring.

An uppercut got through and rocked Hugh. A right cross landed and it was lights out. He fell to the canvas as Fuzz stood over him, yelling something no one could understand. The referee shoved him to a corner as Hugh managed to get on all fours. Looking through the ropes, he made eye contact with Nevin Noll, who was yelling and shaking his fist. *Get up! Get up! Get up!*

Hugh took a deep breath, looked up at the referee, and on the five-count jumped to his feet. He steadied himself with the top rope, wiped his nose with a forearm, and saw blood. He had a choice. Stay under cover on the ropes like a proper boxer and get eaten alive, or go after the bastard.

Fuzz charged like an idiot, growling, hands low, ready to throw everything at his target. Instead of backing up, Hugh took a quick step forward and threw the same left hook he'd nailed Patterson with. It landed perfectly on the mouth and dropped Fuzz onto his butt, as if pulling up a chair. He looked around in disbelief and tried to stand. He stumbled, fell into the ropes, and struggled to steady himself. As the referee counted to ten, the crowd screamed even louder. At ten, Fuzz nodded and began his growling again.

The two met in the center of the ring and brawled like street fighters until the bell saved their lives. The ref rushed to break them up. Both noses were oozing blood. On his stool, Hugh guzzled water and tried to catch his breath while a second crammed swabs up his nostrils. Buster was saying something like, "You gotta cover up! He can't keep going like this." But his words were just part of the noise. Hugh's head was throbbing and it was impossible to think of anything but survival. When the bell rang, he jumped to his feet and noticed how heavy they were.

If Fuzz's corner wanted a slower pace, the advice was ignored by the fighter. He charged again, the instinct to brawl undeterred.

Hugh covered up for a moment on the ropes and tried to slide punches, but there was no fun in getting hit. Because Fuzz fought with his hands at his sides, his head was always exposed. Hugh saw an opening, shot a quick left-right combo, made perfect contact, and watched proudly as Fuzz hit the deck hard and rolled into a corner. The noise from the crowd was deafening. "Stay down, dammit!" Hugh said, but Fuzz could take a punch. He jumped to his feet, flailed his arms in a sign of invincibility, waited for the ten-count, then attacked. Thirty seconds later, Hugh was on the deck, flattened by a wild right that he never saw. He was stunned and groggy and for an instant thought about just staying down. It was safer on his back. A loss in his second real fight was no big deal. Then he thought of his father and Nevin Noll, and Keith and all of his friends, and he got up at five and started bouncing on his toes.

Halfway through the second round, it became obvious that the winner would be the guy still standing at the end of the third. Neither backed away, and for the last ninety seconds they went toe-to-toe and slugged it out. Between rounds, the referee went to both corners to observe the damage. "He's all right," Buster assured him as he wiped Hugh's face with cold water. "Just a bloody nose, nothing broken."

"I don't want to see a cut," the ref said.

"No cuts."

"Has he had enough?"

"Hell no."

Speak for yourself, Hugh almost said. He was tired of fighting and hoped he never laid eyes on Fuzz Foster again. Then a loud chant of "Let's go Hugh! Let's go Hugh!" started again and shook the walls of the gymnasium. The fans were loving the old-fashioned alley fight and wanted more. To hell with gentlemanly boxing. They were after blood.

Hugh got to his feet, heavy as brickbats now, and bounced around waiting on the bell. There was a commotion in the other corner. The referee was yelling at Fuzz's coach.

Buster said, "Boy's got a cut above his right eye. Go for it. Attack it! You hear?"

Hugh nodded and tapped his gloves together. He could feel his own right eye closing and his left one was blurred.

The bell sounded and Fuzz got to his feet. The ref was still talking to his coach, who slid under the ropes. With the threat of disqualification for a lousy cut, Fuzz needed a quick knockout. He came in fast and landed a low shot to Hugh's right kidney. It hurt like hell and he bent over in pain. Fuzz rocked him with uppercuts, and within seconds of the last round Hugh was back on the mat, scrambling to get on all fours and remember his name.

The crowd reminded him with "Let's go Hugh!"

He got to his feet for the last time, shook his head at the ref as if everything was just wonderful, and braced for the onslaught. He and Fuzz swapped punches and commenced beating the crap out of each other while the fans yelled for more. Much to Hugh's surprise, Fuzz went down after a flurry and looked like he was finally out of gas. Hugh certainly was, but there was at least a minute to go. Fuzz lumbered to his feet. The ref made them touch gloves, then signaled for more fighting. They tied up in the center, both too fatigued to throw more punches. The ref suddenly stopped the fight and led Hugh to his corner. He wiped his face and said to Buster, "He's cut. The other boy is cut. Both have busted noses. Both have been knocked down three times. I'm calling the fight. It's a draw. Enough is enough."

The crowd booed loudly when the PA announcer said it was a draw, but the fighters didn't care. Hugh and Fuzz congratulated each other on such thorough beatings and left the ring.

———•———

Two hours later, Hugh was lying on the sofa in the den with ice packs on his face. Carmen was locked in her bedroom, in tears. Lance was outside smoking a cigarette. They had argued and fought and said too much in front of the children. Carmen could not believe her son would ever come home so bruised, cut, and beaten. Lance was proud of the boy and said the ref was wrong to stop the fight. In his opinion, Hugh was on his way to a unanimous decision.

CHAPTER 10

There had always been rumors that Carousel Lounge was for sale. Its owner, Marcus Dean Poppy, was an erratic and unstable businessman who drank too much and had gambling debts. It was not a well-managed business because Poppy was usually too hungover to tend to the details. It made money, though, because of its location in the center of the Strip. Booze, strippers, hookers, gambling; it offered it all and stayed afloat, but barely. What few people knew was that Poppy was in too deep with some Vegas boys and needed cash. He sent Earl Fortier, his trusted lieutenant, to meet with Lance Malco at his office at Red Velvet. Lance, Tip, and Nevin Noll welcomed Fortier, though they were wary of his shifty reputation.

Most of the men they encountered on a typical day had, to some extent, shifty reputations.

They enjoyed a cold beer with Fortier, talked about the fishing, and finally got around to business. It was a simple deal. Poppy wanted $25,000 for Carousel, cash on the table. The club had no debts, all accounts were current.

Lance frowned and shook his head and said, "Twenty-five's too much. I value the club at twenty."

"Are you offering twenty?" Fortier asked.

"Yep, plus Marcus Dean agrees to a non-compete for three years."

"No problem there. He ain't staying around here. Says he's going back to Hot Springs, likes to be near the track."

"Will he take twenty?"

"All I can do is ask. I'll call you tomorrow."

Fortier left and drove to O'Malley's where he met Ginger Red-field alone in her office. She offered a drink but he declined. He said Marcus Dean Poppy was going to sell Carousel and had a deal with Lance Malco for $20,000. Could she top that?

Yes she could. She was delighted at the opportunity and offered what they wanted: $25,000 up front, payable by certified check.

The following day Fortier called Lance and said they had a deal at $20,000 cash. Half up front with a simple buy-sell agreement, the other half when the lawyers finished their mischief in a week or so. Two days later, Fortier was back at Red Velvet with a two-page agreement, already signed by Marcus Dean. Lance's lawyer was in the room and approved the contract. Since real estate was not involved, other than a long-term lease, the final paperwork would be finished without delay. Fortier left with $10,000 in cash and drove straight to O'Malley's where he pulled out another con-tract, one also pre-signed by Marcus Dean Poppy. Ginger read it carefully, signed her name, and handed Fortier a certified check for $25,000. Fortier drove straight to her bank, cashed the check, and entered Carousel, rather triumphantly, with $35,000 cash in his briefcase.

Marcus Dean was thrilled and tipped his boy $2,000. He waited two days and called Lance himself with the terrible news that the IRS had just raided his place and was in the process of slapping tax liens on everything. The deal was off. Lance's surprise quickly turned to anger and he demanded his $10,000 back. Marcus Dean said that would not be a problem, except, of course, there was a problem. The IRS was attaching all the hard cash it could find. Marcus Dean could get him $5,000 in a day or so, with the balance "real soon."

Lance smelled a rat and made a few phone calls. Since he pros-pered in a world of illicit cash, he had no relationship with anyone even remotely connected to the IRS. But his lawyer had a friend who knew someone. In the meantime, word hit the street that

Ginger Redfield had purchased Carousel. It closed temporarily, allegedly because of tax problems.

Marcus Dean disappeared and refused to take calls from Lance Malco. Word eventually got around that the IRS was investigating neither Carousel nor Marcus Dean Poppy.

On the Strip in 1963, swindling a thousand bucks from the wrong person could get one permanently injured—severe head wounds, missing limbs, blindness. At ten thousand dollars, a swindler was as good as dead. Nevin Noll finally found Fortier and delivered the ultimatum: Seven days to return the cash, or else.

———————•———————

A week passed, then another. No one had seen Poppy. Lance was convinced he had indeed fled the area for good and kept the cash. A construction crew hired by Ginger descended upon Carousel and began sprucing it up for a grand reopening.

Fortier was lying low too and had left the Strip, but not the Coast. He was selling used cars for a friend in Pascagoula and living in a small apartment there. Late on a Saturday night, he came home from a party half-drunk, with his girlfriend Rita. They quickly got undressed, hopped in the bed, and were getting steamed up when a man stepped from the closet eight feet away and began firing a handgun. Earl took three bullets in the head, as did Rita, who managed one quick scream before the end.

A next-door neighbor, Mr. Bullington, heard the shots and described them as "muffled thuds," certainly not the wall-splitting sounds of a gun being fired in close quarters. Ballistics would say the gunman probably used some type of silencer, which would make sense for a murder that was carefully planned.

Mr. Bullington also heard the scream and it prompted him to turn off his lights, ease to the rear window in the kitchen, and watch. Seconds later, he saw a man leave their building, hurry across a small parking lot, and disappear around a corner. White, about six feet tall, medium build, dark hair under a dark cap, age about twenty-five. Mr. Bullington waited a moment, then left through his rear door, and, staying in the shadows, followed the man. He heard the sound of a car engine being started, and, hiding behind some bushes, watched as the killer drove away in a light brown 1961 Ford Fairlane, Mississippi tags but too far away to see the numbers.

Fortier was dead in his bed, but Rita was not. For three days her doctors waited to pull the plug, but she hung on. On the fourth day she started mumbling.

The murders were newsworthy along the Coast but not surprising. Fortier was described as a used-car salesman with a checkered past. He had worked in the Biloxi clubs and had served time for aggravated assault. Rita's last job was waiting tables at a steak house in Pascagoula, but her trail quickly led to a long career as a waitress at Carousel. An employee who knew them both said their romance had been on and off for many years. In his opinion, she was only a waitress and had not worked the rooms upstairs. Not that it mattered when she was on life support.

Pascagoula was in Jackson County, the domain of Sheriff Heywood Hester, a relatively honest public servant who loathed Fats Bowman and his machine next door. Hester immediately called in the state police and gave the investigation his full attention. His citizens took a dimmer view of gangland shootings than those in Harrison County and he was determined to solve the crime and bring someone to justice.

A week after she was shot, Rita managed to scrawl on a notepad the name *Nevin*. Avoiding the Biloxi authorities, an undercover cop from the state police hung around the Strip long enough to catch wind of the bad blood between Lance Malco and Marcus Dean Poppy. It was common knowledge that Nevin was one of Malco's underbosses. It was easy enough to find out that he owned a light brown 1961 Ford Fairlane, which Mr. Bullington identified.

In a surprise attack, Nevin Noll was awakened at three in the morning by a knock on his door. He treated every suspicious knock the same, and grabbed a small handgun from under his mattress. At the door, he was informed that the police had a warrant for his arrest and another one to search his apartment. They had the place surrounded. *Come out with your hands up.* He complied and no one was hurt.

He was driven to Pascagoula and thrown in jail with no bond. The police searched his apartment and found a small arsenal of handguns, rifles, shotguns, brass knuckles, switchblades, billy clubs, and every other weapon a self-respecting hoodlum might need. The state police and Sheriff Hester attempted to interrogate him, but he demanded a lawyer.

Lance Malco was furious with Nevin for getting into such serious trouble. Lance had authorized the hit on Fortier by ordering Nevin to take care of the matter, but he assumed a contract killer would be called in. Nevin had been pestering him for years to kill someone, said he was tired of the beatings and wanted to step up, but Lance had scolded him away from such talk. He wanted Nevin to stay where he was, at his side. Contract killings were as cheap as $5,000 a pop. Nevin was worth far more than that.

Lance went to the jail two days after the arrest and met privately with Nevin. After a serious tongue-lashing, in which the boss pointed out the stupidity of killing Fortier in Jackson County instead of Harrison County, where Fats was in charge, and after pointing out other obvious mistakes the boy made, Lance asked about the woman, Rita. She was not supposed to have been there. Fortier lived alone and Nevin had assumed he would return late that Saturday night by himself. Nevin was already in the house hiding when the couple staggered in and started undressing. He had no choice but to kill her, or at least try to.

"Yeah, well you missed, didn't you? She survived and now she's talking to the cops."

"I hit her three times. It's a miracle."

"Miracles happen, don't they? A basic rule is never leave behind a witness."

"I know, I know. Can't we take care of her?"

"Shut up. You're in enough trouble."

"Can you get me outta here?"

"I'm working on it. Burch'll be over tomorrow. Just do what he says."

———·———

Joshua Burch was a well-known criminal defense lawyer along the Coast. His reputation spread from Mobile to New Orleans, and he was the go-to guy when a man with some cash found himself in trouble. He had long been a favorite of the gangsters and was a regular at the nicer bars along the Strip. He worked hard, played hard, but maintained a respectable facade in the community. He was a fierce advocate in the courtroom, cool under pressure and always prepared. Juries trusted him, regardless of the awful things his clients were accused of, and he seldom lost a verdict. When Burch was performing, the courtroom was always packed.

He was thrilled to hear the news of Fortier's murder, suspected it was gang-related, and anticipated the phone call for almost a week. He wanted the cops to arrest someone and solve the crime. Burch wanted to be called upon for the defense.

The first thing he didn't like about Nevin Noll was his stare: cold, hard, uninterrupted by normal blinking, the look of a psychopath who knew no mercy. Look at a juror like that and he or she will vote to convict in a heartbeat. They had to work on the stare, probably beginning with a pair of odd eyeglasses.

The second thing was his cockiness. Locked away in a county jail, the boy was arrogant, unperturbed, and nonchalant about the serious charges facing him. Nothing was wrong, or whatever was wrong could certainly be swept away. Burch would have to teach him humility.

"Where were you at the time of the murder?" Burch asked his client.

"Not sure. Where do you want me to be?"

So far there had been no straight answers. "Well, it looks like the state is putting together a rather compelling case. The cops think they have the murder weapon, though ballistics has yet to report. There are a couple of eyewitnesses, one of whom took three slugs in the face and evidently is claiming you pulled the trigger. We're off to a bad start here, Nevin. And when the proof is stacked against the defendant, it's usually helpful if the defendant has an alibi. Is it possible you were playing poker with some buddies in Biloxi while Mr. Fortier was getting shot in Pascagoula? Or could you have been with a girlfriend? It was, after all, Saturday night."

"What time do they think Fortier got shot?"

"The preliminary estimate is eleven thirty."

"It was closer to midnight. So, yeah, look, I was playing cards with some friends and then around midnight I went to bed with my girl. How about that?"

"Sounds great. Who were your friends?"

"Uh, well, I'll have to think about that."

"Okay, who's your girl?"

"Think about that too. There's more than one, you know?"

"Of course. Get the names straight, Nevin. And these are people who'll be asked to take the witness stand and verify your story, so they have to be rock solid."

"No problem. I got lots of friends. Can you get me outta here?"

"We're working on it, but your bond is a million bucks. The judge takes a dim view of murder, even when it involves a lowlife like Fortier. We have a bail hearing next week and I'll try to get it lowered. Mr. Malco is willing to put up some real estate. We'll see."

——— • ———

Two weeks after Fortier's burial, Marcus Dean Poppy assumed his daily breakfast table in the main dining room of the Arlington Hotel in Hot Springs, Arkansas. He had not attended the rather low-end graveside service; in fact, it did not cross his mind to go anywhere near Biloxi. The murder was a clear warning to Mr. Poppy, who understood the full meaning of it and was making plans to go to South America for a few months. He would already be there but for an incredible run of good luck at Oaklawn, the nearby horse track. He couldn't leave now. His angel was telling him to take his winnings and get out now. His devil had convinced him his lucky streak would never end. For the moment, the devil was in control.

Wilfred, his waiter, in a faded black tux, sat a tall Bloody Mary in front of him and said, "Good morning, Mr. Poppy. The usual?"

"Good morning, Wilfred. Yes, please." He picked up his drink, looked around to see if anyone was watching, then sucked hard on the straw. He smacked his lips, smiled, and waited for the vodka to hurry to his brain and deaden a few cobwebs from the night before. He was drinking too much, but he was also winning. Why tinker with a beautiful combination? He picked up a newspaper, opened to the sports section, and began checking the day's races. He smiled again. It was amazing how quickly the vodka could travel from the straw to the cobwebs.

Wilfred delivered two scrambled with buttered toast and asked if there was anything else. Mr. Poppy waved him away rudely. As he took a bite of eggs, a young gentleman in a handsome suit suddenly appeared and, without a word, sat down across from him. "I beg your pardon," Mr. Poppy said.

Nevin said, "Look, Marcus Dean, I work for Lance and he sends his regards. We've taken care of Fortier. You're next. Where's the money?"

Poppy choked on his eggs and coughed them up. He wiped his

shirt with a linen napkin and tried not to panic. He gulped some ice water and cleared his throat. "The paper said you're in jail."

"You believe everything you read in the papers?"

"But—"

"Got out on bond. No trial date yet. Where's the money, Marcus Dean? Ten grand, cash."

"Well, I, uh, you see, it's not that easy."

Nevin looked around the room and said, "You're living pretty high these days. Nice place here, easy to see why Al Capone was a frequent guest, back in the day. Rooms are not cheap. Ponies are running every day. You got twenty-four hours, Marcus Dean."

Wilfred walked over with a concerned look and asked, "Everything okay, Mr. Poppy?"

He managed a hesitant nod. Nevin pointed to his drink and said, "I'll have one of those."

Marcus Dean watched Wilfred walk away and asked, "How'd you find me?"

"That's not important, Poppy. Nothing is important but the ten grand. We'll meet here for breakfast tomorrow morning, same time, and you'll give me the money. And don't do something stupid like try and run. I'm not alone and we're watching."

Marcus Dean picked up his fork, then dropped it. His hands were shaking and beads of sweat lined his forehead. On the other side of the table, young Nevin Noll was perfectly calm, even smiling. The second Bloody Mary arrived and Nevin hit the straw. He looked at the plate and asked, "You gonna eat all that toast?"

"No."

He reached over, lifted half a slice of bread, and ate most of it.

Marcus Dean finished his drink and seemed to breathe easier. In a low voice he said, "Let's be clear here. When I give you the cash, what happens then?"

"I leave, deliver it to Mr. Malco, the rightful owner."

"And me?"

"You're not worth killing, Poppy. Why bother? Unless of

course you decide to return to the Coast. That would be a huge mistake."

"Don't worry. I'm not going back."

Nevin hit the straw again and continued smiling. Marcus Dean took a deep breath and said, almost in a whisper, "You know, there's an easier way to do this."

"Let's hear it."

Poppy looked around again as if spies were watching. At the nearest table a couple in their nineties stirred their oatmeal and tried to ignore one another. He said, "Okay, the money is upstairs in my room. Sit tight and I'll get it."

"I like it. Sooner rather than later."

"Give me ten minutes." Poppy dabbed his mouth and laid his napkin on the table.

Noll said, "I'll wait here. No funny stuff. I have men outside. You get stupid and I'll rub you out quicker than Fortier. You have no idea, Mr. Poppy, how close you are right now to a bad ending."

On the contrary, Poppy had a very clear idea. He delivered the cash in an envelope and watched as Noll left the restaurant. He drank another Bloody Mary to calm his nerves, then left for the restroom, turned in to the kitchen, took the stairs to the basement, left through a service door, and hid in an alley until he was satisfied no one was watching. He got in his car, drove away, and couldn't relax until he crossed the state line into Texas.

CHAPTER 11

The prosecutor for the Nineteenth District was a solemn and inexperienced young man named Pat Graebel. He had been elected four years earlier and was on the ballot, unopposed, in 1963 when his biggest case landed in his lap. He had never prosecuted anyone for murder, and the fact that Nevin Noll was such a well-known figure in the Biloxi underworld raised the stakes enormously. The citizens of Jackson County, the same voters who had elected Graebel as their district attorney, were proud of their law-abiding reputation and looked down on the riffraff next door in Biloxi. Occasionally the crime spilled over and they had to deal with the mess, which caused even more resentment. The pressure on young Graebel to get a conviction was enormous.

His case at first looked airtight. Rita Luten, the other victim and a solid eyewitness, was mending slowly but steadily. She was paralyzed and could say little, but her doctors expected her condition to improve. Mr. Bullington, the next-door neighbor, was even more certain he had seen Nevin Noll flee the scene. The ballistics expert from the state crime lab said the .22 caliber revolver found in Noll's apartment was the same gun that fired the six shots. Motive would be harder to prove, given the vagaries of the underworld, but the prosecution believed it could produce witnesses from the Strip who would testify, under pressure, that the shootings were the result of a business deal gone sour. Another frightening tale of gangland violence.

Pat Graebel had no idea how thoroughly the mob could sabotage a case. One week before the trial was to begin in the Jackson County Courthouse in Pascagoula, Rita Luten disappeared. Graebel had not bothered to put her under a subpoena, a forgivable but major blunder. He assumed, as had everyone else, that she would eagerly show up and finger the defendant as the murderer who shot her in the face three times. She wanted justice all right, but what she needed even more was money. She voluntarily got in an ambulance late one night and was whisked away to a private rehab facility near Houston where she was admitted under a pseudonym. All contacts, as well as all bills, were directed to a lawyer working for Lance Malco, though this would never be proven. Three months would pass before she was located by Graebel, and by then the trial was long over.

The next witness to disappear was Mr. Bullington. He, like Rita, vanished in the middle of the night, and didn't stop driving until he checked into the Flamingo Hotel and Casino in Las Vegas. Not only did he have some cash in his pocket, he also had the comfort of knowing that he would not be beaten senseless by the two thugs who'd been following him.

The day before the trial began, Graebel demanded a hearing, and during it howled to the heavens about his vanishing witnesses. Joshua Burch played along and seemed genuinely concerned about what was happening, and he assured the court he knew nothing about it. He was far too smart to get his hands dirty intimidating witnesses.

Burch had laid another trap, one that Graebel walked into. He had convinced the judge to try the cases separately, beginning with the murder of Fortier. The shooting and attempted murder of Rita Luten would go to trial a month later. Rita would be an important witness in the Fortier trial, but her absence would not necessarily derail the proceedings.

Burch knew she would disappear at the last moment, though he never admitted this.

At the hearing, Graebel argued loudly that the forces of evil were at work, his case was being undermined, justice was being thwarted, and so on. Absent proof, though, the judge could do nothing. Since the prosecution had no idea where Rita and Mr. Bullington were at the moment, it seemed unlikely they would be found and hauled back to testify. The trial must go on.

A good murder trial could break up the monotony in any small town, and the courtroom was packed when the chosen twelve took their seats and looked at the lawyers. Pat Graebel went first and fumbled badly. In his defense, it was difficult to say what the State intended to prove when the State had no idea which of its witnesses might disappear next. He relied heavily on the murder weapon and waved the pistol around as if clearing out a saloon in the Wild West. Experts from the state crime lab would testify that the gun was used to kill Earl Fortier and grievously injure Rita Luten. And the same gun was found in the apartment of the defendant, Nevin Noll, along with numerous other weapons.

Sputtering and stammering at the end of his opening, Graebel tried to link decades of corruption and organized crime along their "beloved Coast" to the forces of evil still at work "over there," but couldn't tie things together. It was not a good performance in his biggest trial.

Joshua Burch, though, was on center stage in a courtroom where he'd defended many. He wore a light gray seersucker suit, with a matching vest, complete with a pink pocket square, a pocket watch, and a gold chain. Rising from the defense table, he lit a cigar and blew clouds of smoke above the jurors as he paced back and forth.

The State had no proof, no evidence. The State had hauled his client, Nevin Noll, a young man with no criminal record whatsoever, into the courtroom on bogus charges. The law did not require his client to take the stand, but just wait. Mr. Noll was eager to sit right there, take the oath to tell the truth, and tell the jury exactly what he did not do. The charges against him were outrageous. The cops had the wrong guy. The trial was a waste of time because, at that very moment, the man who killed Earl Fortier was out there on the street, probably laughing at the spectacle inside the courthouse.

The State went first and Graebel couldn't wait to score points with the bloody crime scene photos. The startled jurors passed them around quickly and tried not to gawk. The investigators laid out the apartment and the positions of the bodies. The pathologist spent two hours explaining in excruciating detail what killed Earl Fortier, though it was painfully obvious to the jurors and everyone else that the three bullets to the head did the trick.

Joshua Burch knew better than to argue with an expert and he asked only a few minor questions. Nevin Noll sat next to him and managed to appear confident. The cold, hard stare was gone, replaced by a permanent grin, one kept in place by muscle relaxers. Juror number seven was an attractive young woman of twenty-six and their eyes met a few times.

The serious proof came early on the second day when the State's ballistics expert pinned the murder weapon squarely on the defendant. There was no way around it. The .22 caliber revolver taken from Noll's apartment was, without a doubt, the pistol used to kill Earl Fortier and wound Rita Luten.

When the State rested at lunch, its case looked strong.

After lunch, though, it didn't take long for Joshua Burch to begin punching holes in it. He started with a poker game in a back room at Foxy's and called to the stand three young men who testified under oath they had been playing cards with Nevin at the time of the murder, twenty miles away. On cross-examination, Graebel pounced on them and established that all three were friends of Noll's and worked in one of the various enterprises owned by Lance Malco. The three had been carefully coached by Joshua Burch and managed to deflect the insinuations with protests that, yes, they were friends and all but nothing could deter them from telling the truth. They played cards all the time, and, yes, they partied and enjoyed young ladies and consumed beer and good whiskeys. Hell, they were all single and in their twenties, so why not?

Bridgette was next and she stole the show. She told the jury that she and Nevin had been dating for a few months and were beginning to see a future together. On the night in question, she was working as a waitress at Foxy's and planned to meet Nevin when his poker game was over. She did, in fact, and around midnight they were together in a room upstairs. She was quite attractive, full-figured, with lots of long blond hair, and when she talked she sort of cooed into the microphone like Marilyn Monroe.

There were ten male jurors, two female. Most of the men seemed to absorb Bridgette and her testimony, no doubt thinking that the defendant had himself quite an evening. The notion that he would somehow leave her in the bed and race off to shoot two people in the head was preposterous.

Graebel went into her background but got little. She had also been well rehearsed. He was curious about the rooms upstairs and stepped into another trap. Bridgette bristled and snapped, "I am not a whore, Mr. Graebel! I'm a waitress who's working three jobs so I can go back to college." Graebel froze like a deer in headlights and dropped his notes. He suddenly had no more questions for the witness and hurried to his chair.

Now that college had been mentioned, Joshua Burch felt the need on redirect to quiz the young lady about her studies. Her dream was to become a nurse and then, maybe, a doctor. The male jurors could only fantasize about her taking their blood pressure.

The truth was that Doris (real name) was a nineteen-year-old high school dropout who'd been tending to the needs of well-heeled customers in the upstairs rooms for at least two years. With her looks and body she was too good to work as a common prostitute and was quickly elevated to the A-list where the club charged seventy-five dollars an hour for her company. Her men were older and had more cash.

When Joshua Burch was finished with her, she was instructed to step down. Most of the male jurors watched every move as she left the courtroom. They had no trouble buying the defense's alibi.

And the gun could be explained too. Joshua wisely called his client to the stand immediately after Bridgette was gone. Nevin, thoroughly coached, frowned solemnly at the jurors as he put his hand on the Bible and swore to tell the truth, then started lying. He lied about the poker game with his three buddies, lied about the tryst with Bridgette at the precise moment Fortier and Rita were taking bullets, and he lied about the pistol. Sure, it was in his possession, as were plenty of other weapons.

"Why do you own so many guns?" Burch asked dramatically.

"It's very simple," Noll said gravely, earnestly. "In my business, as a security manager for the club, I often have to break up fights and ask some of our louder customers to leave. They often have guns and knives on them. Sometimes I take them away. Other times, I just tell them to leave. It can be a dicey job, especially on a Friday or Saturday night when everybody is in a rowdy mood. Some of these guys come back to the club the next day or so and apologize and ask for their guns. Some of them we never see again. Over the years, I've accumulated quite a collection of weapons. I keep the better stuff, sell the rest."

Joshua Burch walked to the court reporter's table, picked up the Ruger, and handed it to the witness. "Now, Mr. Noll, do you recognize this pistol?"

"Yes sir."

"And when did you first lay eyes on it?"

Nevin seemed to rack his brain for the exact date, though one had been provided for him weeks earlier. "Well, I believe it was the Tuesday after the shooting of Mr. Fortier."

"And tell the jury what happened."

"Yes sir. I was at Foxy's and things were slow, as they usually are that time of the week. These two guys came in, got a table in a corner, ordered some drinks. Two of our girls joined them and they kept drinking. After several rounds, there was an argument with some boys shooting pool, something to do with one of the girls. Before we knew it there was a big fight—chairs, bottles, pool sticks flying. Girls screaming. We tried to break it up. I saw this one guy reach for the gun, this pistol right here, had it in a coat pocket, but before he could pull it out he got hit over the head with a pool stick. Split his head. I grabbed the gun before he could kill anyone and we soon got things under control. I hustled the first two out of the club and got 'em in their car, told 'em never to come back. They were really drunk. The one who owned the gun had blood all over his face. I had never seen 'em before, never seen 'em since."

"And you kept the gun?"

"Yes sir. I took it home, cleaned it up. It's a very nice piece and I waited for the owner to come back to the club and ask for it. As I said, I never saw him again."

"Can you describe him for the jury?"

Nevin shrugged. When you're creating a fictional character, he can be anything you want. "Yes sir. About my height and build, I'd say thirty years old, dark hair."

"Did he drive away?"

"No sir. It was his car, but he was banged up pretty bad and his friend got behind the wheel."

"What kind of car."

"A Ford Fairlane, light brown."

Pat Graebel sunk a few more inches in his chair as his entire case smoldered in ashes. The alibi was sticking. Bridgette and the poker boys nailed it. Now the smoking gun had been lost, explained away, never to be salvaged as clear proof of guilt.

Normally, prosecutors do not get the chance to cross-examine defendants who are known criminals and work for known gangsters. They have records and rap sheets that need to be kept away from juries. Nevin Noll, though, was early in his career and had yet to be convicted of anything significant, or felonious, and he seemed supremely confident he could handle anything Graebel could fire at him.

Graebel asked him, "Mr. Noll, who's your employer?"

"I work for Foxy's Restaurant in Biloxi."

"And who owns Foxy's?"

"Mr. Lance Malco."

"And you said you were the security manager."

"I did."

"And what does that job entail?"

"I manage security."

"I see. Why does a restaurant need security?"

"Why does any business need security?"

"I'll ask the questions, Mr. Noll."

"Yes sir. You go right ahead."

"What type of security issues do you have at Foxy's Restaurant in Biloxi?"

"Well, I just described a fight. We have those from time to time, have to break 'em up, you know, get rid of the rowdies."

"You said the two men were drinking, right?"

"That's right."

"So, alcohol is served at Foxy's?"

"Is that a question?"

"I believe it is, yes."

Noll started laughing and looked at the jurors, most of whom were ready to join him. "Mr. Graebel, are you asking me if we serve alcoholic beverages at Foxy's? Because if you are, then the answer is yes."

"And that's illegal, right?"

Noll smiled and raised both hands. "Go talk to my boss, okay? I don't own the place and I don't serve drinks. You got me on trial for murder, ain't that serious enough?"

Several of the male jurors laughed out loud, which caused Noll to start chuckling again. The humor spread instantly and dozens of spectators joined in the fun.

Poor young Pat Graebel stood at the podium, the butt of the

joke, the fool of the hour, the hotshot prosecutor whose case had vanished into thin air.

Two hours later, the jurors filed back into the courtroom. Most appeared to be amused by the process. The trial had turned into a travesty. All twelve voted "not guilty" and Nevin Noll beat his first rap.

CHAPTER 12

Keith was in right field, half asleep, one eye on the fireflies twinkling in the semidarkness, the other on the action far away. The bases were loaded, the pitcher was in trouble, and no one cared. The game meant nothing. It was a late summer weekend tournament that was intended to draw teams from along the Coast, but most had backed out. The winner would advance to nowhere. The American Legion season was over and the boys were tired of playing. The parents, evidently, were also weary because the stands were empty, with only a few bored girlfriends gossiping and ignoring the game.

A horn honked in the parking lot and Keith waved at his gang. The car was a brand-new 1963 Pontiac Grand Prix, candy-apple red, convertible, perhaps the coolest car in Biloxi at the moment. Its driver was Hugh Malco, and the occasion had been his sixteenth birthday a month earlier. His father had surprised him with the car, and the boys, all of whom were still driving old family sedans, when they were lucky, had never seen a finer gift. Of course they were envious, but they were also thrilled to be cruising the streets in such style. Hugh seemed determined to wear out the 12,000-mile warranty in the first two months. He always had money for gas, cash he earned working for his father, and also a generous allowance.

And he had plenty of time on his hands. He had given up baseball and the other team sports, and for fun trained in Buster's Gym three days a week. He boxed in tournaments around the state and lost as many as he won, but he loved the thrill of the fight. He was also proud of the fact that he was in the ring and his friends were not. They cheered him on, but they didn't have the guts to put on the gloves.

A lazy pop foul drifted down the right field line and Keith took it in stride for the final out. Ten minutes later, he was in the rear seat of the Grand Prix and they were off to the marina. Hugh was behind the wheel, driving with more caution since his second speeding ticket the week before. Riding shotgun was Denny Smith, who was in charge of the beer cooler. Next to Keith in the back was Joey Grasich, another kid from Point Cadet who had started the first grade with Hugh and Keith. Joey's father was a charter captain who fished for a living. He owned several boats, including the twenty-five-foot Carolina Skiff the boys were borrowing for the trip. All parents had signed off on the adventure—an overnight camping excursion to Ship Island.

They unloaded the trunk of the Grand Prix and piled their gear and coolers onto the boat. Hugh hated to leave his new car in the lot at the marina but had no choice. He admired it, wiped a smudge of dirt off the rear bumper, then locked it and bounded down the dock and jumped onto the skiff that was pulling away. The harbormaster whistled at Joey and told him to slow down. He did so as they opened another round of canned Schlitz. They were soon in the Mississippi Sound and the lights of the town were fading behind them.

Ship Island was a narrow slice of land thirteen miles away. It was a barrier island that took the brunt of the many hurricanes that hammered the Coast, but between storms it was popular with campers and day-trippers. On the weekends, families boated out for long picnics. Ferries ran excursions for tourists and locals. Teenagers sneaked away for adolescent games and bad behavior. Soldiers were known to spend drunken weekends on the island, parties that constantly drew complaints.

The four friends knew the island well and had fished the waters around it since they were kids. Floating on a Carolina Skiff with a small outboard motor, it was an hour away. They stripped down to their shorts and relaxed on the deck as they puttered across the water. Each lit a cigarette and sipped a beer. Keith was not a smoker but enjoyed an occasional Marlboro. Other than Hugh and his boxing, Keith was the only serious athlete left. His junior year in high school was approaching and he had a chance to start at quarterback. The dreaded two-a-day practices were just around the corner and he was about to shape up. The beer that was tasting so good would probably ooze through the pores of his skin in the heat and humidity. The thought of a cigarette would make him gag during wind sprints. But for the moment, he was savoring his little vices. The boys were sixteen years old and utterly thrilled to be independent for the weekend, free to do almost anything they wanted.

Joey, the boat captain, had played Little League baseball against Keith and Hugh but never made all-stars. Like his father, he preferred to spend his time on the boat and in the Gulf, preferably stalking game fish. Denny Smith was perhaps the slowest kid at Biloxi High and had never tried team sports. He was a serious musician who could play several instruments. He pulled out his guitar and began strumming as they inched toward the island.

It was well known that Hugh was hanging around the clubs that were strictly off-limits for the others. He was not a braggart, but he let it be known that he had been with some of the girls who worked in the family business. He had never told his friends about Cindy, and would not admit at gunpoint that he had fallen hard for a teenage hooker. She was history now and he had moved on to other girls, with Nevin Noll always watching out for him. The boys joked about sneaking into the clubs with him and watching the strippers. Hugh, though, knew they were serious, and he was determined to one day show his pals the upstairs rooms.

Denny strummed and played "Your Cheatin' Heart" by Hank Williams, one of their favorite singers and a legend who had performed at the Slavonian Lodge several times. He had also been well known in the bars and some of his drinking escapades were legendary. The boys sang along, as loud and as off-key as they wanted. There was not another boat in sight. The Sound was still. The moon was full. Near the beach, Joey raised the outboard and the Carolina skiff quietly floated ashore. They unloaded their gear, pitched two tents, and built a fire. Four thick rib-eyes hit the grill, and of course each of the campers had plenty of advice on how to cook them. They enjoyed the steaks, washed them down with beer, and when they were stuffed they sat in the surf and talked until midnight as the waves broke gently around them. There was another campfire a hundred yards to the east, more campers, and to the west they heard the laughter of girls.

They slept late and awoke to a hot sun. After a morning swim, they went to explore and found the girls. They were a little older and had boyfriends with them. They were from Pass Christian, a town twenty miles to the west of Biloxi, and they were friendly enough but didn't want company.

Joey led them around the island to the pier where a ferry was unloading day-trippers. A vendor was selling hot dogs and sodas, and they enjoyed a light lunch watching the boats come and go. Near an old fort, they saw a group of airmen in the middle of a rowdy game of beach volleyball. They had plenty of beer and invited their new guests to join in the fun. They were about twenty years old, from all over the country, and they were rougher and used coarser language. Keith thought it best if they politely declined, but Hugh wanted to play. After an hour in the sun and humidity, the games were suspended for a beer break and a swim in the ocean.

Late in the afternoon, they returned to their campsite and fell into long siestas. They were tired, sunburned, dehydrated from too much beer, and so it made perfect sense to open another round. As the sun set, they built a fire and roasted hot dogs for dinner.

Early Sunday, Hugh roused the gang from their slumbers and said they needed to hurry. Their weekend had one more adventure, one they had heard of but never experienced. They broke camp, shoved the Carolina skiff off the beach, and headed for the Biloxi lighthouse. An hour later, they docked at the marina and unloaded. Hugh was thrilled to see his shiny new car untouched and waiting.

He drove them out of town, north on Highway 49 for a few miles, then turned onto a county road that led deep into the piney woods. On a gravel trail, they saw other cars and trucks parked haphazardly along the ditches and in the fields. Men were walking toward an old barn with a peeling tin roof. They parked and went with the others until they were stopped by a man with a shotgun. "You boys are too young to be here," he growled.

Hugh was not intimidated and said, "We're guests of Nevin Noll."

He stopped frowning, nodded, and said, "Okay, follow me."

As they got closer to the barn they heard shouting and the voices of excited men. A line waited to get in. They went around to a side door and were told to wait. The guard disappeared inside.

"This is still illegal, right?" Joey asked.

"Illegal as hell," Hugh said with a laugh. "Best cockfights on the Coast."

Nevin appeared and Hugh introduced him to the other three. They knew his name because Hugh had told many stories. Nevin said, "You guys stay in the back, away from the crowd. Got a full house this morning." They eased through the narrow door and entered another world.

The barn had been converted into a cockfighting arena. A large pit filled with sand, perhaps twenty feet square, was dead center and everything else was built around it. It was bordered by a plank wall two feet high, to keep the roosters from escaping, and on top of the wall was a narrow counter where the men with the front-row seats could lean on their elbows and place their drinks. Behind them were rows of benches elevated one after the other so that the spectators were looking down at the action. Behind the last row of benches and in the aisles and exits there was a hodgepodge of lawn chairs, old theater seats, church pews, stools, upside-down barrels, and anything else a man could possibly sit on. Men only. The crowd was packed shoulder to shoulder. A thick layer of cigar and cigarette smoke hung above the cockpit and was not disturbed by several large box fans trying vainly to break up the humidity. The temperature outside was at least ninety, but even higher near the pit. Chewing tobacco was widely in use and some of the men in the front seats spat their juice onto the sand. Almost everyone had a tall paper cup with a drink, and bottles were passed around.

The men were boisterous, talking loud, even yelling at each other across the pit in good-natured fun. They were waiting for the next fight, when their moods would change. In one corner, behind a section of seats, two men in white shirts and ties worked behind a counter, taking in cash, recording the bets, trying frantically to keep straight the rush of gambling. In another corner, the voices grew louder and there were more shouts as two handlers emerged from the outside pens and walked toward the pit. Each carried a rooster, and when they stepped into the pit they held them high for the crowd to admire.

The gamecocks were naturally aggressive toward all males of the same species. The good breeders picked the heavier and faster ones and bred them over and over for increased strength and stamina. They trained them by forcing them to run long distances and obstacle courses, and they fed them steroids and adrenaline to enhance performance. Two weeks before the fight, they were kept in small dark boxes to isolate them and jack up their aggressiveness.

Both handlers were extremely careful because their roosters were equipped with razor-sharp steel gaffs tied to their legs, deadly weapons that resembled small curved ice picks.

A gentleman in a black cowboy hat and matching bow tie was yelling here and there, encouraging all bets to be placed. Hugh said, "That's Phil Arkwright, he owns the place. Makes a lot of money off this racket."

"And you've been here before?" Keith asked, knowing the answer.

"Couple of times," Hugh said with a smile. "Nevin loves these fights."

"What about your dad? Does he know?"

"Probably."

They were behind the back row, looking down at the pit. Hugh felt at home. The other three could only gawk. The two handlers met in the center of the ring, squatted, allowed the roosters' beaks to touch, then turned them loose. They attacked with their beaks, squawked fiercely and crowed, rolled around in the sand as feathers flew. One managed to pin the other and unloaded with the gaffs, jabbing away with both feet. The wounded bird scrambled to his feet and there was blood on his chest. They traded attacks and wounds and neither retreated. The one showing the most blood began to fade and the other moved in for the kill. Half the crowd wanted more blood, half wanted a time-out. No one kept quiet.

The rules did not provide for a clock or any stoppages. At Arkwright's arena, all fights were to the death.

When the loser was motionless, Arkwright entered the pit and beckoned the handler for the winner to come corral his bird. He managed to subdue him without getting slashed and held him high for the crowd to applaud. The gamecock seemed to care nothing for the adulation. He strained to watch the dying bird in the sand and wanted to finish him off. The loser's handler appeared with a burlap sack, carefully scooped him up, and dragged him away to the jeers of those who'd put good money on him. His owner would eat him for dinner.

Packs of men descended on the gambling desk to collect their winnings. A stable boy raked the sand and tried to cover up the blood. Fresh cigars were lit and bottles were passed around.

Hugh said, "You guys wanna play?"

All three shook their heads. Joey asked, "What do the cops think about this?"

Hugh chuckled and pointed at the pit. "See that first row on the other side, big guy in a striped shirt with a green cap? That's our beloved sheriff, Fats Bowman. And that's his reserved seat. He's here every Sunday morning, except during election years when he occasionally goes to church."

"So that's Fats Bowman?" Denny said. "Never saw him before."

"Crookedest sheriff in the state," Hugh said. "Also the richest. Look, it's time to bet and the next fight is the biggest. There's a breeder from up around Wiggins who raises the meanest birds in the state. He's got a new Whitehackle named Elvis who's supposed to be unbeatable."

"Whitehackle?" Keith asked.

"Yeah, one of the more popular breeds of gamecocks."

"Forgive me."

"Elvis?" asked Joey. "They have names?"

"Some do. Elvis has this black plume thing going, thinks he's really pretty. He's fighting a Hatch from Louisiana and is a three-to-one favorite. I'm putting five bucks on the Hatch. That's fifteen if I win. Anybody want some action?"

All three shook their heads and watched as Hugh weaved through the crowd and made his way to the gambling counter. He must have felt lucky because he returned with four bottles of Falstaff beer.

For the main event, the pit grew even louder. Men lined up to place bets as Phil Arkwright harangued them to hurry up, the roosters were getting antsy. They finally made their entrance, with their handlers squeezing their wings firmly to keep them under control. When the birds saw one another they almost jumped out of their feathers. Both breeds were famous for their "no retreat, no surrender" style of life-or-death fighting.

Hugh, now with money on the line, started yelling like the others, as if a rooster a hundred feet away could understand him. The one named Elvis looked nothing like the singer but for some thick black plumage that rose up the back of his neck and topped off his head. His razor-like spurs glistened as if they had been polished.

The beaks touched and the handlers quickly withdrew. The

crowd bellowed as grown men yelled at two birds fighting in the sand. The cocks crowed and attacked, with blood on the line. Elvis stood a bit taller and used his height to peck away furiously. The Hatch knocked him down, rolled him over, and seemed ready to pounce when Elvis suddenly took flight, swooped over the Hatch, and landed on his back, both gaffs hacking away. Blood was suddenly everywhere on the Hatch and he could not get away for a break. Elvis smelled a quick knockout and hit even faster. The Hatch finally managed to scramble away from the onslaught but had trouble walking. It was obvious that he was grievously wounded. The crowd, or at least those who put money on the Hatch, were stunned at how quickly Elvis had cut up their favorite. He lunged at the Hatch, spun him around, and like an expert in martial arts, hacked his throat with a gaff. The blow almost decapitated the Hatch, who was suddenly defenseless.

It was a blood sport and death was part of it. Arkwright was not one to show sympathy or cheat his crowd out of a thrill, so he allowed Elvis to mutilate his opponent for a few more seconds. The mauling lasted less than a minute.

Hugh was speechless, so his buddies came to his rescue. "Great bet there, Hugh," Keith said with a laugh.

"Hang out here often?" asked Denny.

"That wasn't even a decent fight," added Joey.

Hugh, always a good sport, raised both hands in surrender and said, "All right, all right, let me have it. You guys wanna show me how it's done? Let's do a side bet on the next fight. A dollar each."

But they were too broke to gamble. They finished their beers as they enjoyed a few more fights, then headed back to the car. Their long weekend was over. They would tell no one of their visit to Arkwright's, though Lance Malco would find out soon enough. He really didn't care. Hugh was only sixteen but was mature for his age and could certainly take care of himself. He was showing no interest in college and that was fine with Lance as well.

The boy was needed in the family business.

CHAPTER 13

Two days after Thanksgiving in 1966, the body of Marcus Dean Poppy was found in an alley behind a brothel on Decatur Street in the French Quarter. He had been beaten with a blunt instrument and finished off with two bullets to the head. His pockets were empty; there was no wallet, no means of identification. Not surprisingly, no one inside the brothel would admit to having seen him before. No one heard a peep from the alley. It took the New Orleans police two weeks to determine who he was, and by then any hope of finding his killer was gone. It was a rough town with a lot of crime, and the police were accustomed to finding bodies in alleys. A detective poked around Biloxi and put together a brief sketch of the victim, who'd once owned Carousel Lounge but who hadn't been seen in town for over three years. A brother in Texas was located, informed of the death, but had no interest in retrieving the body.

The story finally made its way to the *Gulf Coast Register,* but was easily missed on page three, bottom left-hand corner. The reporter did manage to link the murder to the one of Earl Fortier back in 1963. That one led to a trial in which Nevin Noll was acquitted.

Absolutely no one would comment. The people who knew both Poppy and Fortier back in the day were either long gone or hiding in the shadows. Those who read the story and knew the players in Biloxi's underworld figured Lance Malco had finally settled another old debt. It was common knowledge that Poppy had outslicked him when he sold Carousel Lounge to Ginger Redfield and her gang, and it was only a matter of time before Lance got his man. Carousel had become an even more popular nightclub and casino, one that rivaled Foxy's and Red Velvet, and one that Malco still coveted. Ginger was a tough businesswoman and ran it well. Along with O'Malley's, she had added another club on the Strip and a couple of bars on the north side of town. She was ambitious, and as her empire expanded it was inevitably encroaching on turf that Lance Malco believed was rightfully his.

A showdown was looming. Tension was in the air as both gangs watched each other. Fats Bowman knew the streets and had cautioned both crime lords against outright warfare. Selfishly, he wanted more clubs, more gambling, more of everything, but he was smart enough to understand the need for a peaceful flow of commerce. If and when the shooting started, there would be no way to control it. Hell, they were all making money, and lots of it, so why get even greedier? An old-fashioned gangland shootout would only rile the public, bring in unwanted attention, and possibly provoke outside interference from the state police and the Feds.

———•———

Jesse Rudy read the story about Poppy's murder and knew what had happened. It was another grim reminder of the lawlessness that was growing in his town. He had finally made the decision to do something about it.

Keith was home for the Christmas break, and after dinner one night Jesse and Agnes gathered their four children in the den for a family chat. Beverly was sixteen, Laura fifteen, and both were students at Biloxi High. Tim was thirteen and in junior high.

Jesse said that he and their mother had had many long conversations about their future, and had made the decision that he would seek the office of district attorney in next year's 1967 election. Rex Dubisson, the current DA, was completing his second term and would be a formidable opponent. He was entrenched with the old guard and would be well financed. Most of the local lawyers would support him, as would most of the other elected officials. More importantly, he would be backed by the nightclub owners, mobsters, and other crooks who had controlled local politics for years. His children knew their children.

Hopefully, Jesse would have the support of those on the right side of the law, which should be the majority of voters. But there were many who paid lip service to reform while secretly enjoying the easy life on the Coast. They liked the upscale clubs, the fine restaurants, with cocktails and wine lists, and the neighborhood watering holes away from the Strip. There had been many politicians who campaigned with promises of reform, only to succumb to the corruption once elected. And there were those who had managed to keep their integrity while turning a blind eye. He had no plans to do so.

The campaign would be strenuous and perhaps dangerous. Once the mobsters realized he was serious about reform, there could be threats and intimidation. He would never risk the well-being of his family, but he seriously doubted anyone would be bold enough to threaten real harm. And, yes, they would all hit the streets, knocking on doors and putting up yard signs.

Keith, the oldest and unquestioned leader of the pack, spoke first and said he wasn't afraid of a damned thing. He was proud of his parents for the decision and he couldn't wait to start campaigning. At college, he had grown accustomed to comments about Biloxi. Most students had a romanticized vision of the vice and all the fun it offered. Many had been in the clubs and bars. Few understood the dark side of the Strip. And there were those who viewed anyone from Biloxi with suspicion.

If the idea was good enough for Keith, then Beverly, Laura, and Tim were on board. They could handle any snide comments from kids at school. They were proud of their father and supported his decision.

He cautioned them to keep the plans quiet. He would announce his candidacy in a month or so; until then, not a word. The election would be settled in the Democratic primary in August, so they had a busy summer in front of them.

When the conversation was over, the family held hands and Jesse led them in prayer.

———— • ————

Two nights later, Keith met the old gang at a new downtown bar. The state had finally changed its antiquated liquor laws and allowed each county to vote yes or no to the sale of alcohol. Not surprisingly, the Coast counties—Harrison, Hancock, and Jackson—had quickly voted yes. Liquor stores and bars were soon doing a brisk business. For those eighteen and older, it was legal to drink. This put a dent in vice trade, but the gangsters filled the gap with marijuana and cocaine. Gambling and skin were still in demand. Business on the Strip was still thriving.

Hugh was working for his father and running a construction crew building new apartments, or so he said. The others suspected he was hanging around the clubs. Joey Grasich was home on leave from the navy. Denny Smith was a full-time student at the junior college and had never left home.

The four retired to a table, ordered pitchers of beer, and lit cigarettes. Joey told stories of basic training in California, a place he was quite taken with. With some luck, he would be assigned to a submarine and stay far away from Vietnam.

The boys found it hard to believe they were out of high school and approaching adulthood. They were curious about Keith's baseball career at Southern Miss, and he reported that he'd had a good fall tryout. He had not made the team but he had not been cut either. The coach wanted him to practice every day, starting in February, and see how his arm developed. The team had plenty of pitchers, but then, in baseball, there's never enough pitching.

Hugh had retired as a boxer. In his two-year career, he fought eighteen bouts, won nine, lost seven, and had two draws. Buster, his coach, had become frustrated with his training habits because Hugh admittedly had no desire to lay off the beer, cigarettes, and girls. He always won the first round, lost steam in the second, and held on for his life in the third when his feet got heavy and he had trouble breathing.

As the beer flowed, Hugh said, "Hey, remember Fuzz Foster, my second fight in Golden Gloves?"

They laughed and said of course they remembered.

"Well, I fought him two more times, in the ring. The ref stopped that first fight because we were both cut. A year later I beat him on points in a tournament in Jackson. Two months after that, he beat me on points. I came to really despise the guy, you know? Then, about three months ago we had our fourth fight, and this one was not in the ring. No gloves. He was in Foxy's one night with a bunch of his boys, all drunk as skunks, raising hell. I was working security and trying to stay away from them. Sure enough, a fight broke out and I had to step over. When Fuzz saw me he had a big smile and we acknowledged each other. We got the fight under control, kicked out a couple of boneheads, then Fuzz started this crap about how he'd kicked my ass all three times and got screwed by the refs and judges. He was still boxing and started bragging about winning the state welterweight in a couple of months and going on to the Olympics. Total bullshit. I told him to pipe down because he was too loud. The place was full, other customers were getting tired of his mouth. He got mean, got in my face, and asked me if I wanted another go at it. We had plenty of security and another guy stepped between us. This really pissed off Fuzz and he threw a wild right that bounced off the top of my head, one of those drunk hooks that good boxers duck. But you know Fuzz, always going for the big knockout. I popped him in the jaw and the brawl was on. We slugged it out as his buddies piled on. What a mess. It was wonderful. Fuzz wasn't on his game because he was drunk and unsteady. I got him on the floor and was pounding his face when they pulled me off. We finally got 'em outside and called the cops. Last time I saw Fuzz he was getting hauled away in handcuffs."

"Did y'all press charges?"

"Naw, we rarely do. I went to court the next day, talked to the cops, and got him out. He had a broken nose and two puffy eyes. I drove him home and told him never to come back. I really kicked his ass."

"So you work security?" Joey asked. "Thought you were build-ing apartments."

"That's my day job. Sometimes I work the clubs. A guy's gotta do something at night." His cockiness had only grown worse with age. His father was the king of the underworld, with plenty of money and power, and now he was grooming his oldest son to learn the business. He paid him well and Hugh always had plenty of cash. And fast cars, nicer clothes, more expensive tastes.

They bantered back and forth, then enjoyed more of Hugh's exploits in the clubs. He had the floor and relished telling stories about the shady characters he encountered on the Strip.

Keith listened, laughed, drank his beer, and acted as though all was well, but he knew these moments were fleeting. The friend-ships were about to change, or vanish altogether. In a few short months, his father, and his family, would be in the middle of a rough campaign that pitted new versus old, good versus evil.

For him and Hugh, it was probably their last beer together. The moment Jesse Rudy announced his campaign, the conflict would be clearly defined, and there would be no going back. At first, the underworld would be amused at yet another politician promising to clean up Biloxi, but that would soon change. Jesse Rudy had an iron will and a strong moral compass and he played to win. He would battle the crooks to the bitter end, all the way to the ballot box.

And his family would be at his side.

Keith wasn't sure where the other friends would land. Denny

was already bored with college but would not jeopardize his defer-ment. He and Hugh were talking about renovating some retail spaces together. Denny didn't have a dime, so any financing would no doubt come from Mr. Malco. It was well known that he had his tentacles in many legitimate businesses and used them to launder his dirty money.

Joey's father had once been close to Lance, but was a commer-cial fisherman and stayed away from the mobsters. Keith had no idea how Joey would deal with a split in the gang.

The thought of the friends dividing over politics was unset-tling, but the fault lines were just under the surface.

They left the bar and piled into Hugh's latest sports car, a 1966 Mustang convertible. He drove them to Mary Mahoney's Old French House and paid cash for a big dinner of steaks and seafood.

Keith was prescient in his feeling that it would be their last night on the town together.

PART
TWO

—•—

THE
CRUSADER

CHAPTER 14

On a raw, windy day in late February, Jesse Rudy walked to the Harrison County Courthouse to meet with Rex Dubisson, the district attorney. His office was on the second floor, down the hall from the main courtroom. The two had known each other for years and had worked many cases from opposite sides. On four occasions they had squared off in the courtroom and fought over the guilt or innocence of Jesse's clients. As expected, Rex had won three out of four. District attorneys rarely went to trial with cases they were not confident of winning. The facts were on their side because the defendants were usually guilty.

The two lawyers respected one another, though Jesse's admiration was tempered by the belief that Rex had little interest in fighting organized crime. He was a good prosecutor who ran a tight office and boasted, predictably, of a 90 percent conviction rate. That sounded good at the Rotary Club lunches, but the truth was that at least 90 percent of the folks he indicted were guilty of something.

After coffee was served and they got through the weather, Jesse said, "I'll not beat around the bush. I'm here to tell you that I'm running for DA and will announce my candidacy tomorrow."

Rex looked at him in disbelief and finally said, "Well, thanks for the warning. May I ask why?"

"Do I need a reason?"

"Sure you do. You have problems with the way I run my office?"

"Well, I guess you could say that. I'm sick of the corruption,

Rex. Fats Bowman has been in bed with the mobsters since he took office twelve years ago. He skims from every part of the vice and doles out cash to the other politicians. Most are on the take. You know all this. He regulates the business and allows the likes of Lance Malco, Shine Tanner, Ginger Redfield, and the other club owners to do their dirty business."

Rex laughed and said, "So you're a reformer, another politician promising to clean up the Coast?"

"Something like that."

"They've all fallen flat on their faces, Jesse. So will you."

"Well, at least I'll try. That's more than you've done."

Rex thought for a long time and finally said, "Okay, the battle lines are drawn. Welcome to the fight. I just hope you don't get hurt."

"I'm not worried about that."

"You should be."

"Is that a threat, Rex?"

"I don't make threats, but sometimes I give warnings."

"Well, thanks for the warning, but I'm not going to be intimidated by you, or Fats, or anyone else. I'll run a clean race and I expect the same from you."

"There's nothing clean about politics around here, Jesse. You're being naive. It's a dirty game."

"It doesn't have to be."

———•———

Jesse had envisioned an announcement party in which he would invite friends, other lawyers, maybe some elected officials, and a few committed reformers to declare his candidacy. This proved hard to organize because there was so little interest in such an open display of reform. Instead of launching his campaign with speeches and headlines, he decided to sort of ease into it quietly.

The day after the meeting with Dubisson, he met with a

group that included several ministers, one Biloxi city council-man, and two retired judges. They were thrilled with the news that he would run and pledged their support and a few bucks for the campaign.

The following day, he met with the editorial staff of the *Gulf Coast Register* and laid out his plans. It was time to shut down the clubs and put the mobsters out of business. Gambling and prostitution were still illegal and he promised to use the law to get rid of them. Alcohol was now legal in the county, and, technically, the state liquor board would not grant a license to sell booze if a club allowed gambling. He was determined to enforce the law. One obvious problem was the fact that stripping was not illegal. A club with a valid liquor license could operate freely and employ all the girls it wanted. It would be almost impossible to monitor those clubs and determine when the stripping led to more illicit activities. Jesse acknowledged the challenge and was vague as to any specific plans.

The editors were delighted to have a campaign that would certainly create a lot of news, but they were skeptical of Jesse's optimism. They had heard it all before. They pointedly asked how he planned to enforce the laws when the sheriff had little interest in doing so. His response was that not all cops were on the take. He was confident that he could gain the trust of the honest ones, lean on the state police, and get indictments. Once he had them, he planned to push hard for prosecutions and jury trials.

Jesse was careful to stay away from naming any of his potential targets. Everyone knew who they were, but it was too early to provoke outright warfare by openly challenging the mobsters and crooks. The editors pried here and there, but Jesse refused to call names. There would be plenty of time for that later.

He was encouraged by the meeting and left it with the belief that the newspaper, a major voice on the Coast, would back him. The following day, the front page had a nice photo of him with the headline: "Jesse Rudy Enters DA's Race."

Lance Malco read the story and was amused by it. He had known Jesse since their childhood days on Point Cadet and had once, many years ago, considered him a friend, though never a close one. Those days were long gone. The new battle lines were clear and the war was on. Lance, though, was not concerned. Before Jesse could begin his mischief, he had to get elected, and Fats Bowman and his machine had never lost an election. Fats knew the playbook and was adept at the dirty tricks: stuffing ballot boxes, raising large sums of unreported money, buying blocks of votes, spreading lies, intimidating voters, harassing poll workers, bribing election officials, and voting dead people with absentee ballots. Fats had never been seriously challenged and enjoyed boasting about the need to have at least one opponent in every election. An enemy on the ballot allowed him to raise even more money. He, too, was up for reelection and when an opponent finally appeared he would crank up the full force of his political machine.

Lance would meet with Fats soon enough and have a drink over this latest news. They would map out their opposition and plan their dirty tricks. Lance would be clear, though, about one thing. Jesse and his family were off-limits and were not to be threatened. Not in the first months anyway. If his reform campaign gained traction, which Lance seriously doubted, then Fats and his boys could revert to their old ways of intimidation.

Through the spring of 1967, Jesse hit the civic club circuit and made dozens of speeches. The Rotarians, Civitans, Lions, Jaycees, Legionnaires, and others were always looking for lunch speakers and would invite almost anyone in the news. Jesse honed his skills on the stump and talked of a new day on the Coast, one without corruption and the freewheeling, anything-goes history of unbridled vice. He was a proud son of Biloxi and Point Cadet, had risen from modest means, raised by hardworking immigrants who loved their new country, and he was tired of his town's ugly reputation. As always, he avoided naming names, but quickly rattled off joints like Red Velvet, Foxy's, O'Malley's, Carousel, the Truck Stop, Siesta, Sunset Bar, Blue Ocean Club, and others as examples of "pits of iniquity" that had no place in a new Gulf Coast. His favorite prop was a memo sent from the headquarters at Keesler. It was an official warning to all members of the armed forces, and it listed 66 "establishments" on the Coast that were "off-limits." Most were in Biloxi, and the list included virtually every bar, lounge, club, pool hall, motel, and café in town. "What kind of place do we live in?" Jesse asked his audiences.

He was generally well received and enjoyed the polite applause, though most of those listening doubted his chances.

As busy as his office was, he found two or three hours each afternoon to hit the streets and knock on doors. There were almost 41,000 registered voters in Harrison County, 6,600 in Hancock, and 3,200 in Stone, and his goal was to meet as many as possible. He barely had enough money for brochures and yard signs. Radio ads and billboards were out of the question. He relied on hard work, shoe leather, and a dogged determination to meet the voters. When she was free, Agnes joined him, and they worked many streets together, Jesse on one side, his wife on the other. When school ended in May and Keith came home from college, the four children eagerly grabbed stacks of brochures and canvassed shopping centers, ball games, church picnics, outdoor markets, anywhere they could find a crowd.

It was an election year, time for serious politicking, and every race from governor down to county constable and justice of the peace was on the ballot. Somewhere in the district, there was a rally every weekend, and the Rudy family never missed one. Several times, Jesse spoke either before or after Rex Dubisson, and the two managed to keep things cordial. Rex relied on his experience

and crowed about his 90 percent conviction rate. Jesse countered
with the argument that Mr. Dubisson was not going after the real
crooks. Fats had managed to coerce an old deputy to run against
him, and his machine was in high gear. His presence at a stump
speaking always guaranteed a crowd. The governor's race pitted
two well-known politicians, John Bell Williams and William
Winter, against each other, and when it heated up in midsummer
the voters were even more excited. Observers predicted a record
turnout.

There were few Republican candidates to speak of at the local
level; everyone—conservative, liberal, black or white—ran as a
Democrat, and the election would be determined in the primary
on August 4.

The reform movement Jesse dreamed of did not galvanize. He
had plenty of supporters who wanted change and were eager to
help, but many seemed reticent to be identified with a campaign
that aspired to such a radical departure from the way things had
been done for decades. He was frustrated by this but could not slow
down. By July, he had all but abandoned his law practice and spent
most of his time shaking hands. From six until nine in the morning he was a lawyer taking care of his clients, but after that he was
a political candidate with miles to cover.

He slept little, and at midnight he and Agnes were usually in
bed replaying the day and planning tomorrow. They were relieved
that, so far, there had been no threats, no anonymous calls, no hint
of intimidation from Fats and the mobsters.

The first sign of trouble came in early July when four new tires
on a Chevrolet Impala were slashed and flattened. The car was
owned by Dickie Sloan, a young lawyer who was volunteering as
Jesse's campaign manager. It was parked in his driveway, where he
found it vandalized early one morning as he left for the office. At
the time, he could think of no reason anyone would want to slash
his tires, other than his political activities. Sloan was shaken by the
threat, as was his wife, and he decided to step aside. Jesse was rely-

ing heavily on Sloan's management and disappointed when he got spooked so easily. With a month to go, it would be difficult to find another volunteer willing to commit the time necessary to run the campaign.

Keith immediately stepped into the void, and, at the age of nineteen, assumed responsibility for raising money, directing volunteers, dealing with the press, monitoring the opposition, printing yard signs and brochures, and doing everything else necessary to keep a low-budget campaign afloat. He plunged into the job and was soon putting in sixteen-hour days like his father.

Keith was playing on a semi-pro team in the Coast League and felt like he was wasting his time. He still enjoyed the game but was also accepting the reality that his baseball days were numbered. He was immersed in politics and learning its lessons firsthand. He thrived on the challenge of putting together a campaign and its goal of getting more votes than the opponent. He quit the team, and baseball, and never looked back.

Occasionally he bumped into Joey, Denny, and other old pals from the Point, but he had not seen Hugh Malco in months. According to his friends, Hugh was keeping a low profile and busy working for his father. Keith suspected they were meddling in the local races, but there had yet to be any evidence of it. The slashed tires were the first indication that the mob was getting antsy. And, there was no way to prove who was behind the vandalism. The list of possible suspects was long.

Jesse cautioned his family and volunteers to be vigilant.

Election laws required all candidates to file quarterly reports as to funds raised and moneys spent. As of June 30, Jesse had raised almost $11,000 and spent all of it. Rex Dubisson's campaign reported $14,000 in income and $9,000 in expenses. The reporting laws were riddled with loopholes, and, of course, covered only those funds "above the table." No one seriously believed that Rex was relying on such paltry sums. And, since the next reports were not due until September 30, long after the August 4 primary, the serious money was being hoarded with no worries about reporting laws.

The attack began on July 10, three weeks before the election, when every registered household received in the mail a packet of professionally printed materials, including an eight-by-ten sheet with a large mug shot of one Jarvis Decker, a black man with a menacing scowl. Above it, the question screamed: "Why Is Jesse Rudy Soft On Crime?" Below the mug shot was a two-paragraph story of how Jesse Rudy, only two years earlier, had represented Jarvis Decker in a domestic abuse case and "got the thug off scot-free." Decker, a convicted felon with a "violent past," had beaten his wife, who filed charges, only to see the case "swept out of court" by the shifty legal work of Jesse Rudy. Once free, Decker left the area and drifted to Georgia, where he was convicted of not one but two rapes. He was serving a life sentence and would never be paroled.

If not for Jesse Rudy, Decker would have been convicted in Biloxi, sent away, and been "off the streets." The slanted narrative left little doubt that Jesse Rudy was responsible for the rapes.

The truth was that Jesse had been appointed by the court to represent Decker. His wife, the alleged victim, had failed to show up in court and asked the police to drop the charges. They then divorced, and Jesse never heard from the client again.

But the truth was not important. Jesse, a lawyer who represented many guilty criminals, was soft on crime. A brochure in the packet touted the fierceness of Rex Dubisson, a veteran prosecutor known to be "Tough On Crime."

The mailing was devastating, not only because it barely nibbled at the edges of the truth, but more importantly because Jesse had no discernible means to counter it. Such a mass mailing cost thousands and there was almost no time, and certainly no money, to put together a response.

The large conference room of the Rudy Law Firm had been converted into the campaign's headquarters, with posters and maps covering the walls, and volunteers coming and going. He met there with Keith, Agnes, and a few others, and tried to measure the impact of the mailing. The room was tense and gloomy. They had been punched in the gut and it seemed almost senseless to hustle back to the streets and resume knocking on doors.

Simultaneously, eight prominent billboards along Highway 90 sprang up with a handsome image of Rex Dubisson under the banner: TOUGH ON CRIME. Radio ads began running on the hour touting Dubisson's record as a regular crime-buster.

Driving along the Coast, and listening to the radio, Jesse passed billboard after billboard and acknowledged the obvious. His opponent and his supporters had stockpiled their money, carefully planned the last-minute ambush, and delivered a crushing blow. With less than a month to go, his campaign looked hopeless.

Keith worked all night and mocked up a brochure that he presented to his father early one morning over coffee. The idea was to blanket the district with a mailing that did not mention Dubisson but went after the organized crime that was the real reason for their campaign. It would have photographs of the more infamous nightclubs where gambling, prostitution, and drugs had been allowed to flourish for years. Keith had the details and explained that such a mailing would cost $5,500. They had no time to raise the money from supporters, who were tapped out anyway. Keith, who'd never borrowed a dime, asked if there was any possible way to get a loan.

Jesse and Agnes had casually, and quietly, discussed the idea of getting a second mortgage to help fund the campaign, but were hesitant to do so. Now the idea was back on the table and Keith was all in. He was confident the money could be repaid. If Jesse won the election, he would have no shortage of new friends, along with a powerful position. The bank would be impressed and better terms could be negotiated. If Jesse lost the election, the family could double down with the law practice and find a way to satisfy the mortgage.

Their son's courage convinced them to go to the bank. Keith

went to the printer and wouldn't take no for an answer. Over a long weekend, a team of a dozen volunteers worked around the clock addressing and stuffing envelopes. On Monday morning, Keith hauled almost 7,000 thick packets to the post office and demanded expedited deliveries. Every registered home, apartment, and trailer in the district would receive the mailing.

The response was encouraging. Jesse and his team had learned the hard lesson that direct mail was extremely effective.

CHAPTER 15

As the wealthiest elected official in the state, Fats Bowman owned an impressive portfolio of property. He and his wife lived in a quiet neighborhood in West Biloxi, in a modest home any honest sheriff could afford. They had been there for twenty years and still made monthly mortgage payments, just like everybody else on the street. To get away, they vacationed in their condo in Florida or their cabin in the Smokies, homes they rarely discussed. With a partner, Fats owned beachfront property in Waveland, next door in Hancock County. Unknown to his wife, he also had an interest in a new development at Hilton Head.

His favorite hiding place was his hunting camp deep in the piney woods of Stone County, twenty miles to the north of Biloxi. There, far away from prying eyes, Fats liked to call in his boys and associates and discuss business and politics.

Two weeks before the election, he invited some friends to his camp for steaks and drinks. They gathered on a covered patio at the edge of a small lake and sat in wicker rockers under a rattling ceiling fan. Rudd Kilgore, his chief deputy, chauffeur, and primary bagman, poured bourbon and kept an eye on the grill. Lance Malco was accompanied by Tip and Nevin Noll. Rex Dubisson came by himself.

Copies of the Rudy campaign's recent mailing were passed around. Lance was irritated by the fact that the slick brochure included a color photo of Red Velvet, his flagship club, and the narrative said bad things about it. For Lance, it was the first sign of open warfare from Jesse Rudy.

"Just keep your cool," Fats drawled, a black cigar wedged between two fingers, a bourbon in the other hand. "I don't see any movement in Rudy's direction. Boy's broke and I guess he's borrowing money, but it won't be enough. We got everything teed up." He looked at Dubisson and asked, "How much cash you got?"

"We're okay," Rex said. "Our last mailing goes out tomorrow and it's pretty rough. He won't be able to respond."

"You said that last time," Lance said.

"I did."

"I don't know," Lance said, waving the brochure. "This is getting some attention from the do-gooders. You're not worried?"

"Of course I'm worried," Rex said. "It's politics and anything can happen. Rudy's run a good campaign and worked his ass off. Keep in mind, guys, I haven't run a hard race in eight years. This is something new for me."

"You're doing a good job," Fats said. "Just keep listening to me."

"What about the black vote?" Lance asked.

"Well, there ain't much of it, as you know. Less than twenty percent, if they go vote. I got the preachers lined up and we'll deliver the cash Sunday before the election. They tell me there's nothing to worry about."

"Can you trust them?" Rex asked.

"They've always delivered in the past, haven't they. The preachers will haul their people to the polls in church buses."

"Rudy looks strong on the Point," Rex said. "I was over there last weekend and got a rather cool reception."

Lance said, "I know the Point as well as Rudy. That's his base and he might carry it, but it'll be close."

"Give him the Point," Fats said, blowing smoke. "There's fourteen other boxes in Harrison County and I control them."

"What about Hancock and Stone?" Lance asked.

"Well, first of all, there are four times more votes in Harrison than the other two combined. Hell, ain't nobody to speak of in

Stone County. The votes are in Biloxi and Gulfport, boys, you know that. Y'all need to relax."

"We're okay in Stone County," said Dubisson. "My wife's from there and her family has influence."

Fats laughed and said, "You just keep hitting him with the mail and the radio and leave the rest to me."

———•———

Three days later, the district was blanketed with another flood of brochures. The color photo was of an ailing white woman in a wheelchair, with an oxygen tube stuck to her nose. She appeared to be about fifty years old, with long stringy gray hair, and lots of wrinkles. In bold black print above the photo, the caption, in quotation marks, read, "I Was Raped By Jarvis Decker."

She said her name was Connie Burns, and she described what happened when Decker broke into her home in rural Georgia, tied her up, and left two hours later. After the ordeal and the nightmare of the trial, her world completely collapsed. Her husband left her; her health deteriorated. There was no one to support her, and so on. She was now living in a nursing home and was unable to afford her medications.

Her story ended with: "Why was Jarvis Decker allowed to roam free and rape me and other women? He should have been serving time in Mississippi, and he would have been if not for the slick moves of criminal defense attorney Jesse Rudy. Please don't elect this man. He cozies up to violent criminals."

Jesse was so upset he locked himself in his office, stretched out on the floor, and tried to breathe deeply. Agnes was down the hall, in the restroom, vomiting. The campaign volunteers huddled in the conference room and stared in muted horror at the mailing. The secretary ignored the phone, which rang nonstop.

———•———

Ten days before the election, Jesse Rudy filed suit in chancery court seeking to enjoin Rex Dubisson from distributing campaign materials containing blatant falsehoods. He demanded an expedited hearing on the matter.

The damage was done and the court did not have the power to repair it. The chancellor could order Dubisson to stop future mailings and ads that were not true, but, in the heat of a campaign, such injunctions were rare. Jesse knew he could not win the court battle, but winning was not the reason for the lawsuit. He wanted publicity. He wanted the story on the front page of the *Gulf Coast Register* so the voters could see what a sleazy campaign their district attorney was running. Moments after he filed in court, he drove to the newspaper's office and hand-delivered a copy of his complaint to the editor. The following morning, it was front-page news.

That afternoon, the chancellor called the matter for a hearing and a nice crowd materialized. In the front row were several reporters. As the complaining party, Jesse went first and began with an angry description of the "rape ad," as he called it. He paced around the courtroom, waving the ad, calling it "blatantly false" and a "sleazy campaign trick designed to inflame the voters." Connie Burns was an alias for a woman who was probably paid by the Dubisson campaign to use her fictitious story. The real victims of Jarvis Decker were Denise Perkins and Sybil Welch, and he had copies of the indictments and plea agreements to prove it. He entered those into evidence.

The problem with his case was that he had no real proof, other than the paperwork. Connie Burns, or whoever she was, had not been found, nor had the two rape victims. With time and money, Jesse could have located them and tried to cajole them into either traveling to Biloxi or signing affidavits, but that could not be done with only a week to go.

Veteran trial lawyers knew the old adage: "When the case is weak, go heavy on theatrics." Jesse was angry, indignant, wounded, the victim of a dirty campaign trick. When he finally wound down, he yielded the floor and Rex Dubisson had the chance to respond. He seemed taken aback, as if he'd been caught red-handed. After a few disjointed statements, the chancellor interrupted with "And so who, exactly, is Connie Burns?"

"It's an alias, Your Honor. The poor lady is the victim of a violent sexual assault and does not want to get involved."

"Get involved? She allowed you to use her photograph and statement, didn't she?"

"Yes, but only with an alias. She lives far away and any publicity generated here will not find its way there. We're being protective of her identity."

"And you're trying to blame Jesse Rudy for her being raped, right?"

"Well, not directly, Your—"

"Come on, Mr. Dubisson. That's exactly what you're doing. The sole purpose of this ad is to lay blame on Mr. Rudy and convince the voters that it's all his fault."

"The facts are the facts, Your Honor. Mr. Rudy represented Jarvis Decker and got him off. If he had gone to prison here in Mississippi, he would not have been able to rape women in Georgia. It's that simple."

"Nothing's that simple, Mr. Dubisson. I find these ads repulsive."

The lawyers took turns haggling and the hearing grew even more contentious. When the chancellor asked Jesse what type of relief he wanted, he demanded that Dubisson do another mailing in which he retracted his ads, admitted the truth, and apologized for deliberately misleading the voters.

Dubisson objected hotly and argued that the court did not have the authority to require him to spend money. Jesse retorted that he, Dubisson, evidently had plenty of it to spend.

Back and forth they went like two heavyweights in the center of the ring, neither yielding an inch. It was magnificent theater and the reporters scribbled away. When both were on the verge of throwing punches, the chancellor ordered them to their seats and settled the matter. He ruled: "I do not have the power to undo what has been done with these ads. However, I do order both campaigns to immediately cease the promulgation of ads, either in print or on the air, that are not supported by the facts. Failure to follow this order will result in severe fines, perhaps even jail time for contempt of court."

For Rex Dubisson, the victory was immediate but somewhat hollow. He had no plans for more mailings and attack ads.

For Jesse, victory came the following morning when the front page of the *Register* ran the priceless quote: "I Find These Ads Repulsive."

———•———

The campaign's final days were a whirlwind of stump speeches, barbecues, rallies, and canvassing. Jesse and his volunteers knocked on doors from mid-morning until after dark. He and Keith disagreed sharply over tactics. Keith wanted to take the Connie Burns ad, put in the tagline "I Find These Ads Repulsive," run several thousand copies at the print shop, and flood the district with them. But Jesse disagreed because he thought the ads had done enough damage already. Reminding the voters of his ties to a rapist would only solidify their belief that he had done something wrong.

Over the last weekend of the campaign, "the money hit the streets," as they say. Sacks of cash were delivered to black ministers who promised to deliver voters by the busload. Fats Bowman's ward bosses took more cash and distributed it among their own teams of drivers. Absentee ballots by the hundreds were prepared using the names of those who had died since the last election.

On August 4, Election Day, Jesse, Agnes, and Keith voted early at their precinct in an elementary school. For Keith, a new voter, it was an honor casting a ballot for his father. And it was a pleasure voting against Fats and several other politicians on his payroll.

Turnout was heavy in all precincts along the Coast and the Rudys spent the day visiting their poll workers. There were no complaints of harassment or intimidation.

When the polls closed at 6:00 P.M., the arduous task of hand-counting the ballots began. It was almost 10:00 P.M. before the first precinct captains arrived at the courthouse with their tallies and boxes of ballots, all of which were counted for the second time by election clerks. Jesse and his team waited nervously in his conference room as they worked the phones. Stone County, the least populous of the five, reported its final tally at 10:45. Jesse and Dubisson evenly split the vote, an encouraging sign. The excitement waned when Hancock County went 62 percent for Dubisson.

Fats was known to delay the reporting in Harrison until all other votes had been broadcast. Foul play was always suspected but had never been proven. Finally, at 3:30 A.M., Jesse received a call from an election clerk at the courthouse. He had been soundly thumped in the Biloxi precincts, with the exception of the Point, which he carried by 300 votes, but not enough to do any damage to the Bowman machine. Dubisson received almost 18,000 votes, for a 60 percent shellacking.

Overall, throughout the three-county district, Jesse had convinced 12,173 voters that reform was needed. The others, almost 18,000, were content with the status quo.

Not surprisingly, Fats steamrolled his hapless opponent and took almost 80 percent of the vote.

It appeared as though little would change, at least for the next four years.

———•———

For two days Jesse stewed over the loss as he contemplated contesting the election. Almost 1,800 absentee ballots looked suspicious, but there were not enough to change the outcome.

He had been beaten in a dirty fight and had learned some hard lessons. Next time he would be ready for a brawl. Next time he would have more money.

He promised Keith and Agnes that he would never stop campaigning.

CHAPTER 16

With the election over, and those pesky reformers once again put in their places, 1968 began with a bang. Fats had managed to mollify long-simmering feuds while he worked to control the voting, but things got out of hand soon enough.

An ambitious outlaw named Dusty Cromwell opened a joint on Highway 90, half a mile from Red Velvet. His bar was called Surf Club and at first sold nothing but legal booze. With a liquor permit in hand, he soon opened an illegal casino and expanded into a strip club advertising an all-girl revue. Cromwell had a big mouth and let it be known that he planned to become the king of the Strip. His plans were set back when Surf Club burned to the ground early one Sunday morning when no one was around. After a cursory investigation by the police, no cause of fire could be determined. Cromwell knew it was arson and sent word to Lance Malco and Ginger Redfield that he was out for revenge. They had heard it before and braced for trouble.

Mike Savage was known in the business as the go-to arsonist and was often used in cases involving insurance fraud. He free-lanced and was on no one's payroll, but he hung around Red Velvet and was known to associate with Lance Malco and other members of the Dixie Mafia. He left the club one night and never made it home. After three days, his wife finally called the sheriff's office and reported him missing. A farmer in Stone County noticed a mysterious car parked in the woods on his land and figured something was amiss. The closer he crept to it the stronger the odor became. Buzzards were circling above. He called the law and the license plates were tracked to Mike Savage of Biloxi. When the trunk was opened, the odor nauseated the deputies. Mike's bloated corpse was covered in dried blood. His wrists and ankles were tied together with baling twine. His left ear was missing. An autopsy revealed numerous stab wounds and a viciously slit throat.

A week after the body was found, a package addressed to Lance Malco arrived at Red Velvet. Inside, wrapped in a plastic bag, was someone's left ear. Lance called Fats, who sent a team to have a look.

Motive was easily ascertained, at least by Lance, though there were no suspects, no witnesses, and nothing useful from the crime scene. Dusty Cromwell had delivered a message, but Lance was not one to be intimidated. He met with Fats and demanded he take action. Fats, as always, said that he did not get involved in turf battles and disputes among the mobsters.

"Settle it yourself," he said.

The murder was duly reported by the *Gulf Coast Register,* though details were scarce. Most of those with knowledge of the Biloxi underworld knew it was little more than a gangland payback.

One of Dusty's gun thugs was a bouncer called Clamps, a real brute of a boy who'd spent ten of his thirty years in prison for stealing cars and robbing convenience stores. With Surf Club in ashes, he was out of full-time work and looking for trouble. He had yet to kill anyone, but he and his boss were having conversations. He never got the chance. When Dusty sent him to New Orleans to collect a shipment of marijuana, he was followed by Nevin Noll. The shipment was delayed and Clamps checked in to a motel near Slidell. At three in the morning, Nevin parked his car, now sporting Florida license plates, and walked half a mile to the motel. The front office was closed, all the lights were off, and the handful of customers appeared to be sleeping. He picked a room that was empty for the night, and with a flathead screwdriver unlocked the knob to the only door. The low-end motel did not use either deadlocks or security chains. He left and eased through the darkness to the room where Clamps was sound asleep. He quickly unlocked the door, turned on the light, and as Clamps was trying to wake up, focus, figure out what the hell was happening, Nevin shot him in the face three times with a .22 caliber revolver muffled by a six-inch silencer. He finished him off with three more shots to the back of the head. He gathered Clamps's wallet, cash, car keys, and pistol under his pillow and put everything, including his screwdriver and Ruger, into the cheap overnight bag Clamps was traveling with. He turned off the light, waited fifteen minutes, and drove away in Clamps's car. He parked behind a truck stop, quickly removed the Mississippi license plates, substituted them with a set from Idaho, and drove to a gas station that was closed for the night. He left the car there, walked back to his own car, and returned to Biloxi.

Nine days passed before the Slidell police could identify the victim. His last known address was Brookhaven, Mississippi. The murder went unreported by the *Gulf Coast Register.*

At first, Dusty Cromwell assumed Clamps had picked up the marijuana and absconded with it. Three weeks after the murder, he received a package, a cardboard box with no sender's name or address. Inside was a wallet with a driver's license issued to Willie Tucker, aka Clamps. Under the wallet were his license plates.

The police in Slidell drove to Biloxi and met with Sheriff Fats Bowman, who'd never heard of anyone named Willie Tucker. Fats suspected the boy was another casualty of the escalating tensions along the Strip, but he said nothing of the sort. When it came to mob fights and dead bodies, Fats knew nothing, especially when out-of-town cops were poking around. After they left, he drove to Red Velvet and went to Lance's office.

Not surprisingly, Lance, too, said he'd never heard of Willie Tucker. There were plenty of bad actors on the Coast and the violence was getting contagious. Fats cautioned him about escalating the fighting. Too many revenge killings and they would attract the attention of outsiders. Knock off one or two here and there and it was business as usual. A gangland war was destined to end up in the press.

Dusty proved to be just as ruthless as Lance. He met with a Dixie Mafia hit man named Ron Wayne Hansom and negotiated a $15,000 contract to kill Lance Malco. The down payment was $5,000, the balance promised after the job was complete. Hansom, who operated out of Texas, spent a month on the Coast and decided the contract was too risky. Malco was seldom seen and always protected. Hansom skipped town with the money, but not before getting drunk in a bar and bragging about killing men in seven states. A waitress was eavesdropping and heard the name Malco mentioned more than once. This quickly made its way up the ladder and Lance was alarmed enough to call Fats, who called an old pal with the Texas Rangers. They knew Hansom and picked him up in Amarillo. Dusty learned of his whereabouts and sent two of his boys to have a chat. Hansom denied any involvement with the plot to kill Malco, and since the Rangers had no proof, he was released. He was ambushed by the two thugs from Biloxi and beaten senseless.

Lance was steamed at the idea of another club owner from the Strip ordering a hit on him and sent word to Dusty that if he wasn't out of town in thirty days, he, Lance, would put out his own contract. Dusty didn't back down and said he was looking for another hired killer. Lance knew a few more than Dusty, and for two months things were quiet but tense as the underworld waited for bullets to start flying. The next one went through the front windshield of Lance's car, with Nevin behind the wheel, and both were hit by shattering glass. They were stitched up at the hospital and released.

Hugh drove his father home and talked of nothing but revenge. He was horrified that a bullet had come so close. Every time he glanced over and saw the bandages he felt like crying. At home, Carmen was a wreck and went back and forth between bouts of near hysteria and fits of anger at her husband for getting so involved in criminal activity. Hugh tried to rein her in, tried to referee between his parents, and tried to allay the fears of his younger siblings. Two days later, he drove his father to his office upstairs at Red Velvet and announced that he was now assuming the role as his bodyguard and driver. He pulled back his jacket and proudly showed his father a .45 Ruger automatic.

Through his bandages and stitches, Lance smiled and asked, "Know how to use it?"

"Of course. Nevin taught me."

"Keep it close, okay? And don't use it unless you have to."

"It's time to use it, Dad."

"I'll make that decision."

———•———

Lance was fed up and knew it was time to destroy the enemy. He sent Nevin out of town and on a mission to deal with the Broker, a well-connected middleman known for his talent in selecting just the right hit man for any job. In a bar in Tupelo, they agreed on the price of $20,000 to pick off Dusty Cromwell. Nevin did not know the identity of the killer, nor did he want to.

Before it happened, a street battle erupted when three of Dusty's goons walked into Foxy's with baseball bats and hit everyone who moved, including two bouncers, two bartenders, some customers, and a cocktail waitress who was trying to flee. They broke every table, chair, neon light, and bottle of booze, and seemed ready to finish off a bartender or two when a guard appeared from the kitchen and opened fire with a handgun. One of the goons whipped out his own and a shootout began as they scampered for the door. The guard followed them into the parking lot and emptied his automatic. Bullets were peppering the front of the building and some of the cars parked close by. A bouncer with a bleeding forehead staggered out with a pistol to help the guard. They hopped in a car and chased the goons, who were firing wildly out the windows as they squealed tires and fled the scene. The gunfight continued down Highway 90 as the cars weaved through traffic and horrified drivers ducked for cover. When a bullet came through the front windshield of the chase car, the guard decided it was time to stop the madness and pulled into a parking lot.

Unknown to the guard and bouncer, one of their wild shots got lucky and hit a goon in the neck. He died in surgery at the Biloxi hospital. His two buddies dropped him off then disappeared. Typical for the time, the dead guy had no wallet, no ID. The getaway car, riddled with bullets, was never found. Luckily, no one inside Foxy's was killed, but seven were hospitalized.

Two weeks later, Dusty was walking along the beach on a beautiful Sunday afternoon and holding hands with his girlfriend as they splashed barefoot in the sand. He was sipping a can of beer, his last. From six hundred yards away, an ex–army sniper known as "the Rifleman" took his position on the second floor of a beach motel on the other side of Highway 90. He aimed his trusted Logan .45 caliber military rifle and pulled the trigger. A millisecond later, the bullet hit Dusty in the right cheek and blew off the back of his head. His girlfriend screamed in horror and another couple ran to help. By the time the police arrived, the Rifleman was on the bridge over Biloxi Bay and headed to Mobile.

Cromwell's death was sensational and the *Gulf Coast Register* finally woke up and began digging. The "gangland warfare" had claimed at least four men, all known to be involved in prostitution, drugs, and gambling. All were connected in some manner to the nightclubs along the Strip. There were rumors of other killings, as well as beatings and burnings. Fats Bowman had little to say, but assured the newspaper that his office was actively investigating the murders.

———•———

Like all law-abiding citizens, Jesse Rudy watched the war, and he, too, expected little from the investigations. And while he was frustrated by the efforts of Rex Dubisson to prosecute the murders, he was secretly delighted that the district attorney was showing so little interest. In his next campaign, he would emphasize his opponent's benign efforts to rein in the gangs. More violence would only help Jesse's cause. People were upset and wanted something done.

Nature intervened in an unimaginable way and stopped the killings. The storm blew away the nightclubs on the Strip, as well as most of Biloxi. It dealt a crippling blow not only to the nightlife, but every other industry along the Coast.

It also led directly to the election of Jesse Rudy.

CHAPTER 17

The summer of 1969 was a busy season in the Caribbean, but there was no reason to believe Hurricane Camille would become so deadly. When it skirted north of Cuba on August 15 it was an unimpressive Category 2, with a path projected to find landfall along the Florida Panhandle. As it headed north, it calmed somewhat after Cuba, then intensified rapidly in the warm waters of the Gulf. It wasn't a wide storm, but its lack of size only added to its speed. By August 17, it was a Cat 5 and roaring toward the Coast. All projections were ignored and it took dead aim at Biloxi.

The Gulf Coast was accustomed to hurricanes and everyone could tell stories, everyone had a favorite. Warnings were part of life, and, for the most part, taken in stride. No one had ever seen a twenty-foot storm surge and predictions for one seemed absurd. The residents along the beach tacked plywood over their windows, bought batteries, food, water, and tuned up their radios; the usual precautions. They had been through the routine so many times. They were not being foolish. Those who survived would later say they had simply never seen anything like Camille.

On Sunday afternoon, August 17, forecasters determined that the storm was not veering to the east. Alarms and civil alerts rang out in every coastal town—Waveland, Bay St. Louis, Pass Christian, Long Beach, Gulfport, Biloxi, Ocean Springs, and Pascagoula. The urgent warnings were dire and predicted an unprecedented storm surge and unheard-of winds. The last-minute evacuation was chaotic and most residents were determined to ride out the storm.

At 9:00 P.M., as the winds picked up, the mayor of Gulfport

ordered the jail to open its doors. All prisoners were told to go home, we'll find you later. Not a single one took the offer. Power and phone lines were down by 10:00 P.M.

At 11:30, Camille made landfall between Bay St. Louis and Pass Christian. It was only eighty miles wide, but its eye was tightly formed, its winds historic. It was a Category 5, the second-strongest hurricane to ever hit the United States. Its barometric pressure fell to 26.85 inches or 900 millibars, the second lowest in U.S. history. For one fleeting moment, a full sixty seconds, the wind speed gauges hit 175 miles per hour, then Camille blew them all into oblivion. Experts guessed that the top winds hit 200 mph. They pushed ashore a wall of water twenty-four feet in height. In some places the surge measured almost thirty feet.

The heavier populations to its east—Biloxi, Gulfport, Pascagoula—bore the full brunt of its counter-clockwise rotation. Virtually every building along Highway 90 and the beach was destroyed. The highway itself buckled and its bridges were knocked out. Power and phone lines snapped and disappeared in the raging waters. Six blocks inland from the beach entire neighborhoods were demolished. Six thousand homes disappeared. Another fourteen thousand were severely damaged. The storm killed 143 people, most of whom lived close to the beach and refused to evacuate. Schools, hospitals, churches, stores, office buildings, courthouses, fire stations—everything was gutted.

Camille wasn't finished. She weakened quickly in the Ohio Valley, then turned east for more destruction. Over central Virginia, she merged with a dense low-pressure system that seemed to be waiting for her. Together, they dumped thirty inches of rain in twenty-four hours into Nelson County, Virginia, causing historic floods that wiped out highways, homes, and lives; 153 were killed in Virginia.

The storm was last heard from fading over the Atlantic. Mercifully, there would never be another Camille. Her damage was so unbelievable that the National Weather Service retired her name.

———·———

When the sun rose on Monday, August 18, the clouds were gone. The storm was so fast it disappeared quickly, taking its wind and rain elsewhere. But it was still August in Mississippi, and by mid-morning the temperature was pushing ninety.

People emerged from the rubble and moved about like zombies, shell-shocked by the terror of the night and the devastation in front of them. Screams were heard as they found friends, neighbors, and loved ones who didn't make it. They searched for bodies, automobiles, even houses.

Life had suddenly been reduced to the basics—food, water, and shelter. And health care; over 21,000 people were injured and there were no hospitals, no clinics.

The governor had moved five thousand National Guardsmen to Camp Shelby, seventy miles to the north. By dawn they were hustling south in caravans and listening to the first radio reports. Seventy-five thousand people were homeless. Thousands were either dead or missing. The Guardsmen soon ran into trouble when they encountered entire trees lying across Highway 49. Using chain saws and bulldozers to clear the road, it took almost six hours to reach Biloxi.

The 101st Airborne was right behind them. As the first images of the Coast made their way to the evening news, state, federal, and private aid began pouring in. Dozens of relief organizations mobilized and sent teams of doctors, nurses, and volunteers. Churches and religious organizations sent thousands of relief workers, most of whom slept in tents. Along with food and water, tons of medical supplies arrived, most of it by boat to avoid the impassable roads.

It took a month to restore electricity to the hospitals and schools that could open. Longer, to account for all the missing people. Years, to rebuild for those who wanted to.

For six months after the storm, the Coast resembled a camp for displaced war refugees. Rows of green army tents for hospitals;

rows of barracks; thousands of soldiers hauling debris; volunteers manning food and water distribution centers; large tents filled with clothing and even furniture; and long lines of people waiting to get in.

For a resilient people, the challenge was almost overwhelming, but they tenaciously hung on and slowly rebuilt. The storm was a staggering blow and they were stunned by it. However, they had no choice but to survive. Inch by inch, things improved a little each day. The opening of the schools in mid-October was a milestone. When Biloxi hosted its archrival Gulfport in a football game on a Friday night, there was a record crowd and life seemed almost normal.

———•———

For the mobsters, Camille led to unique opportunities. They were all temporarily out of business but they knew the business would quickly come back. The place was crawling with soldiers, relief workers, and an amazing collection of riffraff that was attracted to disasters and the free goodies handed out. These people were away from home, tired, stressed, and in need of booze and entertainment.

Lance Malco spent no time licking his wounds. His home, one mile inland, was not heavily damaged. However, his clubs on the Strip, Red Velvet and Foxy's, were completely gone, blown away and washed away down to their concrete slabs. The Truck Stop was gutted but still standing. Two of his bars were gone; two others were in decent shape. Three of his motels along the beach were also bare down to the concrete. Sadly, two of his dancers perished in one of them. Lance had ordered them to evacuate. He planned to send their families a check.

As Lance, Hugh, and Nevin inspected the damage to Red Velvet with the first insurance adjuster, they noticed eight large squares of what appeared to be metal embedded in the concrete foundation. The adjuster was curious and asked what they were. Lance and Nevin said they had no idea. The squares were actually magnets that had been hidden under a thick carpet upon which the craps tables were situated. The crooked dice had smaller magnets behind certain numbers. By manipulating various sets of dice, the shifty dealers could increase the chances of certain numbers being put into play.

After all the years of being accused of rigging his tables, Lance had finally been caught, thanks to Camille. But the hapless adjuster didn't gamble and had no idea what he was looking at. Nevin winked at Lance and both had the same thought: No one in the world could guesstimate the amount of hard cash those magnets had netted for the nightclub.

Insurance policies written in Mississippi covered damage by wind, with specific and carefully worded exclusions for damage by water. The wind-versus-water fights were not yet raging, but the insurance companies were already bracing for them. When Lance's insurer denied based on water damage, he threatened to sue. There was little doubt that the storm surge had swamped his nightclubs along Highway 90.

Because he had more cash than the other nightclub owners, Lance was determined not only to open first, but to reopen a much fancier version of Red Velvet. He found a contractor in Baton Rouge with men and supplies.

Before most homeowners had cleared the debris from their lawns and streets, Lance was rebuilding his flagship club. He planned to add a restaurant, expand the bar, build more rooms upstairs. He had lots of plans. He, Hugh, and Nevin firmly believed that most of their competitors on the Strip could not survive Camille. The time was right to spend big and establish a monopoly.

CHAPTER 18

Wind versus water.

On the Sunday afternoon before Camille hit, Jesse and Agnes made the last-minute decision to evacuate. She and the kids would head north to her parents' home in Kansas. Jesse insisted on staying with the house. They hurriedly packed the family station wagon with supplies and water, and, with Keith behind the wheel, waved a frightened goodbye to Jesse.

Twelve hours later he wished he had joined them. He could not remember being so frightened, not even in the war. Never again would he ride out a hurricane.

Their home survived structurally but was heavily damaged. Most of the roof was blown off. The small front porch was never found. Virtually all the windows were shattered. The storm surge pushed floodwaters to within ten feet of the front door. The neighbors down the street, to the south, were not so lucky and took in water. Jesse spent two days clearing debris and waited in line for hours to get two large tarps from a Red Cross distribution center. He hired a teenager looking for work and they labored in the heat to secure the openings in the roof. Much of the furniture was soaked from rainwater and had to be tossed. A team of National Guardsmen arrived and helped him cover the windows with plywood. They also supplied him with bottled water and a case of tomato soup, which he ate from the can because there was no way to heat it. After five days of hot and exhausting work, he waited in line at a Guard station and was handed a telephone. He called Agnes in Kansas and almost wept when he heard her voice. She wept too, as did the children. Since there was no electricity and the days were long and hot, he told them to stay in Kansas until the situation improved.

Volunteers and relief workers were everywhere, and he gathered a crew to clean out his office downtown. The waterline on the downstairs walls was exactly seven and a half feet and everything was ruined. He couldn't imagine practicing law there, but then every office around him was in the same mess. Giving up was not an option, and each passing day brought a small improvement.

Late in the afternoons, as the sun was fading and the air was somewhat cooler, he checked on his neighbors and helped clear debris and make repairs. Almost everyone was checking on someone else. The damaged homes were too hot to sit in, and so they gathered under shade trees that were still standing. Joe Humphrey, three doors down, had somehow smuggled in a case of beer from a National Guardsman, who also sent a bag of ice, and the cold Falstaff had never tasted so good. The neighbors shared everything—beer, cigarettes, food, water, encouragement, and stories.

They had survived. Others were not so fortunate, and much of the gossip on the street was about those who died.

———•———

The Rudy Law Firm reopened on October 2, some six weeks after Camille. Jesse spent most of the first day using his new phone to badger his insurance adjuster. The company, Action Risk Underwriters, was based in Chicago and was one of the four largest insurers on the Coast. In the weeks following the storm, it became apparent to Jesse that ARU and the others were stonewalling all claims and had no intention of honoring the policies in a forthright manner. Their blanket denials were simple: The damages were caused by water, not wind.

When the courthouse reopened for business on October 10, Jesse marched in and filed fourteen lawsuits on behalf of himself and his neighbors. He sued the four largest insurance companies, demanding full payment, plus punitive damages for bad faith. He had been threatening to sue for weeks and the companies would hardly return his phone calls. With at least 20,000 flattened or seriously damaged homes, their exposure was enormous. Their strategy was taking shape. They would deny all claims, sit on their money, drag out the process, and hope most policy holders wouldn't have the means to litigate.

Meanwhile, folks were trying to survive with tarps over their heads and plywood over their windows. Many homes were uninhabitable and their owners were camping in their backyards. Others were living in tents. Still others had been forced to flee and had moved in with friends and relatives throughout south Mississippi. In the woods north of town, an entire community, nicknamed Camille Ville, sprung up overnight and a thousand people lived in tents and campers. Most of them owned valid insurance policies but couldn't find an adjuster.

Jesse was angry and on a mission. When he filed the first wave of lawsuits, he tipped off the *Gulf Coast Register* and happily sat down for an interview. The next day he was on the front page and his office phone began ringing. It would not stop for months.

In terms of making money, the cases were not valuable. In 1969 the average home in Harrison County was assessed at $22,000. Jesse and Agnes had paid $23,500 for theirs four years earlier, and a contractor had estimated its storm damage to be $8,500, not including furniture. His first lawsuits were in that range, and all of them were for wind damage. He had inspected each of the homes and knew damned well that they had not been damaged by the storm surge. In one testy exchange with an adjuster, he had explained that the water damage occurred in a downpour after the roof was blown off. Camille dropped ten inches of rain in twelve hours. Remove the roof and everything below gets soaked. Indeed, with nothing but flimsy plastic tarps as protection, every good rainstorm brought new adventures for the homeowners.

The insurance company denied the claim anyway.

He filed the simpler cases first. The more complicated ones would involve both wind and water damage, and he would pursue those later. There were plenty to choose from. Word spread quickly and clients were pouring in. He was getting much more than he bargained for and worried about covering the overhead. But, that had been a constant worry long before Camille. The second mortgage from his campaign two years earlier had not been fully paid off.

He had little time to worry and there was no turning back. He had cornered the market on Camille cases and was filing a dozen each week. He worked eighteen hours a day, six days a week, and had entered another zone where nothing mattered but the cause. With Keith back in college, for his senior year, and Agnes holding the family together, he was seriously understaffed. His teenage daughters, Beverly and Laura, were at the office after school and often into the night trying to keep the files organized.

To the rescue came the Pettigrew boys, two brothers from Bay St. Louis. Their father had been found dead in a tree the day after Camille. The family home, fully insured, was half a mile from the beach and damaged so severely that it was uninhabitable. Their mother was living with a sister in McComb. The insurance company, also ARU, had denied the claim.

The brothers, Gene and Gage, appeared to be twins but were eleven months apart. They looked alike, sounded alike, dressed alike, and had the odd habit of finishing each other's sentences. They had graduated from law school together at Ole Miss the previous May and opened up a small shop in Bay St. Louis. Camille blew it all away, everything. They couldn't even find their diplomas.

Their tragedy had made them angry and they were looking for a fight. They read about Jesse Rudy, and marched into his office one day and asked for employment. Jesse liked them immediately, promised to pay them whenever he could, and on the spot inherited two fresh new associates. He dropped what he was doing, locked them in the conference room for a training session, and taught them the exciting ins and outs of reading insurance policies. They left at midnight. The following day, he sent Gage to Camille Ville to meet with some new clients. Gene began intake sessions with the daily drop-ins.

Other lawyers along the Coast were taking similar cases, though nowhere near the volume of Jesse Rudy. They watched him carefully and curiously. The general feeling among the bar was to move somewhat slower, allow Rudy to go first, and hope he nailed the companies in the first series of trials. Maybe then the insurers would come to the table and settle the claims fairly.

For Jesse, the litigation was not without risks. It was clear that water from the storm surge had destroyed many of the homes, especially those close to the beach. Prevailing on those claims would be difficult. If he lost at trial, the insurers would not feel as threatened and would deny even more aggressively. His reputation was on the line. His clients were hurting, often irrational, and not only expecting justice but some retribution as well. If he failed to deliver for them, his career as a trial lawyer would be over and he might as well hide in his office and draft deeds.

If he won, though, and won big, the rewards would be plentiful. He would not get rich, not by winning $8,000 claims, but at least his cash flow would improve. Hammering the insurance companies into submission would bring publicity that no amount of money could buy.

By the end of the year, there was a feeling of outright hatred for the insurance companies. Jesse wanted a trial, in his courtroom in Biloxi, and pushed hard for one. The opposition was formidable. The insurers had wisely decided to hire the big firms in Jackson to defend them, staying away from the Coast lawyers. Jesse had filed over three hundred lawsuits in the circuit court of Harrison County. It was nothing short of a bonanza for the defense firms, and they used every tool and trick available to delay and bury him with paperwork.

The Pettigrew boys proved up to the task and learned more about litigation and discovery in three months than they would have in five years on their own. They urged Jesse to keep filing. They would slog through the mail, keep the files orderly, and fire back at the defense firms.

During the small office party two days before Christmas, Jesse surprised everyone by announcing that he was promoting Gene and Gage to junior partners. Their names would go on the letterhead. The sign out front would now read: RUDY & PETTIGREW, ATTORNEYS AT LAW. It was more of a symbolic move than anything else. Real partnerships split the fees, of which there were few.

———•———

Judge Nelson Oliphant, age seventy-one, took the bench, pulled his microphone closer, and looked at the crowd. He smiled and said, "Good morning, ladies and gentlemen. What a nice turnout. Not sure I've ever seen such a crowd for a motion hearing."

Jesse had packed the courtroom with his clients and told them that under no circumstances should anyone smile about anything. They were angry, frustrated, and ready for justice. They were fed up with the insurance companies and their lawyers, and they wanted Oliphant, one of their own from Harrison County, to know they meant business. He would soon be up for reelection.

At the plaintiffs' table, Jesse sat between the Pettigrews. On the other side, packed around the defense table, were at least a dozen well-tailored Jackson boys with associates and secretaries seated behind them in the front row. Somewhere in the pack were insurance executives.

Oliphant said, "Mr. Rudy, you may proceed."

Jesse stood and addressed the court. "Thank you, Your Honor. I've filed several motions for a hearing today, but I would first like to address the issue of some trial dates. I have at least ten cases ready for trial, or I guess I should say I'm ready for trial." He waved an arm at the defense lawyers and said, "Looks like these guys'll never be ready. Today is February the third. May I suggest that we set some cases for trial next month?"

Oliphant looked at the defense squad and at least four of them stood. Before they could speak he said, "Wait a minute. I'm not going to listen to all you guys say the same thing. What's your first case, Mr. Rudy?"

"Luna versus Action Risk Underwriters."

"Okay. I believe Mr. Webb is lead counsel for ARU. Mr. Webb, you may respond."

Simmons Webb stood and took a few steps forward. "Thank you, Your Honor," he said properly. "I appreciate the opportunity to be here in your court today. My client certainly understands the wishes of the plaintiffs to hurry things up and have a trial, but we are entitled to complete the discovery process. I'm sure Mr. Rudy understands this."

Jesse, still standing, said, "Your Honor, we've finished discovery and we're ready for trial."

"Well, Your Honor, we haven't finished. He's only taken two depositions."

"I'll handle my case, Mr. Webb. You handle yours. I don't need any more depositions."

The judge cleared his throat and said, "I must say, Mr. Webb, you have been rather slow at pursuing discovery. It appears to me that your client, ARU, is in no hurry at all to go to trial."

"I disagree, Your Honor. These are complicated cases."

"But Mr. Rudy filed them, didn't he? If he's ready, why aren't you?"

"There's a lot to be done, Your Honor."

"Well get it done, and now. I'm setting this case for trial on Monday, March the second, right here. We'll pick a jury and let it decide the case."

Webb feigned disbelief and leaned down to huddle with another dark suit. He looked up and said, "We respectfully object to such short notice, Your Honor."

"And you are respectfully overruled. What's the next case, Mr. Rudy?"

"Lansky versus ARU."

"Mr. Webb?"

"Well, again, Your Honor, we're simply not ready for trial."

"Then get ready. You've had plenty of time, and God knows you've got plenty of talented legal help on your side."

"We object, Your Honor."

"Overruled. Here's the plan, Mr. Webb, and the rest of defense counsel. I'm setting aside the first two weeks in March to try as many of these cases as possible. I don't see these as long trials. Based on the discovery, there are not that many witnesses. These plaintiffs have the right to be heard and we're going to hear them."

At least five of the defense lawyers jumped to their feet and started talking.

"Please, please, gentlemen," His Honor said. "Sit down. You are free to file written objections. Go ahead and do so and I'll overrule them later."

The others sat down and Webb tried to control his frustration. "Your Honor, this is rather heavy-handed, and it is a clear example of why my client is worried about getting a fair trial in Harrison County."

With perfect timing, Jesse blurted a statement he had prepared and saved for this moment. "Well, Mr. Webb, if your client would pay the claims we wouldn't be there, would we?"

Webb turned and pointed a finger at Jesse. "My client has legitimate grounds to deny these claims, Mr. Rudy."

"Bullshit! Your client is sitting on its money and acting in bad faith."

Judge Oliphant said, "Mr. Rudy, I admonish you for your foul language. Please refrain from such."

Jesse nodded and said, "Sorry, Your Honor. I couldn't help it."

If for no other reason, the hearing would be remembered as the first time a lawyer had yelled the word "bullshit" in open court in Harrison County.

Webb took a deep breath and said, "Your Honor, we are requesting a change of venue."

Calmly, the judge said, "I don't blame you, Mr. Webb, but the people of this county have suffered greatly. They continue to suffer, and they have the right to decide these cases. Motion denied. No further delays."

CHAPTER 19

Through the pre-trial wrangling that followed, Jesse soon realized that Judge Oliphant was squarely on the side of the policy holders. Almost every request made on behalf of the plaintiffs was granted. Almost every move by the insurance companies was blocked.

Oliphant and Jesse were worried that they might be unable to find enough impartial jurors to decide the cases. Every resident of the county had been impacted by the storm, and the bad behavior of the insurance companies was now common chatter at church and in the cafés that were reopening. Folks were out for blood, which obviously was to Jesse's advantage, but it seriously compromised the notion of a disinterested jury pool. Selecting jurors was further complicated by the fact that so many people were displaced.

The two met privately, which under normal circumstances would be forbidden, but the Jackson lawyers were far away in their tall buildings and would never know. The insurance companies had chosen them; another mistake. Jesse had eleven cases against ARU that were ready for trial. They were virtually identical: same insurer, homes damaged by wind, not storm surge, and the same reputable contractor willing to testify as to damages. Judge Oliphant decided to take the first three—Luna, Lansky, and Nikovich—and consolidate them for the first trial. Simmons Webb and his gang squawked and objected, and even threatened to run to the Mississippi Supreme Court for protection. Through back channels, Judge Oliphant knew the Supremes had about as much sympathy for the insurance companies as Jesse Rudy.

On Monday, March 2, the courtroom was again packed, with spectators lining the walls and bailiffs directing traffic. The crowd spilled into the hallway where angry men and women waited for a seat inside. In chambers, Judge Oliphant laid down the rules and impressed upon the lawyers that the trial would be expedited at every turn, and he would not tolerate even the slightest attempt to delay matters.

With effort, forty-seven summonses had been served upon the prospective jurors, and every one of them reported for duty. Using a questionnaire designed by His Honor and Mr. Rudy, thirteen were excused because they had property damage claims pending against insurance companies. Four were excused for health reasons. Two were excused because they were related to people killed in the storm. Three were excused because they knew the families of other victims.

When the pool was whittled down to twenty-four, Judge Oliphant allowed the lawyers half an hour each to quiz the panel. Jesse managed to control his aggression but left no doubt that he was the champion for the good guys and they were fighting evil. Through his growing network of clients, he had learned more about the twenty-four than the defense could ever know. Simmons Webb came across as a folksy old boy, with deep roots in south Mississippi, and he was there just searching for the truth. At times, though, he was nervous and seemed to know that the mob wanted his skin.

It took two hours to seat twelve jurors, all of whom swore to hear the facts, weigh the evidence, and decide the case impartially. Without a break, Judge Oliphant gave the lawyers fifteen minutes for their opening remarks and nodded at Jesse, who was already on his feet and walking to the jury box to deliver the shortest first-round statement of his career. Gage Pettigrew timed it at one minute and forty seconds.

"Ladies and gentlemen of the jury, we shouldn't be here. You shouldn't be sitting where you are and you certainly have better things to do. I shouldn't be standing here addressing you. My client, Mr. Thomas Luna, seated over there in the blue shirt, should not be living in a house with no roof and only a plastic tarp as protection against rain, wind, storms, cold, heat, and insects. He should not be living in a house with black mold growing on the walls. He should not be living in a house with almost no furniture. Same for Mr. Oscar Lansky, that gentleman in the white shirt. He lives two doors down from Mr. Luna, on Butler Street, a half mile north of here. As for my third client, Mr. Paul Nikovich, he shouldn't be living in a barn owned by his uncle up in Stone County. All three of these families should be living in their homes, where they're still paying mortgages I might add, with all the comforts and amenities they enjoyed before Camille, homes damaged over six months ago, homes properly insured with policies written by ARU, homes still sitting forlornly under blue tarps and patched up with sheets of plywood."

Jesse took a deep breath and a step back. He raised his voice and continued, "And they would be living normal lives in their homes but for the despicable actions of Action Risk Underwriters." He pointed to Fred McDaniel, a senior adjuster for the company, seated snugly next to Simmons Webb. McDaniel flinched but did not take his eyes off a file lying on the table in front of him.

"We shouldn't be here but we are. So, since we're forced to gather in this courtroom let's make the most of our time. In a few hours you'll get the opportunity to tell Mr. McDaniel and his big company from up in Chicago that folks here in Harrison County believe a contract is a contract, an insurance policy is an insurance policy, and there comes a time when greedy corporations have to pay up."

Simmons Webb was caught off guard by Jesse's brevity and shuffled papers for a moment. Judge Oliphant said, "Mr. Webb."

"Sure, Judge, I've just found the policy." He got to his feet and walked to the jury box with a phony grin from ear to ear. "Ladies and gentlemen of the jury, this is the homeowner's policy issued by my client to the Luna family. It's basically the same as the ones issued to the Lanskys and the Nikoviches." He held the policy up and made a show of flipping pages. "Now, here on page five the policy clearly states, and I quote: 'Excluded from all coverages stated herein are damages to the principal residential structure as well as appendages such as porches, carports, garages, patios, decks, and outbuildings such as utility sheds, tool sheds, et cetera, caused by floods, rising waters, rising tides, or surges as a result of hurricanes and/or tropical storms.'"

He tossed the policy onto his table and stood before the jury. "Now, this case is not as cut-and-dried as it seems. Storm damage is often complicated because in almost all big storms there are homes that get hit by wind and flooded with water." Webb began rambling about the difficulty of ascertaining what exactly caused damage to a certain structure, and told the jury that he would present expert witnesses, men trained in the field, who would show the jurors what happens in a major storm. He feigned great sympathy for all of the "fine folks down here" who were hit by Camille and claimed that he and his client were there to help. This drew some skeptical looks from the jurors. He got lost a few times and it became apparent, at least to Jesse, that Webb was attempting the old strategy of "If you don't have the facts, then try to confuse them."

"One minute," Judge Oliphant finally said.

When Webb sat down, Jesse was almost giddy. His opponent represented the largest insurance companies doing business in the state and was known as a tough negotiator. However, it was obvious that he settled cases but didn't try them. His opening statement was not impressive.

The first witness was Thomas Luna. Jesse led him through the preliminaries and asked him to describe for the jury the horror of riding out a hurricane with winds estimated at 200 miles an hour. Luna was well prepared by his lawyer and a gifted storyteller. He and his twenty-year-old son stayed behind and several times during the night were in a closet, clutching each other as the house shook violently, certain that it was about to be blown away. The house across the street was lifted from its foundation and scattered for blocks. The storm surge came to within fifty yards of their home. Mr. Luna described the passing of Camille, sunlight, calm winds, and the unbelievable damage on his street.

The jurors knew the story well and Jesse did not belabor it. He submitted repair estimates from a contractor that totaled $8,900. His other exhibit was a list of furniture, furnishings, and clothing that had been destroyed. The total claim was $11,300.

After a thirty-minute lunch break, Mr. Luna was back on the stand and was cross-examined by Simmons Webb, who painstakingly went through the repair estimates as if looking for fraud. Mr. Luna knew far more about carpentry than the lawyer and they bickered back and forth. Twice Jesse objected with "Your Honor, he's just wasting time. The jury has seen the repair estimates."

"Let's move along, Mr. Webb."

But Webb was methodical, even tedious. When he finished, Jesse put on Oscar Lansky and then Paul Nikovich with their similar stories. By 4:30 Monday afternoon, the jurors and spectators had heard enough of the horrors of Camille and the damage it caused. Judge Oliphant recessed for fifteen minutes to allow them to stretch their legs and load up on coffee.

The next witness was the contractor who had examined the three homes and estimated the damage. He stood by his work and his figures, and would not allow Webb to nitpick here and there. He knew from years of experience that rising waters almost always leave a flood line, or a high-water mark, and it is usually easy to determine how much water a building took on. In those three homes, there was no flood line. The damage was by wind, not water.

It was almost 7:30 when Judge Oliphant finally relented and adjourned for the evening. He thanked the jury and asked them to return at 8:00 A.M. ready for more work.

Jesse's first witness Tuesday morning was a professor of civil engineering from Mississippi State. Using enlarged diagrams and maps, he tracked Camille as it came ashore, with its eye between Pass Christian and Bay St. Louis. Using data retrieved from the storm, along with documented eyewitness reports, he walked the jury through the path of the storm surge. He estimated it at twenty-five to thirty feet high at the Biloxi lighthouse, the most famous landmark, and showed large photos of the total devastation between the beach and the railroad track half a mile inland. Beyond the rail line, which was ten feet above sea level, the surge lost its intensity as the waters dispersed over a larger area. One mile inland, it was still five feet in height and was being propelled by horrendous winds. In the area of Biloxi where the plaintiffs lived, the surge was no more than two or three feet, depending on the uneven terrain. He had examined thousands of photographs and videos taken in the aftermath, and was of the opinion that the three homes in question were just beyond the last reach of the surge. Of course, there was extensive flooding in the low areas, but not on Butler Street.

Simmons Webb quarreled with the engineer over his findings and attempted to argue that no one really knew where the storm surge ended. Camille hit in the middle of the night. Filming it at its height and fury was impossible. Witnesses did not exist because no one in their right mind was outdoors.

There was a famous video of a TV weatherman standing in the middle of Highway 90 at 7:30 that evening. The winds were "only 130 miles per hour" and gaining strength. The rain was pelting him in sheets. A gust pummeled him, and for about three seconds his cameraman filmed him tumbling across the median like a rag doll. Then the cameraman went upside down. There was no other known footage of any fool waiting to greet Camille that late in the day.

By mid-afternoon, Jesse was finished with his case. He and everyone else suffered through the monotonous and impenetrable give-and-take between Simmons Webb and his star witness, an expert in hurricane damage who worked for the American Insurance League in Washington. Dr. Pennington had spent a career poking through debris, photographing, measuring, and otherwise researching damage to homes and other buildings caused by severe storms. After a baffling lecture on the virtual impossibility of knowing for certain whether a piece of building material was damaged by wind or water, he then proceeded to give confounding opinions on the cases at hand.

If Webb's goal with Dr. Pennington was to sow doubt and confuse the jury, then he succeeded brilliantly.

Two months earlier, Jesse had deposed the expert for two hours and thought he would make a terrible impression on any breathing person in Harrison County. He was stuffy, pompous, well educated and proud of it. Though he had left Cleveland decades earlier, he had managed to hang on to his nasal, clipped, Upper Midwest accent that was like nails on a chalkboard to anyone south of Memphis.

When the water was as muddy as any storm could make it, Webb tendered his witness and Jesse came out throwing knives. He quickly established that Dr. Pennington had worked for the AIL for over twenty years; that the AIL was a trade organization funded by the insurance industry to research everything from arson to auto safety to suicide rates; that one arm of AIL was also involved in lobbying Congress for more protection; that AIL frequently battled with consumer protection groups over legislation; and so on. After haranguing the expert for half an hour his employer seemed downright evil.

Jesse suspected the jurors were getting antsy and he decided to go for the quick kill. He asked Dr. Pennington how many times he had testified in storm cases where the issue was wind-versus-water. He gave a self-satisfied shrug as if he had no idea, too numerous to recall. Jesse asked him how often he had told a jury that the damage was caused by wind and not water.

When Dr. Pennington hesitated and looked at Webb for help, Jesse walked to the corner of his desk and patted a stack of papers at least eighteen inches thick. He said, "Come on, Dr. Pennington. I have your records right here. When was the last time you testified on behalf of a policy holder and not against one? When was the last time you tried to help the victim of a storm? When was the last time you offered an opinion against an insurance company?"

Dr. Pennington seemed to mumble as he searched for words. Before he could speak, Jesse cut him off with "That's what I figured. No more questions, Your Honor."

———————•———————

The jury was given the three cases at ten minutes after five. A bailiff led them out and into their deliberation room while another one brought in coffee and doughnuts.

Twenty minutes later they were back. Before most could finish a doughnut, and before the lawyers and spectators could finish their visits to the restrooms, a bailiff informed Oliphant that verdicts were ready.

When everyone was in place, he read the notes from the foreman. The jury found in favor of all three plaintiffs and awarded $11,300 to Thomas Luna; $8,900 to Oscar Lansky; and $13,800 to Paul Nikovich. In addition, the jury awarded seven dollars a day as living expenses, per the language of the policy, for the 198 days since the damage. And, for good measure, the jury tacked on interest at the annual rate of 5 percent for the entire claim, beginning with August 17, the day Camille blew through.

In short, the jurors gave the three plaintiffs every penny Jesse asked for, and there was no doubt they would have given more if so allowed.

In chambers, Judge Oliphant took off his robe and invited the lawyers to have a seat. The two-day trial had been exhausting. All jury trials were stressful, but the packed courtroom and looming docket only added to the tension.

The judge said, "Nice work, fellas. I felt confident we could do it in two days. Any ideas on how to streamline the next round?"

Jesse snorted and looked at Simmons Webb. "Sure, tell your client to pay the claims."

Webb smiled and replied, "Well, Jesse, as you know, the lawyer cannot always tell the client what to do, especially when the client has plenty of money and no fears."

"So how do we frighten them?"

"It's been my experience that these companies do what they want without regard to fear."

Judge Oliphant said, "I'm sure that somewhere in the bowels of ARU there's a team of actuaries who've crunched the numbers and told the big guys upstairs that it'll be cheaper to deny the claims and pay the legal fees. Right, Mr. Webb?"

"Judge, I cannot discuss the decision-making process of my client. Even if I knew. And, believe me, I don't want to know. I'm just doing my job and getting paid."

"And you're doing a fine job," Jesse said, but only to be polite. He continued to be less than impressed with Webb's courtroom skills.

The judge asked Jesse, "And you have the next three ready to go?"

"Teed up, Judge."

"Okay, we'll start at eight in the morning."

CHAPTER 20

With a friendly judge cracking the whip, Jesse's assembly-line style of litigation hit full stride. In the first two weeks of March, he tried eleven straight cases against ARU and won them all. It became a grueling ordeal, and when it was over everyone needed a break. Webb and his gang hustled back to Jackson hoping to never see Biloxi again. Judge Oliphant moved on to other pressing business. Jesse returned to his office to tend to the details of a few other non-Camille clients, but it was virtually impossible. The more trials he won, the more ink he got in the *Gulf Coast Register,* and the more people knocked on his door.

The verdicts were satisfying on professional and moral levels, but burdensome financially. Jesse had not managed to squeeze a dime out of ARU or any of the other big insurers. Some of the smaller carriers were spooked and started settling claims, and a few fees dribbled in. He had almost a thousand claims against nine different companies, and all of the fees were on a contingency. Instead of the usual one-third lawyers preferred, he agreed to 20 percent. However, when the checks arrived he could not bring himself to take money from clients who had lost so much. He usually negotiated his position downward and settled for 10 percent.

Later that month, Jesse, his firm, and his clients received the dispiriting notice from Simmons Webb that ARU was appealing the verdicts to the Mississippi Supreme Court, where appeals routinely took two years to resolve. It was frustrating news and Jesse called Webb in Jackson to complain. Again, Webb, who was showing more and more sympathy, explained that he was only doing what his client instructed him to do.

Jesse then called Judge Oliphant, who had just learned of the appeals. Off the record, they cussed ARU in particular and the insurance industry in general.

In late March, His Honor saw an opening in his docket and notified the parties that he was scheduling three more trials, beginning on Monday, the thirtieth. Webb moaned about the unfairness of it all. Judge Oliphant suggested he tap into some of the other talent around the office, or stop complaining. No one felt sorry for the largest law firm in the state. Webb and his team showed up, took the same ass-whippings as in the first eleven trials, and crawled back to Jackson, tails between their legs.

After a two-week break, it was time for another round. Judge Oliphant had expressed concern that they might be reaching a point where they would be unable to find qualified jurors in Harrison County. There were simply too many conflicts, too many strong feelings. He decided to move the next trials forty miles up the road to the town of Wiggins, the seat of Stone County, one of three in his district. Perhaps they could find more neutral jurors there.

It wasn't likely. Camille was still a Category 3 when it crossed the county line and did $20 million worth of damage in and around Wiggins.

On April 16, Judge Oliphant patiently worked through the selection process, and, after eight long hours, found twelve he could trust. Not that it mattered. The good folks of Stone County were evidently just as ticked off as their neighbors to the south, and they showed no mercy on the insurers. Seven cases went to trial over ten days and the plaintiffs won them all.

Webb, thoroughly defeated, informed Jesse that his latest batch of nice little verdicts would also be appealed.

Wiggins was halfway to Hattiesburg, where Keith Rudy was sailing through his last semester at Southern Miss. Instead of going to class and playing with the girls by the pool, he was in the courtroom in Wiggins taking notes, watching jurors, and absorbing every aspect of the trial. He had been accepted to law school at Ole Miss, and would jump-start his studies there by enrolling in summer school. His plans were to join his father's firm in less than three years.

———•———

After twenty-one courtroom fights over what could only be considered "small claims," a few truths were becoming self-evident. First, Jesse Rudy was not backing away and would try a thousand cases if necessary. Second, he would defend his verdicts on appeal to the final gavel. Third, though he was grinding down the defense lawyers and getting some publicity, his strategy was not working. ARU seemed unfazed—its bottom line was well sand-bagged up there in Chicago, while his clients were still living with leaky tarps and black mold. Their frustration was growing. His was at a breaking point.

For months, Jesse had been badgering Judge Oliphant, both in proper filings and off-the-record discussions, to allow him to pursue a claim of punitive damages. The strategy of the big insur-ers had been laid bare in open court: deny all legitimate claims, ignore the policy holders and bully them into submission, then hide behind the best lawyers money could buy. The strategy reeked of bad faith and was grounds for punitive damages. Give Jesse a shot or two at ARU's executives and things might change.

Judge Oliphant was a traditional jurist with conservative views on damages. He had never allowed punitives and was repulsed by the idea of allowing lawyers to dig into a company's assets to extract more than what had been lost. Nor did he believe that punitives would ever deter future bad conduct. But he was sickened by the actions of the insurance companies and had great sympathy for their policy holders who were being mistreated. He finally acqui-esced and gave Jesse the green light.

Simmons Webb was shocked, and threatened to file an inter-locutory appeal with the state supreme court. Punitive damages were unheard-of in Mississippi.

Judge Oliphant convinced him that would be a mistake.

The case was another one Jesse had filed against ARU and it involved damages more serious than most. The home was unin-habitable and the contractor estimated its repairs at $16,400. Jesse wasted no time in drawing blood. The claim's first adjuster was on the stand, and Jesse walked him through a series of enlarged photos of the damage to the home. The young man had evidently been lucky enough to avoid courtrooms, but his lack of experience did not serve him well. He initially adopted the strategy of sparring with his examiner, and Jesse fed him enough rope to hang himself. In photo after photo, the adjuster identified damaged walls, floors, and doors as being flooded with the storm surge, then Jesse asked him to explain the water damage when it had been proven that the surge never quite made it to the house. It became apparent the adjuster would say anything his boss wanted to hear.

His boss, the district manager, was next and was visibly uncomfortable from the moment he swore to tell the truth. ARU had sent three denial letters to Jesse's client, and he asked the dis-trict manager to read all three to the jury. In the third letter, the claim was being denied because of "obvious water damage." Jesse took that phrase and beat him over the head with it until Judge Oliphant asked him to stop. It was clear that the jury loved the annihilation.

An ARU vice president, one who apparently drew the short straw, took the stand to defend the honor of his company. In a blis-tering cross-examination, one which Simmons Webb tried to stop with repeated interruptions, Jesse finally drilled down deep enough to find the truth. When Camille hit, ARU had 3,874 homes insured in Harrison, Hancock, and Jackson counties. Almost 80 percent of the homeowners, or 3,070 to be exact, had filed claims to date.

"And of that number, sir, how many claims have been settled by your company?"

"Oh, I don't know. I'd have to check the records."

"You were told to bring the records."

"Well, I'm not sure. I'll check with counsel."

Judge Oliphant, who had long since abandoned his role as an impartial arbiter, snarled, "Sir, I'm looking at the subpoena. You were instructed to bring all records related to claims filed since the storm."

"Yes sir, but you see—"

"I'll hold you in contempt."

Simmons Webb stood but appeared to be tongue-tied. Jesse quickly decided to help matters by practically yelling, "It's okay, Your Honor, I have the records."

He waved a thin manila file, legal size. The courtroom became deathly still and Webb fell into his chair. With perfect dramatic flair, Jesse approached the witness and said, "Your Honor, I have in this file copies of all of the legitimate claims that have been paid and settled by ARU."

He turned, faced the jury, and opened the file. It was empty. Nothing fell out.

He angrily pointed at the vice president and said, "Not a single one. Not a single claim has been paid by your crooked company."

Webb managed to bolt upward again in protest. "Objection, Your Honor! That language is offensive!"

Judge Oliphant held up both hands and Jesse waited to be rep-rimanded. Everyone watched the judge, who began scratching his head as if struggling to decide if the word "crooked" should be struck from the record. Finally, he said, "Mr. Rudy, the word 'crooked' is inappropriate. Objection sustained."

Webb shook his head in frustration and said, "Your Honor, I move to have it struck from the record." Exactly what Jesse wanted.

"Yes, okay, ladies and gentlemen of the jury, I have admonished Mr. Rudy, and I ask you to continue as if the word 'crooked' had not been uttered." At that moment, and for hours to come, the dominant word in the jurors' thoughts and discussions was, and would be, of course, "crooked."

They awarded the plaintiff $16,400 in actual damages, plus the daily expenses, plus interest from the day after the storm. And, they awarded $50,000 in punitive damages, a record in the state courts of Mississippi.

The verdict made the front page of the *Register,* and it reverberated through the law offices and courthouses along the Coast. It rattled the insurance executives far away in their nice suites. It cracked their stone wall of denials and sent their strategies spinning in different directions.

In the first week of May, Jesse repeated his performance in a crowded courtroom in the Hancock County Courthouse in Bay St. Louis. With a wide variety of clients, he chose one with a policy issued by Coast States Casualty, the fourth-largest property insurer on the Coast and the one he had come to despise the most. Its lawyers, also from a big firm in Jackson, were overwhelmed from the opening gavel. Its executives, frog-marched in from New Orleans by subpoena, were far outside their element and no match for Jesse's grenades. They strenuously avoided courtrooms. Jesse was thriving in them.

An angry jury slapped the company with $55,000 in punitive damages.

The following week, again in Hancock County, Jesse put on his case in the usual rapid-fire manner he had perfected, then lay in wait to ambush the corporate mouthpieces sent down to protect the treasured assets of Old Potomac Casualty. They tried to defend their actions by hiding behind the field reports, all of which clearly proved the damages in question were caused by water, not wind. One executive, startled by the ferocity of the attack by plaintiff's counsel, became so flustered he referred to the storm as Hurricane Betsy, another legendary storm from 1965.

The jury awarded every penny Jesse asked for, then added $47,000 in punitive for good measure.

Like the others, all verdicts were appealed to the Mississippi Supreme Court.

———•———

Keith graduated from the University of Southern Mississippi in May with a degree in political science. He was twenty-two, still single, not really looking for prospects, and eager to start law school at Ole Miss in June. He passed on a trip to the Bahamas with friends and went straight to his father's law office, which had become his usual weekend hangout. He had become fast friends with Gage and Gene Pettigrew, and the long hours brought on by Jesse's brutal trial schedule were not without some fun. Late in the evening, after Jesse had finally gone home, the boys locked the doors and brought out the beer.

During one session, Keith had the brilliant idea of publishing a monthly client newsletter with updates on all aspects of the Camille litigation. Reports of trials, the latest verdicts, reprints from newspapers, interviews with policy holders, recommendations for good contractors, and so on. Of course, Jesse would have something to say in each edition. He was the most popular lawyer on the Coast and had the insurance companies on the run. People wanted to read about him. The mailing list would include all clients, of which there were now over 1,200, but also other lawyers, paralegals, clerks, even judges. And the most brilliant tactic would be the inclusion of *all* policy holders with claims.

Gene argued there could be a problem with advertising, which was still strictly prohibited in the state. Gage didn't see a problem. The newsletter was not an overt attempt to solicit clients. Rather, it was simply a means to share information with people who needed it.

Keith saw it as a rare, perfect moment to (1) keep clients happy, (2) subtly solicit more clients, and (3) remind the voters in the Second Circuit Court district that Jesse Rudy was a badass lawyer they could trust. While avoiding the stickiness of politics, the newsletter could be a beautiful calling card and the first salvo in next year's race for district attorney. He wrote the first newsletter, christened it the *Camille Litigation Report,* and showed it to his father, who was impressed. They argued over the mailing list and Jesse was adamant in his belief that the mailing would be regarded as advertising. He reluctantly agreed to an initial run of 2,000 clients and others who had contacted his office.

The newsletter was a hit. The clients loved the attention and were encouraged to see their lawyer so actively pushing their cases. They passed their copies around, shared them with neighbors. Strangers showed up at the office, holding the newsletter, asking for some time with Mr. Rudy. Unknown to anyone at the firm, Keith ran hundreds of additional copies of the initial newsletter, virtually all of it written by him, and nonchalantly left them around the courthouses, post offices, city halls, and at a makeshift field tent being used as the unofficial gathering place in Camille Ville.

And then it was time to leave for law school. His last night in Biloxi, he met Joey and Denny at a new watering hole in Back Bay, a cheap dive at one end of an old oyster house and cannery. With thousands of relief workers still in town, someone had realized they were thirsty and opened a bar. Oddly enough, there were no strippers, no rooms upstairs, no slot machines.

The Camille cleanup was in full throttle, but it would take years, not months. Many homes, stores, and offices would never be rebuilt. Mountains of debris sat waiting to be hauled away and burned. Denny was working for a government contractor from Dallas and driving a dump truck ten hours a day. Not much of a job, but the pay was okay. Joey talked about the fishing business, which was rebounding nicely. The storm unsettled the Sound for a month or so, but the fish came back, as always. The enormous amount of debris taken away by the surge was now at the bottom of the Gulf and attracting fish for nesting. The oyster crops were especially abundant.

They finally got around to the subject of Hugh. Keith had not seen him in at least three years, certainly not since the last election. And that was a good thing, the other two agreed. They saw Hugh occasionally, and he had made it clear that he and his father had no use for the Rudy bunch. Too much was said in the heat of the campaign. Jesse had promised to take on the nightclubs and shut them down for illegal activity. He had even used a photo of Red Velvet in one of his mailings.

"Stay away from the guy," Denny said. "He's looking for trouble."

"Oh, come on," Keith said. "If Hugh walked up right now I'd buy him a beer and talk football. What's he gonna do?"

Denny and Joey exchanged looks. They knew more than they wanted to tell.

Joey shrugged and said, "He fights a lot, Keith, likes to work the door and intimidate people. As always, he enjoys trading punches."

"His old man makes him work as a bouncer?"

"No, he wants to. Says that's where the action is. Also, he gets the first look at the girls."

Denny said, "He says he'll take over one day and wants to learn the business from the ground up. He drives his old man around, carries a gun, hangs out in the clubs, samples the women. He's a total thug, Keith. You don't want to be around him."

"I thought you guys were in business."

"Maybe before Camille, but not now. He's too big for me, a real tough guy and a real swinger. Not my friend anymore."

To change the subject, Joey said, "You guys read about Todd Foster, kid from over in Ocean Springs?"

Both shook their heads no.

"Didn't think so. Todd Foster was killed in Vietnam a couple of weeks back, the twenty-third casualty from the Coast. He must not have been too bright because he volunteered to begin with, then signed up for two more tours."

"Awful," Keith said, but they had grown accustomed to such stories.

"Anyway, he had a nickname. Take a guess."

"How are we supposed to know? Shorty. Shorty Foster."

"Try Fuzz. Fuzz Foster. The guy we saw in Golden Gloves the night he and Hugh beat the shit out of each other. Referee called it a draw."

Keith was startled and saddened. He said, "How could we ever forget? We were all there, raising hell and yelling, 'Let's go Hugh! Let's go Hugh!'"

"I'll never forget that fight," Denny said. "Fuzz was tough as nails and could take a punch. Didn't they fight again?"

Joey smiled and said, "Remember? Hugh said they had two more fights, split them, then they had a brawl in a club one night when Fuzz got outta line. According to our dear friend Hugh, he won by a knockout."

"Of course. Has Hugh ever lost a fight no one saw?"

They laughed and sipped their beers. They had been together since the first grade on the Point and had shared many adventures. Keith wanted their friendship to last forever, but he feared they were drifting apart. Denny was still searching for a career and making little progress. Joey seemed content following his father and fishing for the rest of his life. And Hugh was gone. Surprising no one, he had slid into the underworld, from which there was no return. Career gangsters like Lance Malco went to prison, or took a bullet, or they died in prison. That was Hugh's future too.

CHAPTER 21

The litigation had found a new reality. The insurance companies could afford to stall the damage claims, but they could not survive angry juries willing to do whatever Jesse Rudy asked. When the value of a $15,000 claim quadrupled with the addition of punitive damages, it was time to wave a white flag. Typically, though, the surrender would be tedious and frustrating.

The break came in the courtroom in Wiggins, just as the lawyers were waiting for Judge Oliphant to take the bench and begin jury selection. Simmons Webb walked to the plaintiff's table, leaned down and whispered, "Jesse, my client's had enough." The words were magic, though Jesse's expression did not change. He said, "Let's go to chambers."

Judge Oliphant took off his robe and waved at the small conference table.

Webb said, "Your Honor, I have finally convinced my client to settle these cases and pay the claims."

His Honor couldn't suppress a smile. He was tired of the nonstop trials and needed a break. "Great news," he said. "What are your terms?"

"Well, in the case before us the policy holder claims damages in the amount of thirteen thousand dollars. We'll write a check for that amount."

Jesse was ready to pounce. "No way. You've sat on this money for almost a year and you don't get to use it for free. Any settlement must include interest and living expenses."

"I'm not sure ARU will do that."

"Then let's start the trial. I'm ready, Judge."

His Honor held up his hands and asked for quiet. He looked at Webb and said, "If you're settling these cases, then it will be done properly. These people are entitled to damages, expenses, and interest. Every jury so far has agreed."

Webb said, "Judge, believe me, I'm aware of that, but I'll need to discuss this with my client. Give me five minutes."

Jesse said, "And there's something else. I've signed up these cases on a twenty percent contingency, but it's not fair for me to take fees out of the money that is desperately needed by my clients. Your company's bad faith required them to file suit. So, your company will pay five hundred dollars in legal fees per case."

Webb bristled and said smugly, "That's not in the policy."

"Neither are punitive damages," Jesse shot back.

Webb stuttered but had no retort.

Jesse fired away with "And since when does your client honor the policy?"

"Come on, Jesse. The jury's not in here."

"No, it's out there and I'm ready to put it in the box and have us another trial. If all goes well I'm going to ask for a hundred thousand in punitive damages."

"Settle down. Give me five minutes, okay?" Webb left chambers, and the judge and Jesse exhaled in unison. "Could it be over?" Oliphant asked, almost to himself.

"Maybe. It just might be the beginning of the end. I met with the lawyers for Coast States last week, up in Jackson, trying to get the cases settled. For the first time there they were willing to talk. The big boys haven't blinked, until now. If ARU and Coast States surrender, the rest will be quick to follow."

"How many cases do you have now?"

"Fifteen hundred, against eight companies. But I've filed only two hundred, those with clear wind damage. The others are more complicated, as you know. They'll be harder to settle because of water damage."

"Please don't file any more, Jesse. I've had enough of these trials. And there's something else that's really bothering me. I'm not impartial anymore, and for a judge that's not good."

"I understand, Judge, but no one can blame you. These damned insurance companies are rotten, and if you hadn't allowed my claim for punitive damages we wouldn't be talking settlement. You made it happen, Judge."

"No, you get the credit. No other lawyer on the Coast has dared to try one of these. They signed them up all right, but they're waiting on you to force settlements."

Jesse smiled and acknowledged the truth. Minutes passed before Webb returned, and he came back a different man. His face was relaxed, his eyes had a glow, his smile had never been wider. He stuck out a hand and said, "Deal."

Jesse shook it and said, "Deal. Now, we're not leaving this room until we have a written agreement, witnessed by the judge, that covers all of my cases and clients."

Judge Oliphant put on his robe, went to his courtroom, and released the prospective jurors. Jesse informed his client that the case had been settled, a check was on the way.

———•———

Weeks passed, though, before anyone saw a check. ARU had written the playbook on stalling claims and it simply turned to the next chapter. Phone calls to adjusters were often not returned and never promptly. An amazing amount of paperwork was lost in the mail. Every letter from the company was mailed at the last possible moment. A favorite ploy was to settle with the folks who'd hired lawyers, and ignore those who hadn't.

Coast States agreed to settle two weeks after ARU, and it

proved just as slippery. By the end of July, almost all of the insurance companies were making offers to settle. Contractors were suddenly busy, and through the ravaged neighborhoods the welcome sounds of hammers and power saws filled the air.

Rudy & Pettigrew received its first batch of checks for the eighty-one clients who had sued ARU. Suddenly, there was a little over $40,000 in fees in the bank, and the money lessened the stress considerably. Jesse rewarded his partners with handsome bonuses; likewise for his secretary and part-time paralegal. He took some money home for Agnes and the kids. He sent a check to Keith in law school. And he tucked away $5,000 for his campaign account, one he had never closed.

The litigation was far from over. His clients who lived closer to the beach suffered damage that was clearly caused by the surge. His position was that the winds, at least 175 miles an hour, blew off roofs and porches hours before the flood came. Proving it, though, would take experts and money.

———•———

On the one-year anniversary of Camille, a crowd gathered on a beautiful morning near the remains of the Church of the Redeemer, the oldest Episcopal Church on the Coast. The municipal band played for half an hour as the crowd gathered. A Presbyterian minister offered a flowery prayer, followed by a priest who was more succinct. The mayor of Biloxi talked about the iron will and fighting spirit of his people along the Coast. He pointed to his right and talked about the rebuilding of the Biloxi harbor. To his left and across Highway 90 a new shopping center was under construction. Most of the rubble had been cleared and every day the sounds of recovery grew stronger. Staggered and wounded like never before, the Coast had been brought to its knees, but it would rise again.

A beautiful memorial to the victims was unveiled.

When Camille leveled the nightclubs and swept away everything but the concrete slabs, there was optimism in some quarters that perhaps God had sent a message, had finally pronounced judgment on the wicked. This was a popular theme among some preachers after the storm. The infamous Biloxi vice was gone. Good riddance. Praise the Lord.

The sinners, though, were still thirsty, and when Red Velvet and O'Malley's reopened three months after the storm, they were instantly packed and long lines waited to get in. Their popularity inspired others and soon there were opportunists everywhere. Once-expensive land that faced the beach was now empty, and many homeowners had no plans to return. Why build an expensive home and risk another Camille? Prices plummeted and that drew even more interest.

By Christmas of 1969, a construction boom was underway along the Strip. The buildings were of the cheap metal variety, barely able to withstand winds from a good summer thunderstorm. They were decorated with all manner of awnings, porticos, colorful doors, fake windows, and neon signs.

The Coast was still busy with construction workers, day laborers, volunteers, drifters, and Guardsmen, not to mention the new recruits at Keesler, and the nightclub scene returned in a hurry. Vice was perhaps the first industry to fully recover after the storm.

CHAPTER 22

Because it was an older building made of concrete and bricks, the Truck Stop withstood the winds and water and was still standing after the storm. Lance put Hugh in charge of its repairs and renovations, and when it reopened in February he decided it would be his new hangout. He needed some distance from his father and Nevin Noll. He was twenty-two years old and looking for a challenge. He was tired of driving his father around and listening to his unsolicited advice. He was tired of breaking up fights at Foxy's and Red Velvet, tired of mixing drinks when a bartender failed to show, tired of his mother's quiet warnings about a life of crime. He wasn't tired of the girls but was curious about a more serious relationship. He had his own apartment, lived alone and enjoyed it, and was getting restless.

Hugh's official job was operating all-night convenience stores that also sold cheap gas. Lance owned several on the Coast and used them to launder money from his clubs. Their inventories were paid for in cash, at discounts, and once the goods hit the shelves they became legitimate stock. Their sales were properly recorded, taxes were paid, and so on. Most of the sales, anyway. The truth was that about half of the gross receipts never hit the books. The dirty money got even dirtier.

Hugh had given up boxing when he realized his strengths—a hard head, quick hands, a love of trading punches—were offset by his bad training habits. He had always enjoyed the gym, but Buster finally ran him off when he caught him smoking for the third time. Hugh enjoyed beer, cigarettes, and the night life too much to stay in fighting shape. Once he retired, his afternoons were spent hanging around the Truck Stop, shooting pool and killing time. He loved poker and thought about going to Vegas and pursuing it full-time, but could never win consistently. He became an ace pool shark, won some tournaments, but there was never enough money on the line.

Honest work had never appealed to him. He met some drug smugglers and dabbled in the trade, but was turned off by the brutality of the business. The money was attractive but the risks were much higher. If he didn't get shot he would probably get busted. Snitching was rampant and he knew men who'd been sent away for decades. He'd also heard of a couple who had been bound, gagged, and dropped in the Gulf.

He was at the pool table one evening when Jimmie Crane entered his life. He had never seen him before and no one knew where he came from. Over beers, Jimmie said he had just been paroled from federal prison after four years for smuggling guns from Mexico. Jimmie was a big talker, charismatic, and funny with plenty of tall tales of prison life. He said his father was a member of the Dixie Mafia and ran a gang of bank robbers in South Carolina. One job went bad and his father got shot, barely survived, and was now serving life in prison. Jimmie claimed to be working on a plan to help him escape. Hugh and the others doubted many of Jimmie's stories but they listened and laughed anyway.

Jimmie became a regular at the Truck Stop and Hugh enjoyed his company. He, too, avoided employment, and said he made good money gambling, though he had always avoided the tables along the Strip. He said everyone in the business knew the Biloxi tables were rigged. He drove a nice car and seemed unconcerned about money. Odd, thought Hugh, for a guy who'd just spent four years in prison.

Hugh had a chat with Nevin, who in turn talked to a private investigator. Jimmie's stories checked out. He'd been busted in Texas on weapons charges and served time in a federal pen in

Arkansas. His father had been a known bank robber. Lance had never heard of him but a couple of old-timers knew his reputation.

Jimmie was convinced a fortune could be made in the weapons trade. Pistols, rifles, and shotguns were being manufactured all over South America, where ownership was not as popular as in the U.S. Notwithstanding the fact that he had just served time for smuggling, he was ready for another foray into the business. Hugh was intrigued and they soon talked of little else.

The first obstacle was cash. They needed $10,000 to buy a truck-load of weapons, the street value of which was at least five times the investment. Jimmie knew the business, the middlemen in Texas, the shipping routes, and the dealers stateside who would buy whatever they smuggled across the border. At first, Hugh was suspicious and thought his new friend was either an undercover agent or a true con man who had dropped in from nowhere and was angling for the Malco money.

With time, though, he began to trust him.

"I don't have ten thousand dollars," Hugh said over a beer.

"Neither do I," Jimmie said, cocky as always. "But I know how to get it."

"I'm listening."

"In every small town there is a jewelry store, sitting right there on Main Street next door to the coffee shop. Diamond rings in the window, gold watches, pearls, rubies, you name it. Owned by Mom and Pop, got a gum-smacking teenage girl working the counter. No security whatsoever. At closing time they lock it all up in a safe and go home. The smart ones take the diamonds with them, put them under a pillow. But most of them ain't that smart, been doing the same thing for years, nothing to worry about."

"You're a safecracker too?"

"No, ass, I'm not a safecracker. There's an easier way to do it and the chances of getting caught are about one in a thousand."

"Gee, I've never heard that before."

"Just keep listening."

———— • ————

They picked the town of Zachary, Louisiana, just north of Baton Rouge and three hours from Biloxi. It was busy enough, population 5,000, with a nice little jewelry store on Main Street. Hugh, in a coat and tie, entered at ten o'clock one morning with his bride-to-be, Sissy, one of his favorite strippers. For her role, she was fully clothed in a plain white dress that plunged a bit low and revealed too much of her ample breasts. Her face was scrubbed of paint and mascara, just a touch of lipstick, hair unteased, the look of a cute little tart, almost wholesome. Mr. Kresky, age about sixty, greeted them warmly and was thrilled to learn they were looking for an engagement ring. What a lovely couple. He pulled out two racks of his finest diamonds and asked them where they were from. Baton Rouge, and they had heard of his store, his wonderful selection and reasonable prices. When Sissy leaned forward and gawked at the rings, Mr. Kresky couldn't help but take in the cleavage and blushed.

She looked around, pointed at some more rings, and he deftly pulled out two more display boards.

Another customer entered, a friendly young man with a big hello. Said he wanted to look at some watches, which Mr. Kresky pointed to in a display before quickly returning to Sissy.

Hugh leaned closer and said to Mr. Kresky, "See that purse of hers. There's a pistol in there." The other customer, Jimmie, stepped over and said, "And I've got one right here." He pulled back his jacket and showed him a Ruger clamped to his belt. Jimmie then stepped to the door, turned the deadbolt, and flipped the OPEN sign to CLOSED.

Hugh said, "Put all these in a bag, now, quickly, and no one gets hurt."

"What is this?" Mr. Kresky asked, wild-eyed.

"It's called a robbery," Hugh barked. "Hurry up before we start shooting."

Hugh walked around the counter, grabbed two large shopping bags, and began snatching every piece of jewelry and watch in view.

"I can't believe this," Mr. Kresky said.

"Shut up!" Hugh snapped.

In seconds the two bags were stuffed, the display cases looted. Hugh grabbed Mr. Kresky and put him on the floor while Sissy pulled a roll of silver duct tape from her purse. "Please don't hurt me," Mr. Kresky begged.

"Shut up and nobody gets hurt."

Hugh and Jimmie wrapped his ankles and wrists, and rather roughly slapped the tape over his mouth and around his head, leaving only a slight gap so he could breathe. Without a word, Jimmie took one bag, unlocked the door, and left. He walked around the corner and hopped into Hugh's 1969 Pontiac Firebird, with a fresh set of Louisiana license plates. If anyone noticed him, he wasn't aware of it. He stopped in front of the jewelry store, Hugh and Sissy jumped in with the other bag, and the getaway was clean and quick. Five minutes later they were out of town, heading north, howling with laughter at their cunning. It had been as easy as taking candy from a baby. Sissy, in the back seat, was already trying on diamond rings.

They drove at a reasonable speed, no sense in taking chances, and an hour later crossed into Mississippi. In the river town of Vicksburg, they stopped at a hot dog stand for lunch, then continued north on Highway 61, through the heart of the Mississippi Delta. At a service station, they put their valuables—two dozen diamond rings, several gold pendants, earrings and necklaces with rubies and sapphires, and twenty-one watches—in a metal box and hid it in the trunk. They threw away the shopping bags and display boards from Mr. Kresky's store. They replaced the Louisiana license plates with a set from Arkansas. At 3:00 P.M. they crossed the Mississippi River and were soon in downtown Helena, population 10,000, with a Main Street that was busy but not crowded.

They parked with the jewelry store in sight and watched for customers coming and going.

Hugh and Jimmie had argued over strategy. Hugh wanted
to carefully case each target and plan their movements. Jimmie
thought it was a bad idea because the more time they spent on-site,
the likelier someone would notice them. He wanted to hit fast and
get out of town before something went wrong. Sissy had no opinion and was just thrilled to be along for the adventure. It was much
more fun than hustling soldiers for drinks and sex.

At 3:30, when they were convinced there were no customers
inside Mason's Keepsakes, Hugh and Sissy, holding hands, entered
the store and said hello to Mrs. Mason, the lady behind the counter.
Before long it was covered with velvet boards displaying dozens of
inexpensive diamonds. Hugh said he wanted to spend some money
and she yelled for someone in the back. Mr. Mason appeared with
a locked box, which he opened and proudly showed the handsome
young couple.

Jimmie entered the store with a smile and asked about watches.
He pulled his Ruger, and within seconds the Masons were on the
floor begging for their lives. When their ankles, wrists, and mouths
were taped, Jimmie left first with a MASON'S KEEPSAKES shopping
bag filled with jewelry. Hugh and Sissy followed minutes later with
another bag. The getaway was easy, with no one giving them a
second look. Two hours later they arrived in downtown Memphis,
got a fine room at the Peabody Hotel downtown, and went to the
bar. After a long dinner, the three slept together in the same bed
and enjoyed a rowdy time of it.

Jimmie, the more seasoned criminal, seemed to have great
instincts and was fearless. He was of the firm opinion that no two
robberies should take place in the same state, and Hugh readily
agreed. Sissy did not have a vote in the planning and was content
to nap in the back seat. The boys allowed her to wear some of the
loot from Mason's and she had a delightful time modeling necklaces and bracelets.

At ten the following morning, they hit a store in Ripley, Tennessee, and four hours later raided Toole's Jewelers in Cullman, Alabama. The only hitch occurred when Mr. Toole fainted at the sight of Jimmie's Ruger and appeared dead when they wrapped him in duct tape.

After four flawless heists, they decided not to push their luck and headed home. They were exhilarated by the ease of their crimes and impressed by their own guile and coolness under pressure. Sissy in particular was a natural at playing the starry-eyed bride-to-be and emanated pure affection for Hugh as she tried on ring after ring. He couldn't keep his hands off her, nor could the men on the other side of the counter ignore her sumptuous features. They began to think of themselves as modern-day Bonnie and Clydes, roaring through small towns of the South, leaving no clues, and getting rich.

When Biloxi was an hour away, they began to bicker about storage. Who would keep the loot, and where? How would they divide things? Hugh and Jimmie had no plans to split things evenly with Sissy; she was nothing more than a stripper, though they enjoyed her company, laughed at her goofiness, and became lightheaded when she undressed. However, both men were smart criminals and knew full well that she was the weak link. If a cop showed up with questions, she would be the first to squeal. They finally agreed to allow Hugh to hide the goods in his apartment for a few days. Jimmie claimed to know a contact in New Orleans who would fence the jewelry for a fair price.

Two weeks passed without a word, no hint of trouble. Hugh went to the main library in Biloxi and scoured newspapers from Louisiana, Arkansas, Tennessee, and Alabama, and saw nothing. News of the robberies had not been reported by the bigger newspapers. The library did not subscribe to the small-town weeklies. He and Jimmie assumed, correctly, that the police in the four towns were not cooperating because they didn't know of the similar crimes.

Hugh parked his Firebird in a public lot one block south of Canal Street in New Orleans. He and Jimmie wandered into the French Quarter and went to the Chart Room on Decatur, and had a beer. Each carried a bulky gym bag filled with their loot. The next step was treacherous because of the unknowns. The dealer was a man named Percival, supposedly a man who could be trusted. But who in hell could be trusted in such a cutthroat business? For all they knew, Percival could be working undercover and perfectly willing to ensnare them in a sting that could send them to prison. Jimmie had worked his contacts and was confident they were headed to the right place. Hugh had sought the advice of Nevin Noll and fed him a line about a friend who needed to fence some diamonds. Nevin drilled deeper into the underworld and came back with the word that Percival was legit.

His shop was on Royal Street, between two high-end merchants of fine French antiques. They entered nervously but tried to appear calm, as if they knew exactly what they were doing. They were impressed by the display cases of rare coins, thick gold bracelets, and gorgeous diamonds. A chubby little man with a black cigar stuck in the corner of his mouth appeared from between thick curtains and without a smile asked, "Help you?"

Hugh swallowed hard and said, "Sure, we need to see Percival."

"What are you looking for?"

"We're not buying. We're selling."

He frowned as if he might either open fire or call the police. "Got a name?"

"Jimmie Crane."

He shook his head as if the name meant nothing. "Selling what?"

"Got some diamonds and stuff," Jimmie said.

"You ain't been here before."

"Nope."

He looked them over and didn't like what he saw. He grunted, blew another thick cloud at the ceiling, and finally said, "I'll see if he's busy. Wait here."

As if there was some other place to wait. He disappeared between the curtains. Low voices could be heard from the rear. Hugh became occupied with a display of Confederate dollar bills while Jimmie admired a rack of Greek coins. Minutes passed and they thought about leaving, but there was no place to go.

The curtains opened and the man grunted, "Back here." They followed him through a cramped hallway lined with framed World War II pin-ups and *Playboy* foldouts. He opened a door and jerked his head to show them inside. He closed the door behind them and said, "Need to search you. Arms out." Hugh raised his arms and the man patted him down. "No guns, right?"

"Nope."

"Last cop who came in here got shot."

Jimmie quipped, "Interesting, but we're not cops."

"Don't be a smart-ass, boy. Arms out."

He patted down Jimmie and said, "Both of you got wallets in your left rear pockets. Take them out slowly and put them on the desk."

They did as they were told. He looked at the wallets and said, "Now, remove your driver's licenses and hand them to me."

He studied Hugh's and grunted, "Mississippi, huh? Figures."

Hugh could think of no response, not that one was expected. The man looked at Jimmie's with the same disapproval, then said, "Okay, here's the way we handle things. I'll keep these until Percival is finished. All goes well, you get them back. Understood?"

They nodded because they were in no position to object. Their loot was worth little if they couldn't fence it, and at the moment Percival was their only prospect. If things did indeed go well, they planned to return soon with another load.

"Wait here. Have a seat." He jerked his head at two dilapidated chairs, both covered with old magazines. Minutes dragged by as walls of the damp room began to close in.

Finally, the door opened and he said, "This way." They followed him deeper into the building and stopped at another door. He tapped it as he opened it and they stepped inside. He closed it behind them and stood guard five feet away.

Percival sat behind a spotless desk in a large chair upholstered in leopard print. He could have been forty or seventy. His hair was dyed a deep auburn color and stood straight on top of his otherwise shaved head. Mismatched rings dangled from his ears. The man loved jewelry. Thick gold bands hung like ropes around his neck and fell onto his hairy chest. Every finger was adorned with a gaudy ring. Baubles and trinkets rattled on his wrists.

"Sit down, boys," he said in a high-pitched, slightly effeminate voice.

They complied and couldn't help but gawk at the creature before them. He eyed them right back from behind a pair of round, red-framed glasses. His cigarette hung from the end of a long, gold holder, with the tip stuck between his yellow teeth.

"Biloxi, huh? Had a friend up there one time. Got caught and they sent him away. It's a rough business, boys."

Hugh felt the need to respond and almost said *Yes sir,* but "sir" just didn't seem appropriate. When neither spoke, Percival waved at the desk and said, "Okay, let me see the goodies."

They emptied the two bags of rings, pendants, pins, necklaces, bracelets, and watches. He made no effort to touch the jewelry, but kept his distance, gazing down his long nose, past his cigarette. He took a drag and said, "Well, well, somebody's been shopping. Looks like mom-and-pop stuff. Don't tell me where you found it because I don't want to know."

He finally reached down and picked up an engagement ring, half a carat, and that's when they noticed his bright red fingernails. He clicked his teeth on the tip of his holder and shook his head as if wasting his time. Slowly, he took a sheet of paper from a drawer and uncapped a heavy gold pen. From behind them, their guard blew a cloud of blue cigar smoke.

Methodically, Percival picked up each item, pulled it close to his hideous glasses, clicked his teeth, then wrote down a number. He seemed to appreciate a pair of ruby earrings, and as he studied them he relaxed deeper into his chair, stretching his bare feet in their direction under the desk. The paint on his toenails matched the polish on his fingers.

Hugh and Jimmie kept their faces grim, but they knew they would laugh all the way back to Biloxi. If, indeed, they made it out alive.

He didn't wear a watch and evidently didn't care for them, but he studiously examined each one and assigned a value. All seemed to freeze as time stood still. They were patient, though, because Percival had the cash.

He worked in silence as he chain-smoked unfiltered Camels. The cigar smoker behind them didn't help matters as he puffed away. After an eternity, Percival kicked back again and announced, "I'll offer four thousand bucks for the lot."

They had estimated the retail value at something close to ten thousand but were expecting a heavy discount.

Jimmie said, "We were thinking five thousand was a fair price."

"Oh you were? Well, boys, I'm the expert here and you're not." He looked at the cigar smoker and said, "Max?"

With no hesitation, Max said, "Forty-two tops."

"Okay, I'll pay forty-two hundred, cash on the table."

"Deal," Hugh said. Jimmie nodded his agreement. Percival looked at Max, who left the room. Percival asked them, "How steady is your supplier?"

Jimmie shrugged and Hugh looked down at his shoes. In doing so, he caught another glimpse of the red toenails.

"There's more," Jimmie said. "You're in the market?"

Percival laughed and said, "Always. But be careful out there. Got a lot of crooks in this business."

Howling with laughter on the ride home, they would repeat this admonition a hundred times.

Max returned with a large cigar box and gave it to his boss. Percival withdrew a stack of $100 bills, slowly counted forty-two of them, and laid them in a neat row. Max handed back their driver's licenses. On the way out, they thanked Percival and promised to be back, grateful that he did not rise or extend a hand.

When they emerged onto Royal Street, they inhaled the muggy air and practically ran to the nearest bar.

———•———

The easy cash was addictive but they fought the urge to launch another crime spree. They paid Sissy $500 and threw in some jewelry to boot. They plotted for a month, and when the timing felt right they left Biloxi early one Tuesday morning and drove three hours east to the town of Marianna, Florida, population 7,200. Faber's Jewelry was a small shop at one end of Central Street, far away from a busy café. They parked on a side street and gave each other a pep talk. Hugh and Sissy entered the store and Mrs. Faber herself greeted them. She was delighted to show the young couple her best engagement rings. There were no other customers in the store and she was even happier when Jimmie walked in and asked about some watches. Five minutes later, Mrs. Faber was on the floor, wrapped in duct tape, and every single diamond was gone.

They spent the night in Macon, Georgia, and had dinner in a downtown café, but the town was too big and there were too many people in the shops. They drove two hours east to Waynesboro, the seat of Burke County, and saw an easy target. Tony's Pawn and Jewelry was on Liberty Street, the main drag, across from the courthouse.

Jimmie had been griping about his limited role in the heists and wanted to swap jobs with Hugh, who considered himself the better actor. Sissy really didn't care. She was the star anyway and could handle herself with either prospective groom. Hugh eventually agreed to stay behind and waited as they entered and went about their routine.

The clerk was a teenager named Mandy who'd worked at Tony's part-time for years. She loved showing engagement rings to brides and pulled out the best ones for Sissy and Jimmie. After five minutes, Hugh left the car, with a small pistol in his pocket. He did not realize that Jimmie had the Ruger on his belt under his jacket.

As Sissy tried on rings, Mandy glanced over and saw the pistol. This startled her but she pretended all was well. When Jimmie asked if there were larger diamonds in the safe, she said yes and left to fetch them. In the office, she informed Tony that the customer had a gun. Tony had been in the business for years and knew his inventory attracted all types. He grabbed a Smith & Wesson .38 caliber automatic and went to the front. When Jimmie saw him coming with the pistol, he panicked and reached for the Ruger.

Hugh was ten feet from the front door when shots rang out inside the store. A woman screamed. Men were yelling in angry, desperate voices. One bullet shattered the large front window as the sounds of others cracked through the air and were heard up and down Liberty Street. Hugh ducked away and scrambled around a corner. His first impulse was to get in his Firebird and leave in a hurry. He heard sirens, more loud voices, people running here and there, total confusion. He decided to wait, blend in with the crowd, and survey the damage. He walked across the street and stood in front of the courthouse with other shocked onlookers. Two cops crouched low and entered the store; others followed. The first ambulance arrived, a second one moments later. Deputies blocked traffic and ordered the crowd to stand back.

Word finally spread and the first accounts came to life. Armed robbers had hit the store and Tony fought them off. He was injured but not seriously. The two thieves, a man and a woman, were dead.

As experienced criminals, Jimmie and Hugh knew to leave behind nothing with their names on it. At that moment, Jimmie's wallet and clothes were in the trunk of the Firebird, along with Sissy's purse and personal effects. The purse she carried into the store had nothing but a pistol and duct tape. Hugh was too stunned to think clearly, but his instincts told him to ease out of town. With his eyes glued to his rearview mirror, he drove out of Waynesboro, Georgia, for the first and last time.

Augusta was the nearest city of any size. When he was certain he had not been followed, he stopped at a motel on the outskirts of the city and spent a long afternoon waiting for the six o'clock news. The botched robbery in Waynesboro was the big story. The chief of police confirmed the deaths of two as-yet-unidentified people, one man, one woman, both about thirty. After dark, Hugh, eager to leave the state, drove to South Carolina, circled west into North Carolina, then to Tennessee.

He had no idea where Jimmie Crane called home but he had mentioned a couple of times that his mother had moved to Florida after his father went to prison. He did not know where Sissy was from, and even doubted that was her real name. Not that it mattered because he wasn't about to notify anyone. With time, he would find a way into the records at Red Velvet and perhaps learn more about Sissy. He had been sleeping with her off and on for two months and had grown fond of her.

Two days later, he finally returned home. Frightened out of his mind and convinced he had been nothing but a complete idiot, he gradually fell into his old habits. Armed robbery was not his calling. Arms dealing was for someone else.

———•———

A month later, two FBI agents paid a visit to Fats Bowman at the sheriff's office. They had finally strung together the trail of robberies, and the first five victims had helped an artist prepare composite sketches of the gang of three. The woman, Karol Horton, stage name of Sissy, had been tracked to her last place of employment, Red Velvet. She was now deceased. Her sidekick, Jimmie Crane, was a convicted felon who had recently been paroled and had a Mississippi driver's license. Address in Biloxi. He was dead too. They were looking for the third suspect.

For once, Fats was completely innocent and knew nothing about the robberies. Why should he? They took place in other states, far away from the Coast.

The third composite bore a close resemblance to Lance Malco's son, but Fats said nothing. The FBI agents could flash the composite all over Biloxi, but the people who knew Hugh would not say a word. After they left, Fats sent Kilgore, his chief deputy, to talk to Lance.

Hugh got a job on a freighter hauling frozen shrimp to Europe and was not seen in Biloxi for six months.

CHAPTER 23

1971 was an election year and Jesse Rudy wasted no time in announcing his candidacy for district attorney. In early February, he rented the VFW lodge and held a reception for friends and supporters. A large crowd showed up and he was delighted with the early support. In a short speech, he again promised to use the office to do what it was supposed to do: fight crime and bring criminals to justice. In broad strokes, he talked about the corruption that had plagued the Coast for decades and the casual attitude of law enforcement toward the rampant vice. He did not mention names because he didn't have to. Everyone in the crowd knew his targets. The name-calling would come later; the speeches would get longer.

The *Register* covered the event and Jesse got himself on the front page for the umpteenth time in the past four years. Since Camille, no lawyer on the Coast had received as much publicity as Jesse Rudy.

Agnes had reservations about her husband seeking office again. The nastiness of his first race against Rex Dubisson was still fresh. The dirty tricks would long be remembered. The element of danger was always in the background, though rarely discussed. With Keith in law school, Beverly and Laura at Southern Miss, and Tim headed for college in the fall, the family budget was as strained as always. The DA's salary was barely enough to handle four kids in college. The law firm kept them above water, so, she argued, why not concentrate on the practice and let Dubisson or someone else ignore the criminals?

Jesse, though, would have none of it. He listened to her concerns, again and again, but was too focused on his mission. Since his defeat in 1967, he was more determined than ever to become the chief prosecutor on the Coast. Keith, still in his first year of law school, was of the same mind and encouraged his father to run.

After his announcement, Jesse met with the editors of the *Register*. The meeting did not go well, because of his aggressive approach. In his opinion, the newspaper had for too long sat idly by and ignored the corruption. It loved the crime. The murders, beatings, and burnings were always front-page news. When the mobsters went to war the *Register* sold even more, but it had rarely dug beneath the violence to explore its causes. And, it was too tepid with its endorsements. Fats Bowman was almost never criticized. Four years earlier the newspaper had endorsed neither Dubisson nor Jesse.

He showed the editors the infamous "I Was Raped By Jarvis Decker" ad that Dubisson had used in 1967. He reminded them of the judge's comment of "I find these ads repulsive."

"This was a false ad," Jesse said, lecturing the editors. "We finally found this woman, this Connie Burns, who of course was not Connie Burns. It took me two years to track her down. Name's Doris Murray and she admitted that someone from the Dubisson campaign paid her three hundred dollars to pose for the photo and tell her lies. It was a devastating ad. You were in court. You covered the hearing, but you didn't do a damned thing to investigate the story. You let Dubisson off the hook."

"How'd you find her?" an editor asked, somewhat sheepishly.

"Hard work. Shoe leather. Knocked on doors. It's called investigative reporting, fellas. And if Dubisson tries it again this time, I'll sue him even quicker. It would be nice if you guys would do some digging."

After some more awkward conversation, the editor-in-chief asked, "So you want our endorsement?"

"I don't care. It means little. You're always quick to pipe up with an endorsement for governor or AG or some office that means little to the people out there on the street, but you claim to be impartial in the local races. Looking the other way only encourages corruption."

He left the meeting and considered it successful. He had made them squirm and stutter.

His next stop was a meeting with Rex Dubisson, a courtesy call with a purpose. With a couple of exceptions, the two had managed to avoid each other for four years. Dubisson was rarely in court, which was part of his problem, in Jesse's opinion. He pulled out the Jarvis Decker ad and promised nasty lawsuits if the dirty tricks started again. Dubisson snapped back that the ad was accurate. Jesse launched into a near tirade and told the story of tracking down Doris Murray. He had an affidavit signed by her in which she admitted taking cash from his campaign in exchange for her photo and false story.

The meeting deteriorated and Jesse stormed out. His message had been delivered.

In their first race, Dubisson had the advantage of incumbency, name recognition, and plenty of money. Now, though, because of Camille and its ensuing litigation, the landscape had shifted, in more ways than one. Jesse Rudy was a household name and viewed by many as a gutsy and talented trial lawyer who fought the insurance companies, and won. In legal circles, the gossip was that his firm was doing well and he was making money. He had been campaigning for four years and had made plenty of friends. His partners, the Pettigrew boys, were from Hancock County and their family was well connected. The tragic death of their father in Camille had touched the entire community. Their popularity would be good for an extra thousand votes.

After he left, Dubisson locked the door to his office and called Fats Bowman. They might have a problem.

During Jesse's initial assault on the insurance industry, he met a young lawyer named Egan Clement. She was thirty years old and worked in Wiggins, up in Stone County, where her family had lived for the past century. Her father was the superintendent of education for the county and highly regarded.

Egan had never sued an insurance company before, but she had clients with property damage claims that were being ignored. Jesse took the time to walk her through the ins and outs of the litigation and they became friendly. He helped with her lawsuits and told her when to settle and when to go to trial.

Stone County had the smallest population in the Second District, and Dubisson had carried it by thirty-one votes. Jesse did not intend to lose it again. He startled Egan with the suggestion that she enter the race for district attorney. A three-way race would further dilute Dubisson's strength and divert some of his attention and money away from Jesse. By running, she would gain name recognition, something every small-town lawyer needed. The deal was simple: If Egan ran and lost, Jesse would hire her as his assistant district attorney.

The deal was hardball politics, but nothing unethical. Jesse had seen Egan in action and knew she had potential. He also liked the idea of having a tough female prosecutor on his team.

In April, Egan Clement officially entered the race for district attorney. The deal was kept quiet, of course, and existed only by virtue of a handshake.

———•———

After his last exam in early May, Keith hustled home to jump into the middle of the campaign. Still motivated by the first loss, he had continually encouraged his father to run again. He had been bitten by the bug, loved politics, and was as determined as Jesse to win and win big. He toyed with the idea of another session of summer school, but needed a break. His first year had gone well, his grades were impressive, but he would rather spend the next three months in the rough-and-tumble world of Coast politics.

He wrote the first campaign ads and had them ready to go when, and if, Dubisson started his direct mail mischief. They didn't have to wait long. In the first week of June, the district was flooded with ads that repeated the theme of an incumbent "Tough On Crime." There were the statistics boasting of a 90 percent conviction rate, and so on. There was a photo, an action shot of Dubisson in court pointing angrily at a witness, unseen. There were testimonials from crime victims expressing their unabashed admiration for the prosecutor who had put away the perpetrators. There was nothing original about the ads, just the usual slick offering from an incumbent DA. They were fair and balanced and did not mention either Jesse Rudy or Egan Clement.

The Rudy campaign countered quickly with a mailing that hit back, and hit hard. The ad listed seven unsolved murders in the past six years. Seven murders that were still in the "unprosecuted" category. The implication was clear: The DA wasn't doing a very good job with the serious crimes. In all fairness, Dubisson couldn't prosecute murders that law enforcement hardly investigated. At least five of them were gang-related, and Fats Bowman had never shown much interest when the mobsters were settling scores. But that wasn't mentioned in the ad. It went on to list the crimes that had led to apprehension and punishment, with heavy emphasis on petty burglaries, small drug deals, domestic violence, and drunk driving. In bold print at the bottom was a tagline that would be remembered and repeated: "Rex Dubisson—Tough On Shoplifters."

The following week, billboards along Highways 90 and 49 were converted to bold ads that read: REX DUBISSON—TOUGH ON SHOPLIFTERS.

Any momentum the DA might have inherited due to his incumbency vanished overnight. He abandoned his "Tough On Crime" routine and struggled to find traction elsewhere. At a huge

July Fourth barbecue and political rally, Rex called in sick and missed the festivities. A handful of his volunteers passed out brochures, but they were heavily outnumbered by the Rudy people. Jesse gave a fiery speech in which he blasted his opponent for being a no-show. Going for the jugular, he introduced the one issue that still frightened every law-abiding citizen. Drugs were pouring into the Coast, marijuana and now cocaine, and the police and prosecutors were ignoring the trade, or profiting from it, or sleeping on the job.

Publicly, he never mentioned Fats Bowman and the nightclub crowd. A war was coming, but he would wait until he was elected to start it. Privately, though, he called them by name and promised to put them out of business.

———•———

Two weeks before the August primary, the Dubisson campaign came to life with radio ads touting his twelve years of experience. He was a veteran prosecutor who had sent hundreds of criminals to Parchman. Seven years earlier, in his finest hour, he had successfully tried and convicted a man, Rubio, who had killed his wife and two children. It was an easy case with plenty of damning evidence, one that a third-year law student could have won. But the jury returned with a capital conviction and Rubio was now at Parchman awaiting execution. For any DA in America's death belt, there was no greater prize than sending a man to death row. In the ads, Dubisson crowed about the conviction and vowed to be there when they led Rubio into the gas chamber. In a state where 70 percent of the people believed in the death penalty, the ads were well received.

Fats Bowman then turned the money loose and Dubisson flooded the airwaves with TV ads. The Biloxi station was the only one on the Coast and few local politicians could afford it. By late

July, the Rudy campaign was almost out of money and could not answer the onslaught. The ads were thirty-second spots, professionally done, slick and convincing. They portrayed Rex Dubisson as a hard-charging DA at war with those sinister drug traffickers from South America.

To his credit, Dubisson stayed away from attack ads. He was convinced that another dirty trick would land him in court. Jesse Rudy was itching to go there and the negative publicity would only favor him. He and his team could only watch and cringe as Dubisson's ads ran seemingly nonstop.

Keith wrote a series of print ads that accused Dubisson of "buying" the election. They ran almost daily in the *Register* and finally broke the campaign's tenuous budget. There was talk of Jesse making another trip to the bank for a last-ditch loan, but he finally vetoed the idea. He was convinced he had the battle won, though the momentum seemed to be shifting. In speeches, and in private conversations with voters, he lamented the use of big money to buy an election.

———•———

When the last votes were finally counted on August 5, Egan Clement was the margin of victory. She carried Stone County by 150 votes and received only 11 percent overall, but took crucial support away from Dubisson. Agnes felt all along that many women would quietly vote for her, and she was right. The Pettigrew brothers delivered Hancock County by a margin of 820 votes. And in Harrison County, the longtime stronghold of the Fats Bowman machine, Jesse collected almost 900 more votes than Rex Dubisson.

With 51 percent overall, he avoided the runoff and became the new district attorney.

Getting Egan Clement in the race had been a risky move. She

could have easily forced a runoff, one that Jesse could not afford to fight. With unlimited cash and access to TV, Dubisson would have been reelected. He graciously conceded and wished Jesse the best of luck.

A week after the votes were counted, Keith packed his car and left for law school.

CHAPTER 24

The sheriff arrived at Baricev's half an hour early and saw some familiar faces. He shook hands and thanked the folks for their votes, promised to keep them safe, and so on. As usual, when he was off-duty he wore his blue suit and a tie and gave the appearance of a prosperous businessman. He seemed to relish his role as the machine boss who always delivered. Everyone knew Fats and enjoyed his routine. He was, after all, quite affable, and his mood was even merrier with his latest landslide. His reputation as perhaps the most corrupt sheriff in the state was well established, but, that aside, he ran a tight ship and was tough with common criminals. His darker side was rarely seen by the average citizen. He kept the vice in check and the mobsters in line, for the most part.

He and Rudd Kilgore, his chief deputy, eventually worked their way to his corner table where they ordered cold beers and a platter of raw oysters. Lance Malco and Nevin Noll arrived on time and the four huddled around the table. More drinks and oysters arrived. The other diners, those from the area, knew better than to try and eavesdrop.

"Haven't seen your boy lately," Fats said. No one had seen Hugh in months.

"He's still at sea," Lance said. "Taking a break. No sign of the Feds?"

"Nope. It's been a while. I doubt they've given up, though."

Fats balanced a fat oyster on a saltine, then gulped it down. He chased it with beer and wiped his mouth with the back of his hand. "Robbing jewelry stores. Where did that idea come from? Something you taught him?"

Lance glared at him and said, "Look, Fats, we've had this conversation at least three times. No sense in covering the same territory."

"Pretty stupid."

"Yes, quite stupid. But I'll take care of him."

"You do that. Ain't none of my business until the Feds show up. I mean, the boy's looking at five counts of armed robbery, if and when the Feds ever put two and two together. They're not a bunch of dummies, Lance."

A waitress stopped by and they ordered broiled crab claws and stuffed flounder, Fats's favorites.

The meeting was not about Hugh and his stupidity. The election of Jesse Rudy had them uneasy. They weren't sure what the new DA was planning, but for them nothing good would come from his election.

"I can't believe Rex lost that race," Nevin said.

Fats was swallowing another oyster. "He didn't do what I told him. He won big last time because he took off the gloves, got dirty. Didn't do it this time. I think Rudy had him spooked. Threatened him with lawsuits and such, and Rex backed down."

"What's Rudy's first move?" Lance asked.

"You'll have to ask him. Me, I'd guess he'll clamp down on the gambling. It's easier to prove. If I were you I'd be careful."

"I've told you, Fats, we're not gambling. I have four clubs and three bars and there's no gambling anywhere. The state liquor boys come around from time to time and have a look. If they see as much as a set of dice they'll pull the liquor license. Can't risk it. We're doing okay with drinks and girls."

"I know, I know. But you'd better tighten things up, know your customers."

"I know how to run the clubs, Fats. You and I have been in

business for a long time. You do your thing, I'll do mine. And by the way, don't let me forget to say congratulations on the landslide."

Fats waved him off with "Nothing to it. The voters know talent when they see it."

"Where'd you find that clown?" Nevin asked. As his career flourished, Fats had proven adept at convincing a string of oddballs to jump in the races against him. Running unopposed was a bad idea in his book. One or two opponents, the weaker the better, allowed him to keep his machine well oiled and his fundraising at top speed. The latest opponent, Buddy Higginbotham, had once been convicted of stealing chickens, long before he tried to go straight and became a constable in Stone County. Eleven percent of the voters found him attractive.

They had some laughs telling Buddy stories and enjoyed a smoke. Fats worked a fat cigar while the other three puffed on cigarettes. The platters of crab claws and flounder arrived and covered the table. When the waitress was gone, Nevin said, "We have an idea."

Fats nodded with his mouth full.

Nevin leaned in a bit lower. "That new place called Siesta, up on Gwinnett, some thug named Andy, been open two months."

Kilgore said, "We've been by, sold him a license."

"Well, he's just opened a little casino in the back. Two dice tables, roulette, slots, some blackjack. They keep the door closed, monitor who they let in."

"Let me guess," Fats said. "You want me to shut it down."

"No, not you. Get the city police to do it. We'll tip them off. They make the bust, get in the news, look good. State liquor pulls the permit. Rudy gets handed an easy case to start his new career. We get to watch him and see how he does things."

Fats chuckled and said, "Sacrifice one of your own, huh?"

"Sure. Andy is a dimwit, already poached two of our girls. Let's put him out of business and let the new DA strut his stuff."

Fats shoveled in a load of flounder and smiled at something, either the fish or the idea. "Who else is gambling?"

Nevin looked at Lance, who said, "Ginger's got a private room at Carousel. Cards and dice. Members only and it's tough to get in."

"We ain't messin' with Ginger," Fats said.

"I wasn't suggesting that. You asked."

Nevin said, "Shine Tanner's got his bingo hall hitting on all cylinders. Rumor is he's offering slots and roulette for the right crowd."

"He ain't too bright," Fats said. "Making a killing on bingo and booze and putting it at risk."

"There's always demand, Fats," Lance said.

Fats laughed and said, "And ain't you happy about that? Let's keep talking about this Andy boy. The problem with handing Rudy an easy case is that it's likely to go to his head. He's nothing but trouble and we don't want to jump-start his career as a crusader."

"Good point," Lance said.

Fats drained some beer and smiled at Lance and Nevin. "You boys look worried. Need I remind you that the graveyard is full of politicians who promised to clean up the Coast?"

———•———

Acting on "an anonymous tip," the Biloxi police swarmed the Siesta late on a Friday night and arrested seventeen men caught red-handed shooting craps and playing blackjack. They also arrested Andy Rizzo, the proprietor. They dispersed the crowd, padlocked the doors, and returned the following day to confiscate the slot machines and roulette and craps tables. All suspects bonded out in a matter of days, though Andy, because of his lengthy criminal record, spent a month in jail as his lawyers scrambled.

Jesse convened his first grand jury and indicted all eighteen men. Speaking to a reporter for the *Gulf Coast Register,* he praised the work of the city police and promised more aggressive action against the nightclubs. Gambling and prostitution were rampant and he had been elected to either lock up the criminals or run them out of town.

For the seventeen, four of whom were airmen from Keesler, he went light and allowed them to plead guilty, pay fines, and serve a year in jail, with all time suspended. For Andy, he refused to negotiate and set the case for a trial. He was itching for a courtroom fight, especially against a defendant who was obviously guilty, but eventually agreed to a seven-year prison sentence. Prison was nothing new for Andy, but the harsh sentence rattled the nightclub owners and they closed their casinos. Temporarily.

The case was too easy and Jesse smelled a rat. He tried to establish a relationship with the city's police chief, but got nowhere. The chief had been in office for years and knew the forces at work.

———————

The idea of using the state's nuisance law originated with Keith. During his course in Chancery Court Practice at Ole Miss, the professor skimmed over a seldom-used law that allowed any citizen to file suit to enjoin another citizen from pursuing activities that were illegal and detrimental to the public good. The case they studied involved a landowner who was allowing raw sewage to drain into a public lake.

Keith sent a memo to Jesse, who at first was skeptical. Proving gambling was difficult enough when the casinos screened their customers. Proving prostitution would be even more of a challenge. But, as the months of his first year passed, Jesse became more and more restless.

He drove to Pascagoula and met with Pat Graebel, the DA for the Nineteenth Circuit, comprised of Jackson, George, and Greene Counties. Jackson was on the Coast, but unlike Harrison and Hancock, it had never tolerated the lawlessness that made

Biloxi infamous. Nine years earlier, in his rookie days, Graebel had been thoroughly routed by Joshua Burch in his defense of Nevin Noll for the cold-blooded murder of Earl Fortier. That loss still stung, mainly because Noll was a free man and doing the dirty work for Lance Malco.

Graebel had nothing but contempt for Fats Bowman, the politicians he controlled, and the mobsters who made him rich. Law enforcement in Jackson County spent far too much time cleaning up the spillover from next door. A year before Camille, a home-grown outlaw opened a nightclub on a country road between Pascagoula and Moss Point. He had a big mouth and boasted that he planned to establish his own "Strip" in Jackson County. He had girls and dice and things were hopping until Sheriff Heywood Hester raided the club one Saturday night and hauled away thirty customers. Pat Graebel played hardball with the owner, got a conviction in circuit court for gambling, and sent him to Parchman for ten years.

The ten-year sentence reverberated through the beer joints and pool halls of Jackson County, and the message was clear. Any local thug with ambitions should either find honest work or move along to Harrison County.

Jesse laid out his plans to go after the Biloxi strip clubs. He needed a handful of honest cops willing to go undercover and get themselves solicited for sex. They would be wired, their conversations recorded, and they would abandon the "date" before the clothes came off. That might be problematic. The girls weren't stupid, indeed most of them were experienced and had seen it all, and they would immediately be suspicious when their johns walked away at the last possible moment.

Pat Graebel liked the plan but wanted to give it some thought. The chief of police of Pascagoula was a close friend, a tough cop, and above reproach. He liked undercover work and was monitoring drug traffickers. Sheriff Hester, too, would probably enjoy some of the action. And Graebel had close contacts with the city police in the town of Moss Point. It was crucial that they use men who would not be identified anywhere in Biloxi.

A month later, two men wearing wires and using the aliases of Jason and Bruce walked into Carousel on a Thursday night, found a table, ordered drinks, began to admire the strippers dancing onstage, and within a minute attracted the attention of two tarts who'd been waiting to pounce.

"Wanna buy a girl a drink?" was the standard come-on and it worked every time. The waitress brought two tall glasses filled with a red sugary punch concoction with no alcohol. The men drank beer. The tarts removed the swizzle sticks and kept them for payment later. Onstage the dancers were gyrating to a Doobie Brothers song blaring from the speakers. Back at the table, Jason and Bruce ordered another round and the women moved in closer, practically sitting on their laps. One finally uttered the next come-on: "Wanna date?"

Getting down to business, all four enjoyed the bantering about what, exactly, a date meant. Various things. They could pair off and go to a back room for a few moments of privacy, sort of sex-light. Or, if the boys were serious, they could rent a room upstairs for fifty dollars a half hour and "do it all."

Jason and Bruce were really off-duty, plainclothes policemen from Pascagoula, both happily married. Neither had ever been tempted to enter a Biloxi nightclub. As cops, they watched everything and it was apparent that the traffic was moving to the back rooms and upstairs. In the midst of the loud music, dancing, drinking, and stripping, the hookers were doing a brisk business.

Once the men felt as though they had been sufficiently propositioned, they delayed further action by claiming to be hungry. They wanted burgers and fries, and promised the girls they would catch up with them later. They moved to the bar, ordered food, and watched the girls retreat for a moment, then descend on two more potential customers.

The undercover operation went on for six weeks as various

agents, all off-duty policemen and deputies from the towns in Graebel's Nineteenth District, ventured into Carousel and chatted up the girls. There was no indication that either the girls or their managers were suspicious. Jesse listened to their recorded conversations and became convinced that he could prove a pattern of criminal activity.

When he had enough proof, he filed suit in chancery court of Harrison County seeking to enjoin Carousel from all operations. He notified the state liquor board and demanded it pull the nightclub's license to sell alcohol. And, he hand-delivered a copy of the lawsuit to the *Gulf Coast Register.* The newspaper obliged with a front-page story. His war had begun.

Not surprisingly, Ginger Redfield hired Joshua Burch to defend her nightclub, and, in a blustery rebuttal, he denied any criminal wrongdoing and asked the court to dismiss the charges. Jesse pushed hard for an expedited hearing, but Burch proved adept at delaying matters. Two months dragged by as the lawyers filed motion after motion and quibbled over a day in court.

Needless to say, the startling move by the new DA rattled the underworld. With gambling seriously curtailed on the Coast, the nightclubs relied on prostitution to rake in extra cash. Most were doing well with drinking and stripping, both still quite legal, but the serious money was made in the rooms upstairs.

Lance Malco was livid and realized the gravity of the assault on his businesses. If Jesse Rudy could close Carousel, any club might be next. Lance got his girls in line with strict instructions to stay away from anyone they hadn't dealt with before. He huddled with Joshua Burch and plotted an aggressive line of defense.

———•———

Chancery court was known as the court of equity and had jurisdiction over such non-criminal matters as domestic relations, probate, zoning, elections, and a dozen other issues that did not require jury trials. It was commonly known as "divorce court" because 80 percent of the docket involved bad marriages and child custody. A nuisance case was a rarity.

The chancellor was the Honorable Leon Baker, an aging jurist jaded by years of refereeing warring spouses and choosing who got the kids. Like many citizens on the Coast, he had grown up with a disdain for the nightclubs and had never set foot in one. When he tired of the lawyers and their maneuvers, he called a halt and set the case for a hearing.

It was a historic occasion, the first time one of the infamous joints from the Strip had been hauled into court in an effort to close it. A crowd gathered in the courtroom, and though most of the gangsters stayed away, they were well represented. Nevin Noll sat in the back row and would, of course, report everything to Lance Malco. As the owner of Carousel, Ginger Redfield had no choice but to sit at counsel table next to Joshua Burch who, as always, was thrilled with the audience.

Jesse Rudy spoke first and promised to lay out a clear pattern of criminal activity. He would call to the stand six men, all off-duty officers, who would testify that they agreed to pay for sex at Carousel. No money changed hands, there was no sex, but the statute was clear that once a price was agreed upon, the crime had occurred. Jesse waved around a stack of papers and described them as valid subpoenas he had issued for the working girls at Carousel. The subpoenas had not been served on the girls because Fats Bowman had ordered his deputies to ignore them.

"You want these ladies in court?" Judge Baker asked.

"Yes, Your Honor. I have the right to subpoena them."

Judge Baker looked at a bailiff and said, "Go find the sheriff and tell him to get here immediately. Mr. Burch."

Joshua rose, properly addressed the court, and launched into a windy explanation of how business was conducted at Carousel.

The girls were merely waitresses serving drinks to the boys, harmless fun. Sure, some of the girls were professional dancers who enjoyed performing while wearing little, but that was not illegal.

No one believed him, not even the chancellor.

The first witness was Chuck Armstrong, a policeman from Moss Point. He told his story of going to the nightclub with a friend, Dennis Greenleaf, also a policeman, and buying drinks for a young lady named Marlene. He never got her last name. They drank and danced and she finally propositioned him by offering half an hour upstairs in a room. For fifty dollars cash, he would get all the sex he wanted. He agreed on the price and the arrangements. There was no question that they made a deal, then he said he wanted to wait an hour and get something to eat. She left to hustle another table and lost interest in him. When she disappeared, he and Dennis made their exit.

On cross-examination, Joshua Burch asked the witness if he understood the term "procuring prostitution."

"Of course I understand what that means. I am a police officer."

"Well, then, you must certainly understand that procuring the services of a prostitute is also a crime, punishable by a fine and jail time."

"I do, yes."

"So you, as an officer of the law, admit here, under oath, that you committed a crime?"

"No sir. It was an undercover operation, and if you knew police work then you'd understand that we are often forced to pretend to be people we are not."

"So it was not your intent to commit a crime?"

"It was not."

"Didn't you go to the nightclub with the full intention of entrapping Marlene into an act of prostitution?"

"No sir. Again, it was an undercover operation. We had good reason to believe there was criminal activity going on, and I went there to see for myself."

Burch tried several times to trap the witness into admitting his own criminal activity, but Jesse had prepared him. Dennis Greenleaf was next and his testimony was virtually identical to Armstrong's. Burch railed at the officer and tried to paint him as the perpetrator, a man of the law preying on young ladies who were only serving drinks and doing their jobs.

The next four witnesses were also off-duty policemen and deputies, and by noon the questions and answers were monotonous. There was no doubt that Carousel was a hotbed of prostitution. Before recessing for lunch, Chief Deputy Kilgore arrived in the courtroom and explained to Judge Baker that Sheriff Bowman had been called away on pressing matters and was out of town. Kilgore was grilled about the failure to serve the subpoenas, routine matters in Baker's opinion. He handed the five subpoenas to Kilgore and ordered him to serve them on the "waitresses" immediately. He promised to do so, and the hearing was adjourned until the following morning.

It was not clear whether the deputies actually went to the nightclub in search of the witnesses, but at 9 A.M. the next day Kilgore reported that none of the five was still working at Carousel. To add to the confusion, the names on the subpoenas were aliases. The girls were gone.

This angered Judge Baker but no one was surprised. Joshua Burch called Ginger Redfield to the stand, and she calmly denied any wrongdoing at her club. She was a smooth liar and explained that she did not tolerate prostitution and had never seen any evidence of it.

Jesse was itching to cross-examine her, his first real shot at a crime boss. He asked her to repeat her testimony about prostitution at Carousel, which she did. He reminded her that she was under oath and asked if she understood that perjury was another crime. Joshua Burch objected loudly and Judge Baker sustained the objection. Jesse asked her about the five waitresses and tried to elicit their real names. Ginger claimed that she didn't know because the "ladies" often used fake names. He grilled her about her record-keeping and she had no choice but to admit that the girls were paid in cash with nothing on the books. She explained that the waitresses came and went, that her workforce was unstable at best, and that she had no idea where the five had gone.

Jesse then questioned her about gambling at Carousel and she again claimed to know nothing of it. No slots, poker, blackjack, no craps or roulette tables. Burch objected to that line of questioning and reminded the court that the alleged nuisance was prostitution. The DA had put on no proof of gambling. Judge Baker agreed and told Jesse to move on. The cross-exam lasted for two hours and was at times contentious, as both lawyers argued back and forth while the witness kept her cool and at times even seemed amused. Judge Baker tried to referee the fight but lost patience. Through it all, it became evident that he didn't believe a word the witness said and had no tolerance for the illicit activities at her nightclub.

The hearing ended before lunch. Both sides expected Judge Baker to take the matter under advisement and mull it over for a few days. He surprised them, though, with a ruling from the bench. He declared Carousel to be a nuisance and ordered it closed immediately and permanently.

Its doors were shut for a week before Joshua Burch filed a notice of appeal and posted a $10,000 bond. The law allowed it to reopen pending appeal, a lengthy process.

Jesse won the battle but the war was far from over. It proved how difficult it would be to fight the nightclub owners. With no help from the local police or Fats Bowman, law enforcement was of little use. Using honest cops from other towns would be time-consuming and risky. Plus, the hookers were hard to catch—no one knew their real names and they could vanish at a moment's notice.

CHAPTER 25

The way Lance figured things, if his business could survive the loss of gambling revenues brought on by the nosy state liquor board, and then the worst hurricane in history, it could certainly survive a new hotshot district attorney. The Carousel affair spooked him and the other owners, but after a few weeks the girls returned, as did their customers. He had the clever idea of requiring "club membership" of the regulars. The doors were open to anyone wanting to drink, dance, and watch the strippers, but if a gentleman desired something more he had to show his membership card. And, in order to get one, he had to be known to the bouncers, bartenders, and managers. The rule slowed the traffic somewhat, but it also made undercover work virtually impossible. Lance had enlarged photos of the six cops sent in by Jesse Rudy to infiltrate Carousel and later to testify. They were tacked to the walls in his clubs' kitchens and the employees were on the lookout. A clean-cut stranger under the age of fifty had at least three sets of eyes on him before he reached the bar and ordered a drink.

The screening worked so well that everyone else followed suit. Before long, a few of the club owners felt so secure they reopened their casinos, but for members only.

———•———

Any sense of security, though, got rattled again when the DA made his next move. Jesse convened his grand jury in secret and presented four of the six officers who had testified in the Carousel trial. By unanimous vote, the grand jury indicted Ginger Redfield on four counts of promoting prostitution by "knowingly enticing, causing, persuading, or encouraging another person to become a prostitute," and "having control over a place and intentionally permitting another person to use said place for prostitution." The maximum penalty for each count was a fine of $5,000 and ten years in prison, or both.

Jesse took the sealed indictment to the chambers of Judge Oliphant and asked him to read it. He needed a favor. The law required the defendant to be personally served with a copy of the indictment, but Fats Bowman could not be counted on. Judge Oliphant called the sheriff, who was notoriously hard to find, and was told the boss was out of town. Chief Deputy Kilgore was running the office that morning and the judge asked him to stop by his chambers immediately. When he arrived half an hour later, Jesse handed him the indictment. Judge Oliphant ordered him to serve it on Ginger Redfield, arrest her, and take her to the jail. Bail was set at $15,000.

———•———

Joshua Burch was at his desk when the call came from Ginger. In a voice that was remarkably calm, she described being arrested at her office at O'Malley's, handcuffed even, led by Kilgore to his patrol car, placed in the rear seat, and driven to the jail where they processed her, took her mug shot, and put her in the only cell for women. It was quite humiliating, but she seemed unfazed.

Burch took off for the jail, smiling all the way at the prospect of another high-profile case. He could almost see the headlines.

Ginger was waiting in a small room where the attorneys met with their clients. She had refused to change into the standard orange jumpsuit and was still wearing a dress and heels. Burch read the indictment with a grim face, and said, "This is nothing but trouble."

"Is that the best you can do? Of course it's trouble. Otherwise I wouldn't be sitting here in jail. When can you get me out?"

"Soon. I've already called a bondsman. How fast can you get a thousand bucks in cash?"

"My brother's on the way."

"Good. I'll get you out in a few hours."

She lit a cigarette and took a long drag. Burch knew her well enough to believe she had ice water in her veins. During the Carousel hearing she had never appeared nervous and at times seemed amused by the proceedings. She slowly blew more smoke and said, "Rudy might have a good case, right?"

A damned good case. The six undercover cops would testify and do a convincing job. Burch had seen them under pressure and knew they would have credibility with any jury. Add the fact that Carousel had been declared a nuisance for its prostitution, and, yes, Jesse Rudy definitely had the upper hand.

But Burch said, "We'll put up a good fight. We'll get the girls in line and have them prepped. I don't lose many cases, Ginger."

"Well, you can't lose this one because I'm not going to prison."

"We'll talk about that later. Right now let's get you out."

"I've just spent two hours in a cell back there and it's not for me. My husband has been locked up for six years and is not doing well. Promise me, Joshua, that I won't go to prison."

"I can't make that promise. I never do. But you've hired the best and we'll put up a strong defense."

"When will I go to trial?"

"Months from now, maybe a year. We'll have plenty of time."

"Just get me out."

Burch left the jail and drove to Red Velvet where he met with Lance Malco and described the indictment. Lance was stunned at first, then his shock quickly turned to anger. When he cooled down somewhat, he said, "I guess he can indict all of us, right?"

"Yes, in theory. The grand jury is usually a rubber stamp for the DA. But I wouldn't expect it."

"And why not?"

"He'll probably use Ginger as the test case. If he can convict her, then he'll look around. As you know, there's no shortage of potential defendants."

"That son of a bitch is out of control."

"No, Lance, I'd say he's very much in control. He has enormous power and can indict almost anyone. Convicting, though, is another matter. It's a huge gamble on his part because if he loses, then he'll have to go back to chasing car thieves."

"You can't let him win, Burch."

"Trust me."

"I do, always have."

"Thanks. In the meantime, shut it down. No gambling, no hookers."

"We're not gambling, you know that."

"Yes, but there's plenty of it going on."

"I can't control the other clubs."

"You won't have to. When they hear about Ginger's arrest, they'll get in line, and quickly. Put out the word that there's no gambling and no girls for the next six months."

"That's exactly what Rudy wants, right?"

"Take a break. Play it straight. You've been in the business long enough to know that the demand always comes back."

"I don't know, Burch. Change is in the air. Now we have a cocky DA who likes to see his name in print."

"The best advice I can give you is don't do anything stupid."

Lance finally smiled as he waved him off.

———•———

Late that afternoon, Lance and Hugh left the Strip and drove north into Stone County. Hugh was behind the wheel, back at his old job after a stint on a freighter and another one on an offshore oil rig, both arranged by his father. The jobs convinced him he was unfit for honest labor. Lance had been merciless with his scolding for the jewelry store heists and promised that one more screwup would land the boy either out of the family business or in prison, or both. Hugh had readily given up his dreams of arms dealing and easily fell back into his old routines of pool hustling, beer drinking, and checking on his convenience stores.

They weaved through the piney woods and parked in front of Fats's hunting cabin. Kilgore was grilling steaks on the deck and Fats was already into the bourbon.

It was time to discuss what to do about Jesse Rudy.

CHAPTER 26

As the assistant district attorney, Egan Clement was assigned by her boss to investigate seven unsolved murders that occurred between 1966 and 1971. Five of them were thought to be gang-related because the victims were involved, at some level, with organized crime. Periodically, the turf battles erupted and one killing led to the inevitable payback. Fats Bowman had a deputy he considered to be his chief investigator, but he was untrained and inexperienced, primarily because the sheriff had little interest in wasting manpower trying to solve gangland killings. The reality was that the cases were cold and no one was digging.

After Jesse was sworn in, it took five months to get a look at the sheriff department's files. For murders, they were quite thin and revealed little. He also badgered the state police for assistance, but confirmed what he had expected—Harrison County was the domain of Fats Bowman, and the State preferred to avoid it. Likewise, the FBI had not been involved. The murders, as well as the plethora of other criminal activity, involved state statutes, not federal.

Egan was particularly bothered by the murder of Dusty Cromwell. His death was no great loss to society, but the manner in which it happened was galling. He had been gunned down on a public beach, on a warm, sunny afternoon, less than a mile from the Biloxi lighthouse. At least a dozen witnesses heard the crack from the rifle shot, though no one saw the gunman. A family—mother, father, and two children—were within forty feet of Dusty when half his head was blown off, and they saw the carnage as his girlfriend screamed for help.

The sheriff department's file had plenty of gory photographs, along with an autopsy report that concluded with the obvious. Witnesses gave statements in which they recounted what they saw, which was little more than a man killed instantly by a single bullet to the head. A brief bio of Cromwell gave the details of a thug with a shady past and three felony convictions. His club, Surf Club, had been torched and he had sworn revenge against Lance Malco, Ginger Redfield, and others, though the others were not named. In short, Dusty had managed to make some fearsome enemies in his short career as a mobster.

Jesse was convinced Lance Malco was behind the murder. Egan agreed, and their theory, or rather their speculation, was that Lance used Mike Savage, a known arsonist, to torch Surf Club. Cromwell retaliated by killing Savage and cutting off his ear. Cromwell then hired someone to take out Lance and the hit was almost a success. The bullet with his name on it barely missed, shattered his windshield, and peppered him and Nevin Noll with bits of glass. Convinced his life was on the line, Lance hired a contract killer to take care of Dusty.

It was an interesting story and quite plausible, but thoroughly beyond proof.

The state's death penalty statute made contract killing a capital offense, punishable by death in the gas chamber at Parchman prison. Lance and his gang had killed several men and there was no reason to stop. They had proven to be immune from prosecution. Only Nevin Noll had been charged and arrested. His murder of Earl Fortier ten years earlier in Pascagoula had landed him in a trial, but he walked away a free man when the jury found him not guilty.

As the district attorney, it was Jesse's sworn duty to prosecute all felonies, regardless of who committed them or how despicable the victims might have been. He wasn't afraid of Lance Malco and his thugs, and he would indict them all when and if he had the proof. But finding it seemed impossible.

With no help from the police at any level, Jesse decided to get his hands dirty. The criminals he was after played a deadly game with no rules and no conscience. To catch a thief, he needed to hire a thief.

The runner's name was Haley Stofer. He was driving carefully along Highway 90, obeying all the laws, when a roadblock suddenly appeared in front of him just west of Bay St. Louis. The sheriff of Hancock County had received a tip and wanted to have a chat with Stofer. In his trunk they found eighty pounds of marijuana. According to the tipster, Stofer worked for a trafficker in New Orleans and was making a run to Mobile. During his second day in the county jail, Stofer's lawyer broke the news that he was looking at thirty years in prison.

Jesse informed the lawyer that he would push hard for the maximum sentence and there would be no plea deal. Drugs were pouring in from South America, everyone was alarmed. Harsh laws were being passed. Tough action was needed to protect society.

Stofer was twenty-seven years old, single, and couldn't fathom the idea of spending the next three decades locked away. He had already served three years in Louisiana for stealing cars and preferred life on the outside. For a month he sat and waited in a hot jail cell for some movement in his case. The traffickers in New Orleans paid for a lawyer who did little except warn him to keep his mouth shut or else. Another month passed and he remained silent.

He was surprised one day when he was handcuffed and taken back to the small, cramped room where the lawyers came to visit. His lawyer wasn't there but the district attorney was. They had glared at each other briefly in court during the preliminary hearing.

Jesse said, "Got a few minutes?"

"I guess. Where's my lawyer?"

"I don't know. Cigarette?"

"No thanks."

Jesse lit one and seemed in no hurry. "The grand jury meets

tomorrow and you'll be indicted for all those charges we discussed in court."

"Yes sir."

"You can either plead guilty or go to trial, doesn't really matter, because you'll get thirty years anyway."

"Yes sir."

"You ever met anyone who's served time in Parchman prison?"

"Yes sir. Met a guy in Angola who served time there."

"I'm sure he was happy to be out of there."

"Yes sir. Said it's the worst place in the country."

"I can't imagine spending thirty years there, can you?"

"Look, Mr. Rudy, if you're thinking about offering me some kind of deal where you'll knock off a few years if I squeal on my colleagues, then the answer is no. I don't care where you send me, they'll have my throat cut within two years. I know them. You don't."

"Not at all. I'm thinking about a different gang. And a different deal that involves no time behind bars. Zero. You walk out, never look back."

Stofer studied his feet, then frowned at Jesse. "Okay, I'm thoroughly confused."

"You drive through Biloxi often?"

"Yes sir. It's been my route."

"Ever stop at the nightclubs?"

"Sure. Cold beer, plenty of girls."

"Well, the clubs are operated by a gang of criminals. Ever hear of the Dixie Mafia?"

"Sure. There were stories about them in prison, but I don't know much."

"It's sort of a loosely organized bunch of bad boys that began settling around here twenty years ago. With time, they took over the clubs and offered booze, gambling, girls, even drugs. And they're still very much in business. Camille blew them all away but they came right back. Gangsters, thieves, pimps, crooks, arsonists, they even have their own hit men. Left behind a lot of dead bodies."

"Where's this going?"

"I want you to go to work for them."

"Sounds like a great group."

"As opposed to your drug traffickers?"

"With a criminal record, I have trouble finding work, Mr. Rudy. I've tried."

"That's no excuse for running drugs."

"I'm not making excuses. Why would I want to work for these boys?"

"To avoid thirty years in prison. You really have no choice."

Stofer ran his fingers through his thick, shoulder-length hair. "Can I have that cigarette?"

Jesse handed him one and lit it.

Stofer said, "Seems like my lawyer should be in on this."

"Fire your lawyer. I can't trust him. Nobody knows about this deal, Stofer. Only the two of us. Get rid of your lawyer or he'll just screw things up."

Blue smoke boiled from both nostrils as the defendant emptied his lungs. He blew the remnants and said, "I really don't like him either."

"He's a crook."

"I gotta think about this, Mr. Rudy. It's pretty overwhelming."

"You got twenty-four hours. I'll be back tomorrow and we'll read the indictment together, though you probably know what's coming."

"Yes sir."

The next day, at the same table, Jesse handed Stofer his indictment. He read it slowly, the pain obvious in his face. Thirty years was inconceivable. No one could survive three decades at Parchman.

When he finished, he laid it on the table and asked, "Got a cigarette?"

Both lit up. Jesse glanced at his watch as if he had better things to do. "Yes or no?"

"I don't have a choice, do I?"

"Not really. Fire your lawyer and we'll get down to business."

"I've already fired him."

Jesse smiled and said, "Smart move. I'll take this indictment and hide it in a drawer. Maybe we'll never see it again. You screw up or double-cross me, and off you go. If you get real smart and run away, there's an eighty percent chance you'll eventually get caught. I'll add ten years and I'll guarantee you right now that you'll serve every minute of a forty-year sentence, with hard labor."

"I ain't running."

"Good boy." Jesse reached down, picked up a small grocery sack, and placed it on the table. "Your stuff. Car keys, wallet, wrist-watch, almost two hundred bucks in cash. Go to Biloxi, settle in, hang around two joints, Red Velvet and Foxy's, get a job."

"Doing what?"

"Washing dishes, sweeping floors, making up the beds, I don't care. Work hard, listen even harder, and watch what you say. Try to get a promotion to bartender. Those guys see and hear it all."

"What's my cover?"

"Don't need one. You're Haley Stofer, age twenty-seven, from Gretna, Louisiana. New Orleans kid. Looking for work. Got a criminal record, something they'll admire. Don't mind getting your hands dirty."

"And what am I looking for?"

"Nothing but a job. Once inside, you keep your head low and your ears open. You're a criminal, Stofer, you figure it out."

"How do I report to you?"

"My office is in the Harrison County Courthouse in Biloxi, second floor. Be there at eight A.M. sharp on the first and third Mondays of every month. Don't call ahead. Don't tell anyone where you're going. Don't introduce yourself to anybody in the office. I'll be waiting and we'll have a cup of coffee."

"And the sheriff here?"

"Drive off and don't look back. I've fed him a line. He's good for now."

"I guess I should say thanks, Mr. Rudy."

"Not yet. Never forget, Stofer, that these guys'll kill you in an instant. Never drop your guard."

CHAPTER 27

In May of 1973, Jesse and Agnes, along with their two daughters, Laura and Beverly, made the six-hour drive from Biloxi to Oxford for a weekend celebration. Keith was graduating from law school at Ole Miss, with honors, and the family was rightfully proud. As with most classes, the top students were headed to the larger cities—Jackson, Memphis, New Orleans, maybe even Atlanta—to work by the hour in big firms that represented corporations. The second tier generally stayed in-state and worked for smaller firms specializing in insurance defense. The majority of the graduates went home, where they joined the family firm, or knew someone in an office on the courthouse square, or gamely hung out a shingle and declared themselves ready to sue.

From the first day of classes, Keith knew where he was going and never bothered with a single interview. He loved Biloxi, worshipped his father, and was excited about helping build Rudy & Pettigrew into an important firm on the Coast. He studied hard, at least for the first two years, because he found the law fascinating. During his third year, though, he fell for a brunette undergrad named Ainsley and found her far more interesting. She was only twenty, younger than both Laura and Beverly, and with two more years of college she and Keith were not looking forward to a long-distance romance.

The spring graduation was a time of law school class reunions, alumni gatherings, judicial conferences, bar committee meetings, and parties and dinners. The campus and town seemed choked with lawyers. Since Jesse had not attended Ole Miss, but rather had pursued the more challenging route of night school at Loyola, he felt somewhat like an outsider. He was pleasantly surprised, though, at the number of judges and lawyers who recognized his name and wanted to shake his hand. Barely a year and a half in office, he had received more attention than he'd realized.

Over drinks, several lawyers joked with him about cleaning up the Coast. Don't get too carried away, they deadpanned. For years they had enjoyed sneaking away for a night or two of fun. Jesse laughed along with their silliness, more determined than ever to resume his war.

After Sunday's cap-and-gown ceremony, the cameras came out. In every shot of Keith, with his family and friends, Ainsley was by his side.

Driving home, Jesse and Agnes were convinced they had just spent the weekend with their future daughter-in-law. Laura found her adorable. Beverly was more amused by how smitten their big brother was with the girl. The romance was his first serious one and he had fallen hard.

———•———

When Joshua Burch had finally emptied his impressive bag of delaying tactics, and when Judge Nelson Oliphant had finally had enough of said tactics, the matter of the *State of Mississippi v. Ginger Eileen Redfield* was set for trial. Jesse's patience had gone out the window months earlier and he was barely speaking to Mr. Burch, though he considered it unprofessional to bicker and pout with opposing lawyers. He was the district attorney, the representative of the State, and it was incumbent upon him to at least strive to behave better than the rest.

On a Wednesday afternoon, Judge Oliphant summoned Mr. Rudy and Mr. Burch to his chambers and handed them the list of prospective jurors he and the circuit clerk had just finished compiling. It had sixty names, all registered voters in Harrison County.

Fully aware of the defendant's background in the underworld and the crowd she ran with, Judge Oliphant was concerned with protecting his pool from "outside influences." He lectured both lawyers on the pitfalls of jury tampering and threatened harsh sanctions if he caught wind of improper contact. Jesse took the lecture in stride because he knew he wasn't the target. Burch absorbed it too without objection. He knew his client and her ilk were capable of anything. He promised to warn her.

Two hours later, Deputy Kilgore parked behind Red Velvet, entered through an infamous yellow door that was partially hidden by some old shipping crates, and hurried to Malco's office.

In the haste to rebuild after Camille, the contractor misread the floor plans and installed a door that was not called for. However, it proved invaluable as it became the secret passage for upstanding men who didn't want to be seen coming and going through the front door of the club. To visit their favorite girls, they parked in the rear and used the yellow door.

Kilgore tossed a copy of the jury list onto Lance's desk. "Sixty names. Fats says he knows at least half of them."

Lance grabbed the list and studied each name without a word. As a quiet businessman, he avoided the public and rarely made an effort to meet a stranger. He had long since accepted the reality that most people viewed him as shady and dishonest, and he didn't care as long as the money rolled in. He was wealthier than all but a handful on the Coast. The only gathering Lance attended was Mass every Sunday.

He checked off six names that looked familiar.

Kilgore recognized fifteen. He said, "You know, I've lived here over forty years and think I know a lot of people, but every time I get one of these jury lists I feel like a stranger."

As Joshua Burch had labored through his maneuvers and delays, he and Lance and Ginger became convinced that her trial was a crucial showdown with Jesse Rudy. He had already won the nuisance case, though it was on appeal and Carousel was busier than ever. But it was still a major victory for him, especially if the Mississippi Supreme Court affirmed the chancellor's ruling and forced the club to close. A criminal conviction for running a brothel would put Ginger in prison, close her clubs, and embolden Rudy to use the same statute to indict and prosecute others.

Though the owners were a ragtag, disorganized gang of crooks who competed against each other, despised each other, and often fought each other, there were moments when Lance could command some respect and get the others to follow for their own good. The trial of Ginger Redfield was that moment.

Copies of the list went out. By nine o'clock that evening, the owner of every nightclub, bar, pool hall, and strip joint had the list and was asking about names.

———•———

The first two witnesses called by the State were Chuck Armstrong and Dennis Greenleaf, the same two off-duty policemen who had testified in the nuisance case ten months earlier. They had gone to Carousel, bought drinks for Marlene and another girl, had more drinks, then negotiated a price for an upstairs visit. They observed other waitresses hustling johns and there was plenty of traffic in and out of the bar. They watched several men do the same thing they had done, except the other guys left with the girls.

Both witnesses had been grilled by Joshua Burch before, and they had been thoroughly prepped by Jesse Rudy. They held their own and stayed cool and professional when Burch accused them of procuring prostitutes and trying to lead young ladies astray.

Jesse kept one eye on the jury as Burch railed away. Eight men, four women, all white. Three Baptists, three Catholics, two Methodists, two Pentecostals, and two outright sinners who claimed no church affiliation. Most of them seemed amused by Burch's overly dramatic insinuation that the officers were corrupting the naive waitresses. Everyone within a hundred miles of the courthouse knew the reputations of the nightclubs. They had heard the stories for years.

Keith's job was to take notes, watch the jurors, and try to keep an eye on the crowd behind him. The courtroom was about half full and he did not see another club owner. At some point, though, during the testimony of Greenleaf, he glanced around and was surprised to see Hugh Malco sitting in the back row. They made eye contact, then both looked away nonchalantly as if neither cared what the other was doing. Hugh's hair was longer and he was growing a mustache. He looked thicker in the chest, and Keith thought it was because of too much beer in the pool halls. They had come a long way since 1960 and their glory years as all-stars, and the divide between them was deep and permanent.

But, in spite of their radically different paths, Keith, if only for a second, had a soft spot for his old buddy.

After the morning recess, Jesse called two more officers to the stand, and their testimony was similar to the first two. More of the same pickup routines but with different girls. More promises of sex at fifty dollars a half hour, double that for sixty minutes.

As Burch went through another performance on cross-examination, Jesse took notes and watched the jurors. Number eight was a man named Nunzio, age forty-three, alleged Methodist, and he seemed detached from the trial, with the odd habit of staring at either the ceiling or his shoes.

Keith, who was not about to miss the excitement, sat in a chair along the bar, behind his father. He passed up a note that read: *number 8, Nunzio, not listening, acting weird. Mind's already made up??*

Lunch was a quick sandwich in the conference room of the law office. Egan Clement was concerned about juror number three, Mr. Dewey, an older gentleman prone to nodding off. At least half the jury, especially the Baptists and Pentecostals, were all in and eager to strike a blow for righteous living. The other half was more difficult to read.

In the afternoon, Jesse finished the State's case with the remaining two undercover officers. Their testimony varied little from the first four, and by the time Burch finished haranguing them, the words "prostitute" and "prostitution" had been bandied about so much, there was little doubt the defendant's nightclub wasn't much more than a regular whorehouse.

At 3:00 P.M., the State rested. Joshua Burch wasted no time in calling his star witness. When Marlene took the stand and swore to tell the truth, she had never looked plainer. Real name of Marlene Hitchcock, age twenty-four, now living in Prattville, Alabama. Her cotton dress was loose-fitting, covered every inch of her chest, and fell well below her knees. Her shoes were plain sandals, something her grandmother might wear. Her face was untouched by makeup, with only a light layer of pink gloss on her lips. She had never worn glasses but Burch found her a pair, and peeking from behind the round frames she could have been a school librarian.

Sitting in the third row and watching now that they were finished, Chuck Armstrong and Dennis Greenleaf barely recognized her.

In a carefully rehearsed back-and-forth, Burch led her through testimony that revealed a tough life: forced to drop out of high school, first marriage to a real loser, low-wage jobs until she arrived in Biloxi four years earlier and got a job serving drinks at Carousel. She had never (1) offered herself for sex, (2) suggested sex to a customer, (3) observed other girls hustling for sex, (4) heard of any rooms upstairs where there might be sex, and so on. A complete, total, and smoothly delivered stonewalling of any talk of sex activities at Carousel. She admired "Miss Ginger" greatly and enjoyed working for her.

Her testimony was so blatantly false that it was oddly believable. No decent human being would take an oath, on a Bible no less, then proceed to launch themselves into such unrestrained lying.

Jesse began his cross pleasantly with a discussion of her payroll adventures. She admitted she worked only for cash tips and reported none of it. There were no deductions for pesky things like taxes, withholding for Social Security, or unemployment insurance. She suddenly began crying as she described how hard it was to make and save a few bucks to send home to her mother, who just happened to be raising Marlene's child, a three-year-old little girl.

If Jesse wanted to score points portraying her as a tax cheat, he failed. The jurors, especially the men, seemed sympathetic. Even dressed down and plain-faced, she was a pretty woman, with a twinkle in her eye when she wasn't crying. The men in the jury box were paying attention.

Jesse moved on to the sex talk, but got nowhere. She flatly denied any suggestion of being in that business. When he probed too hard, she startled everyone by snapping, "I am not a prostitute, Mr. Rudy!"

He wasn't sure how to handle her. The issue was, after all, rather delicate. How does one question the sex life of another, in open court?

Burch smelled blood and moved in. He called five consecutive witnesses, the same five waitresses who had been accused by the undercover officers, and the same five who had vanished from the Coast during the nuisance trial. He put them on the stand. No tight clothing, no short skirts, no teased hair, no mascara, no bleach-blond dye jobs, no jewelry, no flashy hooker's heels. Taken together, the six could have passed themselves off as a young women's choir during Wednesday night prayer meeting.

They sang the praises of Miss Ginger and what a wonderful employer she was. She ran a tight ship, did not tolerate drunks and troublemakers, and protected her girls. Sure, some of the others, the strippers, were up there onstage doing their thing. They were the draw, the girls the boys came to see. But they were untouchable and that was part of the attraction.

Two of the waitresses admitted to dating customers, but only when off-duty. Another of Miss Ginger's many rules. One romance lasted a few months.

The four women on the jury saw through the charade and lost

interest. The men were harder to read. Joe Nunzio liked Marlene but soon grew interested in his shoes again. Mr. Dewey had napped through most of the previous testimony, but the ladies held his attention and he followed every word.

By noon of the second day, Burch had portrayed Carousel as virtually a kid-friendly place with wholesome fun for the entire family.

After lunch, he continued his defense with more of the same. Four more ladies came forth and gave similar testimony. They were just hardworking girls serving drinks, trying to make a living. Little of their testimony could be verified. Since no records existed, they could testify to anything, and there was nothing Jesse could do about it. He tried to pin down their names, current addresses, ages, and dates of employment, but even that was difficult.

During a long afternoon recess, Judge Oliphant suggested to Burch that perhaps they had heard enough. Burch said he had more witnesses, more waitresses, but agreed that the jurors were getting tired.

"Will the defendant testify?" Oliphant asked.

"No sir, she will not."

While Jesse was eager to engage Ginger in a lengthy cross-examination, he was not surprised with Burch's response. During the nuisance trial, she had been cool and calm on the witness stand, but Jesse had not hammered away at her past. With a jury watching, he was confident he could rattle her and trick her into a bad answer. Burch was concerned enough to keep her off the stand. Besides, it was usually a bad idea to allow the defendant to testify.

Judge Oliphant was suffering low back pain and taking medication that often meddled with his alertness, and he needed a break. He adjourned until the following morning.

As they walked to Jesse's car in the lot next to the courthouse, he saw something stuck behind a windshield wiper. It was a small white envelope, unmarked. He took it, got in, as did Egan. Keith, ever the rookie, got in the rear seat. Jesse opened the envelope and removed a small white notecard. Someone had written: *Joe Nunzio got $2000 cash to vote not guilty.*

He gave it to Egan, who read it and handed it over her shoulder. They drove in silence to the law office, cleared out the conference room, and closed the doors.

The first question was whether to tell Judge Oliphant. The note could be a joke, a plant, a prank. Of course, it could also be the truth, but without more proof Oliphant was unlikely to do much. He could quiz each juror individually and try to gauge Nunzio's body language. But, if he'd taken the money he was not likely to confess.

As always, there were two alternate jurors. If Nunzio was excused, the trial would go on.

Jesse could demand a mistrial, a rare move for the State. If granted, everyone would go home and they would try the case again another day. He doubted, though, that Judge Oliphant would grant one. Mistrials were for defendants, not prosecutors.

After brainstorming for two hours, Jesse decided to do nothing. The jury would get the case early the next morning and they would soon know what, if anything, Nunzio was up to.

———— • ————

Jesse began his closing argument with a rousing condemnation of the defendant, Miss Ginger, and her house of ill repute. He pitted the testimony of six dedicated law enforcement officers, undercover and in plain clothes, against that of a veritable parade of loose women who also presented themselves to the jury in plain clothes. Imagine what they looked like when they hustled customers and offered them sex.

Burch was up to the task and railed against the cops for sneaking into Carousel with the sole intent of "entrapping" the waitresses into bad behavior. Sure the ladies came from rougher backgrounds and broken homes, but it wasn't their fault. They were given jobs by the goodness of his client, Miss Ginger, and were well paid for serving drinks.

While Burch paced back and forth like a veteran stage actor, Jesse watched the jurors. It was the only moment in the trial when he could study them full-on without worrying about getting caught sneaking a glance. Joe Nunzio had refused to make eye contact with Jesse during his final summation, but he was watching Burch closely.

The majority of the jurors would vote guilty, but the law required a unanimous verdict, either for guilt or innocence. Anything in between would be declared a hung jury, a mistrial, and would possibly lead to another go at it a few months down the road.

The jury retired to its deliberations shortly before 11:00 A.M., and Judge Oliphant adjourned until further notice. At 3:00, his clerk walked down the hall to Jesse's office and informed him that there was no verdict. At 5:30, the jurors were excused for the evening. There was no indication of which way they might be leaning.

At 9:00 A.M., Judge Oliphant called the courtroom to order and asked the foreman, Mr. Threadgill, how things were going. It was obvious from his face and body language that they were having no fun. His Honor sent them back to work and almost scolded them by saying he was expecting a verdict. The morning dragged on with no news from the jury room. When the judge adjourned for lunch, he asked the lawyers to meet in his chambers. When they were seated, he nodded at the bailiff, who opened the door and escorted Mr. Threadgill into the room. The judge politely asked him to take a seat.

"I take it there's not much progress."

Mr. Threadgill shook his head and looked frustrated. "No sir. I'm afraid we've reached a dead end."

"What's the split?"

"Nine to three. Been that way since yesterday afternoon and everyone's dug in. We're wasting our time, yours too, I guess. Sorry about this, Judge, but it's no use."

Oliphant breathed deeply and exhaled with noise. Like every judge, he hated mistrials because they were failures, nothing but failures that wasted hundreds of hours and necessitated doing it all over again. He looked at Mr. Threadgill and said, "Thank you. Why don't you have your lunch and we'll reconvene at one thirty?"

"Yes sir."

At 1:30, the jury was led back into the courtroom. Judge Oliphant addressed them and said, "I have been informed that you are deadlocked and not making progress. I'm going to ask each one of you the same question, and all I want is a yes or no response. Nothing else. Juror number one, Mrs. Barnes, do you believe this jury can reach a unanimous decision in the matter?"

"No sir," she replied with no hesitation.

No one hesitated and it was indeed unanimous. Further efforts would be a waste of time.

Judge Oliphant accepted the obvious and said, "Thank you. I have no choice but to declare a mistrial. Mr. Rudy and Mr. Burch, you have fifteen days for post-trial motions. We are adjourned."

CHAPTER 28

Two days after the mistrial, Jesse made an appointment with Judge Oliphant. Their offices were on the same floor, two hundred feet apart, with the courtroom in between, and they saw each other often, though they avoided giving the appearance of being too friendly. Most meetings were arranged through secretaries and scheduled on calendars. Their favorite was a late Friday afternoon bourbon or two when everyone else cleared out for the weekend.

After the judge poured two cups of black coffee, Jesse handed over the note he found on his windshield. Long thick wrinkles layered across the judge's forehead and he mouthed the words at least three times. "Why didn't you tell me about this?"

"I thought about it and I wasn't sure what to do. It could've been a prank for all I know."

"I'm afraid not." Oliphant handed the note back and frowned at the table.

"What do you know?"

"I talked to the bailiff, as I always do. They hear a lot. Joe Nunzio was fiercely opposed to a conviction and said as much during the trial, during recesses. He was warned to stay quiet until deliberations, but he let it be known that he thought the prosecution was being unfair to Ginger. He was never going to vote for guilt, and he managed to persuade two others to go along with him."

"So, he took some cash?"

"More than likely." He rubbed his thinning hair and looked almost pale. "I can't believe this, Jesse. Almost thirty years on the bench and I've never seen this before."

"Jury tampering is rare, Judge, but it happens. We shouldn't be surprised given the number of outlaws around here. The problem is proving it."

"You have a plan?"

"Yes. I'm not pushing for a retrial until the supreme court decides the nuisance case. If we win that, then I'll hound Ginger until I get her back in the courtroom and in front of a jury. In the meantime, I'll scare the hell out of Joe Nunzio."

"Paul Dewey and Chick Hutchinson are the other two. But you didn't hear it from me."

"As always, Your Honor, I heard nothing from you."

———•———

The mistrial calmed the Strip like a gin martini. Carousel was still open. Ginger had kicked ass in court, walked out free as a bird, and was back at her desk. The hotshot DA with all of his lofty promises was flaming out, just another fading reformer.

Within days, the working girls were back in the nightclubs offering their services, but for members only.

Stofer reported to Jesse that as soon as the trial was over, it was as if someone flipped a switch and let the good times roll. He had heard other clubs had installed slots and tables and quietly reopened their casinos.

After three months at Red Velvet, Stofer was slowly fitting in. He started as a janitor, with the unpleasant job of reporting each morning at dawn to clean and mop the dance floors, wipe down the tables, chairs, and collect broken bottles and discarded cans. He worked a ten-hour shift, six days a week, and left each afternoon before the happy hour rush. He never missed a day, was never late for work, and said little but heard as much as possible. After a month, he'd moved to the kitchen when two cooks quit and help was needed.

He was paid in cash and, as far as he knew, there were no

records of his employment. The manager had asked if he had a criminal record, and he said yes. For stealing cars. This did not bother the manager in the least, but Stofer was warned to stay away from the cash registers. He kept his head down, his nose clean, and worked overtime whenever he was asked. He found a library book on mixology and memorized every type of booze and every drink, though such knowledge was rarely needed at Foxy's. He made no friends at work and kept his personal life to himself.

He had no gossip or inside info to report. Jesse was pleased with his progress and told him to continue on course. As soon as possible, get in a few hours behind the bar where he could see and hear much more.

———•———

For his new role, Gene Pettigrew wore starched khakis, a wrinkled navy blazer, and pointed-toe cowboy boots, an ensemble he would never try around the office. In his four years as one of Jesse's partners, he and his brother Gage had been in more courtrooms than most lawyers under the age of thirty. They were still fighting insurance companies and usually winning. They had honed their litigation skills, and with Jesse cracking the whip from his other office, they were gaining reputations as aggressive trial lawyers.

Now, though, Jesse needed a favor, a bit of undercover work.

Gene found Joe Nunzio where he worked selling auto parts at a store in Gulfport. He was behind the counter, checking a sheet of inventory, when Gene approached with a smile and said in a low voice, "I'm with the district attorney's office. Got a minute?" He handed over a business card, a new one with a new name designed for his new role. Gene had no training as an investigator but the job couldn't be that complicated. Jesse could hire whoever he wanted, pay for his business cards, and give him whatever title and name he chose.

Nunzio glanced around, smiled, and asked, "What's going on?"

"Ten minutes is all I need."

"Well, I'm busy right now."

"So am I. Look, we can step outside and have a chat, or I'll stop by your house tonight. Eight-one-six Devon Street, right, on the Point?"

They went outside and stood between two parked cars. "What the hell is this?" Nunzio growled.

"Relax, okay?"

"Are you a cop or something?"

"Or something. No, I'm not a cop. I'm an investigator for the district attorney, Mr. Jesse Rudy."

"I know who the DA is."

"Okay, off to a good start. He and the judge, you remember Judge Oliphant, right?"

"Yep."

"Well, the DA and the judge are curious about the verdict two weeks ago in the Ginger Redfield case. They suspect the jury was tampered with. You do understand jury tampering, right?"

"You accusing me?"

"No, don't be so touchy. I simply asked if you understand jury tampering."

"I suppose."

"It's when someone outside the courtroom tries to influence a decision by the jury. Could be by threat, coercion, extortion, or old-fashioned bribery. That happens, you know? Someone might offer a juror something like, say, two thousand dollars cash to vote not guilty. I know it's hard to believe, but it happens. And the bad part is that both parties are guilty. The guy who paid the bribe and the juror who took it. Ten years in prison, fine of five thousand dollars."

"I think you're accusing me of something."

Gene looked deep into his nervous and troubled eyes and said, "Well, I think you look guilty. Anyway, Mr. Rudy would like to talk to you, in his office, a private meeting. Tomorrow after work. He's in the courthouse, just down the hall from the courtroom."

Nunzio took a deep breath as his shoulders sagged. His eyes darted from side to side as he tried to think. "What if I don't want to talk to him?"

"No problem. It's up to you. Either go by tomorrow, or wait until he calls in his grand jury. He'll subpoena you, your wife, your bank records, employment stuff, everything really. He'll put you under oath and ask some tough questions. You do understand perjury, don't you?"

"Another accusation? Seems like I might need a lawyer."

Gene shrugged like a real smart-ass. "Up to you. But they cost a lot of money and usually screw up things. Go talk to Mr. Rudy and then decide about the lawyer. Thanks for your time." He turned and walked away, leaving Nunzio confused, frightened, and with plenty of questions.

The bluff continued the following afternoon when Nunzio appeared at the office of the district attorney, without a lawyer. Jesse showed him to his office, thanked him for stopping by, and made small talk. That ended when he said, "Judge Oliphant is getting some reports of jury tampering in the Redfield case, so he's planning to talk to the jurors. I'm sure you'll be getting a call soon enough."

Nunzio shrugged as if he had nothing to worry about.

"He feels like I proved the case beyond a reasonable doubt, yet three jurors didn't see it that way. The other nine thought it was an open-and-shut case."

"I thought our deliberations were confidential."

"Oh, they are, always. Gotta keep them private. But, word usually leaks out. We know that you, Paul Dewey, and Chick Hutchinson voted not guilty, which is disturbing in light of the overwhelming evidence you heard. The three of you did a fine job of hanging the jury. The question is: Did Paul and Chick get money too?"

"What are you talking about?"

"I'm talking about the two thousand cash you took for a not-guilty vote. Are you denying it?"

"Hell yeah I'm denying it. You got it wrong, Mr. Rudy. I didn't take any money."

"Fine. I'm going to haul you in before the grand jury and ask you all about it. You'll be sworn to tell the truth. Perjury carries ten years, Joe. Same for tampering. That's twenty years in Parchman prison, and the judge and I can guarantee that you'll serve every day of it."

"You're crazy."

"I'm also dangerous. Look, Joe, you've committed a serious crime and I know it. How's your family going to feel when I indict you for jury tampering?"

"I need a lawyer."

"Go hire one. You have the money. What's left of it. But you're leaving a trail, Joe. Last week you bought a new pickup from Shelton Ford, paid five hundred down, financed the rest. That's pretty careless, Joe."

"Nothing wrong with buying a truck."

"You're right. So I won't indict you for that. I like the other charges anyway."

"I don't know what you're talking about."

"Sure you do, Joe. I'm using small words here, nothing complicated. I'm going to indict you for tampering, maybe perjury too, and I'll squeeze like hell until you tell me where the money came from. You're a small fish in a big pond, Joe, and I want bigger trophies. I want the man with the money."

"What money?"

"You got thirty days, Joe. If there's no deal in thirty days, then you'll hear a knock on the door at three in the morning. They'll hand you a subpoena. I'll be waiting in the grand jury room."

CHAPTER 29

After the December 1973 term of circuit court was over, Judge Oliphant continued everything on both his dockets to the new year, and left for Florida and a sunny Christmas. The law business slowed considerably around the holidays. Courthouse clerks decorated their offices and handed out baked goods to anyone who stopped by. Secretaries needed more time off to shop. The lawyers knew better than to ask for a hearing; there wasn't a judge anywhere. So they partied, one office after another, and they invited police officers, rescue personnel, ambulance drivers, even some clients. The parties were often loud and raucous, with no shortage of heavy drinking.

At Rudy & Pettigrew, things were quieter as the firm gathered for a catered meal and the exchanging of gifts. For Jesse and Agnes, it was a proud moment because all four children were already home for the break. Keith had been lawyering for seven months. Beverly was out of college and contemplating the future. Laura would graduate from Southern Miss in the coming spring. Tim, the youngest, was making noise about transferring to a college out west. He was tired of the beach and wanted to see the mountains. His older siblings were cut from the Rudy mold—disciplined, driven, regimented, focused. Tim was a free spirit, a nonconformist, and his parents weren't sure what to do with him.

Since he'd left home two years earlier, Agnes had assumed a larger role in the firm. She was practically the managing partner, though without the benefit of a law license. She managed the secretaries and part-time help. She watched the files and made sure papers were filed promptly. She handled most of the bookkeeping and monitored the fees and expenses. Occasionally, she stepped in to referee a dispute between the lawyers, but that was rare. She and Jesse insisted on good behavior and respectful relations, and the truth was that the four young lawyers liked one another. There was no jealousy or envy. They were building a firm and working together.

The district attorney's position was full-time, but some vagueness in the statute allowed a DA to keep his old office as long as he didn't profit from it. The rule was that the firm could take no criminal clients, not even drunks and shoplifters in city court. Freed from that unprofitable law speciality, the four young lawyers were working the civil side and attracting clients.

Jesse stopped by at least twice a week, if for no other reason than to raid the brownies and cookies in the kitchen. And, he liked to remind his busy team that it was still his law firm, though there was never any doubt about that. He spent a few minutes with Egan and each of the Pettigrews and asked about their cases. Since he talked to Keith every day he knew his business. The firm was like a family, and Jesse was determined for it to grow and prosper.

They enjoyed the Christmas lunch, with no alcohol, and laughed at the gag gifts that made the rounds. The party broke up around 3:00 P.M. with hugs and holiday greetings. Jesse excused himself and said he needed to get back to the DA's office. Seriously? On a Friday afternoon in December?

He drove to the Biloxi harbor and parked on the oyster shells. He put on his overcoat and waited for the ferry to Ship Island. The trip out there and back always cleared his head, and he made it three or four times a year. The air was cool and a blustery wind made it colder, and he thought for a moment the shuttle might be suspended. He rather liked the rougher Sound with an occasional spray of salty water in his face.

He boarded the Pan American Clipper, said hello as always to Captain Pete, walked past a row of slot machines, and found a seat on the top deck, away from the other passengers. He faced south, toward Ship Island, which was not visible. It was almost Christmas and the tourists were long gone. The ferry was practically empty. The horn gave a long, mournful blast and they rocked away from the pier. The harbor was soon behind them.

Jesse's first term was almost over and he considered it unsuccessful. In his project to clean up the Coast, he had barely scratched the surface. Prostitution and gambling were still plentiful in the clubs. The drug trade was increasing. The unsolved murders remained so. He'd won the nuisance case against Carousel, but it was still open and doing a brisk business. He thought he had Ginger Redfield on the ropes but she got away. Her jury had been rigged and he felt responsible for letting it happen. The bluff with Joe Nunzio had gone nowhere. He wouldn't squeal and Jesse didn't have enough proof. As he was learning, cash was impossible to trace, and in the shadows there was plenty of it. He had not laid a glove on Lance Malco, the ruling Boss of the Strip, or Shine Tanner, the current number two. His lone win was closing the Siesta, but it was an inside job and he would always be convinced it was a setup. The anonymous tip to the Biloxi police probably came from someone working for Malco. Ratting out the Siesta gave him one less competitor.

In fifteen months, Jesse would announce his candidacy for reelection. He could almost hear the radio ads from his opponent, whoever it might be. Rudy had not cleaned up the Coast. It was dirtier than ever. And so on. The prospect of another hard race was never appealing, but now he had little success to build a campaign on. He had great name recognition and could play politics as well as anyone, but something was missing. A conviction, and a big one.

He got off the ferry at the dock on Ship Island and went for a walk. He bought a tall coffee and found a park bench near the fort. The wind had died and the sea was calm. For a boy who grew up on the water and loved the Sound, he now spent so little time in a boat. Next year he would do better. Next year he would take the kids fishing, just like he did when they were younger.

Convicting Lance Malco and putting him in prison would now be priority one. Murders, beatings, bombings, and burnings aside, Malco had been operating criminal enterprises in Biloxi for twenty years, and he had done so with impunity. If Jesse couldn't put him out of business, then Jesse didn't deserve the job as district attorney.

But he needed the help of another DA.

———•———

Two days after Christmas, Jesse and Keith drove three hours north to Jackson and arrived half an hour early at the state capitol for a meeting with the governor, Bill Waller, a former prosecutor.

Waller had served as the DA for Hinds County for two terms, and had made a name for himself going after the notorious murderer of a prominent civil rights leader. In his campaigns, he refrained from using the incendiary race-baiting language of his predecessors. He was considered a moderate who wanted real change in education, elections, and race relations in the state. As a former prosecutor, he had no patience for the crime and corruption on the Coast. And, he had met Jesse Rudy and was thankful for his support.

A secretary said the meeting would last for only thirty minutes. The governor was quite busy and had family in town for the holidays. Another secretary escorted Keith and Jesse into the governor's official reception room on the second floor of the capitol. He lived in the mansion three blocks away.

He was on the phone but waved them in. The secretary poured coffee and finally left. He hung up and everyone shook hands. They caught up on a few old friends from the Coast as the minutes ticked by.

Keith pinched himself to make sure it was really happening. He was a twenty-five-year-old rookie lawyer sitting in the governor's office as if he actually deserved a seat at the table. He couldn't help but glance around and take in the large portraits of former governors. He absorbed the setting, the powerful desk, the heavy leather chairs, the fireplace, the aura of importance, the busy staff tending to every detail.

He liked it. He might just give it a shot one day.

He snapped back to reality when the governor said, "I like your nuisance case. Read it last night. Supreme court'll do the right thing."

Jesse was surprised to know the governor was current with cases on appeal. He was even more startled to learn that the state supreme court was on their side. "Well, that's certainly good to hear, Governor."

"A decision is on the way, just after the holidays. You'll like it."

Jesse glanced at Keith and neither could suppress a smile.

"Great idea to use the nuisance statute. Can you go after the other clubs and clean up the mess down there?"

"We'll try, Governor, but we need help. As you know, there's not much support from local law enforcement."

"Fats Bowman belongs in prison."

"Agreed, and I'll try to put him there, but that comes later. My priority is shutting down the clubs and putting the crime bosses out of business."

"What do you need?"

"The state police."

"I know that's why you're here, Jesse. I knew it the day you called. Here's my situation. I'm not happy with my director of public safety. The highway patrol is not well run these days, too much cronyism, a real good ole boys' outfit. So, I'm cleaning house. A bunch of the mossbacks are taking retirement. I want some new blood. Give me a month and I'll have my guy in as head of the state police. He'll come see you."

Jesse was rarely speechless, but he struggled for words. Keith piped in with "I read where you're coming to the Coast in February for a speech."

"Well, the speech is the official reason. What I really want to do is sneak over to a club and shoot some dice, maybe check out the hookers." The governor roared with laughter and slapped his knees. Jesse and Keith were caught completely off guard and howled along with their new friend. Waller laughed until his eyes were moist, then managed to pull himself together.

He said, "Naw, it's some new factory opening up in Gulfport and a buddy of mine owns it. I'll pose for pictures, kiss some babies, that kinda stuff. I can't run for reelection, you know, but once politics gets in your blood you can't give it up."

"What's next for you?" Keith asked, somewhat boldly.

"I don't know right now. Got my plate full with current issues. What's next for you? I've seen you looking around the office. Might try it on one day?"

Keith nodded and said, "Maybe so."

CHAPTER 30

On January 11, 1974, the Mississippi Supreme Court came to life and issued a unanimous ruling that affirmed Chancellor Baker's decision. The proof clearly showed a pattern of criminal activity—prostitution—and the lower court did not err in declaring Carousel a public nuisance. The ruling closed the nightclub immediately.

Though it had taken almost two years, Jesse had his first real victory in his war on organized crime. He had shuttered one of the more popular joints on the Strip, and now he could go after Ginger Redfield again. Lance Malco would be next, though he, as always, would be more complicated.

Jesse planned to present the same evidence against Ginger in another jury trial, but never got the chance. A week or so after the court's ruling, Ginger sold Carousel and O'Malley's to Lance Malco and left town, skipping bail. With plenty of cash, she vanished from the Coast, with no forwarding address. Months would pass before word filtered back that she was living the good life in Barbados, far from the short arm of any Mississippi law or indictment.

Thumbing his nose at the DA, Lance Malco quickly renovated Carousel, renamed it Desperado, and threw a grand opening extravaganza that lasted a week. Free beer, live music, the prettiest girls on the Coast. The nightclub advertised everything but sex and gambling.

Out of curiosity, Jesse drove by one night during the festive week and stopped in the parking lot, which was crowded. He was thoroughly depressed and again felt like a failure. All of his time and effort in closing the place had been wasted. Not only was it open, albeit under another name, but business was booming.

———•———

On schedule, Haley Stofer arrived at 8:00 A.M. on a Monday and walked into Jesse's office without a word to the secretary, who still didn't like the fact that he came and went as he pleased. He'd been undercover for almost a year and had settled nicely into the routine of playing gofer at Red Velvet while reporting to Jesse. He had worked as a janitor, dishwasher, cook, errand boy, and anything else they needed. He kept to himself, said little, heard a lot, never missed work, never griped about not getting a raise, and with time had sort of blended into the scenery as one of the gang who kept the place going.

Stofer reported that on the Strip the rules of engagement changed with the winds. If there was an arrest, or even the rumor of one, the floor managers clamped down and the "members only" ruse was strictly adhered to. No girl could hustle a man who didn't have credentials. The only exceptions were the soldiers in uniform. They weren't cops, wouldn't squeal on anyone, and couldn't wait to get the girls upstairs. But once the threat passed, things invariably relaxed and the good times rolled for everyone, members or not. Stofer said that during his one-year stint at Red Velvet, prostitution had increased and there were more rumors of gambling in other clubs.

With Jesse's coaching, Stofer maintained meticulous records. He kept a daily log of who worked and for how long; cooks, bartenders, waitresses, strippers, hookers, floor managers, door managers, security guards, everyone. He counted the boxes of liquor, the barrels of beer, crates of food and kitchen supplies. He was friendly with the housekeeper, an ex-hooker now too old to charge, and she told wild stories of her glory days. Some nights she labored furiously to keep the sheets clean, and, in her opinion, there was more activity upstairs than ever before. Stofer was friendly with Nevin Noll, Mr. Malco's number two, though no one was close to Noll. He knew Hugh Malco and saw him around the club often.

The big news that morning was that he was being transferred to Foxy's because a bartender had run off with a waitress. Jesse had been pushing this for months and was delighted. From his vantage point behind the bar, Stofer could observe much more.

Jesse wanted the name of every hooker, some of their customers, and a few of the membership cards, if possible.

With the governor quietly pulling strings, it was time to send in the state police. From March through July, four undercover cops visited Foxy's and bought drinks for the girls. They were disguised as bikers, hippies, truck drivers, traveling salesmen, even out-of-town lawyers, and stopped by on the nights when a certain floor manager was on duty, a guy not known as a stickler for the rules. They had fake membership cards but never used them. They made a total of eleven visits and wore wires during every one. They laughed with the girls as they talked about pricing and such, then backed away at the last moment with a variety of excuses. Stofer watched the crowd closely and could not spot the cops. If anyone was suspicious, it was not apparent.

———•———

On July 15, in a clandestine session of the grand jury, meeting for the first and only time in a locked ballroom of a Ramada Inn, the four agents testified and played the audio recordings of their seemingly lighthearted encounters with the girls at Foxy's.

They were followed by the three prostitutes who were questioned by Jesse Rudy. Up front, he explained to the grand jurors that the three were formerly employed at Foxy's but had quit two months earlier in a dispute over pay. They were facing charges of prostitution and, with the advice of counsel, were testifying in return for leniency. None of the grand jurors had ever heard a prostitute speak candidly about her work, and they were riveted. The first one was twenty-three years old, looked about fifteen, and had started at Foxy's four years earlier as a waitress. Because she had a nice body, she was offered a promotion to stripper, which she took. The big money was made in the rooms upstairs, and before long she was hustling johns and earning $500 a week. All cash. She did not enjoy the work and tried to quit, but the money was too tempting. The second one worked at Foxy's for five years. The third, a forty-one-year-old veteran, confessed to working in most of the clubs in town and said she was not ashamed of it. Prostitution was the world's oldest profession. Any mutually beneficial agreement between two consenting adults should not be illegal.

Their testimonies were fascinating, at times salacious, and never boring. Some of the women on the grand jury were judgmental. All of the men were spellbound.

The last witness was Haley Stofer, who testified using an alias. For three hours, he described his career first at Red Velvet, then, and presently, at Foxy's where he tended bar fifty hours a week and watched the crowd. A blind man could monitor the girls and their "dates." He presented a list of thirteen women currently active. To hire one, a gentleman had to present his membership card, which in theory meant he could be trusted. Stofer's second list had the names of eighty-six such gentlemen.

Jesse smiled to himself when he tried to envision the brouhaha that would erupt if that list was ever made public.

Stofer assured the grand jurors that not all of the men cavorted with prostitutes. Some were old-timers who were admitted to the club just in case. The perks of membership also allowed them to do business with their favorite bookies and participate in the occasional poker tournament.

After an exhausting day wading through the seedy side of Biloxi vice, the grand jurors were dismissed by Jesse and sent home. They returned at nine the following morning and spent over two hours reviewing the evidence against the suspects. As noon approached, Jesse finally called for the vote. By unanimous agreement, the grand jury indicted Lance Malco on one count of operating a "place" used for prostitution and thirteen counts of causing and encouraging women to engage in prostitution. The grand jury also indicted Foxy's general manager and two floor managers on the same charges, with each count punishable by a maximum fine of $5,000 and up to ten years in prison. The thirteen women were indicted on felony charges of engaging in more than one act of prostitution.

The roundup began at noon the next day when the state highway patrol descended on Biloxi. Lance Malco was arrested at his office at Red Velvet. Two of the three managers of Foxy's were taken into custody. The third one would be found later. Most of the girls were arrested at their homes and apartments.

When Lance was in jail, Keith drove to the offices of the *Gulf Coast Register* and hand-delivered a copy of the indictments to an editor. Foxy's was cordoned off with barricades and yellow crime scene tape. Reporters were soon on the scene with cameras rolling, but there was no one to talk to.

Fats Bowman suddenly needed to visit an uncle in Florida and disappeared. Most of his deputies scattered. His office phones rang nonstop but went unanswered.

Three days later, Judge Oliphant called a bail hearing for all defendants and braced for a circus. He was not disappointed. His courtroom was packed beyond capacity and overflowed into the hallway. When Jesse entered through a side door he got his first good look at Lance Malco, seated in the front row, a lawyer on each side. The two glared at each other and neither blinked. The two rows behind Lance were filled with his girls, most of whom did not have lawyers. Uniformed state troopers walked the aisle and asked for quiet. The bailiff called court to order and Judge Oliphant emerged from the rear, assumed the bench, and asked everyone to take their seats.

He began with Lance and asked him to come forward. With

Joshua Burch on one side and an associate on the other, Lance moved to the defense table. Jesse spoke first and argued for a high bond because the defendant was a man of means, had many properties and employees, and was a flight risk. He suggested the sum of $100,000, which, of course, Joshua Burch found outrageous. His client had no criminal record, had never fled from anything, and was not charged, in "this rather flimsy indictment," with any crime that involved violence. He was a peaceful man, law-abiding, and so on.

As the two lawyers went back and forth, the reporters scribbled as fast as humanly possible. The story was front-page news and would only get better. It was hard to believe that such an infamous mobster, the alleged Boss of the Dixie Mafia, had actually been indicted and arrested.

Judge Oliphant listened patiently, then split the difference and set bail at $50,000. Lance returned to his seat in the front row, chafing at being treated like a common criminal.

Burch argued on behalf of the three managers as Jesse hammered away at them. It was his show, his courtroom, his indictments, and he left no doubt that he was not intimidated by the outlaws and had no fear of them.

Judge Oliphant let the managers go on $10,000 bonds. He cut the girls some slack and set their bonds at $500 each. After a grueling four-hour hearing, he finally adjourned.

———•———

The phone calls began the day after the arrests. Agnes took one at home and a husky voice informed her that Jesse Rudy was a dead man. Gene Pettigrew took one at the law firm and heard the same message. The secretary in the DA's office hung up on an idiot yelling obscenities about her boss.

Jesse reported them to the state police. He knew there would be more. Unknown to his wife, he was now carrying a gun. The state troopers, in their smartly painted patrol cars, stayed in Biloxi and maintained an impressive show of force.

Governor Waller was, after all, a former district attorney. He had been threatened on several occasions and knew how frightening it was for the family. He called Jesse every other day for updates. The support from the top was comforting.

Both men knew there were a lot of crazies out there.

CHAPTER 31

Foxy's was closed for a week while Joshua Burch spun a dizzying assortment of legal maneuvers to get it reopened. When the barricades and police tape were finally removed, Lance tried to gin up excitement with free beer, live country music, and even more hot women. That fizzled when state troopers arrived in uniform and milled around the front door. They parked their patrol cars in full view of the traffic on Highway 90. The few thirsty customers who showed up could only drink and watch the strippers; the prostitutes were in hiding. The intimidation worked so well that Jesse requested more troopers and before long Red Velvet, Desperado, and the Truck Stop were practically deserted. The Strip was a ghost town.

Lance Malco was livid. His flow of cash had been choked off and there was only one person to blame. His private life was a mess. Carmen was living in a guest room above the garage and hardly spoke to him. She had mentioned a divorce several times. Two of his adult children had left the Coast and never called. Only Hugh remained loyal as he jockeyed for more authority in the business. To make matters worse, the highway patrol routinely parked near the Malco home to draw attention from the neighbors. For fun, they followed Lance to and from work. It was nothing but harassment, all orchestrated by Jesse Rudy, he was certain. Lance was at a breaking point. His empire was on the brink. He was facing criminal charges that could put him away for decades. He spoke to Joshua Burch at least three times a day, not a preferred way to spend his time.

Burch was adamant that he represent the three floor managers, along with Lance. Though the four could possibly have conflicting interests, Burch wanted them under his thumb. His fear was that Jesse Rudy would select one of the managers and start chipping away with threats and offers of leniency. If he flipped one, he might flip another, and the dominoes would fall. Burch could protect all four if he called the shots, but interference from another lawyer could be disastrous. Lance was obviously the biggest target, and his defense could not withstand the ruinous testimony from those close to him.

Burch was not privy to the grand jury testimony but would try like hell to get it. Normally it was not discoverable, and Rudy would fight to keep it private. It was not unusual in a criminal case to have little more than the names of opposing witnesses before the trial started. Undermining their testimony was left to the skill of the defense lawyer, and Burch considered himself a master at cross-examination.

In the preliminary court hearings, he maintained his air of confidence in his clients' innocence as he scoffed at the indictments. He said little to the press but let it be known that, at least in his opinion, the State's case was based on the shaky testimony of a bunch of washed-up call girls who hung around the nightclubs causing trouble. Privately, though, he confided to his associates that Jesse Rudy had them on the ropes. Was there any real doubt that Mr. Malco had built his empire on the backs of prostitutes? Wasn't it common knowledge that he was a wealthy man because of illegal booze, gambling, and hookers? How could the defense possibly pick a fair and impartial jury?

The jury would be the key, as always, and the defense only needed one vote.

———•———

As the shock of the arrests began to wane, and fewer state troopers roamed the Coast, the night life slowly returned. Stofer reported to Jesse that some of the girls drifted in, but they flirted only with the men they knew. They were far less aggressive and ignored strangers. When they sneaked away to the rooms it was with someone they had serviced before. Mr. Malco himself was seen around the clubs at night, making sure all rules were being followed. He worked the floor, shaking hands, slapping backs, cracking jokes, as if he had no worries.

Hugh stayed close to his father and was always armed, though they did not feel threatened at the moment. The gangsters had a new and more serious problem—Mr. Rudy—and gave little thought to another senseless turf battle among themselves. Lance's rivals hunkered down in their caves and hiding places, fearful that more indictments might be coming. The nightclubs had a new appreciation of the law and were following it to the letter.

Hugh was twenty-six years old and finally growing out of his rebellious years. He had stopped fighting and given up hard liquor and jacked-up sports cars, and was dating a young divorcée who once worked as a waitress at Foxy's. He got her away from the nightclubs before she could advance to the more lucrative specialties. She worked in a downtown bank where proper attire was required and strict hours kept. The longer they dated, the more she nagged Hugh about getting away from the Strip and finding honest work. The life of an outlaw might be exciting and prosperous for a while, but it was also unstable, even dangerous. His father was facing prison. His parents were separating. Was a life of crime really worth it?

But Hugh saw little future on the right side of the law. He'd been hanging around the clubs since he was fifteen, knew the business well, and had a general idea of how much money his father had made. It was a lot, far more than anyone else knew, and far more than any doctor or lawyer could earn.

The more they quibbled, the less Hugh liked her.

He was worried about his father and was angry that Jesse Rudy had actually indicted him. He could not comprehend his dad going to prison, though he had gradually accepted that possibility. If it happened, how would it affect their business? He had broached the subject a few times, but Lance was too bitter to talk about it. He was consumed with the likelihood of going to trial and facing a jury. The nightmare they faced was driven by the haunting reality that the charges were based on the truth, and everybody knew it.

———•———

Jesse was not pushing for a speedy trial. Joshua Burch was already clogging the docket with motions and requests that would take time to fight through. He was demanding the grand jury transcript; he wanted the indictment quashed for a number of technical reasons; he wanted separate trials for each of his clients; he wanted Judge Oliphant to recuse himself and asked the Mississippi Supreme Court to appoint a special judge. It was another impressive lesson in the endless ways to confuse the issues and delay a day in court.

Jesse fought back with his own lengthy briefs, but as the months passed it became obvious that a trial was far away. And that was fine with him. He needed time to work in the shadows and explore deals with the three managers and the girls.

And there was another reason not to hurry. He was up for reelection the following year. The trial of Lance Malco would be front-page news for weeks, and Jesse would be in the middle of it. The publicity would be priceless and might frighten away a possible challenger. Jesse was not aware of anyone who wanted his job, but a big, splashy guilty verdict would virtually guarantee an uncontested race.

And he knew quite well how devastating a loss would be.

———•———

Losing came a step closer in early September with the disappearance of Haley Stofer. On the first Monday of the month, he failed to show for the first time since going undercover. Jesse called his apartment and there was no answer. There was no safe way to contact him at work, so he waited two weeks until the third Monday of the month. Again, Stofer failed to show. That night, after Jesse had turned out the lights and kissed Agnes, the phone rang.

Stofer said, "Mr. Rudy, they're after me. I'm hiding but I'm not safe."

"What are you talking about, Stofer?"

"I got a tip from a guy at work, said he overheard Nevin Noll cussing me, calling me a snitch. The guy asked me if I was a snitch. I said hell no. But I disappeared anyway. You gotta get me outta here, Mr. Rudy."

A leak from the grand jury was unlikely, but not impossible. Fats Bowman had more informants than the FBI.

"Where are you?" Jesse asked.

"I can't say right now. Three days ago some men came to my apartment, kicked in the door, wrecked the place. A neighbor told me about it. I can't go back there. I need to leave this place and do it in a hurry."

"You can't leave the state, Stofer. Remember the indictment?"

"What good is the indictment if my throat gets cut?"

Jesse had no response. Stofer had him completely boxed in. If he was telling the truth, and that was entirely possible, then he had to get away from the Coast. Malco and his goons would find him and his death would be ugly. If he was lying, another plausible scenario, his timing was perfect because he could run away with Jesse's blessing. Either way, Jesse had to help him. His testimony would be crucial at Malco's trial.

Jesse asked, "Okay, where do you want to go?"

"I don't know. I can't go back to New Orleans. The gang I was working for is there and those boys aren't happy with me. Maybe I'll go north."

"I don't care where you go but you have to keep in touch. The trial won't happen soon but you'll have to come back for it. Part of the deal, remember?"

"Yeah, yeah, I'll be here for that, if I'm still alive."

"I'm sure you're broke."

"I need some money. You gotta help me."

Three hours later, Jesse parked in the gravel lot of a truck stop east of Mobile. The all-night diner was busy with truckers gulping coffee, smoking, and eating, all while talking and laughing loudly.

Stofer was at a rear table, ducking low behind a menu. He seemed genuinely skittish and kept one eye on the door. Jesse said, "You cannot get stopped or get into trouble anywhere. Understand? The moment you're arrested the cops will see the trafficking charges in Harrison County and they'll throw you under the jail."

"I know, I know, but right now I'm not worried about the cops."

"You're a convicted felon with serious charges pending. You can't screw up again, Stofer."

"Yes sir."

Jesse handed over a wad of assorted bills. "Three hundred and twenty bucks, all I could get my hands on. It'll have to do."

"Thanks, Mr. Rudy. Where should I go?"

"Drive to Chicago, it's big enough to get lost in. Find a bar, get a job for cash and tips, you know the drill. Call my office, collect, every Monday morning at eight o'clock sharp. I'll be waiting."

"Yes sir."

CHAPTER 32

The grand plan to stick together and present a unified defense began to unravel a few weeks after the arrests. Joshua Burch soon learned the lunacy of trying to control the competing interests of Malco, his three managers, and thirteen ladies of the evening.

The first to flip was a stripper with the stage name of Blaze. Wary of Lance and anyone connected to him, she hired Duff McIntosh, a tough criminal lawyer and a friend of Jesse's. Over beers late one afternoon, Jesse made his first offer. If Blaze would plead guilty to one count of prostitution, he would reduce it to a misdemeanor, dismiss the other charges, and let her go with a $100 fine and thirty days in jail, suspended. She would have to agree to testify at trial against Lance Malco and his managers and describe in detail the sex trade at Foxy's. In addition, she would promise to leave the Coast, sort of a "go and sin no more" farewell. Getting out of town would not be a bad idea after her testimony. Since she was out of work and blackballed along the Strip, she was leaving anyway. After a month of negotiation, Blaze took the deal and disappeared.

Word spread quickly and Duff became the go-to lawyer for the girls. When they realized they could walk away with no jail time and no felony conviction, they lined up at Duff's office. Through the fall of 1974, he and Jesse met often for beers and conducted business. Jesse offered the same deal. Eight of the thirteen said yes. Two said no, out of fear of Malco. Two others had different lawyers and were still negotiating. One had not been seen since posting bail.

———•———

Three months after their meeting in Mobile, Jesse had not heard from Haley Stofer. He had no idea where he was hiding and had no time to search for him. His only hope was for the knucklehead to screw up, get himself arrested, then extradited back to Harrison County where Jesse would beat him over the head with the indictment, promise him forty years in prison, and strong-arm him into testifying against Lance Malco.

It was a long shot.

The other possibility was that Malco found him first. In that case, it was unlikely he would be found again.

———•———

In mid-November, Judge Oliphant scheduled another motion hearing to deal with the avalanche of paperwork spewing forth from the typewriters inside the law offices of Joshua Burch. At issue on that day was an aggressive and well-reasoned motion to try Lance Malco separately from his three managers. Burch wanted his star client to go last so he could learn the prosecution's strategies, strengths, and weaknesses. Jesse opposed the idea and argued that having four trials based on the same set of facts was a waste of judicial resources. More than three months had already passed since the indictments, and it would take another year to try all of them piecemeal. What Burch wasn't saying was that he believed the prosecution would have a difficult time finding forty-eight jurors who could not be influenced by the outlaws he represented. One hung jury, one mistrial, and the prosecution's momentum would suffer greatly.

Only a few spectators watched as the lawyers haggled. One of the defendants, Fritz Haberstroh, sat in the back row, no doubt sent by Malco to observe and report. Haberstroh was a floor manager at Foxy's and a longtime employee of the Malco enterprises. He had two felony convictions for fencing stolen appliances, and had served time in Missouri before heading south to find work where no one cared about his past. Jesse was itching to get him in front of a jury.

After two hours of often tense argument, Jesse suddenly changed his strategy and announced, "Your Honor, I see that one of the defendants, Mr. Haberstroh, is with us today."

"He's my client," Burch interrupted.

"I know that," Jesse shot back. "I'll agree to try Mr. Haberstroh first. Let's put him on trial a month from now. The State is ready."

Oliphant, Burch, and everyone else was startled.

"Mr. Burch?" the judge asked.

"Well, Your Honor, I'm not sure the defense can be ready."

"You want separate trials, Mr. Burch. You've spent the last two hours begging for them, so we're going to have separate trials. Surely you can be ready in a month."

Jesse glanced at Haberstroh, who appeared pale, stunned, and ready to bolt.

Burch fumbled some papers, then huddled with an associate. For Jesse, it was a rare moment to enjoy watching the great trial lawyer lose his footing.

Burch finally said, "Okay, Your Honor. We'll be ready."

———•———

Two days later, Keith was leaving the courthouse when a stranger opened the door for him and said, "Say, you got a minute?" He stuck out a hand and said, "Name's George Haberstroh, brother of Fritz."

Keith shook his hand and said, "Keith Rudy. A pleasure."

They walked away from the main entrance and stood under a tree. George said, "This conversation never happened, okay?"

"We'll see."

"No, I need your word. Gotta keep this quiet, you understand?"

"What's up?"

"Well, obviously, my brother is in some deep shit. We're not from around here, you see. He came down years ago after he got out. Always had a knack for finding trouble. I don't think he did anything wrong at the club, you know? He was just an employee, doing what Malco wanted. Now he's facing a pretty nasty indictment. With a bunch of thugs, if you ask me."

Keith, still in his rookie season, wasn't sure what to say but didn't like the situation. He nodded as if to say, "Go on."

Haberstroh continued, "Fritz knows Malco will sell him out to save his own skin. Fritz prefers to save his first. He can't do any more time, especially in one of these prisons down here."

Keith said, "He's got a lawyer, one of the best."

"He doesn't trust Joshua Burch and he damned sure doesn't trust his co-defendants."

"We shouldn't be talking."

"Why not? I'm not the defendant. You're not the DA. My brother wants out, okay? He may be stupid but he's not a criminal and he did nothing wrong at that nightclub. Sure the girls were whoring but he didn't make the rules. He got none of the money. Malco paid him a salary to do what he was told."

Keith almost walked away but realized the opportunity. He knew the indictment inside and out because he and his father had discussed it for months. They had spent hours dissecting the criminal activity, the criminals, and the possible trial strategies by both sides. Jesse indicted Haberstroh and the other two managers for the sole purpose of squeezing their balls until they turned on Malco.

The turning had just begun. "What am I supposed to do?" Keith asked.

"Please talk to your father and get Fritz out of this mess."

"Is he willing to testify against Malco?"

"He's willing to do anything to save his own neck."

"Does he appreciate the danger?"

"Of course he does, but Fritz survived four years in a tough prison in Missouri. He's not exactly a pushover. If he walks, he'll never be seen around here again."

Keith took a deep breath and looked around. "Okay, I'll talk to the DA."

"Thanks. How can I contact you?"

Keith handed him a business card and said, "Call my law firm's number in about a week. I'll have an answer."

"Thanks."

"What about the other two managers?"

"Don't know them."

"Well Fritz certainly does."

"I'll ask."

———•———

The second meeting took place in a coffee shop near the docks in Pascagoula. Keith ditched the coat and tie and tried to look nothing like a lawyer. For George Haberstroh it was easy—old chinos, scruffy deck shoes, a gabardine shirt. He said he worked for a shipper out of Mobile and confessed to visiting Foxy's on occasion. When Fritz was off-duty they enjoyed beers and burgers as they watched the girls dance. He was aware of the activity upstairs but thought nothing of it. He had never been tempted, claimed to be happily married. Fritz had worked on the Coast for years and had talked openly, at least to his brother, about the gambling and girls.

Keith got down to business with "Obviously, Fritz is not the target here. Lance Malco is the biggest crime boss on the Coast and the DA has had him in his sights for a long time. Fritz can certainly make things easier. Is he willing to take the stand, stare at Malco in court, and tell the jury everything about the sex business at Foxy's?"

"Yes, but only if he walks."

"The DA can't promise leniency, okay? You have to understand how important this is. Most of the hookers will sign a plea deal in which they agree to testify and take a hit on a misdemeanor charge. Not a big deal because, well, they're hookers. They'll have credibility issues with the jury. The three managers are different. Take Fritz. When he takes the stand and testifies against Malco, Burch will come after him with a hatchet. First question will be: 'Have you been promised leniency by the DA to testify in this case?' It's imperative that Fritz says no, there's no deal because there's no deal."

"I'm not sure I follow you."

"Fritz is scheduled to go on trial in two weeks, but before that he'll plead guilty to one count, agree to cooperate with the State, and will be sentenced after the Malco trial. If he cooperates fully, then the DA will recommend leniency."

"Seems like a helluva risk for my brother. Plead guilty, go into hiding, then go to trial, dodge the bullets there, hope the jury convicts Malco, then hope and pray the judge is in a good mood."

"At this point everything is a risk for your brother. You ever been to Parchman prison?"

"No. What about Burch?"

"He's gotta go. If Fritz wants to cooperate and maybe walk, then Burch will only get in the way. Here's a scenario: Next week, Fritz fires Burch by writing him a letter of dismissal. Send a copy to the DA, file another copy with the court. Then Fritz hires a guy named Duff McIntosh, a guy we know well, good lawyer. He'll charge you $500 to handle the case. At that point, Fritz is a marked man and lays low. On December thirteenth he'll show up in court, plead guilty to all counts, promise cooperation, and go hide in Montana or someplace until he has to come back and testify."

"When is that?"

"Judge Oliphant has set Malco's trial for March seventeenth."

CHAPTER 33

To avoid a crowd, and to protect the defendant, a hearing was hastily arranged for 1:00 P.M. Friday, December 13, in Judge Oliphant's courtroom. Fritz Haberstroh stood before His Honor with Duff McIntosh on one side and Jesse Rudy on the other. As the DA went through the indictment, Fritz quietly answered "Guilty" to all charges. Duff asked the court to release his client on the same appearance bond. His Honor granted the request and informed the defendant that he would be sentenced at a date to be determined. He was free to go.

Following Jesse and Duff, the Haberstroh brothers left the courtroom through a side door and took the janitors' stairs to the first floor. Near the rear entrance, they all shook hands and said goodbye. The brothers hopped into the rear seat of a waiting car and hurried off.

Joshua Burch was in the courtroom and watched the guilty plea in disbelief. It was not just bad news for Malco's defense, it was devastating. Burch was losing clients rapidly as Jesse Rudy flipped them like pancakes. There was little doubt he would go after the other two managers and probably corral the hookers who had not already caved in. The defense was staring at a firing squad and Rudy was giving the orders.

Burch left the courthouse and walked three blocks back to his office, a beautiful three-story Victorian home he had inherited from his grandfather, himself a prominent lawyer. Joshua had turned it into an office, filled it with associates and secretaries, and enjoyed the perks of a big staff. At the front desk, he growled at the receptionist as he checked his phone messages. She shoved over a package and said it had just been delivered. He smiled as he cradled it. His favorite smuggler, an ex-client, had come through again. He took it upstairs to his magnificent office overlooking downtown, and unpacked a box of black cigars, Partagas, pure Cuban and heavily embargoed. He could almost taste one as he took off the wrapper. He lit it and blew smoke out a window. He called Lance and invited him over.

Three hours later, after the staff had been sent home early, Lance, Hugh, and Nevin Noll arrived. Burch met them at the front door and welcomed them to his conference room on the first floor. It was Lance's favorite room in all of Biloxi: walls lined with walnut shelves that held thousands of important books, large portraits of prior Burch lawyers, bulky and weathered leather chairs around a shiny mahogany table. Burch passed around his new box of Cubans and everyone lit up. He poured bourbon on the rocks for Lance and Nevin. Hugh preferred water.

They talked about Haberstroh's guilty plea and the problems it caused. Burch still represented Bobby Lopez and Coot Reed, both of whom were still employed by Foxy's as the manager and floor manager. They were being watched closely by everyone around them. Neither had ever mentioned the idea of a plea bargain and Burch certainly had not. He had no idea how Jesse Rudy weaseled himself into Haberstroh's orbit and cut the deal. When Fritz fired him, Burch had called Jesse with some questions but got nowhere.

They sipped and smoked and bashed Jesse, but it was all a rehash.

Lance asked, "Have you found him an opponent?"

Burch exhaled and sighed in disgust, shook his head and replied, "No, and we've been through the entire bar. Right now there are seventeen lawyers in Hancock County, fifty-one in Harrison, eleven in Stone. At least half are unelectable because of age, health, race, or gender. There's never been a female DA in this state, nor a black one. Now's not the time to blaze a trail. Most of the others couldn't get ten votes because of incompetence, alcoholism, or contrariness. Trust me, there are some bad apples out there practicing law. About a dozen are big firm guys making plenty of money. We whittled our list down to three young lawyers, guys who might do well in politics and need a steady paycheck. In the past month I've mentioned it casually to all three. There's no interest whatsoever."

"What about Rex Dubisson?" Lance asked.

"He said no. He's built a good private practice, making some money, and doesn't miss politics. That, and he got his ass kicked last time. He thinks Jesse Rudy is the most popular lawyer on the Coast and is unbeatable. That's the current sentiment out there on the street."

"Did you mention the money?"

"I told Rex there would be fifty grand for his campaign, plus twenty-five a year in cash for four years. He said no, without hesitation."

Hugh partially raised his hand like a real smart-ass and said, "May I ask a question?"

Burch shrugged, took a puff.

"Okay, so we're talking about electing a new district attorney, right? Assuming we can pay someone to get in the race, and assuming that person can win, the election is in August. The trial is in March, three months from now. What good is a new DA once the trial is over?"

Burch smiled and said, "We're not going to trial in March. I'm not finished with the delays. Gotta few more tricks up my sleeve."

After a long, heavy pause, Lance said, "Mind sharing with us?"

"How old are you, Lance?"

"Why is that important?"

"Please."

"Fifty-two. How old are you?"

"It's not important. You're old enough for heart trouble. Go see Cyrus Knapp, the heart doctor. He's a quack but he'll do what I say. Tell him since you got arrested you've been having chest pains, dizziness, fatigue. He'll give you some prescriptions. Buy 'em but don't take them."

"I'm not playing sick, Joshua," Lance snapped.

"Of course not. You're building a trail, paperwork, another ruse to keep you away from the jury as long as possible. Go see Knapp and do it soon. Wait a few days, then have chest pains at the office where Nevin and Hugh can see it all. One of you calls an ambulance. Knapp checks you in the hospital, keeps you a few days for observation, runs all sorts of tests that leave all sorts of records. He sends you home to rest. You see him once a month, get some more pills, tell him the stress is getting to you and you're afraid of having the big one. When we get closer to your trial, I'll ask for another continuance, for health reasons. Knapp will file an affidavit, maybe even testify. He'll say anything. Rudy will object again but you can't go to trial when you're laid up in the hospital."

"I don't like it," Lance said.

"I don't care. I'm your lawyer and I'm in charge of your defense. After this morning and that crap with Haberstroh you're a helluva lot closer to Parchman. Things aren't looking so good, Lance, so do as I say. We're desperate here. Start acting sick. You ever seen a shrink?"

"No, no, come on, Burch. I can't do that."

"I know a guy in New Orleans, a real wacko who specializes in treating wackos. Same as Knapp, he'll say anything if the money is right. He'll do a psycho exam and give us a report that'll scare the hell out of any judge."

"On what theory?" Lance snarled.

"On the theory that you've come unhinged since being indicted and getting arrested and looking at a future in prison. The stress, the fear, the sheer terror of going to jail are driving you crazy. Maybe you're hearing voices, hallucinating, all that stuff. This guy can find it, does it all the time."

Lance slapped the table and growled, "Hell no, Burch! I'm not playing the lunatic. I'll see Knapp but not a shrink."

"You want to go to prison?"

Lance took a deep breath as the wrinkles in his face relaxed. With a narrow grin he said, "No, but it ain't that bad. I got friends in the slammer now, and they're surviving. I can take anything the State can dish out, Burch."

The three drinkers reached for their glasses and took long sips. Hugh smiled at his father and admired his toughness. It was an act. No man in his right mind would say that Parchman "ain't that bad," but Lance pulled it off. Privately, the two had begun to discuss the possibility of Lance going away for a few years. Hugh was confident he could run the businesses in his father's absence.

His father wasn't so sure.

Burch exhaled thoughtfully, blew another cloud, and said, "It's my job to keep you out of prison, Lance. I've succeeded for about twenty years. But you gotta do what I say."

"We'll see."

Hugh said, "So it's possible to stall until after the election, right?"

Burch smiled and looked at Lance. "That, sir, depends on the patient."

Noll stated the obvious. "But the election is irrelevant if we don't have a horse in the race."

Lance said, "We'll find one. There are plenty of hungry lawyers out there."

———•———

For decades the FBI had shown little interest in the notorious criminal activity in Harrison County. There were two reasons: First, the crimes violated state statutes, not federal; and, second, Fats Bowman and his predecessors didn't want the Feds snooping around their turf and possibly discovering their own corruption. The FBI had enough business elsewhere and little desire to stir up more trouble in an unwelcoming jurisdiction.

Jackson Lewis was the only Special Agent from the Jackson office who ventured south as far as the Coast and he was rarely seen in Biloxi. Jesse had met him several times, even had lunch with him shortly after taking office. His goal during his next term, assuming he was reelected, was to establish a better relationship with Lewis and the FBI and lean on them.

In the first week of January, Lewis called and said he was passing through and wanted to say hello. The following day, he arrived at Jesse's courthouse office with Spence Whitehead, a rookie agent on his first assignment. For almost an hour they drank coffee and chatted about nothing urgent. Whitehead was intrigued by the history of the Biloxi underworld and seemed ready to jump in the middle of it. There were hints that the FBI was being pressured to establish more of a presence on the Coast. Jesse suspected Governor Waller and the state police were having back-channel conversations with the Feds.

"When is the Malco trial?" Lewis asked.

"March seventeenth."

"How does it look from your point of view?"

"I'm confident we'll get a conviction. At least eight of the girls will testify against Malco and describe the sex business in his nightclub. One of his three managers has flipped and is cooperating. We're squeezing the other two but so far they're playing it tough. His prostitution racket has been common knowledge for a long time and the community is tired of it. We'll convict him."

The agents glanced at each other. Lewis said, "We have an idea. What if we drop in on Malco and have a chat? Introduce ourselves."

Jesse said, "I like it. As far as I know, he's never been confronted by the FBI. It's about time you guys showed up."

Lewis said, "Perhaps, but in all fairness the folks who control the Coast have never wanted us around. You're the first person with real authority who's had the guts to take on these boys."

"Yes, and look where it gets me. These days I'm carrying a gun, one my wife knows nothing about."

Lewis said, "Look, Mr. Rudy, we're in town now. We'll introduce ourselves to Lance Malco, Shine Tanner, and some others."

"I have the list."

"Great. We'll knock on some doors, cause a little trouble, stir up the gossip."

"I know these thugs. Some will scare easily, others less so. Malco is the toughest and won't say a word unless his lawyer is in the room."

Lewis said, "Well, we may go see his lawyer too. Just a friendly drop-in."

"Please do. And welcome to Biloxi."

CHAPTER 34

L ance Malco's declining health took another blow when Jesse
Rudy picked off another underboss. Ten days before the trial
of Coot Reed, the longtime general manager of Foxy's, the pressure finally got to him and he lost his loyalty.

Early on a Friday morning, Coot drove to Gulf Shores, Alabama, and found the beach cottage where Fritz Haberstroh was
hiding. Fritz was under subpoena to return to Biloxi and testify
against Coot, a scenario that neither wanted. During a long walk
on a deserted beach, Fritz described the deal Keith Rudy had laid
out for his brother George. Fritz was of the opinion that the same
deal was on the table for Coot and Bobby Lopez, the other floor
manager, whose trial was three weeks away.

Facing years behind bars and fearing for his life, Coot was on
the verge of a nervous breakdown. Those who stuck with Malco
would go down with Malco. The tide had shifted against them and
the game was over. Jesse Rudy would slay them in front of a jury
and send them away. It was every man for himself. Fritz convinced
him to save his own neck by doing what he had done: plead guilty,
cooperate with Rudy, testify against Malco, then get the hell out
of Biloxi and never look back.

———•———

Joshua Burch's defense strategy was flailing. When he took the
phone call from Duff McIntosh and was informed that he, Burch,
had been fired by Coot Reed, and he, Duff, was now his lawyer,

Burch slammed the phone down and stormed out of his office. He drove to Red Velvet for a tense meeting with Lance, who looked surprisingly well in spite of his mounting cardiac issues. Looks were one thing; his attitude was another. He was livid and accused Burch of bungling the entire defense game plan. Demanding separate trials for himself and his three managers was a boneheaded strategy—just look at the results. It allowed Rudy to put enormous pressure on Fritz Haberstroh and Coot Reed and flip them. Only Bobby Lopez was left and his trial was only weeks away. There was little doubt Rudy was after him too. Lance would be left alone to face the jury with his once faithful employees singing like choirboys and embellishing their testimony in order to impress Rudy and Judge Oliphant with their cooperation.

When he calmed down, Lance fired Burch and told him to leave his office. Nevin Noll escorted him out of the nightclub. As Burch walked to his car, Nevin said, "He'll be okay once he settles down. I'll talk to him."

Burch wasn't so sure he wanted to be rehired.

An hour later, Bobby Lopez was called on the carpet in Lance's office and faced his boss, Nevin, and Hugh. He swore he'd had no contact with the DA's office and was not about to flip. He would stick with Lance regardless of the pressure. He would remain loyal to the end, whatever the outcome. He would take a bullet if necessary.

There was no doubt bullets were being considered. Like all of Malco's employees, Bobby was terrified of Nevin Noll and considered him a cold-blooded killer. Nevin relished the reputation and had always thrived on the intimidation. During the meeting he glared at Bobby with hot, glowing eyes, the same psychopathic gaze that they had all seen before.

Bobby left highly agitated and frightened out of his mind. He drove home and started drinking. The whiskey settled his nerves, calmed him, and allowed him to think more clearly. He thought of his old pals, Fritz and Coot, and their gutsy decisions to turn on

Malco and save themselves. The more he drank, the more sense it made. Going to prison with Lance was certainly better than taking a bullet from Noll, but Fritz and Coot were planning to avoid both outcomes. They would survive the nightmare and start new lives somewhere else as free men.

Then Bobby had a terrible thought, one that almost made him sick. What if Malco decided to eliminate him first and avoid the risk of him flipping and cooperating with Jesse Rudy? In the underworld where they lived and worked, such a drastic move would be perfectly acceptable. Malco had been rubbing out his enemies for years, with impunity, and knocking off a potentially disloyal underboss like Bobby would seem obvious.

By noon Bobby was drunk. He slept two hours, tried to sober up with a gallon of coffee, and forced himself to go to work for the evening shift at Foxy's.

———— • ————

Burch was rehired the following day and immediately filed a motion to consolidate the trials of Bobby Lopez and Lance Malco. Jesse was amused by the chaos he was creating on the other side and knew he had the outlaws on the run. He did not object to the motion. Lance Malco was still the target, not his underlings, and he was relieved at the prospect of only one big trial, not two.

On March 3, two weeks before the trial, Burch filed a motion for a continuance, claiming Mr. Malco was too ill to defend himself. The motion included affidavits from two doctors and a pile of medical reports. Jesse was highly suspicious of the move and spent hours with Egan Clement and Keith discussing how to respond. Over coffee, he and Judge Oliphant considered their options. The gentlemanly thing to do would be to agree to a delay of a month or two with a firm date on the docket. The longer they waited, the harder Jesse could squeeze Bobby Lopez.

Jesse did not contest the motion and a trial was set for May 12. Judge Oliphant informed Joshua Burch, in writing, that there would be no more continuances, regardless of Mr. Malco's medical problems.

At 5:00 P.M. on the fourth day of April, the deadline for filing, Jesse walked down to the office of the circuit clerk and asked if he had an opponent. The answer was no; he was unopposed. There would be no costly and time-consuming campaign. He drove to the offices of Rudy & Pettigrew where cold champagne was waiting.

———•———

Since the FBI's surprise visit to his office five months earlier, Jesse had seen Agent Jackson Lewis only once. He had dropped by in early March for a quick cup of coffee and some interesting stories about showing up at the nightclubs unannounced and flashing his badge.

In late April, Lewis was back, along with Agent Spence Whitehead.

They talked about the upcoming Malco trial and what a spectacle it would be. They planned to be in the courtroom watching it all.

Lewis said, "I don't suppose you've ever heard of the jewelry store robberies, have you?"

Jesse drew a blank and said, "No, I have not prosecuted a jewelry store robbery, yet. Why do you ask?"

"It's a long story and I'll give an abbreviated version. About five years ago three people, two men and a woman, strong-armed five jewelry stores, sort of a smash-and-run game. They chose mom-and-pop stores in small towns, none in Mississippi, cleaned out the display cases, hit the road. Not very sophisticated but pretty successful, until the sixth store. In Waynesboro, Georgia, they picked the wrong place. Owner had a gun, knew how to use it, a gunfight broke out. A thug named Jimmie Crane was killed, as was his girl, a hooker named Karol Horton, last known place of employment was Red Velvet. Crane was a recent parolee and living around here. The third guy was driving the getaway car and fled the town, but six people at the first five stores got a good look at him."

Jesse said, "I missed this story. Again, I have enough crime to worry about around here."

Lewis slid across a police artist's sketch of the third suspect. Jesse looked at it and did not react.

Lewis continued, "The Bureau finally tracked Crane and Horton to Biloxi. Two agents spent a few days around here but got nowhere. No one seemed to recognize this guy, or if they did, they kept it quiet. With time the investigation fizzled and now five years have gone by. Two months ago we busted a fencing operation in New Orleans and picked up some clues. Still can't find this guy, though. Any ideas?"

Jesse frowned and shook his head and did a passable job of showing little interest. He said, "Look, guys, I have enough on my plate right now. I can't be worried by a string of old armed robberies in other states."

He gave them a smile, then returned to the composite and looked into the cold eyes of Hugh Malco.

He asked if he could keep the sketch, said he might show it around. They left after half an hour. Jesse made several copies of it and hid them in his office. He told no one, not even Keith and Egan.

———•———

May 5, 1975, one week before the highly anticipated trial of Lance Malco and Bobby Lopez, Judge Oliphant summoned the lawyers to his chambers for a conference. He had promised to hand over the list of prospective jurors and they were eager to get their hands on it. Jesse and Egan sat on one side of the table. Joshua Burch and two of his associates looked on from the other side. All pre-trial motions had been argued and decided. It was time for the battle and the tension was thick.

Judge Oliphant began with the usual inquiry about a settlement. "Have there been discussions about a plea agreement?"

Burch shook his head no. Jesse said, "Your Honor, the State will offer Mr. Lopez the same consideration we made to Fritz Haberstroh and Coot Reed. In return for a plea of guilty, and full cooperation against Mr. Malco, we will recommend a reduced sentence."

Without hesitation, Burch said, "And we reject the offer, Mr. Rudy."

"Don't you think you should consult with your client?" Jesse shot back.

"I'm his lawyer and I reject the offer."

"Understood, but ethically you have a duty to inform your client."

"Don't lecture me about ethics, Mr. Rudy. I've spent hours with Mr. Lopez and I know his intentions. He looks forward to the trial and the opportunity to defend himself and Mr. Malco against these charges."

Jesse smiled and shrugged.

Judge Oliphant said, "It seems to me as though Mr. Rudy has a point. Mr. Lopez should at least be informed of this opportunity."

Burch replied, somewhat smugly, "With all due respect, Your Honor, I have a great deal of experience in these matters and I know how to represent my clients."

Almost gleefully, Jesse said, "Don't worry, Your Honor, I withdraw the offer."

Judge Oliphant scratched his jaw as he stared at Burch. He shuffled some papers and said, "Okay, what about Mr. Malco. Any chance of a plea agreement?"

Jesse said, "Your Honor, the State has an offer for Mr. Malco.

In return for a plea of guilty to the crime of operating a place used for prostitution, the State will recommend a sentence of ten years and a fine of five thousand dollars. All other charges will be dropped."

Burch snorted and seemed amused. "No thanks. Mr. Malco is not willing to plead guilty to anything."

Jesse said, "Okay, but he's facing thirteen other charges of promoting prostitution and ten of his girls will testify against him. Each charge carries a maximum of ten years and five thousand dollars. Same for Lopez. They could spend the rest of their lives in prison."

Burch replied coolly, "Oh, I know the law, Mr. Rudy. No need for a tutorial. The answer is no."

Judge Oliphant said, "And you don't think you should inform Mr. Malco of this offer?"

"Please, Judge. I know what I'm doing."

"Very well." Judge Oliphant shuffled some more papers and said, "Here are the lists of prospective jurors. The clerk over in Bay St. Louis is confident that this pool is qualified and above reproach."

Burch was startled and blurted, "Bay St. Louis?"

"Yes, Mr. Burch. I'm changing venue. This case will be tried next door in Hancock County, not here in Harrison. I'm convinced the jury in the Ginger Redfield trial was tampered with and we're not running that risk this time around."

"But no one requested a change of venue."

"You should know the law, Mr. Burch. Read the statute, I have the discretion to change venue to any district in the State of Mississippi."

Burch was stunned and couldn't respond. Jesse was surprised and elated, but suppressed a smile. Judge Oliphant handed each a list of the names and said, "There will be no contact with anyone in our pool. None whatsoever." He glared at Burch and continued, "When we convene on May twelve, I will quiz the panel about improper contact. Any hint of it and I'll throw the book at the guilty party. Once we select the twelve, and two alternates, I will lecture them on the criminality of improper contact. Each morning and each afternoon I will repeat my lecture. Am I clear?"

"Crystal clear, Your Honor," Jesse said as he smirked at Burch.

PART THREE

———•———

THE PRISONERS

CHAPTER 35

The courtroom was empty; the lights were off. Big Red, the one-legged courthouse janitor, was fiddling with some wires on the bench. Jesse entered, nodded at him from a distance, walked down the aisle, through the bar, placed his briefcase on his table, and said hello. Big Red mumbled something in return, a man of few words. When Joshua Burch entered through the main door, Jesse asked the janitor for a moment of privacy. Big Red frowned as if irritated at having his important work interrupted, but left anyway.

They sat across the table from one another and skipped the pleasantries. Jesse began with "You're not going to win this trial, Joshua. I have too many witnesses and everybody knows the truth anyway. Malco has been running girls around here for decades and his party is over. When he's convicted, Oliphant will throw the book at him and he'll die an old man at Parchman prison."

Burch absorbed it and chose not to argue. The bluster was gone. The facts were not in his favor and he'd lost his chance for a hung jury when the trial was moved to Hancock County, away from Fats Bowman and the tentacles of his influence.

Burch said, "You asked for this meeting. What's on your mind?"

"A plea deal. Lance is a smart man and he knows his luck has run out. A trial will expose many of his nasty secrets. It'll be embarrassing."

"His health is not good."

"Come on, Joshua. No one believes that, and even if it were

true, what's the big deal? Parchman is full of sick people. They have doctors up there. An alleged bad heart is no defense."

"I've discussed a plea with him, more than once. He tried to fire me again, but he's settled down. I think he's discussed it with Hugh, not sure about the rest of the family."

"I have an incentive, something you and he should know."

Burch shrugged and said, "I'm all ears."

Jesse told the story of young Hugh's brief career as an armed robber. The jewelry store heists, the shootout, the deaths of Jimmie Crane and Karol Horton. Hugh's lucky getaway and his even luckier avoidance of being identified. Five years ago, a lot of time had passed, but the FBI is back.

Burch claimed he knew nothing of the robberies and Jesse believed him. He had never caught a whiff of the story.

He described his recent meeting with the FBI. He handed over a copy of the police sketch and said, "Looks like Hugh to me. If the FBI knew it was him, they would take his photograph to the victims. He'd serve at least twenty years, maybe more."

Burch studied the sketch, shook his head, mumbled the word "Moron."

Jesse moved in for the kill. "I haven't said a word to the FBI, yet. I can keep my mouth shut if I get the deal."

Burch laid the sketch on the desk and kept shaking his head. "This is ruthless."

"Ruthless? Malco's been knee-deep in organized crime for the past thirty years. Illegal liquor, gambling, prostitution, drugs, not to mention beatings, burnings, and who knows how many dead bodies. And you call me ruthless. Hell, Joshua, this is child's play compared to Malco's activities."

Burch slumped a few inches in his chair, then picked up the sketch again. He studied it for a long time and put it down. "It's blackmail."

"Call it blackmail, ruthless, anything you want. I don't care. I want Lance Malco in prison."

"So, let's be real clear, Jesse. You're offering ten years, and if he says no, then you'll go to the FBI with the name of Hugh Malco."

"Not quite. If he says no, then I'll put his ass on trial in Hancock County six days from now and the jury will find him guilty on all counts because he's dead guilty. Then I'll go to the FBI with his son's name. Both will go to prison for a long time."

"Got it. And if he takes the deal, then you say nothing to the FBI."

"You have my word. I can't promise the Feds won't find Hugh some other way, but they won't get his name from me. I swear."

Burch got to his feet, walked to a window, looked out, saw nothing, walked back and leaned on the bar. "What about Bobby Lopez?"

"Who cares? He gets the same deal as Haberstroh and Coot Reed. He pleads guilty, gets probation, a slap on the wrist. Get lost."

"No prison?"

"Not another day behind bars."

Burch walked to the table and picked up the sketch. "Mind if I take this?"

"It's your copy. Go show it to your client."

"It's blackmail."

"'Ruthless' sounds better, but I don't care. You have twenty-four hours."

———•———

Lance Malco stood behind his desk and stared at a wall. Nevin Noll sat in a chair to the side, puffing a cigarette. Hugh stood by the door and looked as if he wanted to cry. Burch sat in the middle of the room under a cloud of smoke. The sketch was in the center of the desk.

Lance asked, "How long would I serve?"

"Roughly two-thirds of the sentence. With good behavior."

"That son of a bitch," Hugh mumbled for the tenth time.

"Any chance of getting moved back here to the county jail?"

"Maybe, after a couple of years. Fats could probably pull some strings."

"That son of a bitch."

Lance moved slowly to his swivel chair and sat down. He smiled at Burch and said, "I can take anything they throw at me, Burch. I'm not afraid of prison."

———•———

Burch called Jesse and tried to chat like they were old friends. The favor he wanted was a quiet and quick hearing to get it over with, but Jesse would have none of it. In his finest hour, he wanted a spectacle.

On May 12, a crowd gathered in the courtroom to witness history. The front row was filled with reporters, and behind them several dozen spectators waited anxiously to see if the rumors were true. Every courthouse had a collection of bored or semi-retired lawyers who missed nothing and were adept at spreading gossip, and all were present. Being officers of the court, they were allowed to enter through the bar, mill about with the clerks, even sit in the jury box when it wasn't being used. Keith was not one of them but he found a chair near the prosecution's table. During a casual glance at the crowd he made eye contact with Hugh. It was not a pleasant exchange. If looks could kill.

Carmen Malco was not present, nor were her other two adult children. Lance didn't want them near the courthouse. The headlines would be brutal enough.

A bailiff called court to order and everyone stood. Judge Oliphant appeared and took his seat at the bench. He motioned for the crowd to sit and called Mr. Rudy to the podium. Jesse announced that a plea bargain had been agreed upon between the State and the defendant Bobby Lopez.

Joshua Burch bounced to his feet and strutted to the bench where he motioned for his client to join him. Jesse stood on the other side. The courtroom listened as the judge read the charges. Lopez pled guilty on all counts and was ordered to return in a month for sentencing. As he returned to his seat, His Honor called, "State of Mississippi versus Lance Malco." The defendant rose from his seat at the defense table and walked forward as if he had nothing to fear. Dressed in a dark suit, starched white shirt, and paisley tie, he could have passed for one of the lawyers. He brushed by Jesse without making contact. He stood between Burch and the DA and looked arrogantly up at the judge.

After he pled guilty to one count of "having control over the use of a place and knowingly allowing another person to use said place for prostitution" he was asked if he was ready to be sentenced. Burch answered that he was. Judge Oliphant sentenced him to ten years in the state penitentiary at Parchman and fined him $5,000. Malco accepted the sentence without flinching and never blinked.

The Judge said, "I hereby remand you to the custody of the county sheriff to be transported to Parchman."

Malco nodded, said nothing, and walked proudly back to his seat. When the hearing was adjourned, he was led by two bailiffs through a side door and taken to jail.

———•———

The bold headline in the *Gulf Coast Register* the following morning said it all: **MALCO PLEADS GUILTY—ORDERED TO PRISON.** A large photo captured Malco in handcuffs as he was led to a patrol car, with Hugh one step behind him.

Jesse bought extra copies and planned to have one framed for the Ego Wall in his office.

———•———

Two days later, a long, brown Ford left the jail at dawn with Chief Deputy Rudd Kilgore behind the wheel, Fats riding shotgun, and the prisoner in the rear seat, without handcuffs. Hugh insisted on making the five-hour trip and sat beside his father. For the first hour, as they drank stale coffee from tall paper cups, little was said. The subject of Jesse Rudy came up soon enough, and there was a general thrashing of the DA.

Fats had ruled Harrison County like a dictator for sixteen years and refused to worry about much, though there was some concern now that Rudy was in bed with the FBI. Lance warned Fats that Rudy was out of control and would only become bolder. If he managed to stop the prostitution and gambling, most of the nightclubs would close and Fats's cash flow would be seriously curtailed. Bars and strip clubs were still legal and there would be no need for protection from the sheriff. Fats assured him he was aware of that.

They stopped in Hattiesburg for a nice breakfast, then set off for Jackson and beyond. As they approached Yazoo City, the hills flattened and the Delta began; mile after mile of some of the richest soil on earth, all seemingly covered with perfect rows of green cotton stalks, knee-high.

Hugh had never seen the Delta before and quickly found it depressing. The deeper they drove into it, the more he hated Jesse Rudy.

Lance was already homesick for the Coast.

CHAPTER 36

O n a warm weekend in late September, the entire Rudy family, along with the law firm and at least a hundred other friends and family members, descended on the city of Meridian, two and a half hours north of the Coast. The occasion was the wedding of Keith Rudy and Ainsley Hart. The couple met at Ole Miss when he was a third-year law student and she was a junior majoring in music. She had recently graduated and was working in Jackson. They had grown weary of the strain of a long-distance romance and finally set a date. Keith confided in his father that he wasn't quite ready to get married because he wasn't sure he could afford a wife. Jesse explained that no one could. If he waited until he deemed himself ready, then he would never marry. Time to man up and take the plunge.

Keith's college friends had lobbied hard for a wedding in Biloxi so they could hit the nightclubs and enjoy the strippers. At first, he thought it was a well-organized prank, but when he realized some were serious he nixed the idea. So did Ainsley. She preferred a proper church wedding at First Presbyterian, where she had been baptized. The Harts were fiercely Protestant. The Rudys were staunch Roman Catholic. During the courtship, the couple had occasionally brought up the issue of church affiliation, but since it was a touchy subject they made no progress and hoped things worked out down the road. They agreed to go their separate ways on Sundays and had no idea what would happen when children entered the picture.

Jesse and Agnes hosted a splendid rehearsal dinner at the country club on Friday night. Eighty guests, in cocktail attire, dined on raw oysters, grilled shrimp, and stuffed flounder, a gift from a wholesaler on Point Cadet, one of Jesse's closest friends. His warehouse stood next door to the cannery where Jesse's father had worked ten-hour days shucking oysters as a kid.

Many of the Presbyterians were teetotalers, though drinking was not as deadly a sin as the Baptists believed it to be, and most of them enjoyed wine with dinner. They were surprised, though, by the amount of alcohol consumed by the folks from the Coast. They'd heard about those people from Biloxi and their laid-back lifestyle. Now they were witnessing it firsthand.

The toasts began and more wine was served. Tim Rudy, with hair to his shoulders and a thick beard, flew in from Montana and arrived just in time. He told humorous stories about his big brother, the perfect kid who never got in trouble. Tim stayed in trouble and often ran to Keith for support when Jesse was ready to kill him. A college roommate told a story that brought down the house, especially in light of Jesse's growing reputation. Seemed that one weekend, when Jesse and Agnes were out of town, a carload of rowdies arrived from Southern Miss and descended upon their home. They collected Keith and hit the Strip. At a joint called Foxy's, they drank and drank but nothing happened. Keith explained that the beer was watered down and the drinks were little more than sugary Kool-Aid. They demanded a bottle of whiskey but the bartender refused. They threatened to go somewhere else but Keith said most of the bars served the same crap. When they made too much noise, a bouncer told them to leave. Imagine—Keith Rudy getting kicked out of a Biloxi strip club! The roommate insinuated that a couple of the boys may have made it upstairs, but Keith certainly did not. Joey Grasich reminisced about their childhood days on the Point and their adventures fishing and sailing in the Sound. He was thankful for lifetime friends like Keith and Denny Smith, Hugh, of course, was not mentioned.

Jesse ended the dinner with a tribute to his son. For a man who'd given a thousand speeches, he barely got through it. When he finished, there were only a few dry eyes.

A soul group livened things up and the party moved to the dance floor. At midnight, Jesse and Agnes left the youngsters and headed to their hotel.

Early the following morning, Ainsley's parents awoke in a panic. They had woefully underestimated the amount of beer, liquor, and wine that would be needed that evening for the wedding dinner. Over three hundred guests would attend, almost half of them from Biloxi, and those Catholics could really drink. Mr. Hart spent the morning raiding liquor stores and buying kegs of beer.

The 5:00 P.M. ceremony went as planned, with some of the eight groomsmen showing obvious distress from the long night. Jesse proudly stood next to his son as his best man. Ainsley had never been more beautiful.

———•———

Haley Stofer was arrested in St. Louis for drunk driving. He put up a cash bail and was almost out of the police station when his name appeared on a wanted list. Apparently, the defendant had had some problems down in Mississippi. There was an outstanding warrant based on an old indictment for drug trafficking. It took a month to extradite him to Harrison County, and when Jesse saw his name on the weekly jail log, he dropped everything and paid him a visit.

A bailiff shoved Stofer into the room where the DA was waiting. Jesse stared at him, took in his unshaven, gaunt face, his faded orange jumpsuit, the handcuffs. He even had chains around his ankles, because he was, after all, a drug smuggler.

"Where you been, Stofer?" Jesse asked.

"Good to see you again, Mr. Rudy."

"I'm not sure about that. Look, I'm not here to rehash the past.

I brought you a copy of the indictment, thought you might want to refresh your memory. What did I tell you back then?"

"You told me to get out of town. The bad guys were after me. I was about to be killed."

"True, but I also told you to call me once a week. The deal was that you would be available to testify against Lance Malco. Instead, you disappeared and left me hanging."

"You told me to run."

"I'm not going to argue. I'll knock off ten years for jumping bail."

"I testified before the grand jury and got the indictments."

"Okay, I'll knock off another fifteen. That leaves fifteen for trafficking."

"I can't serve fifteen years, Mr. Rudy. Please."

"You won't have to. With good behavior you might get out in ten." Jesse abruptly stood, left the indictment on the table, and walked to the door.

Stofer said, pleading, "They'll get me, you know? I couldn't come back."

"That wasn't the deal, Stofer."

"It's all your fault. You forced me to go undercover."

"No, Stofer, you chose to run drugs. Now you pay the price." Jesse left the room.

———— • ————

Following orders Lance left behind, Hugh moved into the big office and took charge of the family business. It included the strip clubs—Red Velvet, Foxy's, O'Malley's, the Truck Stop, and Desperado, formerly known as Carousel—as well as two bars where the bookies gathered, a string of convenience stores used to launder cash, three motels once used to house the hookers but now virtually vacant, two restaurants that, oddly enough, had never been used for illegal activities, apartment buildings, raw land near the beach, and some condos in Florida. Lance retained sole ownership of it all, with the exception of the family home which he deeded to Carmen. She had not filed for divorce and was relieved that her husband was gone. They had agreed that Hugh would support her to the tune of $1,000 a month. Hugh's brother and sister had left the Coast and had little contact with the family.

Lance considered his little sojourn to Parchman nothing more than a temporary setback, a survivable price to pay for his riches. He planned to run his empire from behind bars and return soon enough, far sooner than the ten years Mr. Rudy had in mind. With Hugh in place and managing things, and with Nevin Noll as his right-hand man, he was confident his assets were secure. His troubles would soon be over.

After six months, though, the numbers were soft. With gambling and prostitution severely curtailed, the Biloxi underworld was suffering through another downturn. There were too many clubs and bars and not enough customers. The conviction and removal of Lance Malco sent chills through the Strip. Jesse Rudy was after the crime bosses and no one knew who would be next. To make matters far worse, he had the state police on board and the FBI lurking about.

———•———

Limited by state law to only four years in office, Governor Bill Waller was packing his bags as 1975 came to a close. His term had been successful. Though the state still lagged in education, health care, and especially civil rights, he was the first governor to push a progressive agenda. He wasn't finished with politics and dreamed of serving in the U.S. Senate, but at that time both seats were firmly controlled by John Stennis and James Eastland. He planned to start a private law practice in Jackson and looked forward to a return to the courtroom.

In early December, he invited Jesse and Keith to stop by the governor's mansion for lunch. Waller had followed the Malco case closely and wanted to catch up with the gossip from the Coast. He loved seafood, and as a going-away gift Jesse brought a cooler filled with fresh oysters, shrimp, and crabs. The chef prepared them for lunch and the governor, a big man with an impressive appetite, enjoyed the feast.

They chatted about Malco and he informed the Rudys that his "corrections people" had reported that the inmate was doing well and working in the prison library. He had managed to procure his own cell, though like all the others, it lacked air-conditioning. Jesse quipped that he was hoping Malco would be sent to the fields to pick cotton like the common criminals.

Jesse said, "Tell your people to keep an eye on him. He has plenty of cash and bribery always works in prison."

They had several laughs at Malco's expense. Keith knew his place at the table and said little. He was overwhelmed to be having lunch in the mansion with the governor himself.

Waller grew serious and asked Jesse, "So, do you have any plans after district attorney?"

Jesse was caught off guard and said, "Not really. I have plenty of unfinished work down there."

"Can you get that sheriff? Bowman's been on the take for years."

"I think about him every day, Governor, but he's a slick one."

"You can get him. I'll help any way I can."

"You've done enough. Without the state police we wouldn't be where we are. The people on the Coast owe you a huge debt."

"They voted for me, that's all I could ask." He attacked a raw oyster. After it slid down, he said, "You know, Jesse, the Democratic Party in this state is a mess, not a lot of progressive talent, a pretty thin bench, if you ask me. I'm talking to a lot of people about our future, and your name keeps coming up. I think you should consider running statewide. Attorney general, then maybe this job."

Jesse tried to deflect it with a fake laugh. "Look, Governor, I'm Roman Catholic. We're a distinct minority in Mississippi."

"Hogwash. This state went for JFK in 1960, don't ever forget that."

"Barely, and it's gone Republican ever since, except for George Wallace."

"Naw, we still have the votes statewide. I can't imagine Mississippi ever electing a Republican governor. Your religion won't matter. We just need some new talent."

"I'm flattered, Governor, but I'm fifty-one years old. After this next term as DA, I'll be fifty-six, not exactly a youthful age."

"I'm fifty now, Jesse, and I'm not ready for a nursing home. I plan to run for the Senate if there's ever an opening, which looks doubtful. Sorta gets in your blood, you know?"

"Again, I'm flattered, but I just don't see it."

"What about you, Keith?"

Keith almost choked on a bite of grilled shrimp. He swallowed and managed to say, "I guess I'm on the other end. I'm only twenty-seven."

"Time to get started. I like the way you carry yourself, Keith, and you have your father's personality, not to mention the last name, which could be a real asset."

The conversation was not new. Jesse and Keith had discussed pursuing a seat in the state legislature, the traditional starting place for young, ambitious politicians in the state. Keith could not yet admit to anyone, not even his father, that he dreamed of living in the very mansion where he was now having lunch.

Jesse smiled and replied, "He's thinking about it, Governor."

Waller said, "Here's an idea. A. F. Sumner just got reelected to his third term as attorney general. I don't know why the governor gets only four years when everybody else can serve for life, but that's the law. As you know, the legislature does not want a strong governor. Anyway, I'm close to A.F. and he owes me some favors. Think about coming to Jackson and working in the AG's office for a few years. I'll be around and I can introduce you to a lot of people. It'll be a great experience."

Keith was flattered but he wasn't ready to leave the Coast. "That's quite generous, Governor, but I have this new wife and we've just settled into our apartment. The law firm is growing and we're getting some good cases."

"Send me some business. I'm about to be unemployed."

"But thank you, Governor."

"No rush. The offer stands. Perhaps in a year or two."

"I'll certainly consider it."

Jesse had one last favor to request. It was rumored that the chief of the state police would hang on to his job through the change in administrations. Jesse wanted his continued cooperation for the next four years. The seven unsolved murders, all gang-related in Jesse's opinion, still haunted him. Fats had never shown an interest and the cases were only grower colder. Extra muscle was needed from the state, and Jesse wanted a meeting with the chief to ask for help.

With only a month left in office, the governor would promise anything.

CHAPTER 37

The break came in February of 1976, some seven years after the murder, when a bootlegger named Bayard Wolf doubled over in pain and decided it was time to see a doctor. His wife drove him to Tupelo for tests that did not go well. He was diagnosed with acute pancreatic cancer and given a short time to live.

Wolf lived in rural Tippah County, one of the driest in the state, and for years made a decent living selling illegal beer to thirsty customers, many of them teenagers. As a younger man he had raised hell with the State Line Mob and had once worked in a club owned by Ginger Redfield and her husband. His second wife convinced him to leave that unstable and dangerous world and try to go straight. Bootlegging beer was an easy and harmless crime, one without the threat of violence. The sheriff left him alone because he provided a much needed service and kept the kids off the roads to Tupelo and Memphis.

Unknown to his wife, and to the sheriff, Wolf maintained contacts with the Dixie Mafia and provided a service that few others could. In the business his nickname was "the Broker." For a nice fee, he could liaison between a man with money and a grudge, and a professional hit man. From the obscurity of his quiet little farm near Walnut, Mississippi, he had arranged numerous contract killings. He was the man to go see when murder was the only option.

Faced with imminent death himself, Wolf found a sudden interest in God. His sins were numerous, far more impressive than most, and they became burdens too heavy to carry. He believed in heaven and hell and he was frightened over what he was facing.

During a late-night revival service, Wolf walked down the aisle to the altar where the evangelist met him. In tears, he confessed his sinful past, though he did not, at that emotional moment, give much in the way of details. The congregation rejoiced that a notorious bootlegger and sinner had found the Lord and they celebrated with him.

After his dramatic conversion, which was genuine, Wolf felt enormous relief, but he was still plagued by his past. He felt responsible for many horrible crimes which continued to haunt him. Weeks passed and he deteriorated physically. Mentally and emotionally he was not at peace. His preacher stopped by once a day for a devotional and prayer, and several times Wolf felt the spirit move him to confess everything. He could not, however, muster the courage, and the guilt grew heavier.

Two months after his diagnosis, he had lost forty pounds and could not get out of bed. The end was near and he was not ready for it. He called the sheriff and asked him to stop by when the preacher was there. With his wife sitting by his bed, and the sheriff taking notes, and the preacher laying hands on his blanket, Wolf started talking.

That afternoon, the sheriff drove to Jackson and met with the chief of the state police. The following morning, two officers and two technicians arrived at the Wolf home. A camera and a recorder were quickly set up at the foot of his bed.

In a strained, scratchy, and often fading voice, Wolf talked. He gave details of contract killings that stretched back two decades. He named the men who ordered the hits and the fees they paid. He named their go-betweens. He named their victims. The more he talked, the more he nodded off. Heavily sedated and in enormous pain, he drifted in and out and was occasionally confused. Some of the hits he recalled in detail, others had been too long ago.

The sheriff stood at the door, shaking his head in disbelief.

Mrs. Wolf was overwhelmed and could not stay in the room. She served coffee and offered cookies, but no one was hungry.

Bayard Wolf died three days later, at peace with himself. His preacher assured him that God forgives all sins when they are confessed before him. Wolf wasn't sure God had ever heard such a monumental confession, but he accepted the promises on faith and was smiling when he took his last breath.

He left behind an enormous treasure of facts that would take years to unravel. Nineteen murders in twenty-one years in eight states. Jealous husbands, jealous wives, jealous girlfriends, feuding business partners, siblings at war, scam artists, duped investors, a corrupt politician, even a rogue cop.

And one nightclub owner determined to eliminate the competition.

———— • ————

According to Wolf, a man named Nevin Noll met him in a bar in Tupelo. Wolf was quite familiar with Biloxi and had even visited the clubs in years past. He had never met Malco, but he had certainly heard of him. Wolf knew that Noll was a longtime gun thug for Malco, though he didn't ask where the money came from. That question was always off-limits. Noll gave him $20,000 in cash for a hit on Dusty Cromwell, another outlaw with an even shadier past. Wolf assumed there was another turf war underway in Biloxi and Malco was in the middle of it. Such activities were common down there and Wolf knew some of the players.

Wolf kept 10 percent of the cash, his customary fee, and brokered the killing. His favorite hit man was Johnny Clark, a former army sniper who'd been kicked out of the military for atrocities in Vietnam. His nickname, whispered only in certain circles, was "the Rifleman." Wolf met him in the same bar in Tupelo and handed over the rest of the cash. Two months later, Dusty Cromwell was practically decapitated as he walked along a Biloxi beach with his girlfriend.

Of the other unsolved murders on the Coast, Wolf claimed no

knowledge. Some had all the markings of professional hits; others appeared to be the work of local thugs settling scores.

———•———

In May, Jesse Rudy drove to Jackson for a meeting at the headquarters of the state police. He was given the background on Bayard Wolf and shown a video clip of his narrative about the Cromwell murder. It was a stunning turn of events, one that Jesse had in no way contemplated, and it presented an enormous challenge for any prosecution.

First, Wolf, the star witness, was dead. Second, his taped testimony would never be admitted in court. No judge would allow it, regardless of how crucial it was, because the defense did not have the opportunity to cross-examine the witness. Even though Wolf had been sworn to tell the truth, there was no way a jury would ever see or hear him. To admit his testimony would be clear reversible error.

The third problem, as the police had already learned, was that there was no sign of anyone named Johnny Clark. Wolf believed he lived somewhere near Opelika, Alabama. The locals found three men by that name in the area, but none came close to being considered suspects. The Alabama state police located forty-three more Johnny Clarks living in the state, and eliminated all of them as possible suspects. And, according to Wolf, the Rifleman was responsible for two other hits in Alabama, so the police there had their hands full. The phone number Wolf gave them for Clark had been disconnected three years earlier. It was tracked to a mobile home park in the village of Lanett, Alabama, and to a trailer that was no longer there. It had been registered to a woman named Irene Harris, who evidently disappeared with her trailer. She had not been found but they were still searching.

The state police and Jesse agreed it was safe to assume that a professional killer with a checkered past would move around and hide behind a number of aliases.

According to U.S. military records, twenty-seven men named Johnny Clark served in Vietnam; not a single one was dishonorably discharged. Two were killed in action.

The state police tried to investigate every angle of Wolf's story. They did not doubt the gist of it—the nineteen contract killings. With the names of the victims in hand, it was easy enough to track down the cold cases in eight states. However, it was impossible to verify every detail Wolf gave them.

———•———

Jesse did not remember the three-hour drive back to Biloxi. His mind whirled with scenarios, strategies, questions, and few answers. Contract murder was a capital offense in the state, and the beauty of bringing Lance Malco, Nevin Noll, and others to trial for the killing of Dusty Cromwell would excite any prosecutor. They deserved death row, but putting them there seemed impossible. There were no witnesses to the killing and the crime scene yielded nothing. The high-caliber bullet that entered through Dusty's right cheek and blew off the back of his head was never found. Thus, there were no ballistics, no weapon, no proof of any kind to show a jury.

At the office, Jesse briefed Egan Clement on the meeting in Jackson. There was relief in finally knowing who murdered Cromwell, though Lance had been the suspect from the beginning. The confirmation, though, was a hollow win because there was no clear path to an indictment.

They filed the information away, added memos to files that were much too thin, and waited for the next phone call from the state police. It came a month later and was a waste of time. There was nothing to report. The other eighteen investigations were sputtering along, most with about as much success as the Cromwell case. Wolf's snitching had police in eight states chasing their tails with little to show for it. They were searching for skilled hit men who left cold trails. They were wading through the underworld, where they did not belong. They were trying to bring justice to victims who were also crooks. They were trying to follow cash money trails with no hope of success.

Another month passed, and another with no luck. But the digging caused gossip, and the gossip took on a life of its own. Rumors spread through the darkness and in countless bars and honky-tonks word was passed that Wolf had said too much before he passed.

———•———

For the past fifteen years, Nevin Noll had perfected the rules of engagement when a stranger came to a bar looking for him. Get the name, ask what the hell he wants, and tell him Mr. Noll is not in. He might be back tomorrow, or he might be out of town. Never meet with a man you know nothing about.

But the stranger was no stranger to the ways of crime bosses and was in a hurry anyway. On a napkin he wrote down the name "Bayard Wolf," left it with the bartender, and said, "I'll be back in one hour. Please impress upon Mr. Noll that this is an urgent matter." He left without giving a name.

An hour later, Noll was on the beach, sitting at a picnic table and staring at the ocean. The stranger approached and stood five feet away. The two had never met, but they had met Wolf. The man with a grudge meets the man with a gun.

The stranger talked for two minutes, then left, walked back to the parking lot, and drove away. He told Noll that Bayard Wolf had told the cops everything before he died. They knew Malco ordered the contract and Noll handed over $20,000 to Wolf. They knew the Rifleman pulled the trigger.

The Biloxi DA was investigating the Cromwell killing.

CHAPTER 38

He had learned to build bombs ten years earlier when he joined the Klan. At the time he worked for a contractor who often demolished old buildings to make way for new ones. In his day job, he learned the basics of demolition and became adept at the use of TNT and dynamite. With his hobby, he enjoyed building bombs that leveled black churches and the homes of sympathetic whites. He hit his stride in 1969 when the Klan declared war on the Jews in Mississippi and began an eighteen-month terror campaign. They accused the Jews of funding the civil rights nonsense and vowed to run them out of the state, all three thousand of them. His bombs destroyed homes, businesses, schools, and synagogues. Finally, the FBI moved in and put an end to his fun. He was indicted but acquitted by an all-white jury.

Now he was freelance, picking up work occasionally when a crooked businessman needed a building blown up in an insurance scam. His bombs hadn't killed anyone in years and he was delighted with the challenge.

The name embroidered above the left pocket of his brown shirt was LYLE, and Lyle he would be until the job was over. His real identity was hidden with his wallet, cash, and two pistols under the bed of his motel room a mile away.

At 12:05 P.M., on Friday, August 20, 1976, Lyle waited in the cab of his pickup truck, a dark blue 1973 Dodge half-ton. He was parked on a narrow street near the courthouse with an easy escape route. He picked a Friday in August because the county's legal business came almost to a halt at that time. The courthouse was virtually deserted. The lawyers, judges, and clerks not on vacation were slipping away for a long lunch that would lead to a long weekend. Many would not return for the afternoon.

Lyle didn't want collateral damage, unnecessary victims. Nor did he want witnesses, people who might later claim to have seen a UPS delivery man on the second floor just before the explosion. Russ, the real UPS guy, delivered on Tuesdays and Thursdays and was well known to the courthouse regulars. An odd delivery on a Friday might get a look or two.

From the bed of his pickup he collected three boxes, all brown cardboard. Two were empty and had no labels or markings of any type. The third was ten by fourteen inches and six inches deep. It weighed five pounds and contained a block of Semtex, a moldable, plastic, military explosive. The shipping label addressed the package to *The Honorable Jesse Rudy, District Attorney, Room 214, Harrison County Courthouse, Biloxi, Mississippi.* The sender was *Appellate Reporter, Inc.,* with an address in Wilmington, Delaware. It was a legitimate company that had been publishing law books for decades. Three weeks earlier, Mr. Rudy had received an identical package, delivered by Russ. Inside were two thick, leather-bound books, along with a letter from the company asking him to try a free subscription for six months.

Two nights earlier, on August 18, Lyle had broken into the courthouse, picked the lock to the DA's office, and confirmed that the first two books had been received. They were on display on a shelf with dozens of treatises, most of which gave the appearance of never being used. He also checked the master calendar on the secretary's desk and saw that Mr. Rudy had an appointment at 12:30 on August 20. More than likely the secretary would be out for lunch, as would Egan Clement, his assistant. The target would be hanging around, waiting for his appointment.

Cradling the three boxes with both arms, and using them to partially hide his face, Lyle hurried up the stairs to the second floor, and in doing so did not see another person. As he passed the courtroom door he walked between two lawyers who appeared to be disagreeing quietly. He hurried on, and outside the DA's office he left the two empty boxes in the hallway and stepped inside as he tapped on the door.

"Come in," a man's voice called.

Lyle walked in with a smile and said, "Package for Mr. Jesse Rudy." He placed it on the desk as he spoke.

"That's me," Mr. Rudy said, barely looking up from a document. "Who's it from?"

"Got no idea, sir," Lyle said, already retreating. He had no worries about being recognized and later identified. Later, Mr. Rudy wouldn't be around to point a finger.

"Thanks," he said.

"No problem, sir. Have a good day."

Lyle was out of the office in seconds. He picked up the two empty boxes, used the top one as cover, and walked casually down the hall. The two lawyers were gone. There was no one in sight, until, suddenly, Egan Clement appeared at the top of the stairs. She was carrying a paper bag from a deli and a bottle of soda. She glanced at him as she walked by. Lyle thought, *Oh shit!* and had to make a quick decision. In a few short seconds Egan would be in the office and would become collateral damage.

Lyle dropped the boxes and removed from his pocket a remote detonator. He crouched beside the banister for cover, and pressed the button, at least thirty seconds before he'd planned to.

The thrill of bomb-making was to be close enough to feel and hear it, and sometimes even to see it, but yet far enough away to avoid debris. He was much too close and would pay a price.

The explosion rocked the modern building, which seemed to bounce on its concrete foundation. The sound was deafening and burst eardrums in the clerks' offices on the first floor. It shattered every window on both levels. It knocked people down. It rattled walls and shook off portraits, framed photographs, bulletin boards, notices, and fire extinguishers. In the main courtroom, light fixtures crashed onto the empty spectator pews. Judge Oliphant was sitting alone at a table in his chambers having a sandwich. His tall glass of ice tea tilted, flipped, and spilled. He ran into his courtroom, stepped on bits of broken glass, yanked open the main doors, and was hit with a wave of smoke and dust. Through it, he saw someone move along the floor down the hall. He took a deep breath, held it, and scrambled toward the person, who was moaning. It was Egan Clement, with blood oozing from her scalp. Judge Oliphant dragged her back to the courtroom and closed the doors.

Lyle was knocked off balance and sent tumbling down the steps to the landing halfway between the first and second floors. He took a blow to the head and for a moment was out of it. He tried to collect himself and keep moving but his right leg was white-hot with pain. Something was broken down there. Panicked voices filled the air and he could see people running for the double front doors. Dust and smoke were engulfing the entire building.

The detonator. Lyle managed to clear his head for a second to think about the detonator. If they caught him with it he wouldn't stand a chance. Clutching the stair rail, he struggled down the lower steps and made it to the lobby where he crawled to the front door. Someone helped him outside. Someone else said, "It's a compound fracture, buddy. I can see the bone."

Bone or not, he couldn't hang around. "Can you get me outta here?" he asked, but everyone was hurrying away from the building.

On the courthouse lawn, dozens of dazed people staggered out of the building, and once clear and safe, turned to look at it. Some had dust in their hair and on their shoulders. Some pointed to the DA's office on the second floor where smoke and dust boiled out.

The explosion was heard throughout downtown Biloxi and other people made their way to the courthouse. Then the sirens began to wail, as they would for hours, and this attracted even more onlookers. First the police cars, then the firetrucks, then the ambulances. Several policemen arrived on foot, sprinting and breathing heavily. They secured the exterior doors as the firemen frantically unraveled their hoses. The crowd was growing and the curious were commanded to stand back.

Gage Pettigrew heard the noise and commotion and hustled over to see what was happening. By the time he arrived it was an accepted fact that Jesse Rudy's office had been bombed. No, there was no report of casualties. He tried to get closer and talk to a policeman, but was asked to move away. He ran back to his office and was about to call Agnes at home when Keith walked through the rear door and asked what was happening. He was returning from a hearing in Pascagoula. His first impulse was to run to the courthouse and check on his father, but Gage said he couldn't get near the building.

"Please go home and sit with your mother, Keith. I'll go back over there and ask around. I'll call you when I know something."

Keith was too stunned to argue. Gage walked him to his car and watched him drive away, and kept mumbling to himself, "This cannot be happening." Sirens wailed in the distance.

Other than a nasty blow to the head, Egan appeared to be in good shape. Her wound was treated and she was strapped to a gurney and taken away in an ambulance. A secretary in the chancery clerk's office was injured when a large filing cabinet toppled over and pinned her underneath. She left in the second ambulance. Lyle managed to grapple his way around to the side of the courthouse where he removed his brown shirt and stuffed it and the detonator into a large plastic garbage can. He was determined to get to his truck, drive away, go to the motel, and regroup. And as soon as physically possible, get the hell out of Biloxi. His plans went haywire, though, when he tripped and fell on a sidewalk. A first responder saw him, saw the blood and the exposed bone, and called for a stretcher. Lyle tried to resist, said he was fine and so on, but he was losing strength and fading. Another medic stepped over and they managed to get him on the stretcher and into an ambulance.

The fire was confined to the west end of the second floor and was extinguished quickly. The fire chief was the first one into the district attorney's office. The walls of the reception room were charred and cracked; an interior wall had been blown in half. The desks and chairs were splintered. The metal file cabinets were dented and ripped open. Debris and plaster dust covered the floor and mixed with the water to form sticky mud. The door leading to Jesse's office had been torn, and from where he stood the fire chief could see the victim.

The remains of a corpse had been blown face-first into an exterior wall. The back of his head was missing, as were the left leg and right arm. The white shirt was nothing but shreds, all covered in blood.

———•———

For the Rudy family, the clock had never ticked slower. The afternoon dragged on as they waited for the inevitable. Keith and Ainsley sat with Agnes in the sun room, her favorite place in their home. Beverly and Laura were due any moment. Tim was trying to catch a flight out of Missoula.

Gage and Gene Pettigrew manned the front of the house and kept the crowd away. Friends descended on the home and were asked to please leave. Maybe later. The family wasn't receiving guests. Thanks for your concern.

A Biloxi policeman arrived with the news that Egan Clement was being treated at the hospital and doing okay. She suffered a concussion and a cut that required a few stitches. Evidently she was somewhere near the door of the office when the explosion occurred. The FBI and state police were on the scene.

"Can you keep Fats Bowman away from it?" Gage asked.

The policeman smiled and said, "Don't worry, Sheriff Bowman will not be involved."

The corpse would not be moved for hours. There was no hurry. The crime scene would be examined for days. A few minutes after three, an FBI technician carefully removed the wallet from the left rear pocket of the deceased and confirmed his identity.

The wallet was handed to Biloxi's chief of police, who left the courthouse and drove straight to the Rudy home. He knew Keith well and was burdened with the responsibility of breaking the unspeakable news. The two of them huddled in the kitchen, away from Agnes and the girls.

Keith recognized the wallet and looked at his father's driver's license. He gritted his teeth and said, "Thank you, Bob."

"I'm so sorry, Keith."

"So am I. What do you know?"

"Not much so far. The FBI lab guys are on the way. Some type of bomb that went off somewhere close to your father's desk. He didn't have a chance."

Keith closed his eyes and swallowed hard. "When can we see my dad?"

The chief stuttered and stumbled for words. "I don't know, Keith. I'm not sure you want to see him, not like this."

"Is he in one piece?"

"No."

Keith took another deep breath and struggled to keep his composure. "I guess I gotta tell Mom."

"I'm so sorry, Keith."

CHAPTER 39

Fortunately, at least for the investigation, Special Agent Jackson Lewis was on the Coast when he heard the news. He arrived at the courthouse at 12:45, and quickly established that the FBI was in charge. He made sure the building was locked and secured. Only the front door would remain open, for investigators. He asked the sheriff's deputies to control the crowd and traffic, and he asked the Biloxi police to question the spectators and get the name of every person who was in the building at noon. When two FBI technicians arrived, he ordered them to photograph the license plates of every vehicle parked downtown.

He asked the state police to go to the hospital and take statements of those who were injured. In the ER, they found half a dozen people with cuts severe enough to require stitches. Four were complaining of severe pain in their ears. One unidentified man had a broken leg and was in surgery. Egan Clement was being x-rayed. A secretary was being treated for a concussion.

The officers decided their visit was premature, so they left for two hours. When they returned, they found Egan Clement in a private room, sedated but awake. Her mother stood on one side of her bed, her father on the other. Egan had been informed of Jesse's death and was, at times, inconsolable. When she was able to talk, she told them what she remembered. She had left the office around 11:30 to run a quick errand and stop by Rosini's Grocery for deli sandwiches. Chicken for her, turkey for Jesse. She returned to the courthouse around noon and remembered how it cleared out at lunchtime every Friday, especially in August. She walked up the stairs, and passed a UPS delivery man without speaking, which she thought was odd because Russ always spoke. No big deal. It wasn't Russ. And he was carrying boxes away from the second floor. Odd, too, for a Friday. She glanced back at him, and that was the last thing she remembered. She did not hear the blast, did not recall being knocked out by it.

The officers didn't press and said they would return later. They thanked her and left. She was sobbing when they closed the door.

As the hours passed, more crime scene vans arrived from Jackson and they parked haphazardly in the street in front of the courthouse. Two large tents were erected to protect the team from the August sun and heat and to serve as temporary headquarters. The deputies encouraged those in the crowd to leave. Downtown streets were cordoned off, and as shoppers and employees left for the day, the empty parking spaces were secured with orange cones.

Jackson Lewis asked the Biloxi police to inform the downtown merchants and office workers that they could remain open over the weekend, but there would be no parking. He wanted the area locked down for the next forty-eight hours.

In a brief statement to the press, the chief of police confirmed that Mr. Jesse Rudy, the district attorney, had been killed in the explosion. He would not confirm that it was actually a bomb and deferred further questions until a later, unspecified time.

———•———

The man with the compound fracture and head injury had no wallet or ID on him and was unable to cooperate with the ER team when he was wheeled in. He drifted in and out of consciousness and was unresponsive. Regardless, surgery was needed immediately to repair his leg. X-rays of his head revealed little damage.

Lyle was actually alert enough to talk, but he had no desire to. His thoughts were only of escape, which at the moment looked unrealistic. When the anesthesiologist tried to quiz him, he became unconscious again. The surgery lasted only ninety minutes. After-ward, he was moved to a semi-private room for recovery. An administrator appeared and politely inquired if he could answer a few questions. He closed his eyes and appeared unconscious. After she left, he stared at his left leg and tried to collect his thoughts. A thick white plaster cast began just below his right knee and covered everything but his toes. The entire limb was suspended in midair by pulleys and chains. An escape was impossible, so he lost uncon-sciousness when anyone entered the room.

———•———

Agnes whispered to Laura that she would like to lie down. Laura took one elbow, Beverly the other, and Ainsley followed them out of the sun room and down the hallway to the master bedroom. The shades were pulled tight; the only light a small lamp on a dresser. Agnes wanted a daughter on each side, and they lay quietly together in the dark and unbearable gloom for a long time. Ainsley sat on the corner of the bed, wiping her cheeks. Keith came and went but found the room too heavy and miserable. Occasion-ally, he walked to the den and chatted with the Pettigrew brothers, who were still guarding the front door. Beyond it, out in the street, neighbors were milling about, waiting to see someone from the family. There were several news teams with brightly painted vans and cameras on tripods.

At five o'clock, Keith walked to the end of the driveway and nodded to the neighbors and friends. He faced the cameras and made a brief statement. He thanked the people for coming and showing their concern. The family was trying to accept the horrific news and waiting for relatives to arrive. On behalf of the family, he was requesting everyone to honor their privacy. Thanks for the prayers and concerns. He walked away without taking questions.

Joey Grasich appeared from the crowd and Keith invited him into the house. Seeing a childhood buddy brought out a lot of emotions, and Keith had his first long cry of the day. They were alone in the kitchen. So far, he had shown little emotion in front of the women.

After half an hour, Joey left and drove around the block. Keith checked on the women and said he was going to the hospital to see Egan. He ducked through the backyard and met Joey on the next street. They got away without being seen and drove to the law office where they parked. They walked three blocks to the barricades and chatted with a Biloxi policeman who was guarding the sidewalk.

Behind him, the courthouse was crawling with police and investigators. Every firetruck and patrol car in the city and county was there, along with half a dozen from the state highway patrol. Two FBI mobile crime units were parked on the lawn near the front door.

The window of Jesse's office had been blown out and the bricks around it were charred black. Keith tried to look at it but turned away.

As they were walking back to the office, they saw a woman place a bouquet of flowers on the front steps of Rudy & Pettigrew. They spoke to her, thanked her, and noticed several other arrangements folks had dropped off.

At the hospital, Keith tapped on the door to Egan's room and eased inside. Joey didn't know her and stayed in the hall. Her parents were still there, and she had held her composure for some time, until she saw Keith. He hugged her gently, careful not to touch a bandage.

"I just can't believe it," she said over and over.

"At least you're safe, Egan."

"Tell me it's not true."

"Okay, it's not true. You'll go to work tomorrow and Jesse'll be yelling about something, same as always. This is just a bad dream."

She almost managed a smile, but clutched his hand and closed her eyes.

Her mother nodded and Keith thought he should leave. "I'll be back tomorrow," he said and carefully kissed Egan on the cheek.

As he and Joey left her room and headed for the elevators, they passed Room 310, semi-private. Lying in the first bed, with his leg in the air, was the man who killed Jesse Rudy.

CHAPTER 40

Dinner was a cold sandwich under a hot tent, eaten while standing and waiting. Their midnight snack was a slice of even colder pizza, also under the tent. The FBI teams did not rest during the night. Jackson Lewis kept them there and had no plans to release them until the job was finished. For hours they meticulously scoured every inch of the crime scene and collected thousands of samples of debris. The first explosives expert arrived from Quantico at 9:30. He viewed the bomb site, sniffed the air, and said quietly to Jackson Lewis, "Probably Semtex, military stuff, far more than necessary to kill one man. I'd say the bomber got a bit carried away."

Agent Lewis knew from training and experience that the crime scene yields the best evidence, though it's sometimes overlooked because it's so obvious. This was his biggest case yet, one that could make his career, and he vowed to miss nothing. He had ordered that no one and nothing leave the courthouse without approval. Each of the thirty-seven people identified so far as being in the courthouse had been cleared to go home, but only after their bags, purses, and briefcases were searched. Each would be interviewed later. He had the names and addresses of the injured, now numbering thirteen, with only two hospitalized. All trash baskets and garbage cans were collected and taken to a tent.

Lewis had suffered through three weeks without a cigarette, but he broke under the pressure. At 9:00, after dark, he lit a Marlboro and walked around the exterior of the courthouse, puffing away and thoroughly enjoying the tobacco. His wife would never know. The streets were blocked; there was no traffic. With the 11:00 P.M. Marlboro, he noticed a dark blue Dodge half-ton pickup parked on a side street facing north. It was a nice truck, certainly not abandoned. The nearest store had been closed for six hours. There were no apartments above the stores and offices; no lights were on. Down the street were some small homes, all with plenty of parking of their own. The truck was out of place.

The man with the broken leg had not been identified, and Lewis's suspicion was growing by the hour. The state police had attempted to question him on two occasions, but he was barely conscious.

———•———

Jesse's death was welcome news along the Strip. The club owners and their employees relaxed for the first time in months, maybe years. Maybe now with Rudy gone the good times could roll again. In the strip joints, bars, pool halls, and bingo parlors a lot of drinks were poured and glasses raised. Real drinks, not the feeble stuff they sold to their customers but top-shelf liquor that was seldom touched.

Hugh Malco, Nevin Noll, and their favorite bartender had a celebratory dinner at Mary Mahoney's. Thick steaks, expensive wines, no expense was spared. Because the restaurant was crowded and people were watching, they controlled their euphoria and tried to give the appearance of old friends just having dinner. Occasionally, though, they whispered pleasant thoughts and exchanged grim smiles.

For Hugh, the occasion was bittersweet. He was delighted Jesse Rudy was gone, but so was his father. Lance should be dining with them and savoring the moment.

———•———

Lance heard it on the ten o'clock news out of Jackson. He stared at a fifteen-inch black-and-white television with rabbit ears and took in the face of Jesse Rudy as the anchor breathlessly reported his death.

From across the hall, Monk asked, "Ain't he the guy who sent you here?"

"That's him," Lance said with a smile.

"Congratulations."

"Thanks."

"Any idea who did it?"

"Not a clue."

Monk laughed and said, "Right."

The report switched to a shot of the Biloxi courthouse. A voiceover said, "Although authorities have yet to comment, a source tells us that Jesse Rudy was killed instantly around noon today when an explosion occurred in his office. About a dozen other people were injured. The investigators will make a statement tomorrow."

———•———

At midnight, the truck was still there.

There was a flurry in the tent at 12:45 when the contents of a garbage can were spread on a table for a look. In addition to the usual litter and crap, a small unidentified device was found, along with a short-sleeved UPS shirt once worn by someone named Lyle. The FBI explosives expert took one look and said, "That's the detonator."

The 2:00 A.M. cigarette was forgotten as Lewis supervised the sickening task of removing the corpse. Jesse's remains were pieced together on a stretcher. An ambulance took him to the basement of the hospital where the city leased a room for its morgue. There, he would await an autopsy, though the cause of death was obvious.

At 3:00 A.M. Lewis took a break for another cigarette as he made the same walk around the courthouse. It cleared his mind, got the blood flowing. The truck had not been moved.

It had license plates issued by Hancock County. Lewis waited impatiently through the night and called the sheriff in Bay St. Louis at 7:00 A.M. The sheriff went to the courthouse and to the office of the tax assessor. The license tags had been reported stolen four days earlier.

At 9:00 A.M., the stores were opening, though the streets were still blocked. The courthouse, of course, was closed. Working from his dining room table at home, Judge Oliphant issued a search warrant for the Dodge pickup. Under its seat, FBI agents found a set of license plates issued by Obion County, Tennessee. Hidden under the floor mat was a key to Room 19 of the Beach Bay Motel in Biloxi.

Judge Oliphant issued a search warrant for Room 19. Since Agent Lewis had the key, he did not bother with notifying the manager of the motel. He and Agent Spence Whitehead, accompanied by a Biloxi city policeman, entered the small room and found a pile of dirty laundry and an unmade bed. Someone had been there for a few days. Between the mattress and box springs, they found a wallet, some cash, two pistols, keys on a ring, and a pocketknife. The Tennessee driver's license identified their man as Henry Taylor, address in the town of Union City, date of birth May 20, 1941. Thirty-five years old. The wallet also held two credit cards, two condoms, a fishing license, and eighty dollars in cash.

Agent Lewis placed the two pistols in a plastic bag. They left the other items precisely as they found them, and returned to the courthouse. Technicians collected fingerprints from the weapons, and Agent Whitehead returned them to Room 19.

With a flurry of phone calls, more pieces of the puzzle fell into place. Henry Taylor had been charged with blowing up a black church near Dumas, Mississippi, in 1966, but an all-white jury acquitted him. In 1969, he was arrested for bombing a synagogue in Jackson, but again was acquitted by an all-white jury. According to the FBI office in Memphis, Taylor was believed to still be active in the Klan. According to the sheriff of Obion County, he ran a carpet-cleaning business and had never been a problem. After some more digging, the sheriff reported that Taylor was divorced with no kids and lived just south of town.

Lewis directed another agent to begin the process of obtaining a search warrant for Taylor's home.

Having had no sleep in thirty hours, Lewis and Whitehead left the scene and stopped at a café near the beach. Though they managed to control their excitement, they could not help but revel in their success and marvel at their luck. In about twenty-four hours, they had not only identified the killer but had him under watch in a hospital room.

They slugged coffee. Lewis was too wired to rest. He caught Whitehead completely off guard when he said, "Now that we've got him, we let him go."

Whitehead, slack-jawed, said, "What?"

"Look, Spence, he has no idea we know what we know. We get him released from the hospital with no questions asked, just a bunch of dumb rednecks down there, right? He goes home, assuming he can drive with a broken leg, and considers himself a lucky man. Cops had him under their nose and let him get away. We tap his phones, watch him like a hawk, and, with time, he'll lead us to the man with the money."

"That's crazy."

"No, it's brilliant."

"What if he gets away?"

"Well, he won't. And why should he run? We can pick him up anytime we want."

CHAPTER 41

Gulf Coast Register:
JESSE RUDY KILLED IN COURTHOUSE EXPLOSION

Jackson *Clarion-Ledger:*
BILOXI COURTHOUSE BOMBED: D.A. DEAD

New Orleans *Times-Picayune:*
MOB STRIKES BACK—PROSECUTOR DEAD

Mobile *Times:*
BILOXI DISTRICT ATTORNEY TARGETED

Memphis *Commercial Appeal:*
CRUSADING D.A. KILLED IN BILOXI

Atlanta Constitution:
FAMED PROSECUTOR, JESSE RUDY, DEAD AT 52

Gage Pettigrew collected the morning newspapers from various shops along the Coast and took them to the Rudy home at dawn on Saturday. The house was dark, quiet, and mournful. The neighbors, reporters, and curious had yet to appear. Gene Pettigrew was guarding the front porch, napping in a wicker rocker, waiting for his brother. They went inside, locked the door, and made coffee in the kitchen.

Keith heard them stirring. On the worst night of his life, he had stayed in his parents' bedroom, sleeping fitfully in a chair, watching his mother and praying for her. Laura was on one side, Beverly the other, Ainsley slept upstairs.

He eased from the dark room and went to the kitchen. It was almost 7:00 A.M., Saturday, August 21, the beginning of the second-worst day of his life. He sat at the table with Gage and Gene, drank coffee, and stared at the headlines, but had no desire to look at the newspapers. He knew the stories. Beside Gene's coffee cup was a yellow legal pad, and they finally got around to it. Gene said, "You have some pressing matters."

"Just shoot me," Keith mumbled.

"Sorry." Gage clicked off the most urgent: a meeting with Father Norris, their priest at St. Michael's; a dreaded chat with the funeral home over arrangements; at least two dozen phone calls to important people, including some judges, politicians, and former governor Bill Waller; a meeting with the FBI and state police for an update on whatever they knew about the bombing; the preparation of a statement for the press; the matter of fetching Tim from the airport in New Orleans.

"That's enough," Keith said as he sipped coffee he couldn't taste and gazed at a window. Laura entered the kitchen and sat at the table without a word, as if in another world. Her eyes were swollen and red, and she looked as though she had not slept in days.

"How's Mom?" Keith asked.

"In the shower," she replied.

After a long, heavy, silent gap, Gene said, "You guys have to be hungry. What if I go find some breakfast?"

"I'm not hungry," Keith said.

"Where's Dad right now?" Laura asked.

Gage replied, "He's at the hospital, in the morgue."

"I want to see him."

Gage and Gene looked at each other. Keith said, "We can't do that. The police said it's a bad idea. After the autopsy, the casket will remain closed."

She bit a lip and wiped her eyes.

Keith said to Gene, "Breakfast might work. We need to shower and dress and talk about receiving guests."

Laura said, "I don't want to see anyone."

"Nor do I but we have no choice. I'll talk to Mom. We can't sit around and cry all day."

"That's what I plan to do, Keith, and you need to cry too. Drop all the stoic stuff."

"Don't worry."

———•———

Henry Taylor, the man with no name, suffered the indignity of relieving himself into a bedpan and being wiped by a hospital orderly. His shattered left tibia throbbed in pain, but he was still determined to get out of bed at the first chance and somehow make an escape. When he complained of discomfort, a nurse injected a heavy dose of something into his IV and he floated away. He awoke to the smiling face of a very pretty nurse who wanted to ask him some questions. He feigned semi-consciousness and asked for a phone directory. When she returned an hour later she brought him some chocolate ice cream and flattered him with a round of light flirting. She explained that the hospital administrator was insisting that she gather some basic information so they could bill him properly.

He said, "Name's Alan Taylor, Route 5, Necaise, Mississippi, over in Hancock County. You know the place?"

"Afraid not," the nurse replied as she scribbled officially.

From the phone directory, Taylor had found a bunch of Taylors around Necaise and figured he could blend in. His concussion still made him groggy and the meds didn't help, but he was beginning to think with some clarity. He was an inch away from getting busted for murdering a district attorney and it was imperative to get out of town.

He was horrified when two Biloxi city cops walked in an hour later. One stayed by the door as if guarding it. The other walked to the edge of his bed and asked with a big smile, "So how you doing, Mr. Taylor?"

"Okay, I guess, but I really need to get outta here."

"Sure, no problem, whenever the doctors say go, you can go. Where are you from?"

"Necaise, over in Hancock County."

"That makes sense. We've got this abandoned Dodge pickup down by the courthouse, Hancock County tags. Wouldn't be yours, would it?"

Now Henry was in a helluva fix. If he admitted the truck was his, then the cops would know that he stole the license plates. However, it was Saturday, the courthouse was closed, and maybe they couldn't track the stolen plates until Monday. Maybe. But, if he denied owning the truck, then they would tow it away, impound it, whatever. The truck was his only way to freedom. Because he was from Tennessee, he figured the cops in Mississippi were pretty stupid, and he had no choice.

"Yes sir, that's mine," he said, grimacing as though he might yet again lapse into semi-consciousness.

"Okay, would you like us to bring it over here to the hospital?" asked the policeman with a pleasant smile. Anything to help their out-of-town guest. The semi-private room had been cleared and Mr. Taylor was all alone. His hospital phone was bugged, and another team of FBI technicians was preparing to enter his home 475 miles to the north, just outside Union City.

"That'd be great, yes, thanks."

"You got the keys?" The keys were in the pocket of Special Agent Jackson Lewis, who was in the hallway trying to listen.

"Left them under the floor mat."

Right, not too far from the Tennessee license plates hidden under the seat.

"Okay, we'll drive it over for you. Anything else we can do?"

Taylor was relieved and couldn't believe his good fortune. The locals were not the least bit suspicious. "No, that's all. Thanks. Just get me outta here."

The FBI was leaning on the doctors to reset the cast and reduce its size so Taylor could drive away. They were eager to follow him.

———

Agnes stayed in her dark bedroom and refused to see anyone but her children. She knew her friends wanted to get their hands on her, for a long fierce hug, a good cry, and so on, but she simply wasn't up to it. Maybe later. Maybe tomorrow when some of the shock had worn off.

But she couldn't say no to their priest, Father Norris, and he did not linger. They held hands, prayed, and listened to his comforting words. He suggested a funeral mass next Saturday, a week away, and Agnes agreed. He was gone in thirty minutes.

By mid-morning there was a steady flow of friends and neighbors stopping by with food, flowers, and notes for Agnes and the family. They were greeted at the front door by one of the Pettigrews, relieved of whatever gifts they'd brought, thanked properly, then turned away. Cousins, aunts, and uncles were allowed inside where they sat in the den and living room, eating cakes and pies and sipping coffee while they whispered and waited for Agnes to appear. She did not, but Keith and his sisters emerged from the darkness occasionally to say hello and thanks and pass along a word or two from their mother.

At noon, Gene Pettigrew left for the two-hour drive to the New Orleans airport. He picked up Tim Rudy, who'd traveled all night from Montana, and they headed home. He had a thousand questions and Gene had few answers, but they talked nonstop. Of the four Rudy siblings, Tim seemed the angriest. He wanted blood revenge. As they entered Biloxi and drove past the Strip, he uttered vile threats at Red Velvet and Foxy's and was convinced beyond all doubt that the Malcos had killed his father.

At home, Agnes broke down again when she saw her youngest child. The family had another good cry, though Keith was getting tired of the tears.

As the walls closed in, the family asked for privacy and their visitors slowly left the house. At 6:00 P.M. they, along with the Pettigrew brothers, gathered in the den to watch the local news, which was all about the bombing. The anchor flashed a color photo of Jesse in a dark suit, smiling with confidence, and it was difficult to absorb. The story switched to a live shot of the courthouse where the investigation was still in high gear. A close-up showed the burned-out second-floor window of the DA's office. The chief of police and the FBI had addressed the press hours earlier, and revealed virtually nothing. The newscast ran a small segment in which Jackson Lewis said, "The FBI is still investigating the scene and will continue to do so for a few more days. We cannot comment at this time, but we can say that we have no suspects at this early stage."

The Rudy story consumed almost all of the half-hour news, which was followed by CBS weekend news out of New York. Gage Pettigrew had been approached by a CBS correspondent who asked to speak to the family and had been told to get lost. Gage had also seen an ABC crew downtown trying to get near the courthouse. Thus, they knew the networks were in town.

Near the end of the CBS segment, the anchor reported the murder of a district attorney in Biloxi, Mississippi. He switched to a reporter somewhere near the courthouse who babbled for a moment or so but said nothing new. Back in New York, the anchor informed the audience that, according to the FBI, Jesse Rudy was the first elected district attorney to be murdered while in office in U.S. history.

———•———

There were no plans to attend Mass on Sunday morning. Agnes was not ready to be seen in public and her children didn't want the attention either. Late morning, they enjoyed a family brunch in the sun room with the Pettigrew brothers serving as waiters and mixing Bloody Marys.

As a child, Jesse had attended Mass at St. Michael's Catholic Church on the Point. It was known as the "Fishermen's Church" and had been built in the early 1900s by Louisiana French and Croatian immigrants. He had practically grown up in St. Michael's, rarely missing weekly Mass with his parents. Life revolved around the church, with daily prayers, christenings, weddings, funerals, and countless socials. The parish priest was a father figure who was always there in times of need.

Jesse had brought his bride home from the war and had not been married at St. Michael's. But, Lance and Carmen Malco were married there in 1948, in front of a large crowd of families and friends. Jesse was sitting in the back row.

Two days after the bombing, and with the community still stunned and reeling, St. Michael's was packed for Mass as friends, neighbors, acquaintances, and voters sought refuge and strength in their faith. Everyone needed to offer a prayer for the Rudy family. Jesse was their greatest success story, and his violent, senseless death hit the community hard.

Throughout the Point, Back Bay, and the rest of Biloxi, the Catholic churches were busier than usual on the somber Sunday morning. St. John's, Nativity, Our Mother of Sorrows, as well as St. Michael's, welcomed large crowds of mourners, all firmly believing they had some connection to Jesse Rudy.

CHAPTER 42

Early Monday morning, a nurse juiced Henry's IV again and knocked him out. He was rolled into surgery where his doctors spent an hour resetting his tibia and wrapping his lower leg with a smaller plaster cast. According to those up the hospital's chain of command, it was rather urgent that the patient be patched up as well as possible so he could be on his way. There was no mention of the police or FBI. Indeed, little mention of anything; just the clear message that Henry Taylor needed to be released.

While he was unconscious, two vans owned by a Union City, Tennessee, plumbing company arrived in his driveway. The plumbers walked around his house a couple of times, as if looking for leaking sewage or something, but they were really checking out the neighborhood. He lived on a two-acre lot near the edge of town. The nearest neighbor's home could barely be seen. When they were satisfied no one was watching, they quickly entered the house and began searching drawers, closets, desks, anywhere Henry might keep records. Two agents wiretapped his phone and hid a transmitter in the attic. Another agent copied bank records with a mini camera. Another agent found a key ring and began trying locks.

A large shed in the backyard held carpet-cleaning supplies and lawn care equipment. A partially hidden door with a thick padlock concealed a ten-by-ten room where, evidently, the mad bomber did his mischief. Since none of the agents handled explosives, they were afraid to touch anything. They photographed as much as possible and left the room, leaving it for another day and another search warrant.

Back in Biloxi, Taylor's Dodge pickup was also receiving attention. Careful not to rack up too many miles on the odometer, Jackson Lewis took it to a service garage on the Point and paid the owner a hefty fee to look the other way. Technicians installed a waterproof magnetic tracker between the radiator and front grille and wired it to the battery, none of which could be seen without a thorough search. The antenna was replaced by an identical one that not only received radio signals, so Henry could continue to enjoy his tunes, but also transmitted signals within a ten-mile radius.

If all went as planned, the tracking system would be periodically checked or even replaced in a month or so, one night when Henry was sound asleep.

He slept well after his surgery and finally awoke early on Monday afternoon. He accused the nurse of using too many sedatives and she threatened to juice him again. He was pleased to see a much smaller cast and claimed his leg felt great.

Tuesday morning his doctor made the early rounds and said he could be released. The paperwork was already prepared, and when everything was in place an orderly helped him into a wheelchair for the ride to the front door. There, the same two Biloxi policemen were waiting with a pair of crutches. They helped him walk a short distance to his beloved pickup, got him situated in the driver's seat, commented on his wisdom in buying an automatic and not a clutch, and proudly said that they had filled the tank.

His leg was already killing him, but he smiled gamely as he drove away.

What a couple of dopes!

Other dopes followed the blue Dodge to the Beach Bay Motel where they observed the subject use his new crutches with great difficulty as he managed to waddle, limp, and lurch to the door of Number 19.

Inside, Henry seethed in pain as he pulled up the mattress and retrieved his wallet, cash, keys, pocketknife, and pistols. He had dreamed of them and couldn't believe they had not been found by the housekeepers. He threw them in his duffel, along with his clothes, and was about to start wiping down the room when someone knocked. It was the manager looking for an extra sixty-two dollars for the past four nights. Henry hobbled to the credenza, got the cash, and paid him.

When he was gone, Henry locked the door, wet a towel, and began wiping every surface he might possibly have touched in the past week. Television controls, shades, doorknobs, faucets, commode, and shower handles, light switches, door facings, and toilet paper rack.

He was a bit late. The FBI team had lifted prints from the same surfaces, along with prints from his truck and his hospital room. Few suspects in recent history had provided such an incredible portfolio of fingerprints.

But he blissfully wiped away, smug in his cleverness and secure with the knowledge that he was outsmarting the bumpkins. When he was certain Room 19 was print-free, he threw the key on the bed, hobbled out to his truck, tossed his bag in the rear, wrestled himself into position behind the wheel, and drove away.

They followed him out of town, along Highway 90, then north on Highway 49. Another tail picked him up in Hattiesburg, another in Jackson. Six hours later, Henry was followed as he skirted downtown Memphis on the bypass and picked up Highway 51 north. In the town of Millington, he stopped to fill up his tank and buy a soft drink from the convenience store, hobbling painfully and trying to keep any weight off his bum leg. Two hours later, he was trailed at the edge of Union City and followed until he finally made it home.

Inside, he went straight to the kitchen for a glass of water. He took a handful of pain pills, gulped them down, and wiped his mouth with a forearm. He made it to the sofa where he collapsed. His leg felt like red-hot spears were jabbing into his flesh and muscles.

After a few moments, the pain began to subside and he could breathe normally for the first time in hours. He had replayed his mistakes a thousand times in the hospital and didn't want to go there again. He considered himself extremely lucky to have escaped with so many cops around.

What a bunch of morons down there.

———•———

Late Tuesday afternoon, Keith and Tim drove to the firm's office downtown. They admired the incredible collection of flower arrangements that completely covered the porch and most of the small front lawn. They walked a few blocks to the barricades and checked on the courthouse. Keith spoke to a Biloxi policeman he knew and thanked him for his condolences. Back at the firm, they entered Jesse's office, and for a long moment stood in the center of it, taking in their father's life. On the Ego Wall were diplomas, awards, photos, and newspaper clippings from the Camille days. On his credenza were a dozen photos of Agnes and the children at various ages. The desk, seldom used for the past five years, was in perfect order, with gifts the children had given: a silver letter opener, fancy quill pens he never used, a bronze clock, a magnifying glass he didn't need, and a baseball signed by Jackie Robinson. Jesse had seen him play in an exhibition game in 1942.

Their sense of loss was unfathomable. The emotional devastation was overwhelming; the physical pain, after five days, was numbing. A man they had worshipped because of his unabashed love for his family, his integrity, courage, grit, intelligence, and affability, was gone, taken from them in his prime. They and their sisters had never for once given thought to losing their father. He was an enormous presence in their lives, and he would always be there for them. He couldn't be dead at the age of fifty-two.

Tim, the most emotional of the four, stretched out on the sofa and covered his eyes. Keith, the most stoic, sat at his father's desk for a long time with his eyes closed and tried to hear Jesse's voice.

Instead, he heard a faint tapping at the front door. He glanced at his watch and jumped to his feet. He had forgotten the five o'clock appointment.

He greeted Judge Oliphant warmly and led him to the conference room on the first floor. He was in his late seventies and had always been sharp and spry, but at that moment he looked as though he had aged. He moved with a slight limp, and said no to coffee. His close friendship with Jesse Rudy had begun during the Camille litigation and only grown deeper when the new DA assumed an office just down the hall. They were so close that the judge fretted over the issue of impartiality. Jesse often grumbled that Oliphant was so concerned about being fair that he went out of his way to make it hard for the State. They yielded no ground to each other in open court, then laughed about their theatrics over drinks and cigars.

The judge was devastated by Jesse's death and was obviously grieving. They commiserated for a while, but Keith soon grew weary of it. To keep traffic away from the house and Agnes, he was meeting friends at the office. Each visit began with the usual round of tears and condolences, and they were taking a toll.

"Not only was it a cold-blooded murder," Oliphant was saying, "but it was an attack on our judicial system. They bombed the courthouse, Keith, the very place where justice is pursued. I suppose they could've killed Jesse in any number of places, they seem adept at these matters, but they chose the courthouse."

"And who are 'they'?"

"The same people Jesse went after. The same people he indicted, dragged into court, my courtroom, and frightened them so much they pled guilty."

"Malco?"

"Of course it's Malco, Keith. Jesse's put away more than his share of criminals in five years, same as any other DA, I guess. That's what the job entails. But Lance Malco was the big fish, and he left behind a criminal syndicate that is still operating and capable of getting revenge."

Keith said, "The moment I heard that a bomb had gone off in

the courthouse, I said the word 'Malco.' It's so obvious that you have to wonder if they're really that brazen, or stupid."

"They've flaunted the law for so long they believe they're above it. This shocks me, shocks all of us, but it should not be surprising."

Neither spoke for a long time as they weighed the implications of what they had already decided. Finally, Keith asked, "You think Lance ordered the hit from prison?"

"I'm going back and forth. It would be easy for him to do and he has nothing to lose. But, he's too smart for that. Lance avoided attention, went out of his way to operate in the shadows, didn't like to be seen or read about himself. Right now everybody on the Coast, especially law enforcement, is thinking the same thing: Malco."

Keith was nodding and said, "I agree. Lance is too smart, but Hugh is an idiot. Now he's got the power and wants to prove he's a real crime boss. By murdering the DA he becomes a legend, if he gets away with it."

"It will be difficult to prove, Keith. Contract killings are virtually impossible because the guilty party touches nothing."

"But the cash."

"But the cash, and it's untraceable."

Another pause as they listened to voices outside. More flowers were being delivered.

The judge said, "You know, Keith, Governor Finch will appoint an interim DA to fill the vacancy. I know Cliff. We were in the state legislature together. He also served as DA for eight years. I want you to consider asking him for the job. I'm sure you've thought about it."

"I have, but only in passing. I have not mentioned it to Ainsley or my mother. I doubt either will be too excited."

"So you'll consider it?"

"I've talked to Egan and she has no interest. She plans to take some time off. I can't think of anybody else who'll want the job, especially now. Good way to get hurt."

Oliphant smiled and said, "You'll be a natural, Keith, and you can pick up where Jesse left off."

"And I'll be in the middle of the investigation. Governor Waller called last night with his condolences. As you know, he and Dad had become friends. He promised to talk to Governor Finch and push him to give it priority. The state police and FBI seem to be working together for a change. I want to be there, Judge, in the middle of it."

"I'll talk to Governor Finch."

"And I'll talk to my mother, but not now. Let's wait until after the funeral."

———•———

With Father Norris in control and guiding the family, the proceedings went strictly by the Catholic book. On Friday night, a huge crowd gathered at St. Michael's for the prayer vigil. Father Norris led the prayers and asked several friends to read Holy Scripture. Since there would be no eulogies the following day at the Requiem Mass, they were delivered during the vigil. A childhood friend from the Point went first and broke the ice with a funny story from way back then. Judge Oliphant spoke eloquently of Jesse's humble beginnings, his determination to become a lawyer by taking night classes at Loyola in New Orleans, his drive and ambition. But above all, his courage.

Former governor Waller described what it was like for a DA to receive death threats for simply doing his job. He had been there and he knew the fear. Jesse's courage had cost him his life, but the job he started would one day be finished. The thugs and mobsters who killed him would get their day in court.

Amongst the family, there was no doubt about who would speak. Tim knew he could not keep his composure. Beverly and Laura happily deferred to their older brother. When Keith stepped to the pulpit there was complete silence in the church. In a strong, articulate voice, he thanked everyone on behalf of the family. He assured them that the family would not only survive, but would endure and prevail. His mother, Agnes, and his siblings, Beverly, Laura, and Tim, appreciated the prayers and the outpouring of support.

Jesse taught him many lessons about life, and also about the law. Great trial lawyers aren't born; they're made. The great ones simply tell the jury a story, one that he has a thorough command of. The story must be written and rewritten, and edited some more, to the point where the lawyer knows every word, pause, and punch line by memory. The delivery is smooth but not too polished, not in any way rehearsed. Listening to Keith speak without notes and without a single wasted syllable, it was hard to believe he was only twenty-eight years old and had taken only three jury trials all the way to verdicts.

He told stories of fishing with his father in the Mississippi Sound, of playing baseball in the backyard, of a thousand games with Jesse always in the stands. He never missed one. When Keith was fifteen, Jesse took him to court to watch a trial, and over dinner they discussed every move made by the lawyers and the judge. Many trials followed. By the time he was sixteen he was wearing a coat and tie and sitting right behind Jesse.

Keith's voice never cracked. His delivery was as smooth as a veteran stage actor's. Though he kept his composure, his eulogy was extremely emotional. He ended with: "Our father did not die in vain. His work had just begun, and his work will be finished. His enemies will die in prison."

———•———

The Requiem Mass drew an even larger crowd that overflowed the sanctuary. Those who arrived late were directed to a large canopied tent beside the church building. A PA system relayed the events: the sprinkling of holy water on the coffin as it entered the front doors; the family receiving the coffin at the altar and placing an open Bible on it; the reading of Holy Scripture by Beverly and Laura; a solo by a soprano; a reading from the Gospel of Luke by Jesse's brother; a reflection on the verses by Father Norris, followed by a lengthy homily in which he talked about death in the Christian world and said marvelous things about Jesse Rudy; an organist played a beautiful hymn; Tim read a prayer and managed to get through it; communion took half an hour, and when it was over Father Norris sprinkled more holy water on the coffin as he gave the final commendation.

CHAPTER 43

On the Tuesday after Labor Day the courthouse reopened for business. The west half of the second floor was blocked off with a temporary partition as work crews finished the cleanup and began the repairs. Judge Oliphant was eager to tackle his docket and schedule hearings.

Two days later, in his courtroom, a brief ceremony took place. Pursuant to an appointment by Governor Cliff Finch, Keith Rudy would fill the vacancy left by the death of his father and serve as district attorney for the remainder of the term, through 1979. Judge Oliphant read the appointment and swore in the new DA. Agnes and Ainsley watched proudly, though with plenty of quiet doubts. Both had been opposed to Keith taking the job, but his mind was made up. To Agnes, he was like Jesse in so many ways. When he felt he was right, it was impossible to dissuade him.

Beverly and Laura looked on, along with Egan, the Pettigrew brothers, and a handful of other friends. They were all still sleepwalking through the aftermath of the murder, but Keith's appointment gave them hope that justice would be served. There were no speeches, but a reporter from the *Register* covered it and chatted with Keith when it was over. His first question was one that was obvious: "Can you be fair and objective if you prosecute the person or persons responsible for the murder of your father?"

Keith knew it was coming and replied: "I can be fair but I don't have to be objective. In any murder investigation, the police and prosecutor determine guilt long before the jury, so in that respect they're not exactly objective. I can only promise to be fair."

"If the murder is solved, will you handle the trial?"

"It's much too early to talk about a trial."

"Do you know of any suspects?"

"No."

"Will you be involved in the investigation?"

"At every turn. We'll follow every lead, look under every rock. I will not rest until this crime is solved."

Similar questions dogged him during his first days in office. Reporters hung around Rudy & Pettigrew and were repeatedly asked to leave. A steady flow of friends and well-wishers stopped by for a somber word or two and Keith quickly grew tired of their presence. The front door was eventually locked. Gage and Gene worked in the downstairs conference room and kept an eye on the foot traffic. The phone rang nonstop and was routinely ignored. Clients were asked to be patient.

With most of the DA's records destroyed, one of Keith's first challenges was to reconstruct the files and determine who had been indicted and what was the status of each defendant. Without exception, the local bar rallied behind him and provided copies of all records. Judge Oliphant ran interference and gave no ground to the defense attorneys. Rex Dubisson spent hours with Keith and walked him through the ins and outs of the job. Pat Graebel, next door in the Nineteenth District, did the same and made his staff available.

Keith began each day by taking Agnes to morning Mass at St. Michael's.

———•———

Two days after Keith became the DA, Hugh made another journey north into no-man's-land to visit his father. The cotton was in full bloom and the flatlands were as white as snow on both sides of the highway. It was somewhat interesting to watch the Delta change colors with the season as the crops got ready for the harvest, but he still found it depressing. He perked up at the sight of his first cotton picker, a bright green John Deere mechanized creation that resembled a giant insect creeping through the snow. Then he saw another and soon they were everywhere. He passed a trailer headed for the gin, loose bolls flying into the air and landing like litter on the sides of the highway.

Five miles south of the prison, he saw a sight so startling that he slowed and almost stopped on the shoulder of the road. A prison guard with a shotgun and a cowboy hat sat in the saddle of a quarter horse and watched a gang of about a dozen black inmates pluck bolls of cotton from stalks that were almost chest-high. They stuffed the cotton into thick burlap sacks they dragged behind them.

It was September of 1976, more than a hundred years after emancipation.

Parchman covered 18,000 acres of rich soil. With its endless supply of free labor it had been, historically at least, a cash cow for the state. Back in its glory days, long before the intervention of federal litigation and notions of prisoners' rights, the working conditions had been brutal, especially for black inmates.

Hugh shook his head and moved on, stunned again by the backwardness of Mississippi, and happy to be from the Coast. A different world.

Lance had so far avoided picking cotton, a loathsome job now reserved as punishment. He lived in Unit 26, one of many separate "camps" scattered throughout the sprawling farm. Though the federal courts had repeatedly told the state to desegregate Parchman, there were still a few places where inmates with a little cash could survive without the fear of violence. Unit 26 was the preferred address, though the cells lacked air-conditioning and ventilation.

Hugh cleared the front gate and followed well-marked roads into the depths of the farm. He parked in the small lot of Unit 26, cleared another security post, and entered a red-brick administration building. He got frisked again, then led to the visitation room.

Lance appeared on the other side of a mesh screen and they said hello. Though the visits were supposed to be confidential, Lance trusted no one at the prison and cautioned Hugh about saying too much.

Other than a few more gray hairs and wrinkles around his eyes, Lance had changed little in sixteen months. The cardiac problems that had practically killed him the year before had mysteriously vanished. He claimed to be in good health and surviving the ordeals of prison. He worked in the library, took walks around the camp several times each day, and wrote letters to friends, though all mail was screened. In cautious terms, they talked about the family businesses and Hugh assured him all was well. Fats sent his regards, as did Nevin and the other guys. Carmen was doing much better now that Lance was away, though Hugh downplayed his mother's happiness. Lance feigned concern for her well-being.

They talked about everything but the obvious. Jesse Rudy's death was never mentioned. Lance had not been involved in it, and he was worried sick that his unpredictable son had done something stupid.

All suspicions were on Hugh because there were no other credible suspects.

———•———

Like his predecessor, Bill Waller, Governor Finch had served two terms as a district attorney. The brutal murder of one of their own was unthinkable, and he made its investigation his highest priority. He formed a joint task force with the state police and FBI, and promised full cooperation and funding.

In late September, the task force met in secret for the first time in a hotel in Pascagoula. Special Agents Jackson Lewis and Spence Whitehead were there on behalf of the FBI. The head of the state police, Captain Moffett, presided. He was flanked by two of his investigators. Two more of his men, state troopers in uniform, guarded the door. Keith took notes and said little.

It was significant that local law enforcement was absent. Fats Bowman and his gang would never be included, because of distrust. The Biloxi police were not qualified to take part in such a high-profile and complicated investigation. No one in the room wanted the locals to get involved unless it became necessary. Secrecy was crucial.

Agent Lewis reviewed a report from the lab at Quantico. The experts were certain that the blast had been caused by Semtex, a plastic explosive widely used by the U.S. military. They believed the bomber got his hands on the deadlier stuff and was not altogether familiar with its strength. Their estimate was between five and ten pounds, far more than necessary to kill a man in his office.

As they discussed the damage, the faint sounds of hammers and saws were heard from the repair work down the hall.

Keith struggled to ignore the fact that he was sitting in the courtroom where his father had made his mark suing insurance companies after Camille, and later prosecuting notorious criminals. Not twenty feet away was the bench where Lance Malco had stood when he pled guilty and was sentenced by Judge Oliphant.

Next was a discussion of potential witnesses. Henry Taylor was never mentioned. The FBI had practically driven him out of town, broken leg and all, three days after the murder, then leaned on the state and local police to remain quiet about his existence. The FBI had big plans for Taylor, but it was simply too risky to involve anyone in Biloxi at such an early stage. One stray word could jeopardize Jackson Lewis's scheme. Likewise, Judge Oliphant, who had signed the search warrants for Taylor's truck and motel room, had promised secrecy.

Keith would be told of Henry Taylor in due course. He was grief-stricken, driven by revenge, and thoroughly untested. Keeping him in the dark was a delicate matter, but the FBI had no choice. There was also the complicated matter of Keith handling the prosecution. No one in the room believed he would be allowed to pursue the killer or killers all the way to a trial. A special prosecutor would be appointed by the state supreme court, according to backroom conversations between Captain Moffett and the FBI.

The task force reviewed a summary of every person known to be either in the courthouse or having just left it at the time of the explosion. Thirteen people were injured, most by flying glass. Egan Clement was thrown to the floor and received a gash to her head along with a minor concussion. One Alan Taylor from Necaise was knocked down the stairs and broke his leg. He claimed to have been on his way to purchase car tags from the tax collector's office on the second floor. His story checked out, according to the FBI.

Keith said, "I've spoken to Egan several times and she thinks she saw a delivery man with packages near the stairs at the time of the explosion."

Lewis nodded agreement and said, "Yes, and we've spoken to her at length. As you know, she was knocked unconscious. Her recall is not always the same. Most of her story is rather fuzzy, at best. But we're still digging."

"So, we could have a suspect?"

"Yes, possibly. That man, if he exists, is a priority."

"And no one else reported seeing him?"

"No one."

"How'd the bomb get in the office?"

"We don't know yet. Everything is preliminary, Keith."

Keith was suspicious but let it pass. It was too early to press the investigators but he felt certain they knew more than they were sharing. At least there was the possibility of a suspect.

Joint efforts by state and federal law enforcement were notoriously fraught with suspicions and turf battles. After some shadow-boxing, it was agreed that Jackson Lewis and the FBI would take the lead in the investigation. Moffett feigned frustration, but he was under direct orders from the governor to yield to the Feds.

In the ninety days before the murder, Henry Taylor had either made or received 515 calls. Every number had been checked; most were local to family, friends, a couple of ladies he seemed to know well. Thirty-one were long distance but none were suspicious. Two weeks before the murder, he had received a phone call from a pay phone in Biloxi, but it was impossible to know who placed it.

Taylor ran his business out of a small shop in an old warehouse. A federal magistrate issued another eavesdropping warrant and the office phone was tapped. Its records were collected from the phone company and were being analyzed. Virtually all the calls were business-related; again, none seemed suspicious.

Agent Lewis was puzzled. To pull off such a spectacular bomb blast would almost certainly require phone activity. Where did the explosives come from? How did he get them? Lewis and White-head had searched his little bomb lab behind his home and found no explosives, only residue and gadgets for detonators. There had to be contact with the man with the money, or some go-between.

Several calls from his home revealed that his broken leg was causing considerable trouble and he was unable to work. He chatted with two part-time employees and wasn't happy with either. One claimed Taylor owed some back wages; they argued. He called his doctor and complained. He tried to borrow money from a brother, but the conversation didn't go well. There were fewer and fewer calls to his office from prospective customers.

His story was that he had gone fishing in the Gulf and slipped at a marina, breaking his leg. Six weeks after the murder, he was still on crutches and in constant pain.

He made an interesting call on October 14. A Mr. Ludlow took Taylor's call at the bank and listened to his troubles. He wasn't working much, broken leg and all, and he was in a bind, needed to borrow some money. They seemed to know one another from past dealings. Henry wanted $10,000 and was willing to put a second mortgage on his home. Mr. Ludlow said he would ponder it. He called back the next day and said no.

A target in financial trouble. They kept listening.

CHAPTER 44

The Harrison County Board of Supervisors decided to spend some money repairing its courthouse and went overboard on an office suite for its new district attorney. When Keith moved in a week before Thanksgiving, he was impressed with the remodeling, the fine furniture, the latest office equipment. The walls, floors, and ceilings still smelled of fresh paint. Handsome rugs were on all the floors. Modern art adorned the walls, though he would soon replace it. All in all it was a superb effort and a meaningful gesture.

His most pressing problem was the lack of a staff. Jesse's longtime secretary refused to enter the courthouse and Keith could not coax her out of retirement. Nor was his own assistant ready to return. Egan Clement was depressed and still frightened. A lady from the land records office volunteered to answer the phone for two months.

During the first few days, he fought the emotions that surfaced every time he walked into his father's old office, but finally found the resolve to move forward. Jesse wouldn't want him moping around when there was work to do. The knot in his stomach eventually subsided, then went away. When he wasn't busy he left the office and went for long drives in the country north of town. What he needed was his first jury trial; nothing like a good courtroom brawl to make a lawyer forget his troubles.

He called his first grand jury to order and presented half a dozen cases: small-time drug trafficking, an assault from a nasty domestic dispute, and an armed home invasion that almost turned deadly.

The case of *State of Mississippi v. Calvin Ball* involved a honky-tonk fistfight that turned into a shooting that left one dead. Jesse had barely squeezed an indictment out of his last grand jury six months earlier. Calvin Ball, the winner of the fight, claimed self-defense. No less than eight patrons were involved at some level, and all were drunk, stoned, or getting that way. It happened just after midnight on a Saturday in rural Stone County. Ball's lawyer was pushing for a trial because his client wanted to clear his name. Keith finally said what the hell; a win for either side looked doubtful.

The trial lasted for three days in Wiggins and almost turned into another brawl. After eight hours of heated deliberations, the jury split 6–6 and the judge declared a mistrial. Driving back to Biloxi, Keith managed to find little humor in some of the testimony, and in the fact that he had lost his first trial as DA. He remembered that his father had told stories about the honky-tonk. Jesse did not want to put Calvin Ball on trial.

The following week, Keith got his first win in an embezzlement case. The week before Christmas he got convictions for two bikers from California who jumped a gas station attendant in Gulfport and beat him for no reason.

Keith had practically grown up in the courtroom. He was carrying his father's briefcase to trials when he was a teenager. He knew the rules of evidence long before he started law school. He learned courtroom procedure, etiquette, and tactics from watching a hundred trials. Jesse loved to whisper tips, tricks, and slick maneuvers as if passing along insider information.

A lawyer in a trial facing a jury has a dozen things on his mind. Getting to trial takes meticulous preparation. There was no time to grieve, fret, fear, to feel sorry for oneself. At the age of twenty-eight, Keith was becoming a good trial lawyer, one his father would be proud of.

His first three trials were exhilarating, and they at times diverted his mind from the nightmare.

———•———

Agnes was determined to lift the family's spirits with a merry holiday season. She decorated the house as never before and planned at least three parties. Beverly, Laura, and Tim were home for Christmas. Keith and Ainsley lived four blocks away. Their kitchen became the gathering place as the family came and went and friends dropped by with cakes, flowers, and gifts. Though there were plenty of tears at night, and Jesse was never far from their thoughts, they went about their celebrations as if nothing was out of the ordinary. They sat together during Midnight Mass and were surrounded by friends when it was over.

A new chapter in their lives began the following day during Christmas lunch when Keith announced that Ainsley was two months pregnant. A new Rudy would enter the picture, and he or she was badly needed.

Agnes had managed to grit her teeth and plow through the season, but when she heard the wonderful news that she would be a grandmother, she finally broke down. The emotion was contagious, and in an instant the entire family was having a good cry. Tears of joy.

CHAPTER 45

The apartment was in a large, aging complex. Henry Taylor had cleaned there before. Small, inexpensive units, the kind that attracted renters who often fled in the middle of the night, leaving behind nothing that wasn't nailed down along with plenty of dirt and stains. The guy on the phone said he was moving in and wanted the carpets freshened up. They met at the door at the appointed hour, and the guy handed over $120 in cash for the job. Then he left, said he'd be back later.

Henry was working alone—couldn't find decent help so soon after the holidays—and was limping, struggling, and already cursing his bum leg though it was only eight in the morning. He was carrying two large jugs of detergent into the apartment when a stranger appeared from nowhere at the door and startled him. Coat, tie, hard frown, the kind of look that often startled Henry because of his violent sideline. If folks only knew how easily Henry got spooked. A seasoned bomb-maker with steady hands and a cool head, he often lost a breath when confronted with exactly the type of man now staring at him from the doorway. Without a smile the man said, "Looking for Henry Taylor."

Was he a cop? On his trail? Had Henry finally made some unknown mistake along the way and was about to get nailed by forensics?

"That's me. What do you want?"

Finally, a faint smile. He handed him a business card and said, "J. W. Gross, Private Investigator."

Henry actually exhaled but tried not to show it. The man was offering a card, not a warrant. He took it, examined it, flipped it, found nothing on the back. A private eye with an address in Nashville. He offered the card back as if he had no interest whatsoever, but Gross ignored the gesture.

"A real pleasure," Henry said.

"Same here. Got a minute?"

"No. I gotta job and I'm running late."

Gross shrugged but made no effort to leave. "Two minutes is all I ask and it'll be worth it, maybe."

"One minute and talk fast."

Gross glanced around and said, "Let's step inside."

Inside would certainly mean more than one minute, but Henry stood down and backed away. Gross closed the door behind him and Henry glanced at his watch like a real hard-ass.

Gross said, "I gotta client with a friend who's loaded and needs a job, know what I mean?"

"I have no idea what you mean."

"You come highly recommended, Mr. Taylor. A real pro with a lot of experience, a man who gets things done."

"Are you a cop?"

"No, never have been. Don't even like cops."

"For all I know you're wearing a wire. What the hell's going on?"

Gross laughed, spread his arms wide, and said, "Search me. Want me to take off my shirt?"

"Oh no, I'm seeing enough. One minute's up. I'm busy."

Gross gave another fake smile and said, "Sure. But it's a lot of money. A lot more than Biloxi."

A mule kick in the gut could not have landed harder. Henry's jaw dropped as he glared at Gross, unable to speak.

Gross took in his reaction and said, "Fifty grand, cash. You got my number."

He turned around, left the room, and shut the door.

Henry stared at it for a long time as his mind spun out of control. No one knew about Biloxi but himself and his contact there. Or did they? Obviously so. Henry had told no one; he never did. It was impossible to survive in his business if secrets were divulged. Someone in Biloxi had loose lips. Word had spread through the underworld that Henry Taylor had struck again. Henry, though, didn't care for the reputation. That would only attract cops.

He cleaned the filthy carpets for two hours, then needed a break and some pain pills. He drove to the downtown library in Union City and flipped through the phone directories of the largest cities and towns in Tennessee. In the Nashville yellow pages he found a small ad for J. W. Gross, Private Investigator. Honest. Reliable. Twenty Years' Experience.

He scoffed at anyone who advertised honesty.

He went to his office, took a pain pill, and stretched out on an army cot he often used for naps. The meds finally kicked in and the pain subsided. He picked up the phone and called a friend. The number was traced to a home in Brentwood, Tennessee, in the Nashville metro area.

They were listening.

Henry said, "Say, met a private dick from your hometown. Know anybody named J. W. Gross?"

The friend replied, "Why should I know a private dick?"

"Thought you knew everyone on the shadier side."

"Well, I know you."

"Ha ha. You mind making a call or two, check the guy out?"

"What's in it for me?"

"My everlasting friendship."

"Been trying to shake that for years."

"Come on. You owe me one."

"I'll see what I can find out."

"Don't break your neck. Just want to make sure he's legit, you know?"

They talked about women for a few moments and rang off.

Henry began thinking about the cash. He'd been paid $20,000

to blow up Jesse Rudy and he should have asked for more. Taking out a high-profile elected official was worth twice that much. Who in the world was worth $50,000? And, if the guy was really loaded and offering fifty grand as a starting point, then he could certainly go higher. Greed entered his thoughts, along with survival.

He began to smile and nodded off.

———•———

The skinny on J. W. Gross was satisfactory. Solid reputation, nice little firm with himself at the helm and a couple of younger guys in the office. Worked high-end divorces and did some corporate security. No law enforcement background.

Henry was obsessed with the money. He called the number on the business card and arranged a meeting in the parking lot of a softball field on the east side of Union City. No traffic, no witnesses. It was early January, so no softball.

It was cold and the wind was blowing. J.W. followed Henry, using a cane, to the concession stand where the door was unlocked. They stepped inside to get out of the wind.

"How do I know you're not wired?" Henry asked.

Again, J.W. spread his arms and said, "Go ahead."

"Mind taking off the coat?"

Gross looked frustrated but took off his coat. Under it was a cheap black blazer. Henry stepped forward and began tapping his chest and belt. He stopped at the right hip. "Got a piece?"

J.W. pulled back his blazer and showed Henry an automatic pistol in a holster. "Always carry it, Mr. Taylor. Want to see the permit?"

"That's not necessary. Turn around."

Gross did as he was instructed and Henry patted down his neck, underarms, and waist. "Okay, looks like you're clean."

"Thank you." Gross put on his coat.

"I'm listening," Henry said.

"I don't know the man with the money, don't know his real name, so let's call him Mr. Getty. He's about sixty years old, lives somewhere in this state, but has a collection of fine homes around the country. His wife is twenty years younger, number three I think. Typical setup—older guy with money, younger gal with a body. The good life, except she's got a boyfriend on the side, actually one of her ex-husbands she's still quite fond of. Mr. Getty is upset, heartbroken, angry, and not the kind of man who's accustomed to getting dumped on. Even worse, he also suspects she and her stud might be planning a number on him to get his money. It's complicated. A few years back, Mr. Getty and some rich pals developed a resort near Gatlinburg, in the mountains."

"I know Gatlinburg."

"His wife loves the mountains, likes to spend time there with her girlfriends, sometimes alone. Sometimes with Mr. Getty. And often with her boyfriend. It's their favorite little love nest."

"The job is to blow it up."

"And her. And him. Mr. Getty wants a dramatic event, preferably when they're in the bed."

"That might present timing problems."

"Understood. I'm just passing along the info, Mr. Taylor."

"What about the building?"

"Two-thousand-square-foot condo, one of four units. The other three are weekend places and seldom used, especially in cold weather. My contact will get drawings, plans, photos, whatever. Miss Getty and her boy are under surveillance so we'll know when they retire to the mountains."

"You said your contact was the client of a friend, or the friend of a client. That's pretty vague."

"It'll have to stay that way. I'll never meet Mr. Getty. As I understand things, he's a client of a friend who's in this same business. Private work."

"And who knew my name?"

"I can't answer that."

"Fair enough. Two high-profile targets is worth a lot more than fifty grand."

"I don't have the authority to negotiate, Mr. Taylor. I'm just relaying messages."

"A hundred grand."

Gross flinched a bit and gave a frown, but recovered like a pro. "Don't blame you at all. I'll pass it along."

"What's the time frame?"

"Sooner rather than later. Mr. Getty has plenty of security and he's watching them closely. He is obviously concerned. Also, as warm weather approaches this spring the resort will get busier. He thinks the best time is between now and early April."

"I'll have to check my schedule."

Gross shrugged, wasn't sure how to respond.

"Get me the drawings and photos and I'll take a look."

———•———

The trackers and listeners tightened the net around Taylor.

He left home in his pickup on Saturday, January 22, and drove three hours to Nashville where he met Gross in the parking lot of a shopping center and took a folder with the necessary info. From there he drove four hours to Pigeon Forge and checked into a budget motel in the shadows of the Great Smoky Mountains. He paid twenty-four dollars in cash for one night and used a bogus driver's license as an ID. He walked next door to a grill, ate a sandwich, and drove eight miles to Gatlinburg. He got lost in the steep, winding roads but eventually found the resort at dusk.

While he was away, a team of FBI technicians entered his motel room, tapped the phone, and planted six listening devices.

Taylor had been assured by Gross that the condo would be empty during the weekend and there was no alarm system. He left the resort, drove to a diner, and killed some time drinking coffee. At nine, he returned to the resort, which was virtually deserted, and crept in the darkness to the condo. With little effort he jimmied the lock and went inside.

The FBI trackers were impressed with Taylor's ability to move around without being noticed.

He returned to the motel at 11:00 P.M. and called J. W. Gross. They agreed to meet Sunday morning at a truck stop on Interstate 40 east of Nashville. He made no other calls and went to bed.

Sleet was falling and the truck stop was packed with eighteen-wheelers trying to get off the road. Gross found Taylor's pickup parked near the restaurant, but Taylor was not in it. He waited a few moments as 11:30, their agreed-upon time, came and went. Taylor appeared from the restaurant, walked over, and Gross nodded to get inside where it was warm and dry. Taylor got in the passenger's side and said, "Place is packed in there. Couldn't get a table."

The cab of the truck was wired. The listeners, already on high alert and hiding about fifty feet away, held their breaths. What a lucky break. What a dumb move by Taylor.

Gross asked, "You found the condo?"

"Yes, it was easy," Taylor replied smugly. "I don't see a problem, other than timing. I'll need at least three days' notice."

"In three weeks, February eleventh, Mr. Getty and his wife plan to get away for the weekend. He won't make it, some business emergency. She'll probably go anyway and substitute her boyfriend for a little fun. That looks like our first opportunity. Can you do it then?"

"That works. And you want them both dead?"

"No, personally I don't care. But Mr. Getty wants both of them killed and the condo blown to hell and back."

"I can't guarantee it, you understand?"

"What can you guarantee? I mean, hell, for a hundred grand you gotta make some promises, Mr. Taylor."

"I know that. I also know that no two projects are the same, no two bombs behave alike. It's an art, J.W., not a science. I'll set it for three A.M. when it's safe to assume they'll be in the same bed, right?"

"I guess. You're the expert."

"Thank you. Now, about the money."

———————

Supply chain problems plague every rogue bomber, and phone calls can leave tracks.

On January 26, with the FBI in tow, though he had no inkling of it, Henry Taylor drove to a compound in the Ozark Mountains near the small town of Mountain Home. He had been there before and thought he had some clout. It was the heavily fortified supply base of a man considered by the Feds to be a domestic arms dealer. In a country with tepid gun laws riddled with loopholes, the man was doing nothing wrong and had never been convicted.

Henry couldn't gain admittance and left the area. His followers assumed he was looking for explosives. He drove to Memphis and made calls from three public telephone booths, but the calls could not be traced in time.

On January 30, Gross called Henry at home and asked him to call the next day from a secure line. Henry did so, and Gross told him that the February 11 weekend trip by Mr. Getty and his wife was still on. Henry said he would be ready, but he did not tell Gross that he was having trouble finding explosives.

On February 1, Henry made his biggest mistake. There were six public pay phones within five miles of his home and office. The FBI guessed that he might use those for convenience and all six were tapped. The hunch paid off. Henry drove to a hot dog stand near downtown Union City and stepped into a red phone booth. His call went to a nightclub in Biloxi, a famous one known as Red Velvet. Five minutes later the pay phone rang and Henry grabbed it.

He told Nevin Noll that he was in a bind and needed some

supplies. Noll cursed him for calling the club and hung up. Minutes later he called from his own pay phone and was still angry. In cautious, even coded language, Henry said he needed five pounds. Noll said the cost would be a thousand dollars a pound, delivered.

Outrageous, said Henry, but he had no choice. They seemed to reach a deal and decided to work out the delivery details later.

Jackson Lewis and his team of FBI agents were beyond exhilarated. His scheme and patience had now led them to the Strip. The eighteen-hour days were about to pay off.

—————•—————

On February 8, Henry Taylor drove four hours to an interstate motel south of Nashville. He paid cash for one night and refused to provide any type of ID. He waited in the lobby for an hour and watched every vehicle and every person. At 4:30 P.M. on the dot, J. W. Gross parked his Buick in the lot and walked toward the lobby carrying a briefcase. Inside, he made eye contact with Taylor and followed him to his room on the first floor.

Since they were a team now, Taylor didn't bother with searching Gross for a wire. He wouldn't have found one anyway. The bug was embedded in the belt buckle; its transmitter was hidden in the butt of the pistol. The trackers heard every word loud and clear:

TAYLOR: So what's the latest?
GROSS: Nothing has changed. Mr. Getty says they're all set
    for a romantic weekend in the mountains and excited
    about the weather forecast. Supposed to be beautiful.
TAYLOR: Nice. You got the money?
GROSS: Right here. Fifty thousand cash. I'll have the other
    half waiting as soon as we hear the awful news.
TAYLOR: It should be a real show. You guys ought to pick
    a spot nearby and watch the fireworks. Three A.M. this
    Saturday morning.

GROSS: Thanks. I'll pass it along. I'm usually asleep at that
   hour.

TAYLOR: It's always fun to watch.

GROSS: I take it you found the explosives.

TAYLOR: Got 'em. Let's meet Saturday afternoon for the rest
   of the cash. I'll call when it's over.

GROSS: Sounds like a plan.

They watched J. W. leave the motel, then waited two hours for
Taylor to emerge with his small overnight bag. They followed him
to the town of Pulaski, Tennessee, where Nevin Noll was waiting in the parking lot of a busy grocery store. He was smoking a
cigarette, listening to the radio, watching the traffic, waiting for a
blue Dodge pickup truck. In his trunk were five pounds of Semtex
purchased on the black market near Keesler.

They were watching, and the sight of Noll casually smoking
and flicking ashes on the pavement, with a bomb in his trunk,
made them uneasy. They kept their distance.

The blue Dodge arrived and parked next to Noll. He got in
the truck and the two talked for a few minutes. They got out and
Noll opened his trunk. He handed a box to Taylor, who placed
it in a metal container in the bed of his pickup. Noll closed the
trunk, said something to Taylor, then started his engine and drove
away.

Taylor's plan was to drive all night and stay with a friend near
Knoxville. His explosives were safely tucked away in an airtight,
waterproof metal box, one he had built himself. It would take
about an hour to assemble the bomb.

So much for plans. Five miles outside Pulaski, the highway
was suddenly blocked with blue lights and there were even more
racing toward them. He was arrested without a word, handcuffed,
tossed in the rear of a Tennessee State Police car and driven to
Nashville.

They waited patiently for Nevin Noll to amble back onto Mississippi soil. No need to mess with extradition if it could be avoided. When he crossed the state line near Corinth, some idiot ran up behind him with his lights on bright and wouldn't go around. Then the lights turned blue.

CHAPTER 46

Of course there was no Mr. Getty, no wayward wife, no lover, no love nest in need of detonation. J. W. Gross was a real character who played himself brilliantly and collected a nice fee from the FBI. He enjoyed the adventure and said he was available for the next one. The entire $50,000 in marked bills was recovered.

Jackson Lewis reveled in the success of his undercover operation and knew it would make his career, but there was little time to celebrate.

———————•———————

After a few hours of fitful sleep on a dirty mattress, bottom bunk because the top one was the territory of Big Duke, Henry Taylor was removed from the cell, handcuffed to a wheelchair, shrouded with a black hood, and rolled without a word to a windowless room in the basement of the jail. When he was situated at a table, the hood was removed but the cuffs were not.

Special Agents Jackson Lewis and Spence Whitehead faced him, both frowning.

To lighten an awful moment, Taylor began with "Well, boys, don't know what's going on but you got the wrong man."

Neither smiled. Lewis said, "Is that the best you can do?"

"For now, yes."

"We found five pounds of plastic explosives, military grade and highly illegal, in the bed of your truck. Where'd you get it?"

"News to me. Somebody must've put it there."

"Of course. We picked up your pal Nevin Noll last night in Mississippi. He says you paid him ten grand for the stuff. Coincidentally, he had ten thousand cash in his pocket."

Taylor absorbed the blow but couldn't keep his lips together. His shoulders sagged and he dropped his gaze. When he spoke again his voice was hoarse. "Why'd you put that hood over my head?"

"Because we find your face offensive. Because we're the FBI and we'll do anything we want."

"I suppose you'll keep my money, maybe split it between the two of you."

"The money is the last of your worries, Taylor. Conspiracy to commit murder by contract killing is a capital offense in Tennessee. They use the electric chair here. Down in Mississippi, killing someone for money will get you the gas chamber."

"Decisions, decisions. Do I get a vote?"

"No. You're going to Biloxi. Ever been there?"

"Nope."

Whitehead handed something to Lewis, who laid it on the table. "Recognize this, Taylor?"

"Nope."

"Didn't think so. It's the detonator you left behind at the Biloxi courthouse, the one used to set off the bomb that killed Jesse Rudy. Sloppy, sloppy. Your name was Lyle back then. We found your shirt too, in the same garbage can. There's a partial fingerprint on the detonator that matches the prints taken from your hospital room. Sloppy. Coincidentally, those prints match at least a dozen we found in Room 19 at the Beach Bay Motel in Biloxi, including six taken from the two handguns you tried to hide under the mattress. Coincidentally, those prints match ones we lifted from your Dodge pickup truck, along with several dozen taken from your home, your little bomb lab out back, and your office in the warehouse in Union City. You're a dumbass, Taylor. You left behind enough prints to bring down the entire Dixie Mafia."

"I got nothing to say."

"Well, you might want to reconsider that. Your pal Noll is talking, singing like a bird, trying to save his own skin since he doesn't give a damn about yours."

"I'd like to talk to a lawyer."

"Okay, we'll find one, eventually. We'll keep you locked up here for a few days as we finish things. They're gonna put you in a cell by yourself, no phones, no contact with anyone."

"Don't I get a phone call?"

"That's for drunks and wife-beaters. You get nothing, Taylor, until we say so."

"The food sucks."

"Get used to it. In Mississippi, they keep you on death row in solitary for ten years before they gas you. Twice a day they give you the same meal, sawdust mixed with rat shit."

———— • ————

Four hours later, Lewis and Whitehead arrived in Corinth and parked at the Alcorn County jail. The sheriff met them and they compared notes. He led them to a small room where they waited a few minutes while the jailer fetched their man.

Noll was handcuffed but not hooded. He sat in the chair across the table and sneered at the two agents as if they were interrupting something.

Lewis said, "You're a long way from Biloxi."

"So are you."

"You had ten thousand bucks in your pocket last night. Where'd it come from?"

"I like to carry cash. It's not illegal."

"Of course not, but peddling stolen Semtex is. Where'd you get it? Keesler?"

"I have the right to a lawyer. His name is Joshua Burch. I ain't saying anything else."

———•———

A chartered King Air saved them six hours of driving time to the Coast. They arrived in Biloxi at 3:30 and went to the courthouse. Keith Rudy had been alerted and was waiting. Captain Moffett from the state police and two of his investigators joined them. They gathered in Keith's new office and locked the door. Two uniformed troopers sat outside and dared anyone to come close.

Jackson Lewis was in charge and ran the show. He began with a dramatic "Keith, we have in custody the man who killed your father."

Keith smiled and took a deep breath, but showed no emotion. Given the urgency in throwing together the meeting, he was expecting big news. But nothing could have prepared him for what he had just heard. He nodded and Lewis handed over an enlarged color photo. "Name's Henry Taylor, from Union City, Tennessee. Cleans carpets for a living, builds bombs for a hobby. Ten years ago he was a member of the Klan and blew up a few black churches back in the day, got indicted at least twice but never convicted. Known in the trade as a hit man who favors explosives."

"Where is he?"

"We threw him under the jail in Nashville. Interviewed him this morning up there, but he's not very cooperative."

Keith managed an even wider smile and said, "Okay, let's hear it. How'd you find him?"

"It's a long story."

"I want every detail."

———•———

As the briefing was underway, Hugh Malco left his apartment in West Biloxi and was driving to work in his latest sports car, a 1977 Corvette Sting Ray. Two blocks from home, he noticed a city cop behind him in a patrol car. When its blue lights came on he began cursing. He wasn't speeding. He'd broken no traffic laws. He stopped, jumped out of the car, and was storming toward the officer when he realized the street was being blocked by state troopers. One of them yelled, "Hands up! You're under arrest!"

At least three handguns were aimed at him as they approached. He slowly raised his hands, got shoved onto the hood of his Corvette, spread-eagled, searched, handcuffed, roughed up a little.

"I swear I wasn't speeding," he said.

"Shut up," a trooper barked.

They half-dragged him to a patrol car, tossed him inside, and left the area in a motorcade. Two hours later, he was taken to the county jail in Hattiesburg and placed in a cell by himself.

CHAPTER 47

The main courtroom was again chosen for the occasion. Tables and chairs were moved and a podium was arranged close to the bar and facing the gallery. When the doors opened a noisy crowd poured in, led by reporters and cameramen from several news stations—Biloxi, Jackson, New Orleans, and Mobile. They swarmed the podium and stuck their mikes in plain view, then retreated to the back wall with their bulky cameras. A bailiff herded them into one place. Print reporters jostled for the front rows. Other bailiffs pointed here and there and tried to maintain some level of order. Behind the press the gallery filled quickly with courthouse regulars, the curious, associates of the accused, and folks off the street. Lawyers and clerks milled about behind the podium, pleased with their status as members of the court and thus allowed to come and go. When all the seats were taken, one bailiff closed the door while another stood guard in the hallway and turned away the unlucky.

At 10:00 A.M. sharp, early enough to make the noon news, a side door opened and the district attorney emerged, followed by the FBI and state police. No locals were invited to the show. Keith assumed the podium with Egan Clement standing to his immediate left. They were flanked by Special Agents Jackson Lewis and Spence Whitehead, Captain Moffett, and two investigators from the state police.

Keith began with a smile and thanked the crowd for showing up. He was twenty-eight years old, handsome, trim, well-dressed, and very much aware that he was speaking to a wide audience.

"Yesterday, the Harrison County Grand Jury, meeting in this very courtroom, indicted three men for the murder and contract killing of our former district attorney, Jesse Rudy. The indictment charges that on August 20 of last year, 1976, Nevin Noll, and Henry Taylor did conspire to commit and did indeed commit the murder of Jesse Rudy. Nevin Noll paid a large sum of money to Henry Taylor to carry out the contract killing. Mr. Taylor is a known underworld character and accomplished bomb-maker. The grand jury charges that the murder for hire was a contract killing carried out by Henry Taylor, and, under Section 98-17-29 of the Mississippi Code, is punishable by death at the state penitentiary at Parchman. The State of Mississippi will seek the death penalty for both men. The defendants were taken into custody last week and are being kept in various jails around the state, but not in Harrison County."

Keith paused to give the reporters time to catch up. He tried to ignore the row of cameras against the back wall. The room was packed and quiet; everyone was waiting for more.

"This murder was solved by the brilliant work of our state police, and especially by the investigative prowess of the FBI. Special Agents Jackson Lewis and Spence Whitehead conducted an undercover operation that was nothing short of brilliant. For many reasons I cannot go into details, but I hope that one day the story will be told. We the people of this state owe a great debt to these fine officers. I will not belabor the point here. The purpose of this announcement was to inform the public. I will take a few questions, but only a few."

A reporter in the front row leapt to her feet and yelled, "When will the defendants be in court?"

"Judge Oliphant has set a first appearance for Friday morning, in this courtroom."

The next one yelled, "Will they be allowed to post bail and get out?"

"The State will oppose bail, but that's a decision for the judge."

"Was the investigation hampered by local law enforcement?"

"Well, it certainly wasn't helped. We received some assistance from the Biloxi city police, but we kept the investigation away from the sheriff's department."

"Why?"

"Obvious reasons. It's a lack of trust."

"Will there be additional defendants?"

"No comment. It's safe to say we can expect a lot of legal maneuvers between now and a trial."

"Will you prosecute these defendants?"

"As of now, I plan to. That's my job."

"You don't see a conflict of interest?"

"No, but if it becomes necessary for me to step aside, then I'll do so."

"Do you want these men put to death for killing your father?"

Without hesitation, Keith said, "Yes."

———————— • ————————

The grand jury also indicted Sgt. Eddie Morton, a career air force mechanic who had been stationed at Keesler for nine years. An anonymous tip notified the FBI that Morton had been selling explosives and ordnance out the back door. Morton was in the base jail, facing court-martial and a long sentence, and on suicide watch.

With his lawyer present, he sat down with the air force police and told his story. He has been at Keesler for nine years and had spent too much time in the clubs. He had a serious drinking problem and heavy gambling debts. Mr. Malco down at the Lucky Star had offered to forgive his debts in return for some explosives. On August 3 of last year, Morton delivered five pounds of Semtex to Nevin Noll, as associate of Malco's.

When Keith was told of this, he breathed an enormous sigh of relief. Then he rounded up his grand jury for an emergency session. In a quick meeting, it indicted Hugh Malco for capital murder.

———•———

Joshua Burch couldn't find his clients and no one seemed too concerned about it. He called Keith repeatedly and objected strongly to his hiding all three defendants. He claimed there was some vague constitutional right to be housed in a jail close to home, but Keith politely said that was nonsense.

Burch's immediate quandary was which defendant to represent, though the answer wasn't that complicated; he'd take the one with the most money. When he finally spoke to Nevin Noll by phone he tried to break it to him gently and explain that, in a capital murder situation with three defendants, there were too many possible conflicts of interest for any one lawyer to surmount. He, Burch, was loyal to the Malcos, and he, Noll, would have to find another lawyer. It was a difficult conversation because Noll had been fond of Burch since he'd walked him out a free man following the murder of Earl Fortier thirteen years earlier. It had been Noll's first murder, and, after he was found not guilty, had inspired him to kill again.

Now his trusted lawyer was saying no. Burch promised to find another talented criminal defense attorney, but it would be expensive. Noll assumed the Malcos would cover the costs.

Once his cash disappeared, Henry Taylor had no money to hire anyone, especially a lawyer. For four days he was kept in solitary in the Nashville jail and didn't touch a phone until the third day.

———•———

The news of the indictments received front-page coverage throughout the Deep South, and Keith's stern but handsome face was everywhere. The story was instantly compelling—son seeks revenge for father's death—but it became irresistible when the *Gulf Coast Register* found an old photo of Keith and Hugh posing with their teammates as Biloxi All-Stars in 1960.

Keith was inundated with calls and requests from reporters across the country. He was forced to leave his new office in the courthouse and seek refuge at Rudy & Pettigrew. The frenzy only got worse as they prepared for the initial appearances.

———•———

On Friday, February 18, the courthouse was surrounded by freshly cleaned squad cars from the highway patrol. Troopers were everywhere, some directing traffic. The news vans were parked in one small lot at the rear of the courthouse and the cameras were directed to an area near the back entrance. The Biloxi police assured the camera crews they would be in the perfect position to film the three defendants as they were perp-walked into court.

Indeed they were. At 9:45, three squad cars arrived together. Hugh Malco was extracted from the first, and in handcuffs and ankle chains was escorted slowly into the building. Some reporters tossed banalities at him but he only smiled. He was followed by Nevin Noll, unsmiling; and Henry Taylor, eyes diverted and head hung low, brought up the rear.

Keith had a knot in his stomach the size of a softball. He sat at the State's table with Egan to his left and a quiet throng behind him, waiting for the moment when the defendants would be hauled in from a side door and he and Hugh would have their first good look at each other.

Across the way, Joshua Burch sat with his team and the other defense lawyers, all frowning gravely at documents and occasionally whispering important strategies.

Keith was out of his league and he knew it. In his five months as district attorney he had tried eight cases from start to finish, and though he'd won the last seven they were easy wins. He had never even observed a capital murder trial. His father had served as DA for almost five years and never handled one. They were grueling, complicated, and the stakes were enormous.

Burch, on the other hand, had spent the last three decades in front of juries and projected an air of extreme confidence, regardless of the guilt or innocence of his clients. Jesse had said many times that Joshua Burch was the smoothest trial lawyer he had ever fought. "If I ever get indicted," Jesse had said more than once, "I want Burch."

A side door opened and the police led the way. They escorted the three defendants to chairs near the defense table and removed their handcuffs and ankle chains. Keith glared at Hugh Malco, hoping to convey the message: *You're in my courtroom, under my control, and this will not end well for you.* Hugh, though, kept his eyes on the floor and ignored everyone around him.

Once Judge Oliphant settled in on the bench, he thanked the throng for attending and showing so much interest, and went on to explain that the purpose of the initial appearance was to make sure the defendants understood the charges from the indictment and to check the status of their legal representation. He called Henry Taylor first.

Six months earlier, Taylor had stepped inside the dark and empty courtroom as he scoped out the building and planned his attack. At that time he could not have dreamed that he would ever return, especially in handcuffs, under indictment, and facing the death penalty. He limped to the bench where Keith Rudy was waiting with a scowl. Taylor answered a series of questions from the judge. Yes, he had read the indictment and understood the charges. He pled not guilty. No, he did not have a lawyer and couldn't afford one. Judge Oliphant explained that one would be furnished by the State, and sent him back to his seat.

He called Nevin Noll, who walked forward with Millard Cantrell, a long-haired, radical, capital defense veteran from Jackson who Burch had worked with before. After their first three phone conversations, Keith despised the guy and knew they would not get along. Nothing about Noll's prosecution would be easy. Noll answered the same questions, said he was not guilty, and that he had hired Mr. Cantrell for the defense. Cantrell, being a lawyer in front of a crowd, of course had to pipe up with a request for a bail hearing. His Honor was not pleased and in plain English made it clear that they were not there to discuss bail and that the issue might come later, after a proper motion by the defendant. He sent them back to their seats.

When Hugh's name was called, he walked forward and stood between Joshua Burch and the district attorney. The courtroom artists sketched frantically as they tried to capture the scene. There were no other sounds but for the charcoal pencils scratching the onionskin pads.

The two had once been the same size. In their glory days as twelve-year-old stars they were roughly the same height and weight, though no one bothered to measure back then. As they grew, their genes took charge and Hugh stopped at five feet ten inches. His feet became slower and he grew thicker through the chest, a good build for a boxer. Keith grew four more inches and was still lean, but he didn't tower over his old pal. Hugh moved with the assurance of a man who could take care of himself, even in a courtroom.

Judge Oliphant went through the same formalities. Hugh pled not guilty. Burch said almost nothing. Once back in their seats, Burch stood and requested a hearing on his motion to house the inmates in Harrison County jail. Burch had filed a proper written motion and Judge Oliphant had agreed to hear the matter.

As always, Burch loved a crowd and strutted around as if onstage. He whined that it was patently unfair to "hide" his client in a jail hours away, and even to move his client around so that no one, not even he, the lawyer, knew where his client was. It would be impossible to prepare for trial. He had never encountered such an outrage.

"Where do you suggest?" Judge Oliphant asked.

"Right here in Biloxi! Defendants are always housed in their home counties, Your Honor. I've never had a client taken away and hidden somewhere else."

"Mr. Rudy."

Keith knew it was coming and was ready for a smart-ass retort. He stood smiling and said, "Your Honor, if these defendants are released to the custody of the sheriff of Harrison County, they'll be free on ten dollars' bail within an hour and back at the Red Velvet drinking whiskey and dancing with the strippers."

The tense courtroom exploded with laughter and it took a while for it to subside. Finally, a smiling Judge Oliphant tapped his gavel and said, "Let's have some order please."

He nodded at Keith who said, "Judge, I don't care where they're locked up, just make sure they can't get out."

———•———

The following week, a grand jury in Nashville indicted Henry Taylor and Nevin Noll for the crime of conspiring to commit a contract killing. Keith had convinced the district attorney there to get the indictments, even though there would be no effort to prosecute the two. They had enough problems in Mississippi.

Keith wanted to use the extra indictment as leverage against Taylor.

CHAPTER 48

The legal wrangling began in earnest. Three weeks later, in a bail hearing that lasted an entire day, Judge Oliphant denied releasing the three defendants pending trial, regardless of how many promises they made. Hugh was sent to jail next door in Jackson County, where the sheriff had no use for Fats and his gang and promised to keep his prisoner practically in shackles. It would be a thirty-minute drive for Joshua Burch, who still bitched at the unfairness. Nevin Noll was sent to the Forrest County jail in Hattiesburg to be closer to Millard Cantrell, from Jackson. Henry Taylor became the client of Sam Grinder, a tough street lawyer from Pass Christian. Taylor was sent to the Hancock County jail.

Throughout the initial hearings, Keith insisted that all three defendants be kept away from each other, and Judge Oliphant agreed. Indeed, it seemed as though His Honor would agree to almost anything the State requested, and Joshua Burch was keeping notes. Privately, he had been complaining for years that Oliphant was too close to Jesse. Now that his favorite lawyer had been murdered, he seemed determined to help the State put away the killers. Burch planned to do what everyone expected—file a motion asking the judge to recuse himself.

It never happened. In early May, Judge Oliphant was rushed to the hospital after falling in his office. His blood pressure was off the charts. Scans revealed a series of mini-strokes, none of which would be fatal but the damage was done. After three weeks in the hospital, he was released for home rest and returned to a mountain of paperwork. Per doctors' orders, he would not preside over jury trials in the foreseeable future, if ever. He was urged by his wife to retire because he was, after all, pushing eighty, and he promised to consider it.

In late July, he notified Keith and the defense lawyers that he was voluntarily recusing himself from the three cases. He would ask the state supreme court to appoint a special judge to handle them. The Court agreed to do so but months would pass before a new judge arrived.

Keith was not pushing for a speedy trial. Henry Taylor was in solitary confinement in the Hancock County jail and not doing well. The longer he was confined to a cramped, humid, window-less cell with no air-conditioning, the more he might realize that Parchman would only be worse.

Judge or no judge, Joshua Burch continued piling on the paper-work with a dizzying assortment of motions. He finally asked the court to recuse the district attorney, for obvious conflict of interest. Keith responded quickly and opposed the motion.

For a few wonderful days in early August, he managed to forget about prosecuting criminals. Ainsley gave birth to a healthy baby girl, Eliza, and the Rudy clan gathered at home to welcome the child. Keith was delighted to have a daughter. A son would have complicated matters because of the pressure to name him Jesse.

———•———

In August, almost one year after the murder, Sgt. Eddie Mor-ton was court-martialed and sentenced to fifteen years in prison for selling explosives from the munitions facility at Keesler. Part of his plea deal required him to cooperate with the DA in Biloxi.

In their first meeting, inside Keesler, and with the FBI and state police present and recording, Morton revealed that on August 3, 1976, he gave five pounds of the plastic explosive Semtex to Nevin Noll, a man he had known for a couple years. Morton admitted to a gambling problem and also a fondness for the nightlife over on the Strip. In exchange for the explosives, Mr. Malco promised to forgive his gambling debts.

Five months later, Noll called again and was fishing around for some more explosives.

Morton admitted to selling smaller quantities of Semtex, Harrisite, C4, HMX, PETN, and other military explosives, over the past five years. All in, his little black-market business had netted him about $100,000. Now he was ruined, divorced, disgraced, and headed to prison.

Keith and the investigators were impressed with Morton and thought he would make an excellent witness. The one they wanted, though, was Henry Taylor.

———•———

In September, and while still waiting for a judge, Keith decided to finally approach Sam Grinder with a deal. In Keith's office, he presented the State's case against Henry Taylor. The fingerprint trail alone was enough to overwhelm any jury. The State could easily put Taylor in the courthouse at the time of the blast. And why else would he, a noted bomb-maker, be in Biloxi?

On the one hand, Keith was sickened by the idea of cutting a deal with the man who had actually killed his father. But, on the other hand, his target was Hugh Malco, and to get him he had to build a case.

As always, the plea deal was fraught with uncertainty and suspicion. In return for cooperation, the State would not promise leniency. However, leniency was on the table. First, the indictment in Tennessee would be quashed and forgotten. Taylor would testify against Nevin Noll, the only contact he had dealt with, tell all, then plead guilty and get himself sentenced. The State would recommend a ten-year prison term. The state police would find a soft spot for him in a county jail far away from Biloxi, and Taylor would avoid Parchman. If he behaved himself he would be eligible for early parole and able to find a permanent hiding place.

Otherwise, he was headed for death row and a date with the gas chamber. Keith planned to put Taylor on trial first, before the other two, and get a conviction, one he would use against Noll and Malco.

Grinder was a savvy lawyer who could spot a good deal. He spent hours with Taylor and finally convinced him to take it.

———•———

The truth was that the supreme court was having trouble finding a judge who would volunteer to preside over such a high-profile case against a bunch of thugs who had just bombed the very courthouse where the trial was to take place. It could be dangerous down there!

They finally cajoled a colorful old judge named Abraham Roach to dust off his black robe, come out of retirement, and enter the battle. Roach was from the Mississippi Delta, not far from Parchman, and had grown up in a culture where guns were a part of life. As a child he hunted deer, ducks, quail, and virtually every other wild animal that moved. Back in his prime, and he had served as a circuit judge for over thirty years, he was known to carry a .357 Magnum in his briefcase and keep it close by on the bench. He had no fear of guns or the men who carried them. Plus, he was eighty-four years old, had lived a good life, and was bored.

He arrived in February of 1978 with a bang when he filled two consecutive days with oral arguments covering a range of issues. Because of his age, he took nothing under advisement and ruled on the spot. Yes, the trial would be moved away from Harrison County. No, he would not force Keith Rudy to recuse himself, at least not in the near future. There would be three separate trials and the DA, not the defense, would decide the order.

The murder was now eighteen months in the past. The defendants had been in custody for almost a year. It was time for a trial, and Judge Roach ordered one for Henry Taylor on March 14, 1978, in the Lincoln County Courthouse in Brookhaven, Mississippi, 160 miles northwest of Biloxi.

As the lawyers absorbed the ruling, Keith stood calmly and said, "Your Honor, the State has an announcement. It will not be necessary to put Mr. Taylor on trial. We have signed an agreement with him in which he will plead guilty at a later date and cooperate with the State."

Joshua Burch grunted loudly as if kicked in the gut. Millard Cantrell turned and pointed an angry finger at Sam Grinder. Their underlings absorbed the blow, whispered loudly, scrambled for files. The unified defense was suddenly in disarray, and Mr. Malco and Mr. Noll had just been pushed much closer to the gas chamber.

Burch managed to get to his feet and began whining about the unfairness of the timing and so on, but there was nothing he could do. The district attorney had enormous power to cut deals, pressure witnesses, and crank up the pressure on any defendant he chose to target.

Judge Roach asked, "Mr. Rudy, when was this deal completed?"

"Yesterday, Your Honor. It's been in the works for some time, but Mr. Taylor signed it yesterday."

"I wish you had told me first thing this morning."

"Sorry, Your Honor."

Keith was anything but sorry. He had learned the art of the ambush from his father. It was important to keep the defense guessing.

———•———

Henry Taylor left the Hancock County jail in an unmarked car and was driven by the state police to the town of Hernando, six hours due north, almost to Memphis. He was checked into the

DeSoto County jail under an alias and given a single cell, the only one with air-conditioning. Dinner was a slab of pork ribs a friendly jailer barbecued on the grill out back. The deputies had no idea who he was, but it was obvious the new prisoner was someone important.

Though he was still incarcerated and would remain so for years, Henry was relieved to be far away from the Coast and the constant threat of getting his throat cut.

He had served one year; only nine to go. He could survive, and one day he would walk out and never look back. His fascination with bombs was already a thing of the past. Lucky he didn't blow himself up, though he came close.

———•———

One down, two to go. Judge Roach immediately set the case of *State v. Nevin Noll* for trial on March 14 in Pike County.

Before he left the Coast to return to his farm, he was invited to lunch at the home of Judge Oliphant, a fellow jurist he had known for many years. Keith was also invited, and as they enjoyed ice tea and shrimp salads on the veranda, the purpose of the lunch became clear.

Judge Roach finally said, "Keith, Harry and I share the opinion that it's time for you to step aside and allow a special prosecutor to take over."

Judge Oliphant added, "You're too close to the case, Keith. You're a victim. Your work so far has been exemplary, but we think you should not present the case to the jury."

Keith was not surprised; he was oddly relieved. While alone, on many occasions, he had stood before a phantom jury and delivered his opening statement and final summation. Both had been written months ago and fine-tuned a hundred times. If properly delivered in a hushed courtroom they would move any human to tears, and to action. To justice. But he had never, not even in deep solitude, been able to finish them. He was not an emotional person and took pride in maintaining control, but when talking to twelve strangers about the death of his father, he broke down. As the trials grew closer, he had become even more convinced that he should only observe them.

He smiled and asked, "Who do you have in mind?"

"Chuck McClure," Judge Roach said, without hesitation. Judge Oliphant nodded his agreement. There was no doubt they'd had this discussion several times before inviting Keith.

"Will he do it?"

"If I ask him. As you know, he's never been one to dodge a camera."

"And he's very good," Judge Oliphant added.

McClure had served as district attorney in Meridian for twelve years and had sent more men to death row than any prosecutor in the state's history. President Johnson had appointed him U.S. attorney for the Southern District, where he had served with distinction for seven years. He was currently working at Justice in Washington but, according to Judge Roach, was eager to return home. The Jesse Rudy murder was the perfect case for him.

With great respect, Keith said, "Gentlemen, I defer to you, as always."

CHAPTER 49

With one month to go before the trial of Nevin Noll, his lawyer, Millard Cantrell, opened the mail one dismal morning and was startled to see an order from Judge Roach. He was granting Burch's motion to force out Keith Rudy, a motion Cantrell did not join, and he was replacing Keith with Chuck McClure, a well-known prosecutor.

Cantrell was furious that Burch had managed to screw up again. As Cantrell was learning, Burch's greatness was in the courtroom, where he blossomed, but not in the plotting of pre-trial strategies. He wanted to bury his opponent with paperwork and keep him on the defensive. More and more, though, the paperwork was biting Burch in the ass.

Keith was a rookie with no capital murder experience. McClure was deadly.

Cantrell called Burch looking for another fight, but he wouldn't take the call.

The spectacular collapse of Henry Taylor, and his transformation from a defendant to a State's witness, had severely weakened the defense of both Nevin Noll and Hugh Malco. The arrival of Chuck McClure was another heavy nail in their coffins. The most daunting challenge before them, though, was the simple fact that both were guilty of murdering Jesse Rudy.

However, in the eyes of the law, Nevin was guiltier than Hugh simply because there was more proof. Henry Taylor never met Hugh and had no idea what was said between him and Noll. No one else was in the room when Hugh ordered the hit. But Taylor did know for a fact, and could certainly convince a jury, that Noll had paid him $20,000 to kill Jesse Rudy, and that Noll had provided the explosives.

Cantrell had been Noll's lawyer for a year and had spent dozens of hours with him at the jail. He didn't bother feigning affection for his client and secretly loathed him. He saw him as a cold-blooded killer incapable of remorse, a proud gangster who had never earned an honest dollar, and a psychopath who would kill again if the money was right. He was mob to his core and would never rat out a fellow thug.

But, as his lawyer, Cantrell had a duty to look out for his best interests. In his experienced opinion, Noll was staring at a hopeless trial, followed by ten to twelve years of misery on death row, all to be ended by ten minutes in the gas chamber sniffing hydrogen cyanide. Cantrell wasn't sure he could find a better ending, but it was his duty to try.

They met in a small room in the Forrest County jail, the same room as always. A year in jail had done little to improve Noll's looks. He was only thirty-seven, but there were crow's feet around his eyes and dark, puffy circles under them. His thick black hair was turning grayer by the month. He chain-smoked as if slowly committing suicide.

Cantrell said, "I'll see the judge in a few days, another hearing. Sometime soon he'll ask if there have been efforts to settle the case, any talk about a plea agreement. So you and I should at least discuss this."

"You want me to plead guilty?"

"I don't want you to do a damned thing, Nevin. My job is to present options. Option one is to go to trial. Option two is to avoid a trial by entering into a plea agreement. You admit you're guilty, you agree to help the prosecution, and the judge cuts you some slack."

Cantrell half-expected to get cursed for even suggesting cooperation with the State. A tough guy like Nevin Noll could take any punishment "them sumbitches" could dish out.

But when Noll asked, "How much slack?" Cantrell thought he had misunderstood his client.

"Don't know. And we won't know until we have a chat with the DA."

Noll lit another cigarette and blew smoke at the ceiling. The facade was gone, the bluster, the tough-guy routine, the perpetual smirk that looked down on everyone around him. In the first sincere question since they met, Noll asked, "What would you do?"

Cantrell arranged his thoughts and cautioned himself. This might be his only chance to save his client's life. His words must be chosen carefully.

"Well, I would not go to trial."

"Why not?"

"Because you'll be found guilty, and given the max, and sent to Parchman to wither away on death row. The jury will eagerly convict you. The judge will throw the book at you. Nothing good will happen in trial."

"So you won't be there to protect me?"

"Of course I'll be there, but there's only so much I can do, Nevin. You beat one murder rap thirteen years ago with a lot of help from some friends. Won't happen this time. There's too much proof against you."

"Go on."

"I'd take a deal, cut my losses, try to leave a little room for hope down the road. You're now thirty-seven years old, maybe you can get out when you're sixty and still have a few good years left."

"Sounds awful."

"Not as awful as the gas chamber. At least you'll be alive."

Noll sucked hard on the filter, filled his lungs, then let the smoke drift out his nose. "And you think the State will cut me some slack?"

"I won't know until I ask. And, Keith has a new member to his team, guy named Chuck McClure, probably the best prosecutor in the state. He's sent more men to death row than anybody in history. A real badass in the courtroom, a legend actually, and now he's got you in his sights."

More smoke leaked from his nose and through his lips. Finally, "Okay, Millard, have the chat."

———————•———————

Though officially recused, Keith was still the district attorney and as such would be involved in the prosecution. He would assist Chuck McClure in everything but the trial itself, during which he would sit near the State's table, take notes, and watch the proceedings. He would not be introduced to the jurors and they would not know he was the son of the victim.

The phone call from Millard Cantrell came out of nowhere. They had talked several times on the phone and disliked each other instantly, but when Cantrell said the word "deal" Keith was stunned. He had never, for a moment, considered the possibility that a hardened criminal like Nevin Noll would ever consider a plea agreement. But then, how many of them had ever faced the gas chamber?

The ship was sinking and the rats were jumping overboard.

They met two days later in Keith's office. Cantrell had suggested they meet in Hattiesburg, halfway between, but Keith was the DA and expected all defense lawyers to meet on his terms and turf.

Before the meeting, Keith and Chuck McClure had talked for an hour and discussed strategy. A deal with Nevin Noll would send Hugh Malco straight to death row, with hardly a pause at the formality of a trial. Keith wanted them both on death row, perhaps even executed at the same time in a twin killing, but McClure reminded him that the grand prize was Hugh Malco.

Keith did not offer coffee and was barely pleasant. He frowned at Cantrell and said, "Full cooperation, testimony against Malco, and he gets thirty years. Nothing less."

Cantrell was beaten and both knew it. Somewhat subdued, he said, "I was hoping for something that might appeal to my client. A deal he could accept."

"Sorry."

"You see, Keith, the way I look at it, you desperately need Noll because no one else can pin all the blame on Malco. No one else was in the room. Assuming Malco ordered the hit, no one else can prove it."

"The State has plenty of proof and your client goes down first. No way he avoids the gas chamber."

"I agree with that, Keith, I really do. But I'm not so sure you can nail Malco."

"Thirty years for a guilty plea. Cooperation. The Tennessee indictment goes away. Not negotiable."

"All I can do is discuss it with my client."

"I hope he says no, Millard. I really do. My life will not be complete until I watch them strap Nevin Noll in the gas chamber and flip the switch. I visualize that scene every day and dream of it every night. I pray for it at Mass every morning, without remorse."

"Got it."

"You have forty-eight hours until the offer comes off the table."

CHAPTER 50

The trial of Hugh Malco began on Monday morning, April 3, in the county courthouse in Hattiesburg. Judge Roach chose the town for several reasons, some legal, others practical. The defense, oddly enough, had wanted to change venue because Joshua Burch was convinced the Malco name was toxic along the Coast. Judge Roach hired an expert who polled the three counties and was stunned to learn that almost everyone believed the Malco gang rubbed out Jesse Rudy for revenge. The State wanted to move the trial to keep it away from Fats Bowman and his mischief. Hattiesburg was seventy-five miles to the north, halfway to Jackson, and it was a college town of 40,000 with nice hotels and restaurants. On one of his drives back to the Delta, Judge Roach and his clerk scoped out the Forrest County Courthouse and were impressed with its spacious and well-maintained courtroom. The circuit court judge there welcomed the trial and made his staff available. The county sheriff and chief of police agreed to provide security.

The day before the trial began, Hugh Malco was moved to the Forrest County jail, the same place where Nevin Noll had spent the past year. But he wasn't there; he'd been moved to an undisclosed location and would be hauled in under tight security when needed.

By 8:00 A.M. the news vans were arriving and camera crews were setting up in an area near the front entrance that was cordoned off and watched by plenty of men in uniform. Every door of the courthouse was guarded and the county employees were admitted only by credentials. A numbered pass issued by the circuit clerk was required for spectators. The courtroom's capacity was 200, half of which would be the prospective jurors. The legal teams—Burch for the defense and Keith and McClure for the prosecution—entered through a side door and were escorted to the courtroom. The defendant arrived in a motorcade and was whisked through a rear door, away from the cameras.

When Judge Roach settled onto his throne at precisely 9:00 A.M., he took in the crowd and thanked everyone for their interest. He explained that they would spend most of the day and perhaps tomorrow selecting a jury. It would be a slow process and he was in no hurry. He introduced the participants. To his left and seated at the table nearest the jury box was Mr. Chuck McClure, the prosecutor representing the State of Mississippi. Next to him was his assistant, Egan Clement.

Keith sat directly behind McClure with his back to the bar and was not introduced.

To the right, and only a few feet away, was the defendant, Mr. Hugh Malco, who was wedged between his lawyers, Joshua Burch and his associate, Vincent Goode.

Keith glanced at the front row and smiled at Agnes, who was seated with her other three children. Behind them were two rows of reporters.

The excitement of the opening bell soon wore off as Judge Roach began pruning his jury pool. Though they had been carefully screened to exclude those over sixty-five and those who were ill, others stood with various excuses—job and family demands, additional medical concerns, and reservations about being called upon to impose the death penalty, should it come into play. About half admitted to hearing the news about the bombing of the Biloxi courthouse and the death of Jesse Rudy.

Keith resisted the urge to glare at Hugh, who scribbled nonstop

on legal pads and looked at no one. A sketch from a courtroom artist would show the two men seated only inches apart and staring at
one another, but it would not be accurate.

Judge Roach was methodical, at times painfully slow, and
imminently fair with those who spoke up. By noon he had excused
30 of the 102 prospects, and the lawyers had yet to say a word. He
recessed for a two-hour lunch and promised more of the same for
the afternoon.

For an eighty-four-year-old, His Honor showed remarkable
stamina. He picked up the pace when he allowed Chuck McClure
and Joshua Burch to address the pool. They were not allowed to
argue the facts or begin plotting their strategies. Their job during
the selection process was to approve the jurors they liked and strike
the ones they didn't.

At 6:30, court was adjourned with only the first four approved
and sitting in the jury box.

———•———

The Rudy clan and the prosecution team retired to a hotel,
found the bar, and enjoyed a long dinner. The lawyers—Keith,
Egan, McClure, and the Pettigrew brothers—all agreed that the
first day went well. Agnes had been a nervous wreck in the days
leading up to the trial and had balked at attending, but the children
insisted, and during the day she became fascinated with the selection process. For years she had worked in the law office and knew
the lingo, and she had watched Jesse try cases and was familiar
with the procedure. Over dinner, she shared several observations
about the remaining jurors. One gentleman in particular had bad
body language and a permanent scowl, and this bothered her.
McClure promised to strike him.

———•———

The last juror was seated at 10:45 Tuesday morning. Seven men, five women, eight whites, three blacks, one Asian. All "death qualified" as the lawyers say, meaning all had promised Chuck McClure they could impose the death penalty if asked to do so.

Death was in the air. It had brought them all together, and it would be discussed, analyzed, and threatened until the trial was over. Justice would not be served until Hugh Malco was convicted and sentenced to die.

Judge Roach nodded at Chuck McClure, but he was already on his feet. He stood before the jury and began with a dramatic "The defendant, Hugh Malco, is a murderer who deserves the death penalty, and not just for one reason, but for three. Number one: In this state it is a capital crime to murder an elected official. Jesse Rudy was elected twice by the people on the Coast as their district attorney. Number two: In this state it is a capital crime to pay someone to kill another. Hugh Malco paid a contract killer twenty thousand dollars to kill Jesse. Number three: In this state it is a capital crime to murder another person by using explosives. The contract killer used stolen military explosives to blow up the Biloxi courthouse with Jesse as the target. The proof is clear. It's an open-and-shut case."

McClure turned, pointed an angry finger at Hugh, and said, "This man is a cold-blooded killer who deserves the death penalty."

All twelve glared at the defendant. The courtroom was still, silent. Though the first witness had yet to be called, the trial was over.

Hugh absorbed the words without flinching. He was determined to look at no one, to react to nothing, to do little else but doodle and scratch on a legal pad and pretend to be hard at work taking notes. He appeared to be in another world, but his thoughts were very much in the courtroom. They were a scrambled mess of questions like: *Where did the plot go wrong? Why did we trust an idiot like Henry Taylor? How could Nevin rat me out? How can I find him and*

talk to him? How long will I stay on death row before I make my escape?
He harbored not a single thought of being innocent.

McClure allowed his words to echo around the courtroom,
then launched into a windy narrative on the history of organized
crime on the Coast, with a heavy emphasis on the Malco family's
central role in it. Gambling, prostitution, drugs, illegal liquor, corruption, all promoted by men like Lance Malco, now sitting in
prison for his sins, and then by his son—his successor, his heir, the
defendant. After decades of entrenched criminal activity, the first
public official with the guts to go after the crime bosses was Jesse
Rudy.

McClure spoke without notes but with a full command of his
material. He had rehearsed his opening several times with his team
and each version only got better. He moved around the courtroom
as if he owned it. The jurors watched every move, absorbed every
word.

He dwelt on Jesse and his frustrations in his early days as a prosecutor when he was a lonely warrior fighting crime with no help
from law enforcement; his futile efforts to shut down the nightclubs; and his worries about the safety of his family. But he was
fearless and never gave up. The people noticed, the voters cared,
and in 1975 he was reelected without opposition. He fought on,
trying one legal maneuver after another until he began to win.
He became more than a thorn in the side of the crime bosses; he
became a legitimate threat to their empires. When he put away
Lance Malco, father of the defendant, it was time for revenge. Jesse
Rudy paid the ultimate price for fighting the Dixie Mafia.

Keith had watched his father become a master in the courtroom, but he had to admit at that moment that Chuck McClure
was just as brilliant. And he reminded himself of his own wise
decision to sit on the sideline. He would not be able to be as effective as McClure, whose words evoked too many emotions.

McClure finished in forty-five minutes and everyone took a
deep breath. He had brilliantly won the opening battle without

mentioning the names of Henry Taylor and Nevin Noll. The dramatic testimonies of his star witnesses would seal the fate of Hugh Malco.

Joshua Burch quickly revealed his strategy, though it was no surprise. He had so little to work with. He said his client was an innocent man who was being framed by the real killers, lowlifes from the underworld who had cut deals with the State to save themselves. He warned the jurors not to believe the lies they were about to hear from the men who murdered Jesse Rudy. Hugh Malco was no gangster! He was an entrepreneur who ran several businesses: a chain of convenience stores, a liquor store with a legitimate permit, two restaurants. He built and managed apartment buildings and a shopping center. He had been working since the age of fifteen and would have gone to college but his father needed him as the family enterprises grew.

The murder of Jesse Rudy was the most sensational in the history of the Gulf Coast, and the State was desperate to solve it and punish someone. In its eagerness, though, it had sacrificed the search for the truth by pinning its case on the testimony of men who could not be trusted. There was no other direct link to Hugh Malco, a fine young man who had always respected Jesse Rudy. Indeed, he admired the Rudy family.

Keith watched the faces of the jurors and saw no sympathy, nothing but suspicions.

After Burch sat down, Judge Roach recessed for a long lunch.

———————

In a murder trial, most prosecutors called as their first witness a member of the victim's family. Though rarely probative, it set the tone and aroused sympathy from the jury. Agnes wanted no part of it and Keith thought it unnecessary.

McClure called an investigator from the state police. His job was to show the jury the crime scene and describe what happened. Using a series of enlarged photos, he walked the jury through the blast and the resulting damage. When it was time to show photos of the victim, Keith nodded to a bailiff who walked to the front row and escorted Agnes, Tim, Laura, and Beverly out of the courtroom. It was a dramatic exit, one that Keith and McClure had carefully planned, and it irritated Joshua Burch, who stood to object but decided not to. Calling attention to Jesse's family would only make bad matters worse.

Keith stared at the floor as the jurors cringed at four photos of Jesse's badly mangled and dismembered body stuck to the wall.

A pathologist testified as to the cause of death, though his testimony wasn't needed.

An expert from the FBI lab spent half an hour explaining the impact of detonating five pounds of Semtex in a small room the size of an office. It was far more than necessary to kill a man.

After the first three witnesses, Joshua Burch had not asked a single question on cross-examination.

So far the proof had been delivered in straightforward, matter-of-fact testimonies. McClure kept it short and to the point. The photos spoke for themselves.

During the afternoon recess, Agnes and her family returned to the front row. They would never see the horrible photos of Jesse. Keith had seen them months earlier and would be haunted forever.

Drama arrived with the fourth witness, former air force sergeant Eddie Morton. McClure cleared the air immediately and established that Morton had been court-martialed and was serving time in a federal prison. Morton described his side business peddling military explosives to various buyers over a five-year period. He admitted gambling problems and a fondness for hanging around the strip clubs in Biloxi, and about three years earlier had made the acquaintance of one Nevin Noll. On July 6, 1976, he left Keesler with five pounds of Semtex, drove to a club called Foxy's on the Strip, had a drink with Noll, and collected $5,000 in cash. The two went outside to the parking lot where Morton opened his trunk and handed Noll a wooden box containing the explosives. In February of 1977, he was contacted again by Noll who wanted more of the explosives.

Morton's testimony was mesmerizing and the entire courtroom was captivated.

On cross, Joshua Burch made it clear that the witness was a convicted felon, a thief, a traitor, and a disgrace to his uniform and country. He attacked Morton's credibility and asked him repeatedly if he was promised leniency in return for testifying. Morton steadfastly denied this, but Burch hammered away.

Like all great trial lawyers, Burch maintained his composure and never seemed to lose confidence in his case. But Keith had seen him in action before and knew that some of the cockiness was gone. His client was a dead man and he knew it.

Hugh managed to keep scribbling and never looked up, never acknowledged the presence of anyone else in the courtroom. He never whispered to his lawyers, never reacted to a word from the witness stand. Keith glanced at him occasionally and wondered what the hell he was writing. His mother, Carmen, was not in the courtroom and neither were his siblings. His father was surviving another day in prison, no doubt eager to get the daily newspapers.

Keith and Chuck McClure had strategized for hours about which witnesses to use. One idea was to subpoena some of the other criminals from the Strip and have a field day with them on the witness stand. The goal would be to prove motive. They hated Jesse Rudy and there had been plenty of bad blood. Their greatest idea was to haul in Sheriff Albert "Fats" Bowman and rip him to shreds in front of the jury. In the end, though, they agreed that the facts were squarely in the favor of the prosecution. They had the evidence and the witnesses. No sense in muddying the water. Play it straight, hit hard and fast, and get the conviction.

Wednesday started with a bang when McClure announced the State's next witness, Mr. Henry Taylor. For the occasion, he had been allowed to shed his orange jailhouse jumpsuit and took the stand in a starched white shirt and pressed khaki pants. McClure had spent two hours with him the night before and their back-and-forth was well rehearsed.

Taylor was eager to cooperate, though he knew that for the rest of his life he would keep one eye on the rearview mirror. To a hushed crowd, he told the story of being contacted by an intermediary in July of 1976 with an inquiry about a "job" in Biloxi. A week later he drove to Jackson, Mississippi, and met with an operative named Nevin Noll. They came to terms and shook hands on the contract killing of Jesse Rudy. For $20,000 cash, Taylor would build a bomb, drive to Biloxi, follow Mr. Rudy until he knew his movements, deliver the bomb to his office, and detonate it at the right time. Noll said he had a source for military explosives and could handle the delivery. On August 17, Taylor arrived in Biloxi, met with Noll again, was briefed by him on the best time to do the job, and took five pounds of Semtex. The following evening, he broke into the courthouse, then into the office of the district attorney, and scoped out the site. On Friday, August 20, at noon, he entered the courthouse dressed as a UPS delivery man carrying packages, went to the office, spoke to Mr. Rudy, and left a package in a chair by his desk. He made a quick getaway but things got complicated when he passed Egan Clement, the assistant DA, returning from lunch. He did not want her to be collateral damage, so he quickly detonated the bomb. The blast was far more than he expected and knocked him down the stairwell, breaking his leg. He managed to get outside in the chaos but couldn't walk. He passed out and was transported to the hospital in Biloxi where he spent three long days plotting an escape. He eventually returned home and thought he had dodged a disaster.

The witness had the undivided attention of the courtroom, and McClure took his time. He backtracked some of Henry's movements and fleshed out the story. He asked the judge for permission to have the witness leave the stand and step over to a table in front of the jurors. The jurors and lawyers, and everyone else who could strain enough to see, watched with fascination as Taylor arranged the pieces of a fake bomb. McClure asked questions about each piece. The witness then put the bomb together, slowly, carefully, while explaining the dangers inherent with each move. He set the firing switch and explained what happened when the detonation button was at a distance. He gently placed the fake bomb in a wooden box and pretended to seal it.

Back on the witness stand, Taylor was asked by McClure how many bombs he had detonated. He refused to incriminate himself.

Burch came out swinging and asked Taylor if he was confessing to a capital murder. He bobbed and weaved a bit, said he wasn't sure about the capital element, but, yes, he had killed Jesse Rudy for money. He admitted taking a plea deal with the State in return for his damning testimony, and Burch hammered away relentlessly. Why else would a man admit to a crime punishable by death if he had not been promised a lighter sentence? The cross-examination was riveting, at times breathtaking.

Burch landed blow after blow, picking at every small discrepancy while embellishing the obvious, and finally left little doubt that Henry Taylor was testifying to avoid severe punishment. After two hours of the barrage, Taylor was near the breaking point and the entire courtroom was exhausted. When he was excused, Judge Roach announced a recess.

The time-out did nothing to lessen the drama, and it only intensified when Nevin Noll took the stand. McClure began slowly with a series of questions that told the narrative of Noll's long, colorful history in service to the Malco family. He was not quizzed about his other murders. Such testimony would be problematic in many ways, and McClure did not want to discredit his star witness. There was no doubt, though, that Noll had never avoided violence in his various roles as bouncer, bodyguard, enforcer, bagman, drug-runner, and part-time club manager.

Noll never looked at Hugh, and Hugh never stopped his incessant scribbling.

When his thuggish history was thoroughly confirmed, McClure moved on to the killing of Jesse Rudy. Noll admitted that he and Hugh had discussed eliminating the district attorney as soon as Lance was arrested. Their conversations went on for weeks, then months. When they learned that Jesse Rudy was investigating the contract killing of Dusty Cromwell, they decided it was time to act. They felt as though they had no choice.

"Who made the decision to murder Jesse Rudy?" McClure asked, his question echoing through the hushed courtroom.

Noll took his time and finally replied, "Hugh was the boss. The decision was his, but I agreed with him."

Given the green light, Noll contacted a couple of his acquaintances in the Dixie Mafia. No one wanted the job, regardless of the money. Killing a public official was too risky. Killing a high-profile DA like Jesse Rudy was suicide. Eventually he got the name of Henry Taylor, a man he had heard of in the underworld. They met and agreed on the contract, $20,000 in cash. Hugh got the explosives from Eddie Morton at Keesler.

Absorbing the matter-of-fact details of the plot to kill his father was difficult for Keith to sit through. Again, he was thankful Chuck McClure was in charge and not him. In the front row, Agnes and her daughters wiped their eyes. Tim could only glare with hatred at Nevin Noll. If he'd had a gun he would have been tempted to charge the witness stand.

When the story was finished, McClure tendered the witness and sat down. The courtroom felt exhausted and Judge Roach recessed for a two-hour lunch.

———•———

The afternoon belonged to Joshua Burch. Thirty minutes into a long, brutal cross-examination, he firmly established that Nevin Noll was a career thug who'd never held an honest job and had spent his adult life beating and even killing others in the Biloxi underworld, all in service to the Malco family. Noll never tried to downplay his past. As always, he was cocky, arrogant, even proud of his career and his reputation. Burch eviscerated him and made it plain to all that the man could not be trusted. Burch even waded into the death of Earl Fortier thirteen years earlier in Pascagoula, but Noll stopped the line of questions cold when he said, "Well, Mr. Burch, you were my lawyer back then and you told me to lie to the jury."

Burch yelled back, "That's another lie! Why can't you tell the truth?"

Judge Roach sprang to life and called down both men.

But Burch was undeterred. At full volume he boomed, "How many men have you killed?"

"Only one, and that was in self-defense. You got me off, Mr. Burch. Remember?"

"Yeah, and I regret it," Burch shot back before considering his words.

"That's enough!" Judge Roach practically yelled into his mike.

Burch took a deep breath and walked to his table where he consulted with his co-counsel, Vincent Goode. Ever the professional, though, Burch rallied nicely when he calmly walked Noll through a long series of stories about men he'd bullied, beaten, or killed. Hugh remembered them well and had fed the information to Burch. Noll, of course, denied most of the barrage, especially the killings.

How could the jury believe anything he said?

———•———

The defense began with a whimper early Thursday morning when Joshua Burch called to the stand one Bobby LaMarque, a career errand boy for the Malco gang. Burch puffed up his résumé by adding such descriptions as "executive vice president," "manager," and "supervisor." The gist of his testimony was that he was extremely close to Hugh Malco and had been on the inside for years, beginning with Lance. He had dealt with Hugh and Nevin Noll on a daily basis and knew as much about the club business as anyone else. He had never heard Hugh or Nevin discuss Jesse Rudy. Period. Nothing good, nothing bad. Nothing. If there had been a plan to eliminate the district attorney, he, LaMarque, would certainly have known about it. He'd watched young Hugh grow up in the business and knew him well. He was a fine young man who worked hard running the legitimate businesses while his father was away. LaMarque had never, in fifteen years, seen a violent streak, unless, of course, when Hugh was boxing.

McClure made quick work of the witness by pointing out that he was still on the Malco payroll, as he had been for the past eighteen years. He dropped out of school after the ninth grade. Along with the highbrow jobs mentioned by Mr. Burch, LaMarque admitted to working as a cook, janitor, bartender, delivery boy, and driver. He also admitted to dealing blackjack back in the old days.

LaMarque was slow off the mark and nervously cut his eyes at the jurors, as if he himself should've been on trial for some crime. The real reason he had been chosen to defend Hugh was that he was one of the few Malco employees with no criminal record.

If Hugh's life depended on men like LaMarque, then the defendant was as good as dead.

The second star witness was even worse. Hoping to impress the male jurors, or even startle them, Burch called Tiffany Barnes to the stand. Onstage with her clothes off she went by Sugar, but when properly dressed and being a good girl she was Tiffany. Whether or not she was properly dressed could be debated. Her tight skirt stopped several inches above her knees, revealing long shapely legs that were impossible not to notice, if only for a second. Tight low-cut sweater, ample cleavage, lovely face with a sparkling smile. Half of her testimony was revealed just in the presentation.

The lying started immediately. Her story was that she and Hugh had been dating for three years, engaged for two, living together for one, and planned to get married the following month. Assuming, of course, he would be able to get married. She knew his innermost thoughts—his dreams, worries, fears, prejudices, everything. Her fiancé would never harm another human being; it simply wasn't in his genetic makeup. He was a caring, loving man who went out of his way to help others. She had never heard him mention the name Jesse Rudy.

It was a splendid performance, and the jurors, at least the men, enjoyed it, if only for a moment.

Chuck McClure destroyed her in less than five minutes. He asked, "Miss Barnes, when did you and Hugh apply for a marriage license?"

Big smile, perfect teeth. "Well, we haven't done that yet, you know? Kinda hard when he's in jail."

"Of course. Hugh has two sisters. Do you know their names?"

The smile vanished as her shoulders and breasts sagged a bit. She glanced at the jury box, the panicked look of a deer in head-lights. "Yes, one is Kathy. I haven't met the other."

"No, sorry. Hugh has only one sister and her name is Holley. Does he have any brothers?"

"I don't know. He doesn't talk about them. The family is not close."

"Well, surely he talks about his mother. She lives in Biloxi. What's her name?"

"I just call her Mrs. Malco. That's the way I was raised."

"Of course. But what is her first name?"

"I've never asked."

"Where does she live in Biloxi?"

"In the western part."

"What street?"

"Goodness, I don't know. I can't remember street names."

"Nor first names. You've dated for three years, been engaged for two, shacked up for one, and you don't know where his mother lives in the same town."

"As I said, she's in the western section of Biloxi."

"Sorry, Miss Tiffany, but Carmen, her first name, Carmen Malco moved to Ocean Springs two years ago."

"Oh."

"Do you know where you live?"

"Of course I do. With Hugh."

"And what is your address?"

Perhaps tears might save her. She glared at McClure, summoned up a wave, and began wiping her cheeks. After a long painful silence, McClure said, "Your Honor, I have no further questions."

———•———

Late Thursday afternoon, the jury deliberated for all of forty-seven minutes and found Hugh Malco guilty of capital murder. On Friday morning, the sentencing phase began when Chuck McClure called Agnes Rudy to the stand. With firm resolve and only a few quiet tears, she did a fine job of getting through the script she and Keith had memorized. She talked about her husband, their life together, their children, his work, and, most important, the unimaginable emptiness his death left behind.

She missed her husband dearly, even painfully, still, and had not really accepted his death. Perhaps when those responsible for his murder were put away for good, then she could begin to move on.

A second mother followed the first. Carmen Malco had avoided the trial so far and had no desire to make an appearance. But Joshua Burch had convinced her that she was the only person who might be able to save her son's life.

She was not. In spite of her emotional plea to the jurors, they deliberated again for less than an hour and returned with a verdict of death.

PART
FOUR

———•———

THE
ROW

CHAPTER 51

January of 1979 began slow but ended with some excitement. On the seventeenth, Ainsley Rudy gave birth to child number two, another girl, and the proud parents went to the book of baby names and selected one with no family connections whatsoever. Little Colette Rudy weighed in at five pounds, one ounce, and came almost a month early, but she was healthy and had the lungs to prove it. When Agnes finally got her hands on the child the parents were not sure they would get her back.

On January 20, the attorney general's office notified Keith that Hugh Malco's lawyers had completed the filing of his direct appeal to the state supreme court. It was the first step in an appellate process that would take years.

Joshua Burch considered himself a pure courtroom lawyer and had no interest in appellate work. He and Hugh parted ways after the trial, by mutual consent. As much as Burch loved the spotlight, he was fed up with the Malcos and wanted to pursue bigger fees in civil litigation. He referred Hugh to a death penalty firm out of Atlanta and washed his hands of his client. Burch and his staff knew there was little to argue on appeal. The case had tried "cleanly," as they say in the trade, and Judge Roach had been spot-on with his rulings.

By state law, death penalty cases were handled by the Criminal Appeals Division of the attorney general's office in Jackson. A week after the guilty verdict in Hattiesburg, Keith happily boxed up his Malco files and sent them to the AG. As long as he was the DA, he would remain in the loop and be kept abreast of all developments. He would not, however, be required to (1) plow through the 5,000-page trial transcript looking for issues, or (2) write thick briefs in response to whatever Hugh's appellate lawyers cooked up, or (3) participate in oral arguments before the state supreme court two years down the road.

For the moment, Malco was off his desk and out of his office, and he could concentrate on more pressing matters. On January 31, he filed papers with the circuit court clerk and announced he would seek election for his first full, four-year term. He was thirty years old, the youngest DA in the state, and arguably the best known. The tragedy of his father's sensational death and the spectacle of Hugh's trial had kept the family name in the headlines.

After the trial, he'd been generous with his time and sat through many interviews. He was coy about his plans, but it wasn't long before he was being asked about his political ambitions.

He was not expecting opposition in his race for DA, and as the weeks passed there was no hint of any. His grand jury met in March and returned a pile of indictments, the usual assortment of drug possessions, car thefts, home burglaries, domestic dust-ups, aggravated assaults, and petty embezzlements. Two rape cases looked legit and serious.

Not for the first time, Keith asked himself how long he would be content prosecuting small-time criminals and sending them to prison where they served three years before getting out, only to break the law again. He had seen the packed courtrooms and felt the near-suffocating pressure of big league litigation, and he missed it. But he plodded on, doing the job he was elected to do and enjoying the life of a young father.

He kept an eye on the Strip and folks were behaving, for the most part. The state police sent in spies from time to time to appraise the activities. There was no visible gambling. There were plenty of naked girls dancing on stages and such, but it was impossible to know what happened upstairs. Informants assured Keith and the police that the prostitutes had left the Coast and the gamblers had fled to Vegas.

————•————

On a cold, windy day in late March, Lance Malco was handcuffed by a guard and led to a ragged and dented prison van that was at least twenty years old and unfit for highways. A trustee drove it while two guards watched Lance in the back. They bumped along dirt and gravel roads through the vast fields of Parchman, passing other camps encircled in chain-link and razor wire and crawling with inmates in prison garb going about their useless activities. Killing time. Counting days.

For Lance, his days were now on the downhill side. His sentence was half over and he was scheming to return to the Coast. He and Fats had a plan to get him transferred to a medium-security facility in south Mississippi, and from there Fats was certain he could swap a prisoner or two and move his old pal back to the Harrison County jail. They had to keep their plan quiet. If Keith Rudy got wind of it he would raise hell, call the governor, and torpedo everything.

Lance had never been to Unit 29, known simply as "the Row." It was three miles from his unit, but it could've been a thousand. Parchman didn't give tours to other inmates. The request to visit his son had languished for thirteen months in the warden's office before it was approved.

Death row, though, was the source of much gossip and legend, and it seemed as if every inmate at Parchman knew someone on "the Row." The fact that Lance now had a son there gave him an elevated status, one he cared nothing for. Every prisoner cursed the DA who put him away, and killing one made Hugh a legend at Parchman, but Lance was not impressed. Almost three years after the murder, he still found it hard to believe that Hugh could have done something so stupid.

As dust boiled from the bald tires, they passed Unit 18, a World War II–style barracks unit used to house German POWs back then. According to a source, and Lance was still trying to verify it, Nevin Noll was assigned to the unit, but under an alias. During his first four months at Parchman, he had been in protective custody, according to the same source. Then he had been eased out into the general population with a new name.

Lance was on his trail, bribing guards, trustees, and snitches with cash.

Lance, Hugh, and Nevin, together again, sort of. They were scattered over a wretched and forlorn plantation with 5,000 other lost souls, trying to survive another miserable day.

The Row was a flat, squat building of red brick and tarred roof far away from the nearest camp. The trustee parked the van and they got out. The guards led Lance in through the front door, got him properly signed in, removed the cuffs, and walked him to an empty visitation room divided in two by a long section of thick wire mesh.

Hugh was waiting on the other side, seated nonchalantly in a cheap metal chair, with a big smile and a friendly "What's up, Pops?"

Lance couldn't help but smile. He fell into a chair, looked through the wire, and said, "Aren't we a fine pair?"

"I'm sure Mom's proud of us."

"Any contact with her?"

"A letter a week. She sounds good. Frankly, after you left home she really perked up and became another woman. I've never seen her so happy."

"Didn't bother me either. I wish she would go ahead and file for divorce."

"Let's talk about something else. I'm assuming someone is listening to us right now, is that correct?"

Lance looked around the dingy and semi-lit room. "Legally,

they're not supposed to listen, but always assume they are. Don't trust anybody here—your cellie, your friends, the other inmates, the guards, the trustees, and especially the people who run this place. Every person can knife you in the back."

"So no chatting about our problems, then? Past, present, or future?"

"What problems?" Both managed a smile.

Hugh said, "Cellie? Who says a I have a cellie? My little room is eight feet by ten, with one bunk, a metal commode, no shower. Certainly no room for another person, though I think they tried that once. I'm in solitary twenty-three hours a day and never see anybody but the guards, a bunch of animals. I can talk to the guy to my right but can't see him. The guy on my left checked out years ago and speaks to no one."

"Who's the guy on your right?"

"White dude named Jimmy Lee Gray. Raped and killed his girlfriend's three-year-old daughter. Says he killed others. Real prince of a guy."

"So he admits his crimes. I thought most of the guys here claimed to be innocent."

"No one's innocent here, Lance. And these guys love to brag about their murders, at least to each other."

"And you feel safe?"

"Sure. Death row is the safest place in prison. There's no contact with other inmates. I get one hour a day in the yard, a little sunshine to work on my tan, but I'm all alone."

Both lit cigarettes and blew clouds at the ceiling. Lance was filled with pity for his son, a thirty-year-old boy who should be enjoying life on the Coast, chasing the girls he'd always chased, running the clubs that practically ran themselves, counting the days until his father came home and life returned to normal. Instead he was locked in a cubbyhole in a terrible prison and would probably die in a gas chamber just around the corner. Pity, though, was something Lance had learned to put away. They, father and son, had made their choices. They fancied themselves tough gangsters and had flouted the law for decades. They believed the old adage: "Don't do the crime if you can't do the time."

And for Lance Malco, at least, the crime wasn't finished.

CHAPTER 52

The elections of 1979 were quieter than usual. Fats Bowman was unable to convince anyone to run against him, so he coasted to another four-year term, his fifth. With gambling and prostitution under control, his "protection" rackets were seriously curtailed and the criminals didn't need him. The strip clubs and bars were still busy, but with nothing illegal to offer they had little to fear. The pesky state police maintained a presence with undercover agents and informants. The city of Biloxi had a new administration and its chief of police was determined to keep the nightclubs in line. The Malco boys were serving time and their underlings still ran the businesses, but the other crime lords were content to obey the laws. The DA was a hotshot who wasn't afraid of them.

In need of revenues, Fats envisioned a gold mine working with drug traffickers.

———•———

In April of 1980, the Mississippi Supreme Court unanimously upheld the capital murder conviction of Hugh Malco. His lawyers filed thick briefs and asked the Court to reconsider, another step on a long road. Months would pass before the Court ruled again.

———•———

In June, Keith received a phone call from a stranger who claimed to have a letter smuggled out of Parchman. He drove to a café in Gulfport and met with a man with only one name: Alfonso. His story was that he was a close friend of one Haley Stofer, a drug runner Jesse had sent to Parchman for fifteen years in 1975.

Nothing about Alfonso warranted even the slightest level of trust, but Keith was intrigued. The man explained that he had visited Stofer at Parchman and was asked to deliver a letter to Keith. He handed over a sealed envelope with D.A. KEITH RUDY printed in block letters on the front, then lit a cigarette and watched Keith open it.

Dear Mr. Rudy: Sorry about your father. He sent me away five years ago on a drug smuggling charge, of which I was guilty. So I have no ill will toward him. At the time I was involved with some traffickers out of New Orleans. Through contacts there, I am in possession of highly valuable information regarding the involvement of your sheriff in smuggling operations. The drugs, primarily cocaine, enter the country through New Orleans and are air-dropped to a certain farm in Stone County, property owned by your sheriff. I can provide more information, but in return I want out of prison. I swear I know what I'm talking about. I swear I am legitimate. Thanks for your time, Haley Stofer.

Keith thanked Alfonso, left with the letter, and returned to his office. Since Jesse's files had been destroyed in the bomb blast, Keith went to the circuit clerk's office and dug through the old records. He found the Haley Stofer file and read it with great interest.

In his third year of law school at Ole Miss, Keith had visited Parchman on a field trip with a class in criminal justice. One visit was enough and he had never thought about going back. However, the letter from Stofer intrigued him. He also had a perverse desire to see how awful the place was now that so many of his enemies were there. As a DA, he would have no trouble gaining access to death row. He could even arrange a meeting with Hugh, though he had no desire to do so.

A week after meeting with Alfonso, he took the day off and drove alone five hours to Parchman. He enjoyed the solitude, the absence of constantly ringing phones, and the daily grind around the courthouse. He thought a lot about his father, which was not unusual when he was in the car by himself. He longed for the lost friendship of a man he practically worshipped. Typically, when those thoughts became burdens, he popped in a cassette and sang along with Springsteen and the Eagles.

North of Jackson, when the hills flattened and the Delta began, his thoughts turned to Lance and Hugh Malco, two men he had known his entire life and who were now locked away in a miserable prison far from their beloved Coast. Lance had been there for five years and by all accounts was surviving as well as could be expected. He was in a safer camp in the general population, had his own cell with a television and a fan and better food. With more money than anyone else at Parchman, he could bribe his way into almost anything but freedom. And, after five years, there was little doubt he was scheming to manipulate the parole board and get out. Keith was watching as closely as possible.

Hugh, on the other hand, was stuck in an eight-by-ten cell for twenty-three hours a day, in suffocating heat in the summer and freezing cold in the winter.

Keith had seen death row and had sat on an empty bunk, with the door still open, as had all the law students on his field trip. He could not imagine how anyone, especially a person raised with such privilege, could survive from one day to the next.

A fleeting image made him smile as he neared the prison's front gate. The two boys, Biloxi All-Stars, blasting back-to-back home runs in a playoff game against Gulfport.

Keith parked and managed to purge the Malcos from his thoughts. He checked in at the administration building and was practically waved through. Because he was a district attorney, the authorities brought Haley Stofer to him. For two hours he listened as the inmate told his remarkable story of being forced undercover by Jesse in return for a lighter sentence. Stofer took full credit for getting the indictment against Lance Malco for prostitution, the charges that finally nailed him. He admitted he skipped out on Jesse, was later captured and returned to Harrison County, and faced the full wrath of the DA when he met him. Jesse showed some gratitude and agreed to a fifteen-year sentence. The max was thirty. Now, Stofer had served enough time, in his opinion, and wanted out. His contact in New Orleans was a cousin who still worked for the traffickers and knew everything about their smuggling routes into Mississippi. Sheriff Bowman was a key figure and was about to get even richer.

———•———

Such a major bust would be too complicated for the DA's office, so Keith called FBI agents Jackson Lewis and Spence Whitehead. They in turn contacted the Drug Enforcement Agency, and a plan came together.

Keith leaned on the state police and arranged for Stofer to be transferred to the jail in Pascagoula, in Jackson County. It took him a month to make contact with the cousin in New Orleans. So far, everything Stofer said was verified by the DEA.

———•———

Just after midnight on September 3, Fats Bowman, with his longtime chief deputy Rudd Kilgore behind the wheel, took a leisurely drive north from Biloxi and arrived at one of Fats's farms in rural Stone County. Two other deputies blocked the only gravel road leading to the farm. Fats and Kilgore met two operatives in a pickup truck with a camper over its bed. The four men waited at a hay shed near an open pasture, drinking beers, smoking cigars, and watching the clear, moonlit sky.

A team of DEA agents materialized from the woods and quietly arrested the two deputies guarding the gate. A dozen more heavily armed agents moved through the darkness and monitored what was left of the little gang. At 1:00 A.M., on schedule, a Cessna 208 Caravan swept low over the pasture and circled. On its next pass, it dipped to less than a hundred feet off the ground and dropped its cargo, six plastic boxes heavily wrapped in thick plastic. Fats, Kilgore, and the two operatives quickly loaded the packages into the pickup and were about to leave when they were surrounded by some serious-looking men with plenty of firepower. They were arrested and whisked away to an undisclosed location.

The following day, at the federal courthouse in Hattiesburg, the U.S. Attorney for the Southern District presided over a crowded press conference. Standing beside him was Keith Rudy, and behind them was a row of federal agents. He announced the arrests of Sheriff Albert "Fats" Bowman, three of his deputies, and four drug traffickers from a New Orleans syndicate. On display were one hundred and twenty pounds of cocaine with a street value of $30 million. He alleged that Sheriff Bowman's cut was 10 percent.

U.S. Attorneys were notorious for hogging the spotlight, but he was quick to give credit to Keith Rudy and his team from Biloxi. Without Mr. Rudy, the bust would not have been successful. Keith spoke and returned the thanks, and said that the work his father began in 1971 had come to fruition. He promised more indictments in state court for the elected officials and criminals who had run roughshod over the law for so long.

The story was huge and had legs, and for days the *Gulf Coast Register* and other newspapers in the state ran follow-ups. Keith's handsome face was splashed on front pages from Mobile to Jackson to New Orleans.

At Parchman, Lance Malco cursed the news and faced the reality that he would not be getting out of prison anytime soon. Hugh eventually heard the news but had other concerns. His appeals in state court had been turned down and he faced years of habeas corpus appeals in federal court.

After six months in a county jail, Fats Bowman pled guilty to drug trafficking in federal court and was sent away for twenty years. Before leaving jail, though, he was given a weekend pass to go home and say goodbye to his family. Instead, he drove to his hunting cabin in Stone County, went to the lake, walked to the end of the pier, pulled out a .357 Magnum, and blew his brains out.

Haley Stofer was paroled and ran for his life. The state police coordinated a witness protection program with federal agents and sent him away, with a new name, to live peacefully in Northern California.

CHAPTER 53

With Lance and Hugh Malco tucked away, and Fats Bowman freezing in Maine, and life relatively quiet on the Strip, Keith became bored with his role as the chief prosecutor on the Coast. The job was his for the foreseeable future, but he wanted a promotion, and a big one. Since having lunch with Governor Bill Waller as a young lawyer, he had dreamed of seeking statewide office, and an opportunity was brewing.

Late in 1982, he drove to Jackson and had lunch with Bill Allain, the current Attorney General, hoping to discuss the future. Allain was rumored to be preparing for a run for the governor's office and Keith pressed him on it. Allain, ever the politician, would not commit, but Keith left the lunch convinced the AG's race would soon be wide open. He was only thirty-four and felt too young for such an important office, but he had learned that in politics timing was everything. Mississippi had a tradition of reelecting its attorneys general until they died in office, and if the position was about to be vacant, it was time to make his move.

The AG's job would certainly be more challenging than that of a local DA, but Keith knew he could handle it. He would have an entire office of dozens of lawyers representing the state's legal business, civil and criminal, and there would be new challenges every day. It was also a high-profile office, one that could lead to an even higher one.

The only aspect of the job that Keith would not discuss with anyone was the specifics of its Criminal Appeals Division. As the boss, he would have ultimate control over all death penalty appeals. Specifically, those of Hugh Malco.

Keith dreamed of witnessing the execution of the man who killed his father. As the attorney general, he could almost guarantee that day would come sooner rather than later.

The appeals were mired in the usual, interminable delays of post-conviction strategies. But the clock was ticking, if ever so slowly. Malco's appellate lawyers had so far impressed no one with the merits of his defense. There was little to argue. The trial had been free of serious errors. The defendant had been found guilty because he was in fact guilty.

———•———

In January of 1983, Lance Malco filed an application for parole. He had served eight years of his sentence for prostitution, had been a model prisoner, and was eligible for parole.

The five members of the parole board were pressured by Keith, Bill Allain, and many others, including the governor, to say no. By a vote of 5–0, parole was denied.

For Keith, the relief was only temporary. Because of his good behavior in prison, Lance's sentence would soon end, and he would be free to return to the Coast and resume operations. With Fats now behind bars, and honest men running both the sheriff's office and the city of Biloxi, no one knew what mischief Lance would create. Perhaps he would attempt to go straight and stay out of trouble. He had plenty of legitimate properties to oversee. But whatever he decided to do, Keith would be watching.

With her husband's return imminent, Carmen Malco finally filed for divorce. Her lawyers negotiated a generous settlement, and she left the Coast and moved to Memphis, only two hours from Parchman. She visited her son on death row every Sunday.

She did not visit her ex-husband.

In February, Keith, Ainsley, and the rest of the Rudy clan threw a large announcement party at the Broadwater Beach Hotel near the Strip. The main ballroom was packed with family and friends, most of the local bar, the courthouse gang, and an impressive group of business leaders from the Coast. Keith gave a rousing speech and promised to use the AG's office to continue to fight crime, specifically the drug trade. Cocaine was raging through the country, and south Mississippi was riddled with distribution points that changed weekly. The cartels had more men and money, and the state, as usual, was lagging behind with its interdiction efforts. Without getting too carried away, Keith took a generous share of the credit for cleaning up the Coast, but warned that the old vices of gambling and prostitution were nothing compared to the dangers of cocaine and other drugs. He promised to go after not only the narco-traffickers and street pushers, but also the public officials and cops who looked the other way.

From Biloxi, Keith and Ainsley flew to Jackson for another announcement event. He was the first candidate to qualify for the AG's race and the press was interested. He drew a nice crowd at a Jackson hotel, then met with a group of trial lawyers who had money and were always politically active.

Keith had about a hundred friends from law school scattered around the state, and for the past six months had been priming that network for support. Since he was not challenging an incumbent, his friends were eager to get involved and most of them signed on. From Jackson, Ainsley went home and Keith hit the road in a leased car, alone. For eighteen straight days he crisscrossed the state, meeting with volunteers recruited by his lawyer pals, glad-handing his way through courthouses, speaking at civic clubs, talking with editors of small-town newspapers, and even hustling votes in busy shopping centers. He stayed with friends and spent as little as possible.

In his first campaign trip, he visited thirty-five of the eighty-two counties and signed up hundreds of supporters. The money started trickling in.

His strategy was to run hard in the southern half of the state and carry the Coast by a wide margin. One likely opponent was from Greenwood, in the Delta. Another was a state senator from a small town near Tupelo. Several others were being discussed, but all of them lived north of Jackson. There was no clear favorite for the vacant office, not until a newspaper editor in Hattiesburg informed Keith that he had placed first in an unofficial poll. When this became a story, on page four of the first section, Keith ran a thousand copies of the article and sent it to his volunteers and supporters. The same editor told Keith the Rudy name was highly recognized. The candidate embraced his role as the front-runner and worked hard to convince everyone else.

Since losing to Jesse in 1971, Rex Dubisson had built a high-powered law practice specializing in offshore oil rig injuries. He was a making a fortune and was active in the lawyers' organizations. He leaned on his fellow tort stars and passed the hat. When he felt like they weren't serious enough, he passed it again. Then he hosted a cocktail party at Mary Mahoney's and informed Keith that he had raised $100,000 and was promising at least that much by summer. Rex was also busy picking the pockets of national trial lawyers and tort firms, and was optimistic that even more money could be raised.

Over a quiet drink, Rex told Keith that the trial lawyers needed a friend and they saw him as a rising star. He was young, but youth was needed. They wanted him in the governor's mansion to help with their fight against the rising tide of tort reform.

Keith made no promises but happily took the money. He quickly hired a Jackson consulting firm to organize his campaign. He hired a driver/gofer and opened a small office in Biloxi. By late

March there were four other men in the race, two from Jackson and two from further up north. Keith and his consultants were delighted by the growing field and hoped that even more would join the fray. Their internal polls continued to show him ahead and extending his lead. Roughly 40 percent of the state's population lived in the twenty southernmost counties, and the Rudy name was recognized by 70 percent of those polled. Number two came in at a whopping 8 percent.

But the best campaigns were fueled by the fear of losing, and Keith never slowed down. Beginning in April, he left Egan in control of the DA's office and hit the road. He kissed Ainsley goodbye before dawn on Monday and gave her a big hug when he returned after dark on Friday. In between, he and his team swarmed every courthouse in the state. He spoke at rallies, churches, backyard cookouts, bar lunches, judges' conferences, and had coffee in the offices of countless small-town lawyers. Every weekend, though, he was at home with Ainsley and the girls, and every Sunday the family attended Mass with Agnes.

His thirty-fifth birthday fell on a Saturday in April. Rex Dubisson hosted a beach party and invited two hundred friends and campaign workers. July Fourth fell on a Monday, and a huge crowd gathered for an old-fashioned stump speech at the Harrison County Fairgrounds. Bill Allain and five others were in a hot race for the governorship, and all six were on the card. Keith was well received by the home crowd and promised virtually everything. Two of his opponents spoke as well. Both were older men and veteran politicians who seemed to realize they were trespassing on Rudy territory. The contrast was revealing. Youth versus age. The future versus the past.

Two weeks later, on July 17, the *Gulf Coast Register* and the *Hattiesburg American* ran editorial endorsements of Keith Rudy. It proved contagious. The following week a dozen county newspapers, almost all of them near the Coast, followed suit. Not surprisingly, the Tupelo daily endorsed the state senator from that part of the state, but on Sunday, July 31, two days before the primary election, the state's largest paper, *The Clarion Ledger* in Jackson, endorsed Keith.

On August 2, almost 700,000 voters went to the polls in the Democratic primary. With massive support from the southern end of the state, Keith led the ticket with 38 percent of the vote, double that of his second-place opponent. As usual, success attracted money, and it came from all directions, including some powerful business groups eager to make friends and join the parade. The Rudy consultants were ready, and within three days the campaign was running slick television ads in the biggest markets. His opponent was broke and could not answer.

In the August 23 runoff, Keith Rudy walked off with 62 percent of the vote, a landslide that not even his consultants predicted.

In November's general election, he would face much weaker opposition from a Republican. At thirty-five, he would become the youngest AG in the state's history, and the youngest in the country.

CHAPTER 54

The post-election partying came to an abrupt halt a week later when a far more sensational story gripped the state. The winners and losers were suddenly forgotten when it became apparent that Mississippi was about to use its cherished gas chamber for the first time in over ten years. A notorious murderer ran out of appeals and his date with the executioner became front-page news.

In 1972, the U.S. Supreme Court, in *Furman v. Georgia,* stopped all executions. The Court split 5–4, and in a bewildering hodgepodge of opinions, concurrences, and dissents, left little guidance for the states to follow. The law was cleared up somewhat in 1976 when the Court, again split 5–4, but with a different composition, gave the green light for the death states to resume the killing. Most did so with great enthusiasm.

In Mississippi, though, officials became frustrated with the slow pace, and from 1976 to 1983 there was not a single execution at Parchman. Politicians of every stripe and from every corner of the state railed against the system that seemed soft on crime. At least 65 percent of the people believed in the death penalty, and if other states had been turned loose, then what was wrong with Mississippi? Finally, one death row inmate lost his appeals and emerged as the likeliest contender.

His name was Jimmy Lee Gray, and a more perfect villain could not have been found on any death row in the country. He was a thirty-four-year-old white drifter from California who had been convicted of murder in Arizona when he was twenty years old. He served only seven years, was released on early parole, and made his way to Pascagoula where he kidnapped, raped, and strangled a three-year-old girl. He was caught, convicted, and sent to Parchman in 1976. Seven years later his luck ran out and state officials excitedly began preparing for his execution. On September 2, Parchman was swarming with law enforcement officials, reporters from around the world, and even a few politicians trying to wedge into the act.

At the time, the gas chamber had a vertical steel pole that ran from the floor to the top vents, directly behind the chair. As witnesses watched from crowded observation rooms, Gray was led into the cramped chamber, a cylinder barely five feet wide. He was secured by leather straps and left alone with the door open. The warden read the death warrant. Gray refused last words. The door was shut and locked securely, and the executioner began his work. There was no strap to secure Gray's head, and as he breathed the cyanide he began thrashing and banging against the steel pole. He hit it repeatedly with the back of his head as he struggled and groaned loudly. Eight minutes after the gas was released, officials panicked and cleared the observation rooms.

Far from a swift and painless death, the execution was botched and it was clear that Gray suffered greatly. Several reporters described the scene in detail, one calling it nothing but "cruel and unusual punishment." The State took so much flak it quickly switched to lethal injection, but only for those inmates sentenced after July 1, 1984.

When his time came, Hugh Malco would not be lucky enough to die peacefully by lethal injection. He had been sentenced in April of 1978, and the gas chamber was still waiting for him.

Because the men were in solitary confinement twenty-three hours a day, and showered and exercised alone, friends were hard to make on death row. Hugh never considered Jimmy Lee Gray a friend, but their cells were adjacent and they talked for hours daily. They traded cigarettes, canned food, and paperback books when they had them. Gray never had a dime but never asked for anything. Hugh was perhaps the wealthiest inmate ever sent to death row and was happy to share with Gray. A secretary back at Foxy's sent him $500 a month, the maximum allowed, for better food and a few extras. No one else, other than perhaps his father, had access to such funds.

Gray's execution, less than a hundred feet away, saddened Hugh far more than he expected. Like most inmates on the Row, he was expecting a last-minute miracle that would delay things for years. When Gray was led away, Hugh said farewell but was certain nothing would happen. After Gray died, his cell was empty for a week and Hugh missed their long conversations. Gray had a miserable childhood and was destined to have a rough life. Hugh had a wonderful childhood and was still asking himself what went wrong. Now that Gray was gone, Hugh was surprised at how much he missed him. The hours and days were suddenly longer. Hugh fell into a deep depression, and not for the first time.

The Row was much quieter following Gray's execution. When the inmates heard what happened in the "Death Chamber," and how the State had botched things, most were suddenly aware of what they might one day face. The joke around the Row had been that the State was too incompetent to kill an inmate, but that was over. Mississippi was back in the killing business and its leaders demanded more.

Jimmy Lee Gray's appeals took less than seven years. Hugh's had been active for only five, but his appellate lawyers seemed to be losing enthusiasm. With his enemies gaining power, he began to worry about actually being put to death. He had arrived at Parchman confident that his father's money and contacts could somehow spare his life, perhaps even buy freedom, but a new reality was settling in.

———•———

If the execution cast a pall over the Row, it had little impact elsewhere around Parchman. Over at Unit 18, only two miles away across the cotton fields but a different world, life went on as if nothing had happened. When Nevin Noll heard the news about Jimmy Lee Gray, he actually smiled to himself. He was pleased to hear the State was finally back in the execution business. Maybe they would get to Hugh sooner rather than later.

But Noll spent little time thinking about the Malcos. He was convinced they would never find him, and even if they did he would be ready. His alias, one chosen by the prison officials, was Lou Palmer, and if anyone succeeded in finding his bogus file they would learn that he was serving a twenty-year sentence for selling drugs around Jackson.

In his five years at Parchman, Noll had solidified his member-ship in an Aryan gang and was a rising lieutenant. It took only two fistfights to catch the attention of the gang leaders, and he survived the initiation with little effort. Not surprisingly, organized crime suited him well; he'd never really known anything else. The gangs were divided by color—blacks, browns, and whites—and survival often depended on who was watching your back. Violence sim-mered just under the surface, but outright warfare was frowned upon. If the guards were forced to pull out their shotguns, the punishments were severe.

So Nevin Noll washed dishes for five dollars a day, and when the cooks weren't watching he stole potatoes and flour which he funneled to a distillery run by his gang. The home-brewed vodka was quite popular around the camp and provided income and pro-tection for the gang. Noll figured out a way to traffic the stuff to other camps by bribing the trustees and guards who drove the vans and trucks. He also set up a pot-smuggling route by using contacts on the Coast who mailed the drugs in packages to a post office in Clarksdale, an hour away. A guard retrieved them and sneaked them into Unit 18.

Noll at first had no interest in the sex trade and was startled at how vibrant it was. Since the age of twenty, he'd had unlimited access to loose women and had never been exposed to sex among men. Always enterprising, though, he saw opportunity and established a brothel in a restroom of an old gymnasium that was now used as a print shop. He controlled it with strict rules and kept the guards away with bribes of hard cash and fruit-flavored vodka.

Bingo was popular, and before long Noll had restructured the game and offered small jackpots of pot and junk food stolen from a central warehouse.

In short, after a couple years at Parchman he was doing the same things he'd always done in Biloxi. After five years, though, he was ready for a change of scenery.

His goal had never been to take over a gang. Nor was it to make profits. From the day he arrived at Parchman he had been planning his escape. He had no intention of serving thirty years. Long before he could ever think about parole, he planned to be hiding in South America and living the good life.

He watched everything: every vehicle that entered and left the camp; every changing shift of the guards; every visitor who came and went; every inmate that was assigned to the camp and everyone who left. After a few months in prison, the men slowly became institutionalized. They fell into line without complaint because complaining only made their lives worse. They followed the rules and the schedules made by the officials. They ate the food, did their menial jobs, took their breaks, cleaned their cells, and tried to survive each day because tomorrow was another step closer to parole. Almost all of them stopped waiting, noticing, counting, plotting, wondering, and scheming.

Not Nevin Noll. After three years of careful scrutiny, he made the important decision of selecting Sammy Shaw as his running mate. Shaw was a black guy from a tough Memphis neighborhood who'd been caught smuggling drugs and pled guilty to forty years. He, too, had no plans to hang around that long. He was savvy, tough, observant, and his street smarts were second to none.

Noll and Shaw shook hands and began making plans. A prison that sprawled over 18,000 acres was impossible to guard. Its borders were porous. The traffic in and out was barely noticed.

Parchman had a long and colorful history of escapes. Nevin Noll was biding his time. Watching, always watching.

CHAPTER 55

On January 5, 1984, Keith Rudy was sworn in as Mississippi's thirty-seventh attorney general. It was a quiet ceremony in the supreme court chambers with the chief justice doing the honors. Ainsley and their two daughters, Colette and Eliza, stood proudly beside Keith. Agnes, Laura, Beverly, Tim, and other relatives watched from the front row. The Pettigrew brothers, Egan Clement, Rex Dubisson, and a dozen close friends from law school clapped politely after he took the oath, then waited for their chance to be photographed with the new AG.

During the previous holiday break, Keith and Ainsley had completed the move to Jackson and were now unpacking in a small house on a quiet street in Central Jackson, close to Belhaven College. His daily commute to his new office on High Street across from the state capitol was fifteen minutes.

At 7:30 the following morning, he was in his office with his jacket off and ready for his first appointment. Since 1976, Witt Beasley had run the AG's Criminal Appeals Division, and in that capacity was in charge of defending the convictions of the thirty-one inmates currently on death row. The excitement of Jimmy Lee Gray's execution had only increased the pressure on Beasley and his team to wrap up the cumbersome delays and give the green light to the executioner at Parchman. After years in the trenches, Beasley knew full well the complications and frustrations of death penalty litigation. Politicians did not. He also knew his new boss had a burning desire to speed along the appeals of Hugh Malco.

Keith began with "I've reviewed your capital caseload, all thirty-one cases. It's difficult to say who might be next in line."

"Indeed it is, Keith," Beasley said as he scratched his beard. He was twenty years older than his boss and was not being disrespectful. Keith had already implemented a first-name policy for the forty-six lawyers currently on his staff. The secretaries and clerks would be expected to stick with "Mr." and "Mrs."

Beasley said, "Jimmy Lee Gray's appeals were finished rather quickly, relatively speaking, but he didn't have much to argue about. As of today, I don't see another execution for at least two years. If I had to guess, I'd go with Wally Harvey."

"What a horrible crime."

"They're all horrible. That's why they got the death penalty. That's why the people out there are clamoring for more."

"What about Malco?"

Beasley took a deep breath and kept scratching his beard. "Hard to say. His lawyers are good."

"I've read every word."

"I know. Right now we're five-plus years post-verdict. We should win the habeas in federal court this year, maybe next. They don't have much to argue: the usual ineffective assistance of counsel at trial, verdict against the overwhelming weight, that sort of thing. They're doing a nice job of whining about the proof. As you know, the only real witnesses were Henry Taylor and Nevin Noll, two ex-confederates singing to save themselves. Malco is making a decent argument, but I can't see the court falling for it. Again, I'd say two years to get to the finish line with the Feds, then the usual Hail Marys. These guys'll try everything and they are experienced."

"I want it to have priority, Witt. Is that asking too much?"

"They all have priority, Keith. We're dealing with men's lives here and we take these cases seriously."

"I know that, but this is different."

"I understand."

"Put your best people on it. No delays. Right now, I'm guaranteed only four years in this office. Who knows what happens after that."

"Understood."

"Can we do it in four years, Witt?"

"Well, it's impossible to predict. We've had only one execution since 1976."

"And we're lagging behind. Texas is burying them right and left."

"They have a much larger death row population."

"What about Oklahoma? They've had five in the past three years and we have more men on death row."

"I know, I know, but it's not always left up to the AG's office. We have to wait on a bunch of federal judges who, as a group, loathe habeas work. They are notoriously deliberate and uncooperative. Their clerks hate death penalty cases because there's so much paperwork. This is my world, Keith, and I know how slow things move. We'll push as hard as we can, I promise."

Keith was satisfied and offered a smile. "That's all I ask."

Beasley eyed him carefully and said, "We'll make it happen, Keith, and as soon as possible. One question, though, is whether you're ready for it. You're considered the victim of the crime, you and your family. It's a unique case in which the victim wields such enormous power over the machinery of death. Some observers have already brought up the issue of a conflict of interest."

"I've read every word, Witt, and I understand what they're saying. I'm not bothered by it. The people elected me as their AG knowing full well that my father was murdered by Hugh Malco and it would be my responsibility to defend the State against his appeals. I will not be distracted by a handful of critics. Damn the press."

"Very well."

Witt left the meeting and returned to his office a few doors away. Alone, he chuckled to himself at the AG's rather lame effort to feign disinterest in the press. Few politicians in recent history had shown greater affection for cameras than Keith Rudy.

———•———

For the first three months of each year, the electorate held its collective breath as the state legislature convened at the capitol. The city of Jackson felt under siege as 144 elected lawmakers, all veteran politicians, arrived from every corner of the state with their staffs, entourages, lobbyists, agendas, and ambitions.

Thousands of bills, virtually all of them useless, were thrashed about in dozens of committees. Important hearings drew little attention. Floor debates dragged on before empty galleries. The House spent weeks killing the bills passed by the Senate, which, at the same time, was busy killing the bills passed by the House. Little was accomplished; little was expected. There were enough laws already on the books to burden the people.

As the State's attorney, Keith's office had the responsibility of representing every agency, board, and commission in existence, and it took three dozen lawyers to do so. At times during his first months in office, he felt like nothing more than a well-paid bureaucrat. His long days were filled with endless staff meetings as proposed legislation was monitored. At least twice a day he stood at the large window of his splendid office, gazed across the street to the capitol, and wondered what the hell they were doing over there.

Once a week, at precisely 8:00 A.M. on Wednesday, he had a fifteen-minute cup of coffee with Witt Beasley and got the latest update on the appeals of Hugh Malco. With glacier-like speed, they were inching along the federal docket.

In early May, he was informed that Lance Malco would be released in July, eight years and three months after pleading guilty to operating a house of prostitution. Keith admitted it was a harsh sentence for a relatively harmless offense, but he didn't care. Lance had committed far more serious crimes in his violent career and deserved to die in prison like his son.

Of far more importance, Keith would always be convinced that Lance ordered the hit on Jesse Rudy. Short of a dramatic confession, though, it would never be proven.

———————

As if to herald his return to civilian life, or perhaps to simply limber up for the tasks ahead, Lance, still in prison, sent a message.

For the past six years, Henry Taylor had served his time in a series of county jails throughout the state. With each transfer he was given a new name and a slightly modified background. Each new sheriff was leaned on by the state police and told to take care of the boy, treat him well, perhaps even allow him to help around the jail as a trustee. The sheriffs were assured the inmate was not dangerous but had simply run afoul of some narco-traffickers somewhere along the Coast. Each sheriff ran his own little kingdom and rarely shared notes with his colleagues next door.

Late one afternoon, Henry was running errands. He left the circuit clerk's office with a stack of juror subpoenas to be taken to the sheriff's office for service the following day. As a trustee, he wore a white shirt and blue khakis with a white band down the leg, a warning to all that he was a resident of the Marshall County jail. No one cared. Trustees came and went and were common sightings around the courthouse. As he was about to leave through the rear door, a steel club landed at the base of his neck and knocked him out cold. He was dragged to a small, dark utility closet. With the door locked, he was choked to death with a two-foot section of nylon ski rope. His body was stuffed in a cardboard box. His assailant stepped out of the closet, closed the door, locked it behind him, and eased into a restroom with two urinals and one stall. At 4:50 P.M., a janitor entered, glanced around, and turned off the light. The assailant was in the stall, crouching on the lid of the toilet.

Two hours later, as the empty courthouse began to darken, the assailant tip-toed along the downstairs and upstairs corridors and saw no one. Since he had scoped out the building, he knew there were no guards, no security system. Who breaks into rural courthouses?

Taylor should have returned to the jail two hours earlier and was probably already being missed. Time, therefore, was becoming crucial. The assailant walked to the rear door, stepped outside, signaled to his accomplice, and waited for him to drive a pickup truck to the door under a small veranda. It was long past closing time and the shops and offices around the square were empty and dark. Two cafés were busy but they were on the other side of the square.

The corpse was oozing blood so they wrapped his head with some dirty shop-rags. They carried him in the cardboard box and quickly placed him in the rear of the truck. Back inside, the assailant, wearing gloves, tossed the subpoenas along the rear hallway and made no effort to wipe away Taylor's blood. Three miles south of the town of Holly Springs, the pickup turned onto a county road, then onto a dirt trail that disappeared into the woods. The body was transferred to the trunk of a car. Six hours later, the car and the pickup arrived at the Biloxi marina where the body of Henry Taylor was carried to a shrimp boat.

At the first hint of sunlight, the trawler left the dock and headed into the Sound in search of shrimp. When there was no other boat in sight, the body was dumped onto the deck, the clothing was stripped, and a string of netting was wrapped around its neck. It was hoisted on an outrigger boom for a moment as photos were taken. After that, the boom swung over the water, the netting was cut, and Henry was fed to the sharks.

Just like in the old days.

———•———

Henry's disappearance from the Marshall County Courthouse was a mystery with no clues. A week passed before the state police stopped by the AG's office to inform Keith that their protected witness had not been so protected after all. Keith had a good idea of what had happened. Lance Malco was about to go free and he wanted his enemies to know he was still the Boss.

Like his father, Keith had no fear of the Malcos and relished the idea of going after Lance if he resumed his old ways.

And, he was not altogether bothered by losing Henry Taylor. He was, after all, the man who had "pulled the trigger" and killed Jesse Rudy.

———•———

The photo was a five-by-seven black and white, and it was smuggled into Parchman by a guard working for Lance Malco. He admired it for a day and wished he had another one just like it. Bloody, naked, dead as a doornail, hanging from an outrigger, the incompetent bomber who'd snitched on his Hugh and sent him to death row.

Lance bribed another guard for a white-gloved hand delivery of the photo to one Lou Palmer, aka Nevin Noll, currently housed in Unit 18, Parchman prison.

No message was included; none was needed.

CHAPTER 56

On June 7, Keith and an assistant got into the rear seat of a brand-new unmarked highway patrol car for the ride down to Hattiesburg. One perk of being AG was a chauffeured ride anywhere he wanted, with an extra bodyguard thrown in. On the downside were the recurring threats of bodily harm, which usually came in the form of half-crazed, barely literate letters, many of them sent from prisons and jails. The state police monitored the mail and, so far, had seen nothing to worry about.

Another perk was the rare use of the state jet, an asset coveted by a handful of elected officials but controlled exclusively by the governor. Keith had been on it once, enjoyed it immensely, and could see himself riding it into the future.

The gathering was at the federal courthouse in Hattiesburg. The occasion was an oral argument in front of the judge handling the habeas corpus petition filed by Hugh Malco. Two reporters, without cameras, were waiting in the hall outside the courtroom and asked Keith for a word or two. He politely declined.

Inside, he sat at the State's table with Witt Beasley and two of his top litigators.

Across from them Hugh's appellate lawyers from Atlanta busied themselves with paperwork. So far, their voluminous filings had produced nothing beneficial for their client. They had lost in the state supreme court by a vote of 9-0. They had lost on a petition for a rehearing, a formality. They had appealed to the U.S. Supreme Court and lost when it refused to hear the case. Round Two was a petition for post-conviction relief back in the state supreme court,

which they lost. They petitioned for a rehearing, another formality, and lost. They appealed that to the U.S. Supreme Court, which
again declined to take the case. With the required state filings out
of the way, they entered Round Three in federal court with a petition for habeas corpus.

Hugh had been convicted and sentenced to death in the circuit
court of Forrest County, Hattiesburg, in April of 1978. Six years
later, in the same town but a different courthouse, both he and his
case were still alive. According to Witt, though, both were in jeop-
ardy. The finish line was in sight. Hugh's high-powered lawyers
were bright and experienced, but they had yet to gain any traction
with their arguments. Keith, who still read every word that was
filed, agreed.

As they waited for His Honor, more reporters gathered in the
front row behind the lawyers. There wasn't much of a crowd. It
was, after all, rather dry and monotonous appellate maneuvering.
When the notice had arrived a month earlier, Keith had wanted
to handle the oral argument himself. He knew the case as well as
Witt and was certainly capable of going toe-to-toe with the habeas
boys, but he realized it was not a good idea. His father's murder
would be discussed to some degree, and he and Witt agreed that he
should stay in his chair.

Hugh wanted to attend the hearing and his lawyers had made
a request. However, the custom was for such a request to be either
approved or disapproved by the attorney general, and Keith happily said no. He wanted Hugh to leave the Row in a box, and not
before. It was a pleasure denying him even a few hours outside his
miserable little cell.

His Honor finally appeared to call things to order. As the
aggrieved and appealing party, Hugh's lawyers went first and spent
the first hour describing in boring detail the lousy job Joshua Burch
did defending their client at trial. Ineffective assistance of counsel
was customarily relied on by desperate men and was almost always
presented on appeal. The problem was that Joshua Burch was not

some court-appointed public defender assigned to an indigent client. He was Joshua Burch, one of the finest criminal defense lawyers in the state. It was clear His Honor wasn't buying the attack on Mr. Burch.

Next, a different lawyer argued that the State's witnesses had severe credibility problems. Henry Taylor and Nevin Noll were originally co-defendants before they flipped in an effort to avoid the gas chamber themselves.

His Honor appeared to doze off. Everything that was being said had already been submitted in the brick-like briefs filed weeks earlier. For two hours the lawyers droned on. Months ago Keith and Witt had realized that Hugh and his team had nothing new: no surprise witness, no novel strategies, no brilliant arguments missed by Joshua Burch at trial. They were simply doing their jobs and going through the motions for a client who was clearly guilty.

When His Honor had had enough, he let it be known and called for a coffee break.

As a thirty-year veteran of appellate arguments, Witt Beasley had long since learned to make his case with concise and logical written briefs, and say as little as possible in court. He believed that all lawyers talked too much, and he also knew that the more crap a judge heard, the less patience he had.

Witt hit the high points, finished in less than an hour, and they left for lunch.

Knowing the judge as he did, Witt predicted an opinion within six months. Assuming it would be in the State's favor, Hugh would then appeal another loss to the Fifth Circuit in New Orleans. The Fifth had the reputation of being a fairly industrious court and often ruled in less than a year. If it upheld the State, then Hugh's next and probably final appeal would be to the U.S. Supreme Court, where he'd already lost twice.

Keith wasn't counting the months until an execution date

could be set, but he was counting the years. If things fell into place for the State of Mississippi, Hugh Malco would be strapped down while Keith was still the attorney general.

———•———

Lance Malco's euphoria upon leaving Parchman was tempered by his reentry into civilian life on the Coast. His family was gone. Carmen lived in Memphis to be closer to Hugh. The other children had scattered a decade ago and had almost no contact with either their father or Hugh. After the divorce, the family home had been sold, at Lance's direction. His faithful lieutenants were either working elsewhere or had left the Coast altogether. His rock, Fats Bowman, was dead. The new sheriff, along with the new city officials, had already let it be known that Mr. Malco's return was not welcome and that he would be watched closely.

He still owned his clubs—Red Velvet, Foxy's, Desperado, O'Malley's, and the Truck Stop—but they were run-down and in need of renovation. They had lost their popularity to newer, splashier joints along the Strip. Two of his bars had closed. In a world where cash was king, he knew almost for a certainty that he had been robbed blind by managers, bartenders, and bouncers. He'd found it impossible to run things from prison. If Hugh and Nevin had not screwed up, they could have controlled the empire and kept the others in line. With them gone, though, no one had the guts or smarts to step up, take orders from the Boss, and protect his interests.

The euphoria lasted only days before Lance realized he was falling into a state of depression. He was sixty-two years old, in decent health, notwithstanding eight years in prison, which ramped up the aging process. His favorite son was on death row. His marriage was long gone. Though he still had plenty of assets, his empire was in serious decline. His friends had deserted him. The few people whose opinion he coveted were certain he was behind the death of Jesse Rudy.

The Malco name, once feared and respected by many, was mud.

He owned a row of condos on St. Louis Bay in Hancock County. He moved into one, rented some furniture, bought a small fishing boat, and began spending his days on the water, catching nothing and not really trying. He was a lonely man with no family, no friends, no future. He decided to hang around and spend whatever was necessary to save Hugh, and if that proved unsuccessful he would sell everything, count his money, and move to the mountains.

The Strip seemed like a thousand miles away.

CHAPTER 57

The long-awaited opening came in late September when Sammy Shaw noticed that prisoners working in the print shop had loaded some empty cardboard boxes into the dumpster, which was almost overflowing. When Sammy saw the dilapidated sanitation truck arrive at the side gate to collect the dumpster, he signaled Nevin Noll, who was ready. They had walked through this first phase of their escape a hundred times. Each carried a brown paper sack filled with supplies as they jumped into the dumpster and burrowed deep under the cardboard boxes. The dumpster was used by the kitchen and the laundry, and they were instantly covered with rotten food and other filth. Step One was successful—they had not been noticed.

Cables rattled as the driver latched the dumpster, then a motor whined as it tilted up and began jerking forward onto the bed. It clanged and rattled into place, then became still. Nevin and Sammy were four feet down in the muck with no light anywhere, but they were relieved when the dumpster began moving. The truck stopped, the driver yelled, someone yelled back, a gate banged, and they were moving again.

The landfill was nothing but a gigantic quagmire of garbage and mud, dug miles from the units, as far away as possible. Each unit had a fence with guards and razor wire, but the entire prison farm did not. When the truck cleared another fence, the escapees knew they were free and clear, for the moment. Step Two was successful.

The unloading would be the trickiest part. The rear door

was unlatched and the dumpster began tilting sharply. Nevin and Sammy began their slide, one that would either lead to temporary freedom or get them shot on the spot. They had cut and jerry-rigged the cardboard boxes and were completely hidden inside them. Mixed in a wave of garbage bags, loose bottles and cans and jars, they gained speed, slid hard out of the dumpster, fell about ten feet into the landfill and into the vast acreage of rotting food, dead animals, and noxious vapors.

They stayed frozen in place. They heard the dumpster fall back onto the truck. The truck left and they waited. In the distance, they could hear a bulldozer tracking over the latest loads of garbage and filth, packing it all down to make room for more.

Carefully, and trying to stifle their gagging, they inched their way upward to daylight. The dozer was a hundred yards away, crisscrossing. When it turned away from them, they scampered out of the pile, and, staying low, moved until the dozer turned and they hid again. In the distance, another sanitation truck was heading in their general direction.

Though speed was everything, they could not afford to get in a hurry. It was about 1:30. The first bed check was at 6:30.

Dodging the bulldozer and the sanitation trucks, they eventually made it out of the landfill and into a gorgeous field of snowy white cotton with stalks chest-high. Once there they began running, a slow measured jog that took them off the prison land and onto someone else's property. Step Three was working; they were technically out of prison, though far from free.

If most prisons could be jailbroken, then why were most escapees caught within forty-eight hours? Nevin and Sammy had talked about it for hours. In general terms, they knew what to expect within the prison. Outside of it, they had almost no idea what they would encounter. One fact was certain: they could only run so far. Jeeps, three-wheelers, helicopters, and bloodhounds would soon be on their trail.

After two hours they found a muddy pond and collapsed into

it. They peeled out of their stinking prison clothes and changed into jeans and shirts they had stolen and hidden months earlier. They ate cheese sandwiches and drank canned water. They rolled their dirty clothes into tight wads, wrapped them with baling wire, tied them to a rock, and left them in the pond. In their paper sacks, they had food, water, one pistol, and some cash.

According to Sammy's brother, Marlin, the nearest country store was on Highway 32, about five miles from the western boundary of the prison. They found it around 4:00 P.M. and called Marlin from the pay phone. He left Memphis immediately, for a rendezvous that in his opinion would probably never happen. According to the plan, he would drive to an infamous honky-tonk called Big Bear's on the north side of Clarksdale, an hour from the prison. He would have a beer, watch the door, and try to convince himself that his older brother was about to walk in.

It was 4:30. Two hours from bed check and alarms, assuming, of course, they had not already been seen. They left the store and walked two miles out of sight. They hid under a tree and watched for traffic. Most of the people who lived in the area were black, so Sammy became the hitchhiker. With the pistol. They heard a car approach and he jumped onto the shoulder and stuck out a thumb. The driver was white and never slowed down. The next vehicle was an old pickup driven by an elderly black gentleman, and he never slowed down. They waited fifteen minutes; it was not a busy highway. In the distance they saw a late-model sedan and decided Nevin should play the role. He stuck out a thumb, managed to look harmless, and the driver took the bait. He was a fortyish white man with a friendly smile, said he was a fertilizer salesman. Nevin said his car had broken down a few miles back. As they approached the same store, Nevin pulled out his pistol and told the guy to turn around. He turned pale and said he had a wife and three kids. Great, said Nevin, and you'll see them later tonight if you just do as you're told. "What's your first name?"

"Scott."

"Nice, Scott. Just do what I say and nobody gets hurt, okay?"

"Yes sir."

They picked up Sammy and headed west on Highway 32. Nevin said over his shoulder, "Say, Eddie, this here is Scott, our new chauffeur. Please tell him we're good boys who don't want to hurt anyone."

"That's right, Scott. Just a couple of Boy Scouts."

Scott was unable to speak.

"How much gas?" Nevin asked.

"Half a tank."

"Turn here."

Nevin had memorized maps and knew every county road in the area. They zigzagged in a general northern direction until they left the town of Tutwiler. Nevin pointed to a farm road and said, "Turn here." A hundred yards down the road, he made Scott stop and change seats. Nevin gave the pistol to Sammy in the rear seat who kept the barrel touching the back of Scott's neck. On a deserted farm road between two vast cotton fields, Nevin stopped the car and said, "Get out."

"Please, sir," Scott pleaded.

Sammy poked him with the gun barrel and he got out. They led him down a row of cotton, stopped, and Nevin said, "Get on your knees."

Scott was crying and said, "Please, I have a beautiful wife and three gorgeous kids. Please don't do this."

"Give me your wallet."

Scott quickly handed it over and dropped to his knees. He bowed his head and tried to pray and kept mumbling, "Please."

"Lay down," Nevin said and Scott did so.

Nevin winked at Sammy who put the gun in his pocket. They left Scott crying in the cotton field. An hour later they parked the sedan in front of a convenience store in a rough part of Clarksdale. The keys stayed in the ignition. Two blocks away, Nevin waited outside in the dark while Sammy strutted through the front door of Big Bear's and hugged his brother.

Marlin drove them to a motel in Memphis where they took long, hot showers, ate burgers and fries and drained cold beers, and changed into nicer clothes. They split their loot: $210 in cash they had saved in prison; $35 from poor Scott. They threw away his wallet and credit cards.

At the bus station, they said goodbye without a hug. No need to call attention to themselves. They shook hands like lost friends. Nevin left first on a bus to Dallas. Half an hour later, Sammy left for St. Louis.

Marlin was relieved to be rid of both of them. He knew the odds were against them, but for two men who were facing years if not decades at Parchman, why not take the risk?

———•———

Two days later, Keith was informed by the state police. A prison escape was always unexpected, but Keith was not surprised. After the mysterious disappearance of Henry Taylor, he knew the pressure would mount against Nevin Noll. And, he was confident he would eventually be found.

Still, it was unsettling to know that Noll was loose. He was as guilty of killing Keith's father as Taylor and Hugh Malco, and belonged in a cell on death row.

———•———

Sammy Shaw was arrested in Kansas City after the police received a Crime Stoppers tip. Someone who knew him needed $500 in cash.

A month passed with no sign of Nevin Noll. Then two months. Keith tried not to think about him.

Lance Malco wasn't worried either. The last place Noll would surface was the Coast. Lance had put a $50,000 contract on his head and he'd made sure Noll knew it.

If he had good sense, which he did, he would find his way to Brazil.

CHAPTER 58

Like a boxer hanging on the ropes, beaten, bloodied, but refusing to go down, Hugh Malco's legal defense took one blow after another and came back for more. In October of 1984, the federal judge in Hattiesburg rejected every claim. The lawyers dutifully appealed to the Fifth Circuit, which affirmed the lower court in May of 1985. With nowhere else to go, the lawyers appealed to the U.S. Supreme Court, again. Even though the Supremes had already said no to Petitioner Malco on two previous appeals, it took them seven months to say no for the third time. They ordered the State of Mississippi to set a date for the execution.

Keith was at the capitol preparing to testify before the state senate judiciary committee when Witt Beasley found him. Without a word he handed him a scrap of paper on which he'd scrawled, *Execution set, March 28, midnight. Congratulations.*

The news raced around the state and picked up steam. Almost every newspaper ran the headlines and archival photos of Jesse Rudy on various courthouse steps. The *Gulf Coast Register* re-ran the old team photo of Keith and Hugh as Little League all-stars, and that background proved irresistible. Stories flourished about their childhood on the Point. Former coaches, teachers, friends, and teammates were tracked down and interviewed. A few declined to comment, but most had something colorful to add.

Keith was inundated with requests for interviews, but as much as he enjoyed the exposure he said no to every one. He knew there was still a good chance the execution would be delayed.

———— • ————

In their two years in office, the governor and the attorney general worked well together. Bill Allain had held the AG's office four years before Keith, and was always ready for advice if needed. He had enjoyed his term as AG; his current gig was another matter. In a nasty campaign, he had been slandered with allegations of grotesque sexual misconduct, and, though he received 55 percent of the vote, the dark cloud would never go away. He longed for the private life of a country lawyer in his hometown of Natchez.

The white men who wrote the state's constitution in 1890 wanted a strong legislature and a weak governor; thus, a four-year limit. No other elected office in the state had a one-term restriction.

Bill Allain was leaving office, and not soon enough.

He and Keith had a standing lunch date for the first Tuesday of each month at the governor's mansion, during which they tried mightily to avoid any talk of politics. Football and fishing were favorite topics. Both were Catholic, oddities in a state that was 95 percent Protestant, and they enjoyed jokes about Baptists, tent preachers, snake handlers, even the occasional cheap shot at a priest. In February of 1986, though, there was no way to avoid the biggest story in the state.

Being the governor, and a natural storyteller to begin with, Allain did most of the talking. As the AG, he had been in the middle of the execution of Jimmy Lee Gray, and he enjoyed recalling the drama. "It gets crazy at the end. Lawyers shotgunning motions and petitions in every possible court, talking to the reporters, trying to get on camera. Politicians chasing the same cameras, screaming for more executions. Governor Winter was getting hammered with human rights folks on one side, death penalty hawks on the other. He got something like six hundred letters from twenty different countries. The Pope weighed in, said spare the boy's life. President Reagan said gas him. It became a national story because we hadn't executed anyone in a long time. The liberal press was eating us for lunch. The conservative press was cheering us on. With two days to go it looked as though it might really happen, and Parchman became a zoo. Hundreds of protesters came out of nowhere. On one side of Highway 49 there were people yelling for blood, gun nuts waving rifles, on the other side there were nuns and priests and kindlier folks who prayed a lot. Every sheriff in the state found an excuse to rush up to Parchman for the big party. And that was just a warmup. Malco's will be an even bigger circus."

"He filed a petition for clemency yesterday."

"I just saw it. It's on my desk, somewhere. How do you feel about it?"

"I want him executed."

"And your family?"

"We've discussed it many times. My mother is somewhat hesitant, but I want revenge, as do my three siblings. It's that simple, Governor."

"It's never simple. Nothing about the death penalty is simple."

"I disagree."

"Okay, I'll prove how complicated it is. I'm punting this one over to you, Keith. You'll make the decision on clemency, not me. I can go either way. I knew your father and had great respect for him. The contract murder of a district attorney was an attack on the very core of our judicial system and cannot be tolerated. I get that. I can make that speech; indeed I have. I understand revenge. I can pull that switch. But, on the other hand, if killing is wrong, and we can all agree that it is, then why do we allow the State to kill? How does the State become so self-righteous that it rises above the law and sanctions its own murders? I'm confused, Keith. As I said, it's not a simple issue."

"But clemency is your issue, not mine."

"That's the law, yes, but no one has to know about our little arrangement. It's a handshake deal. You make the decision. I'll make it public and take the heat."

"And the fallout?"

"I'm not worried about that, Keith, because I'll never again run for office. When I leave here, and it won't be soon enough, I'm done with politics. I have it from a good source that the legislature is serious about allowing gubernatorial succession. I'll believe it when I see it, but it won't affect me because I'll be gone. My days of looking for votes are over."

"Well, thanks, I guess. I didn't ask for this and I'm not sure I want the responsibility."

"Get used to it, Keith. You're the odds-on favorite to get this job in two years. There are at least four death row cases coming down the pike."

"More like five."

"Whatever. My point is that the next governor will have his hands full."

"I'm not exactly an unbiased player here, Governor."

"So, you've made your decision? If you say no clemency, then Malco will get the gas."

"Let me think about it."

"You do that. And it's our secret, okay?"

"Can I tell my family?"

"Of course you can. I'll do what you and your family want and no one will ever know about it. Deal?"

"Do I really have a choice?"

The governor flashed a rare smile and said, "No."

CHAPTER 59

The governor generously offered the state's Learjet and the attorney general immediately accepted. When the last appeal was denied shortly after 8 P.M., Keith left his office in Jackson and flew to Clarksdale, the nearest town with a runway long enough. He was met by two state troopers who walked him to their patrol car. As soon as they left the airport, Keith asked them to turn off the flashing blue lights and slow down. He was in no hurry and in no mood for conversation.

Alone in the rear seat, he watched the endless flat fields of the Delta, so far away from the ocean.

They are twelve years old.

It is the most glorious week of the year: summer camp on Ship Island with thirty other Scouts. The disappointing end to the baseball season is long forgotten as the boys camp, fish, crab, cook, swim, sail, hike, kayak, sail, and spend endless hours in the shallow water around the island. Home is only thirteen miles away but it's in another world. School starts in a week and they try not to think about it.

Keith and Hugh are inseparable. As all-stars they are greatly admired. As patrol leaders they are respected.

They are alone in a fourteen-foot catamaran with the island in sight, a mile away. The sun is beginning to fall in the west; another long lazy day on the water is coming to an end. Their week is half gone and they want it to last forever.

Keith has the tiller and is tacking slowly against a gentle breeze. Hugh is sprawled on the deck, his bare feet hanging off the bow. He says, "I read a story in Boys' Life *about these three guys who grew up together near the beach, North Carolina I think, and when they were fifteen they got this wild idea to fix up an old sailboat and take it across the Atlantic when they finished high school. And they did. They worked on it all the time, restored it, saved their money for parts and supplies, stuff like that, and the day after they graduated they set sail. Their mothers cried, their families thought they were nuts, but they didn't care."*

"What happened to them?"

"Everything. Storms. Sharks. No radio for a week. Got lost a few times. Took 'em forty-seven days to get to Europe, landed in Portugal. All in one piece. They were broke, so they sold their beloved boat to buy tickets home."

"Sounds like fun."

"One guy wrote the story ten years later. The three met at the same dock for a reunion. Said it was the greatest adventure of their lives."

"I'd love to be on the open sea for a few days, wouldn't you?"

"Sure. Days, weeks, months," Hugh says. "Not a care in the world, something new every day."

"We should do it, you know?"

"You serious?"

"Why not? We're only twelve, so we have, what, six years to prepare?"

"We don't have a boat?"

They think about this as the breeze picks up and the catamaran glides across the water.

Keith repeats, "We don't have boat."

"Well, those three didn't either. There must be a thousand old sloops dry-docked around Biloxi. We can find one cheap and get to work."

"Our parents won't allow it."

"Their parents didn't like it either, but they were eighteen years old and determined to do it."

Another long pause as they enjoyed the breeze. They were drawing closer to Ship Island.

"What about baseball?" Keith asked.

*"Yeah, that might get in the way. Do you ever wonder what'll happen
if we don't make it to the big leagues?"*

"Not really."

*"Neither do I. But, what if? My cousin told me that this year, 1960,
there's not a single player from the Coast in the majors. He said the odds of
getting there are impossible."*

"I don't believe that."

*"Okay, but let's say something happens and we don't make it. We
could have our sailing adventure as a backup. We'll set sail for Portugal the
day after graduation."*

"I like it. We might need a third mate."

"We have plenty of time. Let's keep it our secret for a couple of years."

"Deal."

———————

From a few miles away they saw the blinking lights of two
helicopters hovering over the prison like fireflies. Highway 49 saw
little traffic on the busiest of days, but by 9 P.M. cars were backed
up north and south of the main entrance. The shoulder on the west
side was covered with protesters holding candles and hand-painted
signs. They sang softly and many of them prayed. Across the road,
a smaller group watched and listened respectfully and waved their
own signs. Both sides were monitored closely by what seemed like
an entire army of county deputies and highway patrolmen. Directly
across from the gate was a makeshift press compound with a dozen
news vans. Cameras and wires ran here and there as reporters scurried about waiting for news to break.

Keith noticed a brightly painted van from WLOX-Biloxi. Of
course the Coast would be there.

His driver turned at the gate and waited behind two other
patrol cars. County boys. It was an execution, a big night for law
enforcement, and an old tradition was being revived. Every sheriff

in the state was expected to drive to Parchman, in a late-model patrol car, and sit and wait for the good news that things had gone as planned. Another murderer had been eliminated. Many of them knew each other and they gathered in groups and gossiped and laughed while a team of inmates grilled burgers for dinner. If and when the good news came, they would cheer, congratulate one another, and drive home. The world was safer.

At the door of the administration building, Keith brushed off a reporter, one who had enough credentials to get inside the prison. Word spread quickly that the attorney general had arrived. He qualified as a victim and was permitted to witness the execution. His name was on the list.

Agnes had asked him not to go. Neither Tim nor Laura had the stomach for it, but they wanted revenge. Beverly was wavering and resented the governor for putting pressure on the family. The family just wanted it to be over.

Keith went straight to the superintendent's office and said hello. The prison attorney was there and confirmed that the defense lawyers had surrendered. "There's nothing left to file," he said somberly. They chatted for a few minutes, then climbed into a white prison van and headed for the Row.

———•———

Two folding chairs were in the center of a small, windowless room. A desk and an office chair had been shoved to the wall. Keith sat and waited, jacket off, tie loosened, sleeves rolled up. It was a warm night for late March. The door latch snapped loudly and startled him. A guard walked in, followed by Hugh Malco, then another guard. Hugh's eyes darted around. He was visibly rattled by Keith's presence. He was handcuffed and ankle-chained and wore a white shirt and pants, which appeared to be well-ironed. The death outfit. Burial clothes. He would be hauled back to Biloxi and laid to rest in the family plot.

Keith did not stand but looked at the first guard and said, "Take off the handcuffs and chains."

The guard balked as if asked to commit a crime. Keith snapped, "You want me to get the warden?"

Both guards removed the cuffs and chains and laid them on the desk. As one opened the door the other said, "We're right outside."

"I won't need you."

They left and Hugh sat in the empty folding chair. Their shoes were five feet apart. They stared at each other, neither blinking, neither willing to show the slightest uneasiness.

Hugh spoke first. "My lawyer said you'd be a witness. Didn't expect you to drop by for a visit."

"The governor sent me. He's struggling with the clemency issue, needs some help. So he gave me his proxy. It's my call."

"Well, well. That should suit you just fine. Life and death hangs in the balance. You get to play God. The ultimate ruler."

"Seems an odd time to start the insults."

"Sorry. You remember the first time you called me a smart-ass?"

"Yes. Mrs. Davidson's sixth-grade class. She heard me, marched me into the hall, gave me three licks for foul language, and you laughed about it for a week."

Both managed a brief smile. A helicopter buzzed low, then went away.

Hugh said, "Quite a scene out there, huh?"

"Quite. Are you watching it?"

"Yep. Gotta small color unit in my cell, and because the guards are so swell around here they're giving me some extra time on the last night of my life. Looks like I'll go out in a blaze of glory."

"Is that what you want?"

"No, I want to go home. As I understand things, the governor has four options. Clemency, no clemency, a reprieve, or a full pardon."

"That's the law."

"So, I've been thinking about one of those full pardons."

Keith was in no mood for levity or nostalgia. He glared at him and asked, "Why did you kill my father?"

Hugh took a deep breath, dropped the stare, and looked at the ceiling. After a long pause, he said, "It wasn't supposed to happen like that, Keith, I swear. Sure we hired Taylor to bomb the office, but nobody was going to get hurt. It was a warning, an act of intimidation. Your father sent my father to prison, and Jesse was investigating the Dusty Cromwell killing. He was coming after us and we felt the heat. Bombing his office in the courthouse would be the ultimate warning. I swear we had no plans to hurt anyone."

"I don't believe that. I heard every word Henry Taylor and Nevin Noll said in court. I watched their eyes, their body language, everything, and there was no doubt in anyone's mind that you and Nevin hired Taylor to kill my father. You're still lying, Hugh."

"I swear I'm not."

"I don't believe you."

"I swear, Keith." The tough criminal facade cracked a little. He wasn't pleading, but he sounded like a man telling the truth and desperately wanting for someone to believe him. Keith stared at him, neither blinked, and the first trace of moisture appeared in his eyes. They had not spoken to each other in years, and Keith was hit hard with the realization that perhaps things would be different if they had kept talking.

"Was Lance involved in the killing?"

"No, no, no," Hugh said as he shook his head, an honest reaction. "He was here in prison and knew nothing about it. And it was not supposed to be a killing."

"Tell that to my mother, Hugh. And my brother and sisters."

Hugh closed his eyes and frowned, his first pained expression. He mumbled, "Miss Agnes. When I was a kid I thought she was the most beautiful woman in Biloxi."

"She was. Still is."

"Does she want me dead?"

"No, but she's nicer than the rest of us."

"So, the family's split?"

"That's none of your business."

"Really? Sure feels like it's my business. It's my neck on the chopping block, right? So am I supposed to be begging for my life here, Keith? You have the king's power, up or down, life or death, off with my head or just let me keep it. Is that why you stopped by before the main event? You want me to grovel?"

"No. Did Lance take care of Henry Taylor?"

"I don't know. Believe it or not, Keith, I don't get a lot of gossip from the Coast here on the Row, and I've had other more pressing matters on my mind. But no, it would not surprise me if Lance took care of Henry Taylor. That's the way our world works. That's the code."

"And the code said it was time to get rid of Jesse Rudy."

"No, wrong again. The code said it was time to teach him a lesson, not to hurt him. That's why we chose to bomb the courthouse, a rather brazen attack on the system. Taylor blew it."

"Well, I for one am glad he's dead."

"That makes at least two of us."

Keith glanced at his watch. There were voices in the hall. A helicopter hummed in the distance. Somewhere, a clock was ticking.

Keith asked, "Will Lance be here tonight?"

"No. He wanted to be with me till the end, but I refused to approve him. I can't stand the thought of either of my parents watching me die like this."

"I'm not going to watch either. I gotta go."

"Look, Keith, I, uh, I'm at the end, okay, and I'm cool with it. I've spent time with the priest, said my prayers, all that. I've been here for eight years and if you or the governor granted clemency, then I would get off death row and go live out there in the general population for the rest of my life. Think about that, Keith. You and I are thirty-eight years old, not even halfway there yet. I don't want to spend the next forty years in this awful place. That would be worse than dying. Don't beat yourself up. Let's pull the plug and get it over with."

Keith nodded and saw a tear trickle down Hugh's left cheek.

Hugh said, "But look, Keith, there's one thing. You gotta believe me when I say I didn't intend to kill Jesse Rudy. Please. I would never harm anyone in your family. Please believe me, Keith."

It was impossible not to believe him.

Hugh went on, "I'm a dead man, Keith. Why would I keep lying? Please tell Miss Agnes and the rest of the family that I didn't intend to do it."

"I'll do that."

"And you believe me?"

"Yes, Hugh, I believe you."

Hugh wiped both eyes with the back of a sleeve. He gritted his teeth and struggled to regain his composure. After a long pause he mumbled, "Thank you, Keith. It'll always be my fault. I put everything in motion, but I swear there was no plan to harm Jesse. I'm so sorry."

Keith stood and walked to the door. He looked down at his old friend, a man he had hated for the last ten years, and almost felt sympathy. "The jury said you deserve to die, Hugh, and I agreed then. I agree now. For a long time I've dreamed of watching your execution, but I can't do it. I'm flying to Biloxi to sit with my mother."

Hugh looked up, nodded, smiled, and said, "So long, pal. I'll see you on the other side."